AETHER SPARK

BOOK ONE OF THE CLOCKWORK CALAMITY

NICHOLAS PETRARCH

AETHER SPARK

Copyright © 2018 by Nicholas Petrarch

Pelorus Books, LLC
6905 S 1300 E #496
Cottonwood Heights, Utah 84047
info@pelorusbooks.com
www.pelorusbooks.com

Pelorus Books can bring authors to your live event! For more information or to book an event, contact us at info@pelorusbooks.com.

Publisher: Pelorus Books, LLC
Editor: Jana S. Brown
Interior Design: Douglas Speck
Cover Design: Biserka Design
Illustrations: Wendy Speck
Maps: Douglas Speck
Author Photo: GinnyMae Photography

ISBN: 978-1-7320642-0-1 (ebook)
ISBN: 978-1-7320642-1-8 (paperback)

1. Fiction/Science Fiction/Steampunk 2. Fiction/Urban

First Edition
Published by Pelorus Books

To my loving wife, Eleena,
Without whom I wouldn't have had the courage to see this dream through

To Asher, Catie, and Morgan,
For encouraging me during the times when writing wasn't so glamorous

And to my family,
They've always believed in me, but I think I still surprised them with this

ACKNOWLEDGEMENTS

They say it takes a whole village to raise a child. Well, it takes almost as much to publish a book. *Aether Spark* was my first authoring endeavour, spanning five years since the story's conception in college when it was no more than a stray thought captured on the back of a 3x5 card.

Since that day, there have been many individuals who have influenced this project. I suppose you could say everyone I met shaped this story in some way as I drew characters and details from life experience. This is my humble attempt to thank my community for helping me share this story (and apologize to those I've failed to thank along the way).

I don't believe there is a word to express the appropriate measure of gratitude I feel for my wife. It was early in our marriage that she helped me "unstuck" myself and finally take strides to publish this first book. Without her, I wonder if I would ever have overcome my apprehension to putting myself out there. It's true what they say, "being deeply loved by someone gives us strength, while loving someone deeply gives us courage." Thank you, Eleena, for our story and all it's blessed me with. I couldn't have asked for a better companion on this journey.

Thank you to my father for being a stalwart example of integrity in the face of opposition, and for an early conversation which opened the world of Hatteras to be so much more than could fit on that early note card. He inspired the first of three major rewrites which added new characters, conflicts, and reasons to continue the story into future books.

Thank you to my mother for the many times she has listened to my ramblings over the years, her never ending encouragement, and for her willingness to pitch in and help me with things like the chapter heading images. No mother ever receives the praise they fully deserve, but she remains a testament to me that even we who claim to be amateurs can still produce some truly amazing things.

My writing group was paramount in the process of weeding through the heap of bad writing advice and gifting me courage to continue telling the story while in those first few awkward drafts. Did I say awkward? I'm sorry, I meant dismal. Thanks Asher, Catie, Morgan, Amanda, and Pete for helping me lay the foundation of my authoring career.

My beta readers were timely and on point, offering me a healthy dose of criticism while showing genuine interest in the story. Thanks Wendy, Doug, Beka, Jess, Erin and Jules for helping me catch those pesky plot holes and for guessing what happens next in the story.

A huge thanks to my early patrons over on Patreon who believed in me enough to help offset some of the publishing costs which daunted me as a new indie author. Thank you Jared, Amanda, Brian, Scot, Stacey, Wendy, and Tom for making this phenomenal cover and hiring an editor possible!

And a shout out to the mentor writing group at Paradigm High School. They were always willing to comb through a stray chapter here and there and have been patiently waiting for the full story. Thank you for all you do and sacrifice for your students and peers.

And lastly, thank *you* for taking the time to read my story! Enjoy!

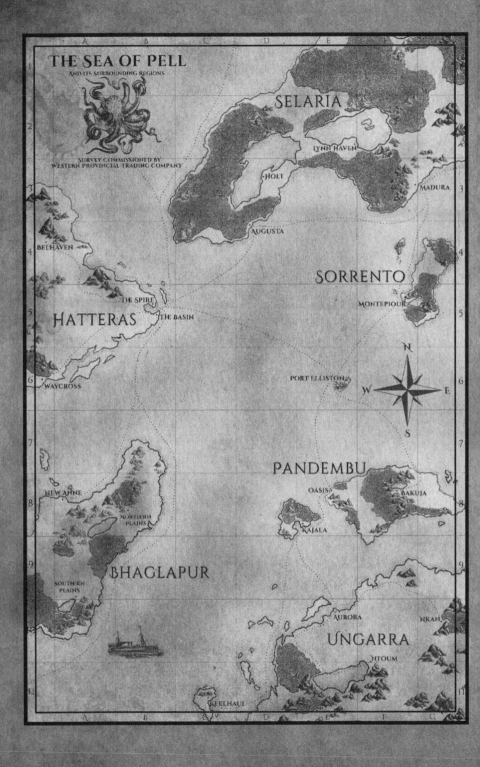

CONTENTS

AETHER SPARK

BOOK ONE OF THE CLOCKWORK CALAMITY

NICHOLAS PETRARCH

PROLOGUE

*There are few bonds as enduring as a childhood friendship, even
under great pressure.*

— Alchemical Proverb

B lack waves crashed through the rocky crags of the shoreline
as the bay's tidal surges dashed against the cliffs of Hatteras.
The magnificent city sprawled along the coast, following the
haphazard slope from the rocky beaches of the Basin all the way to the
peak of the Spire.

Chance sat upon the iron sea-wall, his eyes closed as he listened
to the din rising from below. The power of the waves reverberated
through the wall with each impact. It awakened in him an awful reverence toward the unfathomable force within those darkened waters.

The sun had yet to sink below the horizon, but the city's electric
lights were already coming on. Chance's gaze followed their illuminated
trail as it traced the cliffs around the bay. It astonished him the way
Hatteras had been built, nestled carefully into the cliffs so that the city
resembled a series of steps leading all the way to the top of the Spire—a
plateaued overhang that towered over the bay.

From the shipyard, Chance watched the iron barges coming in

from the sea and great winged dirigibles ferry their precious cargos inland. He watched as one of the smaller ships lifted away from the boatyard and rose into the sky. The craft wasn't much more than a wooden dinghy suspended under a balloon.

Not a vessel intended for long travel, he judged.

Its path curled along the crooked cliffs away from the Basin before it turned inland and was lost between the towering buildings. Chance suspected it was on its way to one of the upper markets, either to deliver some wanted commodity or to ferry some important gentleman.

Septigonee's guess as to whom or what.

With the dinghy gone, Chance's attention turned back to the sea. His reedy hands kept moving from his side to his vest pocket, each time patting it three or four times before returning to rest on the wall. The wait was murder. A half-hour had passed already and he was growing twitchy—and not just because a constable might spot him loitering.

He noticed a fleck of briny rust on the wall and picked at it absentmindedly.

The truth was he would wait through the evening if he had to. It had been nearly three months since he'd last seen his closest friend, Ringgold. Despite how he resisted letting it show, he'd missed him. He missed seeing him at school and the frequency with which they used to make trouble together.

He expected the news tonight would determine just how long it would be until their next meeting.

"Ahoy!" a voice called.

Chance turned to see Ringgold climbing over the rocks. He was wearing his school uniform: crisp white trousers and a long-sleeved shirt. The sleeves were rolled up and he carried his coat draped over the crook of his arm.

He carried a couple small bottles in his hands too. Struggling to keep his grip on them, he shot Chance a quick salute and Chance returned it.

"Come off the wall," Ringgold called. His voice hardly carried to Chance's ears against the noise of the surf. "You're not supposed to be up there."

"We're not supposed to be here at all," Chance responded.

"I know. But it's dangerous up there. You don't want to get washed away, do you?"

Chance smirked. He wasn't in any real danger. The bay offered the safest harbor for leagues around, and only the rare rogue storm ever threatened to overtake the seawall. Nevertheless, Chance flicked the piece of rust into the waves and swung his legs around.

"About time you showed up," he said, dropping down on the rocky sand. "I was about to give up on you. Another ten minutes and I'd have bolted."

"No need to do that," Ringgold said, embracing Chance. "It was difficult getting away tonight; most of the family came by to hear the news. I couldn't excuse myself until father went out to the den for drinks. I did manage to smuggle a few bottles away for us."

Ringgold waved two plum colored bottles before him. Chance recognized the contents immediately: a potent violet liquor. The news must have been good.

"By smuggled you mean asked politely for?" Chance quipped, taking one of the bottles.

"Yes. Well, that's my way I guess." Ringgold laughed.

They used the edge of the rocks to pry the caps away and each took a swig. The viscous liquid crept down Chance's throat, burning as it went. Ringgold choked on his.

"Careful now," Chance warned. "We don't need you knocking yourself out with this stuff."

"I'll be fine," Ringgold coughed.

"It was good news then?"

Ringgold grinned, and Chance suspected he was drawing out the suspense as long as he could.

"And?"

"You're looking at the newest admittee to Hamilton Academy," Ringgold said, flourishing his arm.

Chance was taken aback. "The military institute?" he asked.

"That's the one," Ringgold beamed. "Father is ecstatic! He hasn't been off the wire for more than ten minutes since we heard from the

Board. Mother is less excited, I think, though she wouldn't admit it. She still has her heart set on me attending Solair and becoming a mechanist. She thought I'd make a fine engineer."

It was true. Ringgold had a knack for designing mechanisms. He'd received many endorsements in school over the years, and it was no doubt in part why Hamilton had taken an interest in him.

Chance felt a familiar sense of jealousy pitting in his stomach.

"I always thought that was what you wanted."

"It's been a decent hobby growing up," Ringgold admitted, "but they're going to put me through an *academy* program. All I have to give them in return is my time."

"You mean your life."

"There haven't been any real conflicts for a quarter of a century," Ringgold reasoned. "Not since the Great War, anyways. I won't be in any danger."

"But what about the colonies? What if they ship you off to Madura, or Aurora?"

"I wouldn't mind seeing a bit more of the world."

Chance's brow furrowed. "Fine. But, even if you aren't killed, you'll be taking orders for the rest of your life. Do you really want to put up with that?"

"Have a little faith," Ringgold said. "I'm not planning to remain a foot soldier for long. I have a real opportunity to prove myself to the city. Nearly everyone in the meritocracy has some form of military background. I bet you I come back from my service an officer!"

Chance turned his head and cursed under his breath. He couldn't abide Ringgold's veneration toward distinction.

"Can't you see it?" Ringgold asked, oblivious to Chance's reaction. "An officer in the Navy. And who knows where that could lead? You never thought you'd see me in a naval uniform, did you?"

"Actually, I always thought the costumes they gave you quite fitting," Chance said. "You've always had that certain pomp needed to fill one. It comes naturally."

Ringgold frowned.

"No, you're right!" Chance jeered. "I don't know why I didn't see it before—you standing guard somewhere all shipshape and pretty. You'll make a fine watchdog. In fact, I bet they recognize your talents in the first week and skip deploying you altogether. Perhaps they'll have you following at the heels of some gentleman lord somewhere. That would be a great use of your time."

"Chance," Ringgold said, his voice stern.

"I know! Mention our friendship and maybe they'll promote you on the spot. That's almost six years experience babysitting already? Good luck to anyone trying to compete with that as a new recruit."

Chance took a bitter swig from his bottle.

"The way you carry on, it's little wonder you needed me to look after you all these years."

"Well, count yourself fortunate. That job won't be yours anymore."

"What is that supposed to mean?" Ringgold asked.

"Don't be daft. You know as well as I do Hamilton is on the Spire. You'll move on and pursue your grand dream, and I'll be left here in the Basin. This is the end of our friendship, and you're acting like I should be excited."

"It's not like I'm dying." Ringgold said. "Just because I'm living on the Spire doesn't mean our friendship has to end."

"But it will," Chance sighed. "Sneaking away to the beach today is one thing, but there's no way I'm getting near that place—even if I wanted to. And there's no way you'll be getting away to come back and visit with the regimen they'll keep you under."

"So it might be a while till we see each other next," Ringgold shrugged. "That doesn't negate the past few years, does it?"

"No," Chance conceded. "It's just disappointing."

A heavy silence fell over them as the weight of the unknown future settled on them, interrupted only by sound of the waves. Neither knew what would happen, and it was suddenly difficult to talk about. They endured the awkward silence in the comfort of their bottles.

Despite the mood, Chance chuckled at a thought and cast a side-long grin at Ringgold.

"You know, you and I could stir up some trouble on the Spire. You'll be my inside man. Think of what mischief we could manage.

Might be a lot of fun with the stakes raised."

Ringgold's frown deepened.

"Do you really think I'd pull one of our old stunts there?" he asked. "Septigonee's Well, Chance! This isn't a public program anymore. They're offering me a prestigious future. I'm not going to jeopardize that for the sake of giving you a thrill."

"I didn't mean it like that."

"Sure you didn't," Ringgold chuckled weakly, shaking his head. "Here's a novel idea. Why don't you try the conventional approach rather than jumping straight to planning a break-in? You still have a shot at an academy placement. Take an extra year to study. Refocus. Then reapply for the next term. Quit acting like you don't care about the Board, and perhaps they'll care a little more about you."

"It's that simple, huh?" Chance asked, rolling his eyes.

"I don't see why it couldn't be."

"The Board made it clear what they think of me when they stripped my endorsement. I'm not about to go back and grovel in front of them."

"So, don't grovel. You show them you haven't given up and that you're ready to commit to a program. You've got talent. They know that. They'd have a hard time ignoring you if you just tried a little harder."

"I can't."

"Sure you can," Ringgold assured him. "I bet I can speak to our old mentors and ask them to recommend an appeal. And my father knows a few—"

"I took an apprenticeship," Chance interjected.

"Oh?" Ringgold said, surprised. "And when were you going to tell me this?"

"I haven't started yet. I'll begin on the first of the month."

Ringgold leaned against the seawall, contemplating the new development.

"Well, that's not a *bad* move," he said. "You'll get some experience under your belt; that should impress the Board. Show them you're willing to work hard. It's not unheard of for an apprentice to terminate an agreement early if he has a chance at an academy placement."

"I'm apprenticed to an alchemist," Chance clarified. "A free-merchant here in the Basin." He slumped his shoulders as he anticipated Ringgold's response, taking another swig from his bottle and staring hard at the ground.

"What?" Ringgold's bottle nearly slipped from his hands. "Why?"

"My father was friends with a man who owns his own lab. I saw him a few weeks back and he remembered me. He agreed to take me on."

"You're kidding me, right?"

Chance saw the hope in Ringgold's eyes, hoping he wasn't serious—that this was an attempt to make light of the situation. A jest for old times' sake.

Chance took another swig of his liquor.

"Chance, that's insanity! You were one of the brightest—you had promise! You have promise!"

"I know."

"So, why pursue a dead craft? They're a bunch of misers pushing snake oil and sugar water. This isn't just botching your academy placement—you'll ruin any chance of ever having a good opinion in society."

"I know."

"And you what, don't care?"

"Lay off it," Chance warned. "At least I'll be doing something with my time, rather than sitting around waiting on a bunch of rusty cogs to tell me just how little they think of me."

"You mean squandering your time." Ringgold's voice rose steadily. "Honestly, Chance, you fall in with that lot and you risk falling out of society entirely."

"And how does that differ from where I am now?" Chance snapped. "They turned me away, Ringgold. I didn't make the cut. You know as well as I do what that means for my future."

"Oh, don't act like you're a martyr," Ringgold scoffed. "If blame rests anywhere it's on you for that. You're the one who turned your back on everyone before they ever turned on you. While we were working, do you remember where you were? You were destroying yourself."

"I said lay off it."

"No," Ringgold insisted. "I won't. It's one thing for you to give up on placement, but what about this?" Ringgold's hand shot forward and seized a small copper tin from Chance's breast pocket. Chance scrambled to recover it.

"Give that back!"

"No," Ringgold said, shaking it in front of him. "You've got a habit, Chance. And working with an alchemist is going to help you with that how? Oh, I guess you won't have to go through so many hoops to get your hands on it. Odds are you'll be mixing your own."

"I said lay off it!"

Chance threw his bottle at Ringgold's head, who ducked just in time. It shot over his shoulder and smashed upon the rocks behind him. He only had a second to react before Chance was on him, wrapping his arm around Ringgold's neck and pulling him down in a headlock.

Ringgold dropped his bottle and the tin as he grappled with Chance's middle. Planting his feet, he pushed hard and ran Chance backwards against the seawall.

Chance's knee came up and caught Ringgold in the chest, knocking the wind out of him. Before he could recover, Chance twisted his body and threw Ringgold to the ground.

He rolled in the rocky sand and onto his back, putting his feet up defensively as Chance pounced on him again. With a kick, Ringgold lifted Chance off the ground and tossed him roughly to the side. Chance rolled across the loose rock. It cut into his back and arm, but he didn't care. He scrambled to his feet and squared off again.

"Chance, stop this," Ringgold warned.

He didn't listen. Chance rushed him again, but Ringgold was ready. Weaving his hand through Chance's left arm, he sidestepped deftly and kneed him hard in the side—throwing him off balance. Chance hit the ground face first, and Ringgold dropped on top of him, pressing a knee into his back. He snatched Chance's flailing arm and twisted it behind him.

Chance was pinned.

He struggled under Ringgold's weight, trying to turn himself over, but all he managed to do was swallow sand. Ringgold's grip was like iron fetters. Each twist sent pain through Chance's arm. Despite himself, tears welled up in his eyes. Not because of the pain, but because it burned him to be on the losing side once again.

He couldn't deny it, Ringgold had always been the better fighter.

Reluctantly, Chance's struggling ceased. Ringgold released him and stepped back as Chance lifted himself to his knees and brushed off the sand from his clothes.

"You see? Some things never change," Chance wheezed, picking loose rocks from his arm. "You'll never quit being my watchdog."

"And you," Ringgold said, shaking his head and breathing heavily. "You'll always be an ass." A smile crept across his face as he offered a hand and lifted Chance to his feet.

"Only as much as you."

"Perhaps," Ringgold admitted. "I do keep you around. That says something about me."

The two collected themselves, Chance catching his breath while Ringgold straightened his clothes. He walked to where he had dropped the tin and picked it up reluctantly. His face turned up in disgust as he held it in his open palm, but he offered it back to Chance.

"I suppose I couldn't convince you at least to try working for the city? Alchemy's a dead craft full of backwards thinkers. Anything useful that came from it is used by the city's chemists now. That's where the future lies. You'd have a more respectable place in society as a chemist."

"My place is *outside* of society," Chance insisted. "I won't live my life with a group of cogs looking over my shoulder and telling me what to do. I won't."

"I thought not." Ringgold sighed, looking at the broken bottles on the rocks. "Perhaps we should continue this celebration elsewhere?"

"Fine by me."

The two of them walked back up the beach and into the city. When they were free of sand and their feet tromped on paved streets, Ringgold turned to Chance with a serious look.

"Just because we can't muck around like we used to doesn't mean we aren't friends," Ringgold assured him.

"I know," Chance said.

"Let's make a promise then, shall we?" Ringgold suggested. "No matter where we end up, we'll be there to look out for one another. Agreed?"

He offered his hand to Chance.

"Agreed," Chance promised, spitting into his own hand and clasping Ringgold's firmly.

Ringgold cringed, as he always did when Chance pulled that one on him. He shook his head and wiped the spittle off on Chance's shoulder. The two of them laughed and made their way up the city street.

PART I

CHAPTER ONE

Mishaps

Who considered the boy who stood alone upon the edge of something great? Who sees the potential of a thing before it manifests itself?

— Excerpt from *Mechanarcissism*

Chance bent low over his worktable, struggling to see in the dim light. A single electric bulb burned overhead, illuminating— if only somewhat—his makeshift laboratory. He called it his laboratory, though it was little more than a poorly furnished work shed.

Vials and cases of every size and shape were gathered around him haphazardly, but he ignored them as he focused through his leather-bound goggles on a single beaker. It was secured on a thin iron stand set over a double-boiler where a small, controlled fire burned.

With one hand he worked a miniature, stitched-canvas bellows to keep the fire burning hot and evenly. In his other, he held a ceramic saucer containing a murky gas much like the fog that rolled in from the bay in the early morning hours. He balanced the saucer above the wide brim of the beaker as he consulted the recipe he'd jotted down earlier.

His brow furrowed in deep concentration. Alchemy was a precise science, and the margin of error was unforgiving.

Breathing out slowly, Chance focused on his hands and counted down from ten. When he reached one they were still as stones suspended over the beaker. He tipped the dish slightly and watched the heavy gas drift down the molded channel and spill into the beaker.

He began counting up.

One. Two. Three.

The gas rested stubbornly upon the surface of the liquid.

Six. Seven. Eight.

Chance lifted a piece of paper from the tabletop on which a tiny pile of ground powder lay and dusted it over the beaker with quick, deliberate taps of his forefinger.

Eleven. Twelve. Thirteen.

The gas sank below the surface as the powder fell through it. Chance's body remained tense as he watched the mixing with unbroken attention.

And then his lips curled into their first smile in days. The murky contents in the beaker were clearing. He pulled the saucer away and set it aside among the other dirty and disregarded instruments.

After three days of painfully calculated preparation, the mixture was finished. He lifted the beaker and swirled its contents judiciously as he watched the change spread evenly throughout.

It wasn't anything particularly awe inspiring or daring—just a curative salve, meant to treat the wealth of infections common among citizens living in the Basin. However, expenses had to be met and demand was high. He couldn't afford to scoff at any job that helped offset the costs of maintaining his laboratory. It wasn't exactly lead to gold, but it paid the bills.

Leaning back in his chair, he pulled his goggles down around his neck and wiped his brow with a portion of sleeve. He could feel the indents left around his eyes from the goggles and he scrunched his face to try and relieve them.

Sitting up, he became aware of how greatly his back ached, and how dry his mouth was. He'd been at it a while. Sorting through the mess before him, he retrieved his pocket watch and checked the time.

Seven thirty-eight. He'd lost another day.

Not that he had any other pressing demands. Ashworth, his mentor, was accustomed to leaving him to his own pursuits these days. He called on him only when there was a particularly difficult task or urgent order to fill. It was one of the benefits Chance enjoyed most about become a full partner. He'd taken well to the freedom afforded him.

He was just beginning to tidy up when Chance noticed a slight change in the contents of the beaker. The transparent liquid was putting off a faint light, and Chance felt his insides tense.

"The reaction's speeding up," he said aloud. "Why is the reaction speeding up?"

His mind raced through his procedure. The components were clean. Heat was sustained. Catalysts had been added in the right sequence. The retardant—

That was it, he realized. He hadn't added enough salt copperas to restrict the reaction. His hands sprang for a small wooden box on the corner of the desk and flipped open the lid.

Empty.

Chance leapt from his stool, knocking it to the ground as he scrambled to his shelves. One by one he shuffled through each of the drawers, searching for more of the retardant. From behind, the compound produced a gargled hiss.

"No!" he cried. "Don't do this to me. Please, don't do this to me."

He was pleading with nothing, anything, everything he could, but every shelf and drawer turned up empty. Turning around, he watched helplessly as the glowing liquid squelched and dulled into nothing more than a sickly grey paste.

Throwing his hands up in the air, Chance fell back against the shelves and slumped down into a dejected heap on the floor. Three days wasted. His hands wrung his hair, tugging until his scalp hurt, and he bit his lip until he tasted blood.

Perhaps he'd been foolish to work with such large quantities. He didn't want to calculate the cost of the spoiled components—not yet—but he could only anticipate how far this botched mixing would set him back.

How could he have let himself run so low on salt copperas? Granted, the task of restocking the laboratory's components fell upon

Ashworth's new apprentice, Rhett, but Chance should have known to double-check his stores. He had, after all, spent six years in those same shoes. He couldn't count the number of times during his apprenticeship when he'd left Ashworth fumbling over empty vials.

It was the unwritten way of the apprentice.

The thought of Ashworth made Chance's stomach turn over. He'd borrowed some of the more expensive components for this mixture from Ashworth's personal stores. Now he had nothing with which to replace them. Why had he been so self-assured?

He wasn't looking forward to explaining to Ashworth why his calcinated hartshorn now resembled a putrid foot grease.

After giving himself a moment to wallow, Chance rose to his feet and paced the room. He would have to replace the spent components out of his own savings. That was easier said than done. What he possessed scarcely covered his costs of living, much less the cost of maintaining his laboratory.

Pausing before his cloudy mirror, Chance gave himself a once over. He looked terrible. His hair was shaggy and unkempt, his shirt untucked and hanging out the bottom of his faded vest. His face and clothes were dusted with a fine layer of soot and powders of sundry colors.

He stared at himself, disgusted by his pale, emaciated complexion. No, the years working in the laboratory had not been kind to him.

Splashing some water from the wash bin on his face, he wiped it dry with a rag. "I'll get to it tomorrow," he said decidedly, tossing the rag to the side.

He was about to leave when the mixture made a series of faint popping sounds. He only had a second to glance at it before the beaker shattered, sending fragments of glass in all directions and knocking some of his instruments onto the floor. They hit the ground with the crackle of more breaking glass.

Chance unclenched himself from the ball he'd tucked himself into. Glass covered the floor and speckles of grey paste dotted nearly every surface. He surveyed the mess with a look of utter exasperation.

"You've got to be kidding me," he sighed.

CHAPTER TWO
A Familiar Story

If there's one thing you can rely on, it's unreliability.

— Alchemical Proverb

After he'd cleaned up the mess, Chance stepped out into the enclosed walkway which connected his laboratory and Ashworth's home. He was in a sour mood, but he took a moment to collect himself before he went in, breathing deep and savoring the fresh air.

He gazed through the aged glass panes up into the sky. The sun was approaching the horizon, its buttery tint staining everything its light touched.

The alchemist's hour, Chance thought. *When all the world turns to gold.*

From the walkway, he spotted Rhett digging in a few potting jars set up in the corner by the retaining wall. He was a quiet, optimistic little fellow, always trailing along in Chance and Ashworth's shadows and ducking his head whenever he was noticed.

At times the boy grated on Chance's nerves. But, he was generally an eager, curious boy. Those were important virtues in an alchemist. Confidence was something he could acquire over time.

"Rhett," Chance called out, pushing on one of the panes in the walkway wall. It stuck, and Chance had to give it a firm thump with his palm to get it to swing open.

Rhett perked up, craning his head around.

"Go on and call it a day. You've been at it long enough."

"But Ashworth said to tend the garden," Rhett said, pointing with his spade at the half dozen plants still unpotted. Each had a fresh batch of weeds clinging to the small clumps of soil at their base.

"If you'd gotten to it when he told you to this morning you wouldn't be out here this late," Chance said. Rhett's head sank deeper into his shoulders. "You can finish it up tomorrow. Come in and have something to eat."

"Just..." Rhett hesitated, his hands still in the pots. "One minute! I can get it done!" He turned back and frantically tore the weeds from the clumps that remained.

Chance shook his head and continued into the house.

It was a precarious building, built from brick recycled from a fire years before and added onto so many times that each room seemed to grow out of the others with no thought to any prior style or material. It made for an exceptional space, in a dizzying sort of way.

Chance often wondered if he might wake one morning to find himself buried underneath its rubble—a thought which inspired his habit of sleeping on the couch in his laboratory most nights, rather than in his own bed.

Inside, Chance was greeted by a series of enthusiastic barks as their hound tore down the hall and threw the full weight of her body up against his legs. The force of her greeting nearly knocked him to the ground.

"Yeah, I see you," he said rubbing her head roughly as he tried to push her away. But she pivoted around his hand and pressed him up against the door again. "Wretched mutt! Why is she even inside?" Chance asked, struggling to free himself.

"As I recall, you were the one who brought her home in the first place."

Ashworth sat at the kitchen table reading the evening paper, a cup of broth beside him. He was an older fellow, more gentlemanly in his demeanor than most in their part of the city. Though he looked frail, his voice possessed a calming air which gave each of his words a deliberate, singular quality.

"She followed me home," Chance protested. "It's completely different."

"Mmhmm," Ashworth grinned. "And it was Rhett who fed her, I suppose."

Chance took a stick from beside the door and threw it against the opposite wall. The hound leapt after it, pushing it along the wall before trapping it against the doorpost.

Chance smiled as he watched her struggle with it. They'd never named her. They'd taken to calling her Mutt, and Mutt she remained. Yet, despite her lack of a name, she'd come to be one of them.

Chance rummaged through the cupboards for something to eat. The room had been a breezeway before, but Ashworth had converted it to a kitchen shortly after Rhett's arrival to make room for another workspace. Retrieving a half-loaf of bread and the clay jar where they kept the butter, he joined Ashworth at the table.

"Good afternoon, Ashworth."

"Evening, you mean," Ashworth corrected, nodding to the clock on the wall. "Though I trust that the afternoon was, indeed, a good one. How did that mixing go?"

"To be honest, not well," Chance admitted. "Let's just say we won't be needing any grease for these cabinet hinges for a while."

"I'm sorry to hear that." Ashworth rested his paper in his lap. "But, you know that a setback isn't such an uncommon thing. You can't expect things to go flawlessly every time. You'll just have to learn from your mistake and give it another go—but I'm certain you're already doing that."

Chance nodded.

"Fortunate this was only a simple mixture, and you weren't working with anything irreplaceable."

Chance swallowed hard. The knot in his stomach was tightening.

"About that..." he began.

"Oh dear, here we go," Ashworth sighed.

"I took some calcinated hartshorn from your workshop the other day. I meant to replace it with what money I made off this batch, but—"

"Chance," Ashworth frowned. He tossed the paper down on the table. "How much did you take?"

"Twelve measures. It would have been replaced by tomorrow, I swear!"

"Is something gone?" Rhett asked, entering the room. He carried a bundle of herbs haphazardly in his arms, pieces of loose dirt falling to the floor as he walked. He looked curiously from Chance to Ashworth.

"Don't worry about it," Chance said, slumping down in his chair. He stabbed at his bread with his knife, the dry crust flaking as the blade pierced its hardened shell.

"Are you just now finishing in the garden?" Ashworth asked Rhett.

"Um... yes?"

"I expect those to be cleaned and hung to dry before you turn in tonight. They should have been hung hours ago. I hate to think what else you didn't get to if you're only coming in now with those. What about the rats?"

"I couldn't find any," Rhett shrugged.

"None?" Ashworth's pursed his lips. "What is it you've been doing all day?"

Rhett's head sank even lower. Honestly, sometimes Chance couldn't tell if the boy had a neck.

"You see, this is exactly where your problem lies," Ashworth continued, turning to include Chance in the lecture. "Somehow you two have the notion trapped in your heads that you've got everything under control. That you'll have enough time, enough money, or just enough dumb luck to do whatever it is that weasels its way into those minds of yours when the truth is that there are dozens of variables beyond your control and not one of us can account for them all.

"If there's one lesson you ought to learn as an apprentice it's that you can't count on any given outcome. Not in alchemy. Not in life. We work with the volatile! The less you fool yourself into believing you govern the outcome and the more you focus on the tasks at hand then the more likely you'll be to accomplish something despite that unforgiving fact."

Chance felt his own neck sinking into his shoulders, and he tried to straighten up to preserve some of his dignity.

Ashworth sighed and pulled at his chin.

"Alchemy is a profession based on respect," he emphasized. "Respect for the elements and respect for fate. And, most of all, a respect for those who've gone before you. Have you ever thought that I might have made some of these same poor decisions myself and am trying to guard you from doing the same?

"But, I suppose you have a right to learn for yourselves firsthand," Ashworth concluded. "Go ahead. Do what you will. I've had enough for tonight." He opened his paper again as though it were a shield from any further conversation.

Rhett seized the opportunity and vanished through the open door leaving Chance to bear the brunt of Ashworth's silence alone.

Chance's face grew hot. He wanted to argue. He wanted to tell Ashworth how close he'd come. He was even tempted to point out Rhett's neglect to refill his components, but he refrained. It wouldn't have done any good anyway. Rhett didn't deserve more trouble than he already caused for himself.

"Had things gone better, we'd have had enough money to restock our components for a month," Chance grumbled when he couldn't bear the silence anymore.

"Yes, well, in the craft of alchemy how many good intentions have gone up in flames before yours?"

The frustration in Ashworth's voice had dissipated some. He leaned forward and spoke with a voice of sincere concern.

"Chance, I can't have my personal stores going missing. When that happens, it puts me in a poor position. A poor position indeed. What would happen if a concoction called for hartshorn, and I discovered too late that it was gone? Unlike you, I work with time sensitive components. They can turn on you in a moment."

Chance sat buttering his bread quietly. He understood that problem better than Ashworth knew.

"Oh well," Ashworth said. "No sense crying over past mistakes. Septigonee knows there's enough misfortune coming tomorrow not to carry today's along with us. Best to learn and let it lie. There's some money in the coffee tin inside the pantry. Tomorrow morning, you and Rhett run down to the Exchange and buy what we need to resupply. You can start again in the morning. I don't have the energy to deal with this tonight anyway."

Chance nodded. He wanted to protest the idea of using Ashworth's money for the purchases, but there was no way he could afford it alone. He ate his bread quietly, glancing at the headlines on the back of Ashworth's paper.

It was Ashworth's daily ritual, reading the news. Three separate papers were delivered to the house every day, one of them both a morning and evening edition. Chance didn't understand what he found so fascinating. It seemed to him that anything that happened in Hatteras was either too dull to be of interest, or else about the meritocracy and therefore of little consequence to those who lived in the Basin.

Ashworth had explained once that he found it diverting to find the inconsistencies between papers—like it was some secret game. Chance thought the practice rather mind-numbing.

Tonight, however, Ashworth wasn't leafing through as he usually did. He seemed to be hung up on one particular article. After a long moment, he set the paper down and stared off at the wall, his brow creasing and his fingers interlocked.

"Something wrong?" Chance asked.

"A familiar name in the obituaries," Ashworth said. "An old friend passed away earlier this morning."

"Who's that?"

"Captain Willard Harper. A comrade of mine from years back. About the time of the Great War."

"A soldier?" Chance asked, giving Ashworth a queer look. "I didn't know you fought in the war." Chance had long before accepted there were things about his mentor he didn't know, yet something in his mind's eye made it difficult to picture Ashworth in uniform wielding a flintlock and saber.

"Goodness, no," Ashworth corrected. "Even back then, I was just a simple alchemist. Perhaps comrade was the wrong word. He was a good friend, and a fine soldier. He returned with quite a few distinctions for his bravery overseas, though they cost him dearly."

"What do you mean?"

"Well, like most of the men who were sent to fight, he was injured. An explosive, and a primitive one at that, wounded him just months before the conflict was over. Nearly tore him apart. I don't believe many thought he'd make it. But Willard, he wasn't the type to go peaceably down to Septigonee's Well. He held on long enough for them to fly him back to Hatteras to undergo more... drastic procedures.

"Even on what we all considered his deathbed he was a fighter," Ashworth mused, sipping his broth. Chance suspected it had already gone cold.

"Seems like a lot of effort to keep just one soldier alive."

"Not just a soldier," Ashworth explained. "A war hero. He'd become something of a symbol of everything Hatteras was fighting for across the sea—the embodiment of its independent spirit. They called him 'the good captain'.

"The people were too invested in breaking from Selaria to let their symbol of resistance die. They worked on him for days, bringing in doctors, alchemists, and even a few mechanists to try and save him. Clockwork mechanics were not as advanced then as they are now, but the mechanists managed to reconstruct his shoulder and build an artificial support to his heart and lung—all while we alchemists did our best to sustain him throughout the procedure."

"You worked on him?"

"I did."

Chance shuddered. He had seen wounded veterans in the streets on occasion, with their lifeless mechanical prosthetics. The sight of metal merging with bone and tissue unnerved him, and the thought set a hook in the back of his throat.

"That sounds horrible."

"It wasn't pleasant," Ashworth agreed. "But, it did preserve his life."

"What did he look like? After his recovery? It must have been horrifying."

"I'm not sure exactly. We weren't on speaking terms once the war began, and he made no effort to see me when it was all over. I only heard about his recovery through the papers. He went on to be quite the figure among the new meritocracy, as I read. The city is what it is today in part because of him. But what it must have been like to live out his life with that twisted mess we built of him..."

"I would rather they'd let me die," Chance said, "rather than having to lug about a hunk of dead-weight like that."

"But it wasn't dead weight!" Ashworth's eyes lit up. "It was one of the most remarkable feats of medicine and mechanism that I've beheld to this day. You see, the mechanism they built for him was so piecemeal—they'd built it into him in such a way that it was difficult to tell exactly where he began and the mechanism ended.

"And then, somewhere in the process of it all, something... took. It was as if the mechanism itself became a part of him." He leaned closer to Chance and whispered in a low voice. "He moved the arm."

Chance stared at Ashworth.

"He moved it," he said again, when Chance failed to react. "Goodness, boy. The arm! He moved the arm as if it were his own!"

"But," Chance struggled to wrap his head around the thought. "How is that possible?"

"We hadn't the slightest idea!" Ashworth let out a humored laughed. "It baffled everyone who witnessed it. But regardless, something about that operation connected the two, and he could move the mechanism as if it had always been a part of him.

"We'd never done anything like it before, and it's never been repeated. They never could go back to work on it for fear of undoing what they'd done. It would have been too risky. But," Ashworth's eyes grew wide as he considered it, "what a feat to behold—the merging of man and machine. Never had I seen anything like it. Nor likely will again."

"Sounds unnatural to me," Chance said.

"I agree. Natural is certainly not the word I would use—though the prosthetic functioned nearly as naturally as the limb it replaced."

"I suppose mechanists are good at what they do."

"You know, I may have kept some of my notes from that surgery," Ashworth said. "Some of my thoughts and observations. Perhaps I could dig them up for you? You might find it interesting."

"No thanks," Chance said. "I don't make it a habit to spend my time worrying about what mechanists do with theirs. I've got my own work to worry about."

"A mechanist's work and ours isn't so different. Might do you some good to stretch your mind a little. Perhaps it will help you come at your own work from another angle. I'm sure Welch would be happy to explain some of it to you. You'd be surprised what our crafts have in common."

Chance couldn't keep his eyes from rolling. "The last thing I'd want is to work with Welch. Besides, he's not a real mechanist; he's just a tinkerer."

"Gleaning a little knowledge from other fields isn't a poor use of time," Ashworth insisted. "Often it's the little clues we pick up along the way that help unlock the real mysteries."

"Maybe," Chance shrugged.

They sat in silence again. Chance nibbled at his bread while Ashworth sipped his broth. Chance mind wandered as he thought of what it might be like to live with a prosthetic. To have a portion of yourself made of brass gears and copper plating. It was a strange thought.

"So, what killed him?" Chance finally asked. "In the end?"

"What we'd all expected from the beginning." Ashworth pushed the column to Chance. "It was only a matter of time; the prosthetic was built too haphazardly to last. They were trying to replace it when he died th—"

Ashworth had a sudden fit of coughing.

"Are you alright?" Chance asked, but Ashworth waved his hand dismissively. It was a moment before he caught his breath again.

"—this morning," he finished. He stood and fetched some water from the pump.

"You sure you're alright?"

"I'm fine," Ashworth said, wiping his eyes.

Chance glanced over the article. "When did you last speak to him?"

"Twenty-five years ago," Ashworth sighed. "It sounds so long when I say it. I did try to contact him a few years back, but he wouldn't see me. He's become something of a hermit these days. I felt like I owed it to him to try though."

He took his seat again and leaned back with a heavy look. "And now he's gone," he said.

"So, you were never able to fix things with him?"

"It's my greatest regret," Ashworth confided. "We may have had our falling out, but I still considered him a good friend. The war was a shame, but the way it divided Hatteras was, I believe, the greatest ill that came of it. It would have meant a great deal to me to speak to him again and set things right between us."

"I'm sure he understands," Chance assured. He didn't really buy what he was implying, but it seemed like the right thing to say at a time like this. Either way, the conversation was making him uncomfortable.

"I still couldn't imagine what it would be like to live with a prosthetic," he said. "Can you imagine trying to write a letter with a mechanical hand? Or use the john? It's hard enough to aim with a good hand."

Ashworth frowned. The joke hadn't had the desired effect.

"Sorry," Chance said. "I was just trying to lighten the mood."

"It's alright," Ashworth said. "I'm not much in a mood to laugh. Though I didn't mean to infect you with my melancholy either. I think... I think I could use a walk." He rose from the table.

"But it's getting late."

"Oh, don't worry about me. I'll be fine." Ashworth fumbled in his pocket and pulled out a few loose coins, handing them to Chance. "In case there isn't enough in the tin to replace what you lost."

"We should have enough."

"Good. Be sure you clean up whatever mess you've left in the lab before you turn in, and keep an eye on Rhett. Perhaps give him a hand? I don't want to think of what else he might have neglected to do today."

"Where are you going?"

"Umm... nowhere, I suppose," Ashworth said. "I've just got things on my mind. Some air might do me good." He pushed the cold broth over to Chance. "You can finish this if you'd like."

Ashworth retrieved his coat from where it hung on a knob by the back door and popped into his workroom. A few minutes later, Chance heard the latch on the front door as it opened and closed.

Chance looked over the captain's obituary, gleaning a few more details about his life and service. He'd never seen so many honors in one paragraph. His mind turned to his old friend Ringgold. He was probably off building his own collection of medals in some colony somewhere.

An itch tugged at the back of his throat. His conversation with Ashworth had surfaced the memory without him realizing it. Swallowing hard, Chance pushed the thought of his once friend to the recesses of his mind.

"Is he still mad?" Rhett asked, poking his head through the door.

"Not at you," Chance said. "He's just having a rough day."

Rhett nodded, as if he'd been there the whole time—which he probably had—and sat on the edge of the countertop.

"So why did you lie to him?" Chance asked.

Rhett's face turned red, and he folded his arms over his stomach. "I didn't lie."

"About not having a rat?"

Rhett looked up fearfully.

"You're alright, Rhett," Chance assured him. "I won't tell Ashworth."

"You promise?"

Rhett's eyes nearly broke Chance's heart. There may not have been much backbone in the boy, but Chance admired his measure of heart. He nodded, and Rhett smiled with relief.

Reaching into his shirt, Rhett pulled out a stout brown rat and deposited it on the table. Its hair was matted and its tail had a few nicks cut out of it. The rodent tried to scurry off the table, but Rhett built a barrier around it with his arms.

"Did you name him?" Chance asked.

"No."

"How are you going to tell him from the others without a name?"

"He knows who I am. He comes when I talk to him," Rhett explained. He put a bit of butter on the tip of his finger and let the rat lick it off.

"We really need to work on our naming things. People will think we're lazy." Chance took the rest of his bread and threw it to the mutt, who'd curled up on a loose blanket in the corner. She snapped the crumbs midair.

"You can keep that one," Chance said, "but tomorrow we're setting fresh traps again. We need something to test with if we're going to sell anything this week."

"You'll help me catch some?"

"Sure," Chance said, swirling the cold broth in Ashworth's cup. He got up and poured it back into the pot on the stove top. "I have a few deliveries I need to make down by the docks anyway. We're bound to catch a few there. You can tag along."

"Thanks!"

"Don't thank me yet," Chance grinned. "You've got cleanup to-night."

CHAPTER THREE
Brooding

Some took to scrutinizing my work in those early days, and what should I have expected? Men are nearsighted. They comprehend the future only one day at a time. They cannot fathom what I've brought within arm's reach.

— Excerpt from *Mechanarcissism*

Doctor Stoddard stooped low over the fireplace, a portion of his oiled hair falling loose in front of his face as he poked at the fresh logs. He watched the glow of the coals spread into flames across the new fuel.

It wasn't quite autumn yet, but the morgue possessed a chill not easily dispelled—and the agitation of his mind only increased his present discomforts.

Not that the room was wholly unpleasant. Where the rest of the morgue was harsh in its sterile simplicity, some effort had been made to furnish this specific room. A heavy oak table stood in the middle, with a few cushioned chairs in conference around it. The walls were the same crusty-white plaster, but a few paintings had been hung to variegate them.

One in particular stood out to Stoddard each time he visited the morgue. It depicted the God of heaven as an elderly clockmaker, stooped over his work. Stoddard often paused under that painting whenever he found himself delayed by some bureaucratic process.

But today, he had been too distracted to follow his normal routine and hadn't even remembered the painting hung above him. Instead, he leaned heavily on the hearth and gazed into the fire, rubbing his weary eyes.

He was a stoic figure, possessing a certain formality which communicated itself in the way he held himself. No one passing by at that moment would have perceived the distress with which his mind grappled. They would have seen a handsome man, thoughtful and collected, the glow of the fire accentuating the sharp angles of his cheekbones and the strong slope of his nose.

Stoddard, however, perceived himself as both disagreeable and troubled.

Once the logs were burning steadily he returned to his seat. Reports, medical records, and correspondences lay open in front of him, spread across the table in a web-like sequence only he could connect.

Most important were a stack of accounts from nearly two dozen witnesses who'd attended Captain Harper's procedure earlier that day. He took one of the folders from off the pile and flipped it open. He'd read over them multiple times, searching for what he feared each would inevitably possess.

Fault.

Yet, he found none directed toward himself or his work. Not openly, at least. The witnesses agreed unanimously that Harper's death was nothing more than the result of his aged feebleness. The good captain simply hadn't been strong enough to undergo such a complicated surgery.

Yet, Stoddard sensed a faint dissatisfaction. They had obviously expected more of him. Hadn't he?

He flipped the folder closed and clenched his fingers together under his chin. He could still envision the witnesses circled above him in the medical dome. Judging his work. Judging him.

But who were they to judge him? Those men knew nothing of his labors—of the design he'd perfected over years and the mechanism he'd created. It was beyond the imaginations of any mechanist who'd dared dream before.

And the weakness of one old man had stolen away his moment of recognition. Instead of cheering him on, Stoddard could already anticipate his sponsors, one by one, readying themselves to discard him as an ill investment and move on to other auspicious work.

"Damn you, Harper," he brooded. "Damn you to Septigonee's Well."

He sat like that for some time, cursing the good captain and cursing his own misfortunes. He wasn't one to let his emotions get the better of him, but in that moment he allowed his mind to degenerate in his frustration. It sank into depths he'd not frequented for what felt like eons, until he was quite certain he might not recover himself.

But then, somewhere in those depths, he struck a thought which resonated with such fervor it replaced his feelings of defeat. If this was truly the moment when his worth was to be judged by the meritocracy then he would not leave it in their hands alone. He would make clear his accomplishment—prove it to them, whatever it required. He would not allow himself to be discarded easily, not until his great contribution to the city was made.

"Donovan!" Stoddard called.

There was no response from the hallway. The man had been assigned him from the Bureau of Sciences months before to help with the more mundane tasks as Stoddard prepared for the operation. It was relief Stoddard had taken liberal advantage of.

"Donovan!" he repeated.

Cursing under his breath, he rolled up his sleeves and pulled the typewriter sitting nearby closer. His hands hovered over the keys. It was imperative he reach out to his most influential contacts first if he was going to retain their funding. He needed to show them his work did not end with Harper.

Thinking through his list of sponsors, he made a mental list and began to type the first of many letters.

> *Lord McCallister,*
> *I write in regards to the recent events surrounding*

the...

No, he thought. His tone was all wrong. He cursed and tore the page from the typewriter, replaced it with a fresh sheet, and began again.

> *Lord McCallister,*
>
> *No doubt by now news of the death of the late Captain Harper has reached you. His untimely passing is a profound loss to our city, and we can only praise his many contributions during his life.*
>
> *I'm sure at this time you are curious to know the outcome of your investment. As always, I offer my profoundest gratitude for your lasting support these long years. Rest assured that, despite this unfortunate setback, our prosthetic was flawless in its design. It is both my opinion—and the opinion of those present as witnesses, as you're sure to confirm in coming days—that our good captain's death was a direct result of old age combined with the complications of his previous injuries, and not a fault of the mechanism itself.*
>
> *I remain confident that the mechanism would have replicated the link with Captain Harper as his previous prosthetic miraculously did at the hands of my mentor so many years ago.*
>
> *I wish to reassure you that, as future opportunities present themselves, we will see this most revolutionary work distinguish our great city as the forerunning scientific epicenter of the world. For that purpose, I urge you to continue your dialogue amongst the meritocracy on our behalf and to maintain your generous support.*
>
> *With greatest regard,*

Pulling the page from the typewriter and glanced over it for errors. Once satisfied, he signed it Dr. J. Collins Stoddard and gently blew on the ink.

A knock sounded at the door and his assistant let himself in. Donovan carried a few newspapers under his arm and a steaming cup of coffee in the opposite hand.

"Good evening, sir," he said briskly.

"I needed you earlier," Stoddard said, doing nothing to mask his impatience.

"My apologies." Donovan bowed, setting the coffee on the table. A bit of it sloshed over the side and onto the saucer. "I was just collecting the evening papers, as you'd requested—any that referenced Captain Harper." He set them on the table as well.

"And?"

"Almost every one of them mentioned the captain to some extent. I have here the more noteworthy for your review. With the delays on the rails this evening, I had opportunity to peruse them myself. Apparently, some poor fellow threw himself on the tracks. Quite the grisly ordeal."

"Transit stories don't interest me at the moment," Stoddard said, lifting one of the papers up to the light. He ignored the coffee. "What was your impression?"

"Most of the papers touched only briefly on the captain's death. None ventured to speculate the cause prematurely. I was able to contact those who might have early enough to dissuade them from being too overzealous. They were willing to wait with the expectation you'd provide them with a more engaging story.

"In the meantime, they've taken to printing longer accounts of the captain's life—service in the military, contributions to the city, and the like. I didn't find any negative mention about the procedure itself, or in regards to yourself."

"Good," Stoddard said, satisfied. He continued to scan the articles, a few words leaping out at him as he did so.

Tragic loss.

Valiant efforts.

A complex procedure.

Stoddard tucked the phrases away in his mind so that he might echo the popular vernacular in his interactions over the next few days.

"These aren't the only papers in print," Stoddard pointed out.

"No, sir. I thought you'd only be interested in the more reputable presses."

"That's not enough. I want you to search every press from the Spire to the Basin that has so much as printed his name in an obituary. I want to know what *everyone* is saying. We leave it to chance and we risk the public jumping to a conclusion ill considered. Now is a time for excessive vigilance."

"Yes, sir. I'll make it my first priority."

"Good."

"I also have tomorrow's schedule here. There are a few pending requests for your consideration. Shall I read them now?"

Stoddard nodded.

"A few members of the meritocracy have requested an audience tomorrow at the Pavilion de Lucarne. I'm under the impression this will be an informal social event—no doubt to inquire firsthand about the captain's procedure."

"No doubt," Stoddard agreed. "Is there anyone in attendance who might be a valuable contact?"

"The invitation was distributed by Gentleman Merryfield."

Stoddard waved his hand dismissively. "Merryfield is hardly advantageous. He's likely seeking to appear more influential than he is with his invitation."

"Agreed, sir. But, I have it on good authority that he's already received confirmations from Dempwolf, Lafern, and Marklevitz. I suspect they were compelled to accept the invitation by the promise of an opportunity to meet you."

Stoddard pondered the proposal. He took it as a sign of good fortune if members of the meritocracy were eager enough to meet with him that they'd subject themselves to Merryfield's invitation. He was a bumble of a socialite, yet Stoddard couldn't fault the man for his prompt exploitation of the circumstance.

With luck, it would prove advantageous to them all.

"Send Merryfield a letter accepting his invitation," Stoddard said.

Donovan made a note of it.

"A meeting with the governor has been scheduled to follow immediately afterward. Apparently, he's entertaining foreign delegates from the colonies in the early morning. However, I believe he wishes to thank you personally for your efforts to save the good captain. I've already informed him you'd meet with him at his earliest convenience."

"Good."

"And you have quite a few invitations for lunch," Donovan continued. "I've sorted through them and selected those I felt would be of most interest to you."

He handed Stoddard a stack of four invitations, which Stoddard skimmed through quickly. As he read the third, he paused and looked up at Donovan. A ridiculous grin was plastered across the man's face.

"This is from Elector Sinclair," Stoddard said, taken aback.

"Indeed. I thought you'd be particularly interested in that one."

"Accept it," Stoddard said, ignoring the others.

"Yes, sir."

Stoddard pressed his hands together in thought. If an elector, one of the very highest members of the meritocracy, was requesting his presence he could only take it as a very good sign indeed. It meant that, despite the unfortunate turnout of the operation, he'd managed to catch the eye of the uppermost circles of the meritocracy—the men who held the keys to the city itself.

Perhaps he'd been too pessimistic, expecting the worst.

He was beginning to see pieces laid out before him and a stratagem was devising in his mind. First, he needed to satisfy the press. They were bloodhounds for news, and it would only be a matter of time before they tried to dig up something meatier if they weren't appeased. He couldn't have them muddling things up.

Stoddard drew out a folder from one of his many piles and handed it to Donovan. "See that these records make their way into the press's hands," he instructed.

"Sir?" Donovan glanced over the documents briefly. "But, these are Harper's personal records."

"Yes, they are," Stoddard said, finally accepting the coffee. He drank deeply, the hot liquid hardly fazing him as it went down. "You'll also find a detailed account of the procedure. The meritocracy I can win over personally, but I want the public to understand how invested I was in Harper's condition—the inherent risks we entered into with this procedure.

"If I've learned anything about maintaining one's reputation it is never to leave it to speculation—particularly when it comes to the common masses. They're a dim lot with less sense than the boors in the colonies. I expect to see those facts published in the morning editions."

"Yes, sir," Donovan said. "Am I to understand these documents have been approved for release then?" Stoddard gave him a look and Donovan nodded knowingly, tucking the folder under his arm.

"Also, I would like to schedule a postmortem of the body," Stoddard added. "Schedule it for Thursday. I'd do it sooner if I wasn't otherwise occupied, but it cannot be helped. Notify Doctor Franklin that I'll need him to perform the procedure."

Donovan hesitated. "Is a postmortem really necessary? There were plenty of witnesses in the dome."

Stoddard frowned, setting his coffee down on the table.

"As long as anyone might possess even a sliver of doubt that I did all in my power for the captain it absolutely is," he snapped. "The mechanism would have functioned perfectly; I and a dozen mechanists can testify to that—and the public won't dispute it. They're ignorant when it comes to clockwork mechanics. The profession is too difficult for them to understand.

"However, what I must ensure is that the public is assured his death was no cause of my own. For whatever reason, they're much more willing to speculate regarding medicine. So, we will discourage them with hard facts. Leave them no room to wonder. What part of that was unclear?"

"None of it, sir," Donovan said, standing a little straighter.

Stoddard sat, contemplating the day's events. His finger tapped fitfully against the side of his cup. He might have staunched the threat of the papers, and he was encouraged with regards to leveraging his position with the meritocracy, but there was one matter that still distressed him.

He hadn't been able to test his mechanism.

It gnawed at his mind—not knowing if he could replicate the miraculous link that had tapped into the captain before. Everything leading up to the operation had suggested the prosthetic would have functioned perfectly. Yet, the captain had died, and only moments before Stoddard could test it. Thirteen long hours in surgery, and he had overshot his window by mere minutes.

"How frail are our bodies," he sighed.

"Sir?"

"Nothing," Stoddard said. "Just thinking to myself. Tell me, Donovan, did you know you'd be what you are now when you were young?"

"I'm not sure I follow."

"When you were young. Was it your aspiration to assist others in this capacity?"

"I was raised to be whatever I was needed to be," Donovan said.

"Well said. Each of us a part to play—a role to fill. That is the singularity that distinguishes us from the rest of the world. You knew your role would be to serve, another's to lead, and others yet to labor. But I..." Stoddard paused. "I never intended to be a doctor."

He laughed a short laugh when he saw Donovan's look of concern.

"In fact, I find the time I invest in the profession entirely disagreeable," he continued. "My mind has always had an affinity for gears and springs, ever since I was a youth. I always knew I would create. Had I known then what that would require of me I might have hesitated."

"You regret the role you've played, sir?"

"Not entirely," Stoddard said. "But, sometimes I consider what it would have been to have given my entire focus to clockwork mechanics. There's a permanence about it. Where is Sir Jamison Walt now? Dead, as all are bound to be. Nevertheless, his rails still carry cargo from the shipyards through the city. And Master Walcott? Just as lifeless, yet his circuits illuminate our streets. Their legacies are built into the very infrastructure of this city."

Stoddard closed his eyes and imagined it, picturing the city from a bird's-eye view, yet with a privileged insight into its most intimate workings. It was beautiful, a city so perfect in design that it breathed life of its own.

"What kind of contributions might I have made to this city, I wonder?"

"What you're doing for the city is significant," Donovan assured him.

"Yet unfulfilled," Stoddard scowled. He rose from his chair and paced near the fire. "I've married my success to an unreliable bedmate. Ever since I began to study medicine it's been a profoundly distressing condition to wrestle with—the frailty of our mortality.

"There's no permanency in it," he pointed out, gripping his hand into a tight fist to emphasize his point. "It doesn't matter if you treat someone's cough; they're soon to develop another. And blood saved today is only blood spent tomorrow. Then that great incurable brute, Death, looms with his dreaded ultimatum in the end. Everyone dies, Donovan. No amount of medicine prevents the final cut of mortality—the very same cut that plucked this greatest victory from me today."

Donovan remained quiet where he stood.

"It's not a subject I expect many wish to dwell on for long," Stoddard said. "Better to simply ignore the fact altogether and let it stalk us silently from the shadows. But that our infinite intelligence would be cursed with such an imperfect form—" He relaxed his fist. "Nature goads reason."

"It is a conundrum," Donovan agreed.

"But, there are moments... fleeting moments when I nearly believe I've figured it out? There's a solution there. Here," he said, tapping the papers before him. "I might have had more of the answer now had the good captain bought me a few minutes more."

A thunderclap sounded outside, shaking the room with a faint rumbling.

"Was it storming as you came in?" Stoddard asked.

"No, sir."

"That's enough for tonight, I think." Stoddard collected some of his papers and placed them in his briefcase, latching it closed. He left the rest strewn across the table. "Keep me informed of any new developments. Tomorrow we'll do what we can to put our best foot forward with the meritocracy. Perhaps, we'll come out favored in this after all."

"Yes, sir. Would you like me to fetch you a coach?"

"Quickly." Stoddard switched off the lamp and locked the room as they left. In the hall, he paused at the reception desk while Donovan stepped outside.

"Is that everything for today, Doctor?" the young receptionist asked.

"For tonight," Stoddard said. "Leave the office locked for me. I'm leaving my things here. I'll be back for them tomorrow evening."

"Certainly, doctor. Don't get caught in the storm on your way out," she said as he donned his coat and followed Donovan into the rain.

CHAPTER FOUR
The Spark

Had I known then where that first step would take us, I might have reconsidered how I let it fall.

— Excerpt from *Mechanarcissism*

Ashworth walked with a labored gait—his hands buried deep in his pockets and his shoulders pulled tight into his body. He wandered through familiar streets with only a vague sense of direction, his mind trailing somewhere a few steps behind.

His hand clutched the cold cylinder in his pocket. Its presence left no room to doubt the intention that had set him on his way. Yet, he questioned his resolve. The thought which had entered his mind had been so abrupt, and at the same time strangely premeditated. He feared if he dwelt on it too long he might abandon it altogether.

With great effort, he relaxed his grip and directed his mind to other things.

Ashworth pulled his coat tighter around him. The chill which numbed his hands and bit at his cheeks seemed disregarded by those he passed. A disadvantage of his age, he knew. The great clock was winding down.

How much time did he have left? A few more years, perhaps? Days?

With Harper's passing, it was all the more apparent how time worked against him, and how soon he too would make his way down to Septigonee's Well.

He expelled a forceful cough and kept walking.

There were still quite a few people out on the streets—mostly simple, uninteresting folk from the Basin. They drifted by like wisps of fog from the bay, their faces sullen and private. Occasionally, he'd greet a passerby with a courteous nod, and they'd return it in kind. Or with a grunt. Or even occasionally a mumbled greeting. It was routine, those brief unspoken exchanges. In the Basin, they served to take the temperature, so to speak, of the city—assessing moods and gauging intentions.

If one was listening, danger could typically be sensed well before it was encountered.

Tonight, the city felt groggy. Lethargic. People shuffled around facelessly, and Ashworth took comfort in it. Soon, however, as he climbed the long serpentine path of the main road, he was exchanging greetings with cleaner, more established folk.

And then no one exchanged greetings at all.

It was odd to him, that such distinct cultures as the Basin and the Spire could exist so near each other. He could even name the street which separated the two worlds. As he crossed it, he abandoned his attempts at cordiality altogether.

It was getting late. Ashworth's progress was slowed by the rests he was forced to take. His feet ached and his throat was raspy from his heavy breathing. The thought of taking one of the rails which ran through the city crossed his mind, yet every time he neared a station he would pass it by, caught up in the rhythm of his footsteps and the memories playing in his mind.

"Do you really have to go?"

The words echoed in his mind, so hauntingly real that Ashworth turned about half-expecting to see someone standing there. But he was alone, and he kept on.

"Who else will go it if I won't?"

"There are thousands of others who will fight. Let them go."

"It'll be alright. I'm proud to serve Hatteras. She's been good to us. It'd be bad grace not to honor her."

Ashworth turned up the street, pulling his trench coat up against his neck to shield himself from the steady wind.

"You think you're better than I am?"

"I never said that."

"You never had to. It's dripping from your lips with every word. What is it about my choice that makes you so bitter? If you had any loyalties at all you'd be standing with me."

"It's my loyalty that compels me!"

"No! It's your fear that keeps you from staying."

There was a deafening boom as a bolt of lightning struck a building somewhere nearby. Ashworth jerked to a halt. His heart beat fast and heavy. A steady rain began, growing in ferocity until it came down with a vengeance.

"I'm no coward."

"But you're no hero."

Ashworth had spat those last words with such venom that he could taste their rancor as he recalled them. How they haunted him after so many years.

Stopping under an awning, he wiped his mouth on a dampened sleeve and surveyed the street. Apart from a single coach, it was deserted. The rest of the world was taking shelter to wait out the storm.

Then, as sudden as the storm's appearance, Ashworth realized where he stood. With stubborn eyes, he peered through the heavy sheets of rain at his destination—the morgue.

The light from a single window spilled out into the night, peering back at Ashworth through the dark. Despite being in a wealthier part of the city, the building was old and worn. Likely, it had been converted from some vacant structure at one time or another. The crumbling brick was set back away from the street, wedged between two neighboring buildings, neatly obscured in their shadows.

If one wasn't looking, they'd have missed it entirely.

Mustering his courage and weary limbs, Ashworth hurried across the street. He was just beginning to climb the stairs when the doors opened and two men exited the building. Ashworth turned away as they passed and tried to look uninteresting, waiting while one of the men helped the other into a carriage. Only once the driver urged on the horses did Ashworth finish his climb.

Rapping his knuckles against the heavy doors, he shook what water he could from his coat. He heard the latch raise and a sliver of light appeared as the door cracked open.

"Ashworth?" the young woman said in a surprised tone. "What are you doing out in this rain? You'll catch your death on a night like this."

"Good evening, Ambre," Ashworth said, removing his hat. "I thought... or rather I'd hoped you might be here tonight. I was wondering if you might help me with something. A favor, if you would."

"I didn't realize you were coming by tonight." She peeked out around the door, glancing up and down the street. "What do you need?"

"I'm here to see Captain Harper."

Ambre's eyes grew wide.

"No," she said, shaking her head. "No, I can't let you. They've scheduled a postmortem. They'll know you were here! It was risky enough the last time you came by." She spoke fast, her voice panicked as she withdrew back into the building.

"Ambre," Ashworth said, trying to calm her.

"It didn't work. You know that. It didn't work!"

"Ambre," Ashworth said louder, interrupting her rambling. "I'm not here for a test. I'm here as a friend."

"I can't," she said. The door began to close and Ashworth put a hand out to stop her.

"Ambre, he was my friend," he repeated. "I haven't seen him for years because of a disagreement we had. I've held onto it all of my life and it's eating away at me. It's all I can do not to tear my hair out thinking about it since he died. Please, let me see him. For mercy's sake, it would ease an old man's spirit."

"But..." she started.

"He would have wanted me to come," Ashworth lied.

Ambre hesitated. Ashworth saw the fear in her eyes. He'd been fortunate in obtaining her help before, but even he knew how much more of a risk he was asking her to undertake.

"Please."

Finally, with a sigh, she let the door open wide enough to allow him to slip in. She closed it on his heels, nearly catching the tail of his coat, and latched it behind him.

"Hurry," she urged.

"Where is the body?" he asked. He pooled water with each step, but it couldn't be helped.

"Over here." She guided him past the reception area and down a corridor. "You can't stay long. Someone could come by."

"I wouldn't have thought you'd get many visitors to a morgue this late at night."

"I got you," Ambre pointed out as she slid a heavy door open and ushered Ashworth inside.

The room was larger than the reception area, with two slab tables erected in the center. Each had a small channel along the edge that led to a center drain and a light suspended above it. Beside them stood tables full of the tools and instruments of a mortician's trade.

It was in a setting very much like this one when Ashworth had last seen his friend, opened like a book and struggling for life. The thought struck him with an uncharacteristic queasiness, and he stepped away from the slabs.

Heavy steel doors lined two of the walls, like a series of vaults. Each had a large latch which hooked across the front to seal it. Ambre lifted one and swung the door open wide. The sound of metal scraping against metal cut through the silence of the room as she rolled the body out.

"Is everything alright?" she asked, noticing Ashworth's hesitation.

"I'm fine. It's just..." He stumbled, trying to make sense of his feelings. He saw the outline of the captain's body through the thin sheet and the asymmetry of his shoulder. "I just haven't seen him for some time."

Ambre nodded and carefully folded back the sheet so that Harper's head lay uncovered.

Ashworth stepped forward and looked upon the face of his old friend. He'd almost convinced himself he would see the same man he'd known before. Yet, the face before him was aged—devoid of any emotion which might have betrayed the feelings he'd died with.

It dawned on Ashworth just how much his friend had changed over the years. His skin was tough, like that of a veteran, but it had also grown loose and wrinkled so his frailty was all the more apparent. Neither of them were young men anymore.

"How long since he was brought in?" Ashworth inquired.

"About seven hours. You were close?"

"Once upon a time."

The two of them stood in silence, gazing upon the captain. Ashworth cleared his throat.

"Would it be possible to have a moment? Alone, please?"

Ambre's lips pursed.

"To say my goodbyes," Ashworth added. "It won't take but a moment. I just have some personal things I'd like to get off my chest."

"Fine," she said. "But only to say your goodbyes. Let me know when you're finished." She stepped toward the doorway. "And please hurry," she added. "You aren't supposed to be here, remember?"

"Of course," Ashworth agreed.

"If anyone comes, pretend that you're family," she suggested. Ashworth nodded, and she retreated down the corridor to give him his privacy.

Ashworth sighed as he leaned over the cold body. So many years had passed since he'd seen his friend. Nearly a lifetime. And yet he still felt a closeness despite the passing of time.

"It's been a while," he said. His voice sounded strange as it echoed in the sterile room. "Remember me? I wonder if you would, if we were meeting in better circumstances than this."

Harper's body lay unresponsive, and Ashworth nodded. With slow reverence, he pulled the sheet back, exposing the captain's torso.

"Remarkable work," he whispered, admiring the new prosthetic. His memory wasn't as good as it once was, but he saw plainly the improvements of the new mechanism. The bulk alone was remarkably less, and the merging of the machine and flesh cleaner. He saw the fresh scars of surgery mixed with those of Harper's aged war wounds.

Lightly he touched the casing which surrounded Harper's shoulder, fingering the pressure gauge set into it. It read zero.

It amazed him how the engineers had merged their metallic craft with the organic tissue of the body so perfectly. He imagined the many gears and levers under the surface of that casing, still and silent in their metal cage.

But, perhaps not for long.

"I know I'm probably the last man you would want to be here right now," Ashworth began. "I hope you'll find it in your new heart to forgive me for this."

Ashworth ran his fingers over the metal plates which anchored the captain's heart in place while his other hand fumbled in his coat. With a shaking hand, he produced a double-chambered syringe. The separate glass barrels contained a thin, rust-orange serum and a translucent, watery one.

With a firm twist of the plunger, Ashworth cracked the barrier separating the two and the liquids merged. The resulting reaction crackled with energy, tickling his fingertips and giving off a vibrant blue light.

He only had a moment.

Tapping the chamber a few times with his finger, Ashworth removed the protective cap from the needle end.

"I'm not sure if this will work or not, but it's the best I can do for you. If you're fortunate, you'll have many more years to resent your old friend for it."

Ashworth pressed the needle into the captain's chest, leaning his weight into it and driving it deep into the heart. With a deliberate squeeze, he pressed the plunger down, the contacts in the plunger producing a spark which shot through the chamber as it released the mixture. The serum seeped out of the barrel with some resistance, but after a few seconds the chamber was empty.

"So don't you die on me, you old cog!" Ashworth said, drawing out the needle again.

The glow of the serum shone through the captain's skin, concentrated around Harper's heart. Ashworth waited for something to happen, for some evidence the serum had worked. But the captain's body gave no indication of any change. Soon the light faded and all returned to as it was before.

Ashworth let out a sigh.

Stuffing the syringe back into his coat pocket, he covered the body with the sheet. It had been a long shot to try the serum again. He'd known that. Yet, disappointment hung heavy over him. If there was ever a moment he'd wished fortune would favor him, it was then.

Dejectedly, he pushed the metal slab back into the dark compartment. He was about to close the door when he noticed light was still shining through the thin sheet, ever so faintly in the darkened chamber.

Ashworth peered inside the compartment, perplexed. The reaction usually dispersed by then. Reaching inside, he lifted the sheet away from the body. Sure enough, light shone through the cracks and seams of Harper's new arm. It pulsed, swelling in intensity before flickering until it was nearly out.

Ashworth watched, mesmerized by what he was witnessing, when the captain's prosthetic hand thrust forth and seized his arm in a fierce grip. Ashworth jumped and let out a cry as the body under the sheet shook and twisted, flailing against the chamber walls. Ashworth grasped the handle of the door to keep from being pulled in. The captain's grip was vice-like, and Ashworth feared his arm might be torn away completely.

And then, as suddenly as the throes began, they ended, and the body lay still once again.

Ashworth breathed in quick, shuddering breaths, his heart racing in his chest and pounding in his head. Carefully, he reached in and pried the captain's hand from his arm.

Footsteps echoed in the hall as Ambre came running. She burst into the room and shrieked when she saw Ashworth. "What happened?" she asked, running to Ashworth and crouching down beside him. "Oh, my goodness! Your arm!"

Ashworth cradled his arm. His sleeve was torn and wet with blood where his skin had broken under the grip of Harper's mechanical hand. But, Ashworth paid it no mind. He was focused on the body inside the chamber, watching the steady rise and fall of the captain's chest under the sheet.

"It worked," Ashworth whispered, and for the first time in his life he felt a very real fear.

CHAPTER FIVE
Deliveries

Determination is an admirable trait when blended with
ambition, but a poor substitute for conscience.

— Alchemical Proverb

N o," Chance said, pointing again. "The poultice goes in that
bag. The repellent goes with the corrosives."

His finger guided Rhett to the respective parcels as the
boy corrected his error. The sun was just coming up as they sat on
the steps sorting out the deliveries for the day. They were both a little
groggy, but the cold morning air helped to startle their bodies awake.

Around their feet were a series of bags, cases, and kits full of alchemical components, as well as two small wire cages. Rhett wrapped
the glass containers in swaths of cloth to keep them from breaking
in transit while Chance double-checked each order to ensure nothing
was forgotten or misplaced. When all seemed correct, he buckled each
tightly into their carrier.

"I think that's everything," Chance said as Rhett tied up the last
bundle and dropped it into its case.

"I'll carry it," Rhett volunteered as Chance loaded himself up.

"You sure you got it?" He watched the boy rub sleep from his eyes.

Rhett was still not accustomed to their early morning routine.

"I know how to carry a bag," Rhett said indignantly.

They'd had the same conversation dozens of times. For some reason it gave Chance pleasure to tease Rhett. He knew Rhett could carry the bags. The boy had only ever dropped one before, and that hadn't really been his fault—the strap had broken as he'd boarded one of the rails.

"Alright, you can carry these today," Chance said, handing him two of the larger satchels. "Hold them tight. Those are going to pay for our components at the Exchange this afternoon."

Rhett slung the satchels over his shoulder and tightened the straps. "What about the money jar?"

"I'm hoping we can get by without it." Chance grabbed the two small cages and the rest of the bags. "Let's go."

Locking up the house, the two of them headed east toward the bay. It was a cramped part of the city, filled with confined corridors and back-alley holes. Makeshift hovels could be seen erected in whatever crevice could be found. As long as the inhabitants didn't attract too much attention to themselves the constables overlooked their existence.

They walked for a quarter of an hour before they found a good spot to set up the first of their rat traps, nestling it into the crumbling brick of a general store. They were searching for a spot for the second when Rhett tugged on Chance's sleeve.

"Look!" he said, craning his neck and pointing up between the buildings. Chance's eyes followed the boy's finger. Visible through a gap in the canopy was a dirigible, powered by two massive propellers, drifting toward the bay.

"A sky-ferry," Chance guessed.

The well-to-dos who had business in the Basin District often used sky-ferries to avoid the streets. They hopped from dock to dock among the rooftops, descending below only when necessity demanded it—which was rare. Most of the serious business within the Basin took place in the uppermost parts of those buildings.

The result was a forgotten and decaying underbelly.

"Someday, I'm gonna fly like they do," Rhett said.

"You want to captain a ship?" Chance smirked, kneeling down between two stairwells. He placed the other trap amidst some trash and baited it with a hunk of smelly cheese, partly molded. "You'd have to grow a head or two before you'd fit behind a helm. You'd hardly clear the bow."

"I don't want to fly one," Rhett said quietly.

"There's nothing wrong with having a dream. I've thought about flying my own ship a few times."

"I don't want to fly a ship."

Chance rolled his eyes.

"I didn't mean to embarrass you. If that's your dream, go on and dream it. Chase it if you really want to. Septigonee knows, it would be more glamorous than all of this."

He kicked some loose trash away from the cage, and the two of them continued on.

Rhett kept quiet, his gaze toward the ground. Chance didn't understand why he got like this sometimes. He'd clam up and retreat into himself on the most offhanded comment. It irked Chance to no end.

"You make no sense to me sometimes, Rhett," Chance said, shaking his head as he turned up the steps to a residence. He knocked on the door and pulled a kit from his satchel. The door opened, and a shrunken woman peered out at them.

"Oh! It's you," she said, opening the door fully. "I hoped you'd be coming by soon. And little Rhett along too. How are you, dear?"

"Fine," Rhett said, hiding behind Chance.

She beckoned them inside, and they followed her in through a narrow hallway. The space was cramped, and the wallpaper heavily yellowed by age. In many places it was coming loose from the wall and curling slowly on its way to the floor. Chance could smell the stale moisture which clung to those walls, and his stomach turned.

There were others in the hallway—laborers from the factories—who'd set up small beds in whatever floor space they could find. A few were asleep, but others sat quietly in an almost thoughtless gaze, staring at something indistinguishable on the floor or walls.

Chance and Rhett skirted around them, offering unregistered apologies.

Homes like this were inseparably linked with misfortune and illness in Chance's mind. He was all too aware he wasn't in a much better circumstance, but these people had given up any hope to improve themselves. It was one of the qualities Chance felt distinguished him from the sorry lot that surrounded him.

Ashworth often reminded him that it was these people's very misfortune which employed his craft and sustained their livelihood. He'd reiterated the point every time he'd taken Chance on a delivery when he was an apprentice, and Chance could hear echoes of his voice as though he were a third in their little party.

Regardless, this was the sort of place Chance avoided setting his coat down in.

"How is he doing?" he asked, following the woman deeper.

"Not well, I think," she explained. "He's been off his feet for a while. He can't even get his shoes on. A man can't work that way. What do they expect us to do? He can't work. Not like that."

She led them into a single room at the end of the long hallway. It was only twelve feet across, with a small woodstove against the far wall and a washtub set up beside a makeshift bed. The bed was piled high with blankets. Chance would never have supposed it was occupied except for the pair of uncovered feet which poked out from under them.

The woman knelt beside it and touched the pile of blankets.

"Dear? The boys with the medicine are here." She gently rustled the pile where Chance supposed a shoulder might be. "Dear?"

"I heard you," came a muffled voice. The blankets moved and a face peeked out at them.

"He's been in so much pain," she explained.

"You'll forgive me if I don't stand up," the man said, rolling over.

"That's alright," Chance said. "Let's see how you're doing."

He knelt and examined the man's feet. It was clear they'd not improved since his last visit. Open blisters had formed across the bottom and the skin was flaking away, leaving behind raw, red scabs. Chance suspected the rot had spread even further under the blankets.

Rhett gagged and turned away.

"We've had to sleep in turns," the woman explained. "He can't bear to have them covered, and the rats bite his feet if I'm not up to chase them away."

Chance's heart sank, and he bit down on his tongue to keep from reacting visibly. "I'm afraid we don't have anything with us to cure the rot."

The woman's face flushed. "But the infection," she explained. "It's getting worse! He can't work! If he doesn't work then we won't have enough even to pay you to treat it."

"I'm sorry."

"He could lose his leg! Don't you realize what this is doing to—" The woman stopped herself when she saw Chance's sinking expression. "He can't work," she repeated.

The man took her hand in his and squeezed it tightly.

Chance clenched his fists. He could see that familiar expression surfacing in the woman's face, like the sores on the man's feet—the slow surrender to fate. She was steeling herself for the inevitable course of events. It had only taken a few seconds.

"Rhett," Chance said. "Give me your kit."

Rhett did so, and Chance selected an ointment. Dumping a liberal amount into his hands, he rubbed them together and applied it directly to the man's sores. The man cringed at the touch but relaxed visibly as the ointment brought some relief.

"I'm gathering the components I need for a salve to combat the rot," Chance explained as he pushed the blanket up and rubbed the man's calves. "As soon as it's mixed I'll bring it by myself."

He handed her another vial from Rhett's kit.

"These should help ease the pain in the meantime. Do your best to keep the sores clean. If you've got rat problems, Rhett can come back with a few traps to catch them for you. I know it isn't much, but it's the most we can do right now."

His eyes fixed on the man's as he said it.

"Thank you," the man said.

"Yes, thank you," the woman said. "I'm sure it will help, like you said. How much do we owe you for this?"

"Nothing yet," Chance assured her. "You just hold onto those until we have the salve ready. We don't charge for half an order."

Tears brimmed at the edge of her wrinkled eyes.

"Thank you," she said again.

On the street, Chance didn't waste any time as they set off toward their next delivery. He wanted to put as much distance between himself and that place as possible. His pace was quick, and Rhett struggled to keep up—encumbered as he was with his parcels.

"I want you to collect the traps we set today and bring them back here," Chance instructed.

Rhett nodded.

"You didn't take their money," he said after a moment had passed.

"No, I didn't."

"And you used our own supplies to help them."

"We'll just have to replace what we used." Chance kept up the pace. He didn't want to think about it.

"But," Rhett kept on. "How are we going to buy things at the Exchange?"

"Rhett!" Chance snapped. His toes caught a loose stone, and he felt a torrent of profanities welling up inside him, threatening to hurl themselves at the boy. But, he held back—long enough for the words to settle into his own heart. Their familiar poison numbed his frustration, if only to protect Rhett.

"Never do what I do," he said with strain in his voice. "You got that? Anything you see me do, you do the opposite. Unless you want to end up like me, you do it *right*."

"Okay," Rhett said quietly, and fell in behind Chance.

The two of them continued in silence along the street to the next house. It pained Chance to have to teach the boy such a hard lesson. He liked to believe he'd been able to hold onto some shred of decency, as Ashworth always had. Yet, there were times he came dangerously close to tipping over the edge. Septigonee knew that with all the ill luck they'd inherited, it was a trial every time he was moved by compassion.

"I just wanna ride in one," Rhett said suddenly.

"What?"

"The dirigible," Rhett explained. "I don't wanna fly one. I just wanna ride in one. I think it would be neat to see the buildings from the top. That's all."

"Wait." Chance looked at him, perplexed. "You've never even ridden in one before?"

"No."

Chance smiled. Despite his mood, the gravity of the moment dispersed some. How did the boy manage to do it?

He rubbed Rhett's head playfully. "Your dreams need some work, kid."

CHAPTER SIX
Old Acquaintances

It's bound to work out... but wear the goggles anyway.

— Alchemical Proverb

Thee rest of the morning Chance and Rhett tromped back and forth throughout the district delivering salves, tonics, and an abundance of mundane concoctions. By the time the sun was high they were feeling a little better about their growing collection of coins and banknotes.

"Do you think we have enough?" Rhett asked as they paused to consolidate their parcels.

"By the time we've unloaded all of this we might have a bit extra, actually," Chance said. The surprise in his voice was genuine. He'd expected the worst given their start, and yet somehow fortune had been on their side. "Perhaps we'll take a sky-ferry back to the house?" he suggested.

Rhett looked at Chance with cautious uncertainty. His eyes betrayed his excitement, but it was quickly held back as the idea settled on him.

"We don't have to," he said.

"Why not?" Chance asked, passing under an alcove and nearly

bumping into a man smoking a pipe against the wall. Chance apologized and the man grunted in annoyance.

"Don't you need the money?" Rhett asked.

Chance shook his head. "I can make do with what I have. In a week I'll make twice this much once I mix a few more batches."

"But what about Ashworth? Won't he be mad you wasted the money?"

"If I know Ashworth, he isn't against the occasional diversion. After all, how often do we get to fulfill a lifelong dream on a bit of spare change? I bet you he'll enjoy hearing about it tonight over supper. We'll call it an early birthday present. Or a late one. Doesn't really matter which."

"You mean it?" Rhett shook with excitement. "We're going to ride in a dirigible?"

"We'll be no worse off if we do," Chance reasoned. "Perhaps a little better, even."

Rhett walked with a bounce in his step as they continued down a side street. It was nice to watch the boy get excited about something. It was easier at his age, before he was grounded too much to the reality of their circumstance.

Chance smiled as he walked with him.

And then, like a broken spring rocketing from a machine, the joy went out of Chance's entire body. He swallowed hard and his palms became clammy. He'd recognized that man from somewhere. He glanced behind them, hoping against all hope that he was mistaken.

There, not more than a dozen paces behind, the man with the pipe tailed them.

Chance tried to stay calm. Rhett kept jabbering, wondering whether they'd be able to collect some of the clouds in a jar. Chance let him drone on, trying to think of ways to avoid what was coming. They were in a bad spot, walking down a longer corridor with few connecting streets.

He'd strolled right into this one.

Just as he expected, two men stepped out from the shadows a short distance ahead of them, barring the road. He held a hand out to stop

Rhett, who only then noticed the men. Turning about, Chance faced off with the man coming up from behind.

"Morning," the man grinned as he dumped the contents of his pipe and pocketed it in his worn suit-vest. "I thought I recognized you. Chance, wasn't it? You remember me? I told you we'd run into each other again someday."

"Who is that?" Rhett asked.

"Quiet," Chance snapped. Every hair on his neck stood on end. He was going to have to play it carefully if they were going to walk away from this one.

"You know why we're here," the man continued. "So, let's make this easy, shall we? We've been down this road before."

"Odd," Chance said, his face expressionless. "You'd think I'd have remembered this part of town then."

The man ignored Chance's attempt at humor.

"According to my men, it's been a good day for you two," he said.

"Yeah?" Chance frowned. "Funny how fortune turns, isn't it?"

"It is," the man grinned. "And it's important to remember that no matter how bad things turn out, they can always get worse. Now, how about you just hand over that purse and we'll avoid any unnecessary unpleasantness."

Chance bit his lip, glancing about him for any exit. There were none except on ahead and back the way they'd come.

"Don't try it, boy," the man warned. "You know we mean business."

Chance let out a heavy sigh. He removed his satchel from his shoulder and held it out reluctantly. The man approached with a grin, but as he reached for it Chance swung the bag wide at his head. The man flinched backwards as it grazed his cheek.

"Rhett, run!" Chance yelled. He grasped the boy's shoulder, barreling into the man and knocking him to the side. Both of them sprinted as fast as they could back the way they'd come.

"Who was that?" Rhett asked, his eyes wide with panic. Chance ignored his question, keeping a firm grip on the boy as they ran. He heard the two others giving chase behind them. Their booted footfalls came loud and quick, reverberating off the alley walls.

Chance knew their best hope was to make it to one of the busier streets. Perhaps they could find a constable, or the crowd would discourage the pursuit.

He wasn't used to such sudden exertion, and his lungs ached. His breaths came in sharp wheezes and his veins pulsed with his frustration toward the whole situation. He couldn't outrun them, he realized, but they weren't going to take him without a fight. He could give them that much.

As the closest thug came up behind them Chance forced a sudden stop, digging his feet in and turning about as he swung his fist wide. The back of it connected with the side of the thug's head.

The impact dropped him to the ground with a surprised grunt.

Chance seized a discarded piece of metal scrap and waved it at the other thug, who'd stopped just outside of Chance's reach.

"Keep going, Rhett!" Chance instructed. The thug circled him, eying the scrap he held and glancing at his friend.

Rhett kept running, looking over his shoulder as he turned the corner.

"What's the matter?" Chance shouted, swinging the scrap a few times. "This is what you wanted, right? Come on then!"

He lunged at his opponent and swung wildly, but the thug caught the scrap and seized Chance's wrist. Pain shot up Chance's arm as the thug gave it a twist. The pain was so sharp Chance fell to his knees, dropping the scrap. His whole body twisted under the pressure. The brute held him there, twisting harder every time Chance struggled.

Looking about him in desperation, Chance caught the eyes of a man and woman, staring out at him from their hovel. He wanted to call out to them, to beg their intervention, but he could see how little use they were to him. They kept silent in the shadows, watching impassively as the scene played out before them.

"Now, Chance," the man with the pipe said, approaching with a slow, smug gait. "You know better than that. You're making this a lot more difficult than it need be. Vince, get up, you bolt." He kicked the brute on the ground. "Go get the kid."

The brute clambered to his feet and gave Chance a dark look as he touched his hand to his swelling cheekbone. "Little whelp!" he spat as he lashed out with his boot and caught Chance across the face. Chance's head jerked backwards, and he collapsed the rest of the way to the ground, his arm twisting free of its hold.

He let himself lay there against the rough stone, tasting blood.

"Now!" the boss commanded.

The thug reluctantly gave chase after Rhett. Chance could only hope the boy had enough mind to keep running until he was home, or at least until he found a constable.

The second thug pulled the satchel off of Chance's shoulder and rummaged through it.

"Still with us?" the boss said as he moved Chance's chin with his foot.

Chance let out a groan.

"That wasn't a smart thing to do. Not at all. You see, I need my men to make our living. You're lucky you only bruised him. Imagine what would have happened if you'd done something more serious—gouged his eyes with that piece of scrap, maybe. Gives me the shivers to think of a man deprived of his means to his livelihood."

"That is our living you're taking from us." Chance spat away some of the blood on his lips.

"We're hardly keeping you from working."

"You're not making it any easier."

"Check your luck." The man crouched down so that his shadow shrouded Chance. "Nobody's got it easy, kid. Not here. Not now. Not ever. If you think you're exempt, then you're fooling yourself. You've got yourself a good thing going, no doubt about that. But, everyone's got to pay their dues eventually. Call it a redistribution of the wealth— and we're here to collect."

"Jackpot," the thug said, recovering their money purse from the satchel. He tossed it to his boss.

"Ah," he beamed. He shook the purse a bit, listening to the jingle of the coins. "Now that's a sound I've come to love. Looks like my men were right after all."

"It's slag like you that make this place the dump it's become,"

Chance said.

"Trust me, you all took care of that long before we arrived. We're just making a slightly less than honest living. It's work just as honest as the rest of you. A foreigner's tax on the humbler parts of the city for all the contraband that we deliver from overseas. It's just the natural order of things."

"You have an awfully high opinion of yourself, "Chance said. "Seems a bit wasted on some forgotten highwayman."

"You can't tell me you haven't leeched off of anyone else's misfortune in your lifetime. Can you, kid?"

Chance ignored his question, but deep in his heart the answer pained him. He thought of Ashworth and all the times he'd been sustained only at his mentor's expense.

"I thought so," the boss grinned. "Ah, here's the little guttersnipe now!"

The other thug returned holding Rhett in a tight grip around the collar. Ripping away his satchel, he pushed him down onto his knees.

"Sit still," he barked. The two thugs rummaged through Rhett's pack, pulling vials and tubes out and weeding through what they deemed valuable.

"Don't worry," the boss said, rising so that he loomed over Chance's prone form. "You'll bounce back from this. You free-merchants are a resilient batch. But injure one of my men again..."

He stomped down hard on Chance's hand and ground his boot into it. Chance cried out in pain and jerked his hand free.

"You get the message, I think."

Chance clutched his hand to his chest, watching as the men loaded up with his work. He winced. Some of the skin had been scratched away from his knuckles and fingertips. It stung exposed to the air, and he slipped it into his coat to protect it.

It brushed up against the carrier kept secure at his side.

Every alchemist carried such a carrier, meant to be a quick resource when away from their workshops. Chance's was a hardened leather case not the length of a parchment piece, and about half the width. It tucked easily underneath his coat into the space under his arm. It had three flaps which folded over the center and buckled with a pressure clasp. Inside, individual buckles held all of his ready-made compounds tightly in their place.

And, in all the commotion, they'd forgotten to search his person. A dangerous oversight. Carefully, Chance unclipped a flask and slipped it into his good hand.

"You all need to label these better," the boss said. "How in all of this mess do you even know what you're working with? It's impossible to tell what half this stuff is."

"Recognize this?" Chance growled. The men looked up from the bag and considered Chance. He rose up from the ground, the flask cocked above his head, his expression one of raw malice.

All three men took a few steps back.

"Try to run off with our stuff and you'll lose more than your eyesight!" Chance warned, and the men stopped. They glance nervously from Chance to their boss.

"Hold on now," the boss began. "Let's keep our heads about us. There's no need to escalate things this way. Wouldn't do you any better if you throw that flask than if you didn't. The constables would lock you up for the rest of your measly life. Then what would become of you, or your little friend there?"

"At least I'd be at peace knowing your remains are scattered across these streets." Chance's arm shook as he gripped the vial. "Rhett, come here."

Rhett rose from the ground and hurried to get behind Chance.

"You're playing a dangerous game right now, lad." The boss grinned, revealing a row of withered teeth. "And I think you're bluffing."

"Try me, and we'll see what a desperate man will do when pushed far enough. Come on!" Chance snarled. "Call my bluff!"

The seconds passed slowly and neither side made a move. The boss was too calm, clearly weighing the odds. Chance kept his eyes locked on the man's, his hatred seething out from behind them.

"Alright," the boss said, raising his hands in defeat. He tossed the money pouch and satchel unceremoniously on the ground. "You win then. We'll be on our way. Come on, lads. Let's leave them to their misery."

Chance kept the flask raised high as the two thugs followed their leader away. The bruised one spat on the ground as he glared at Chance once more. Chance didn't move until they'd disappeared at the end of the street. Once they were out of sight, he collected the purse and satchel from the ground. The bottom of the bag was leaking a mess of liquids and he heard the tinkle of broken glass. He rummaged through to check if any of the vials hadn't broken.

"Good thing you had that flask bomb," Rhett said, brushing himself off. "They'd have gotten away with everything."

Chance chewed on his tongue. "It's all broken," he scowled. He checked the purse. Inside were the coins, but the banknotes were missing. "And they took the banknotes!"

"All of them?"

"He must have taken them out when I was on the ground." Chance's jaw twitched as he twisted the purse in his hands.

"You should'a just thrown the flask," Rhett said. "Blown them all up!"

Chance couldn't speak. His eyes were wet as they burned with a white-hot rage. He squeezed the flask in his hand and hurled it against the nearest wall. The glass shattered violently, but there was no explosion—only wetted brick and the weak smell of calamus.

CHAPTER SEVEN
The Pub & Brawl

*A good old-fashioned guffaw is a decent retardant in the
face of despair.*

— Alchemical Proverb

O f all the cowardly filth these streets produce!"

Chance and Rhett sat in the backroom of Liesel's Pub
& Brawl, a finer establishment amidst the shoddy businesses
bordering the factory districts. The room was filled with crates and barrels of fresh foodstuffs, and kegs full of assorted liquors stacked high
against one of the walls.

Liesel, one of Chance's closer friends, fetched a few rags from one
of the cupboards while the cook worked to unpack a supply of vegetables and salt and season raw steaks for the evening meal.

"Here, hold this to your cheek," Liesel instructed, taking a slab of
the fresh cut meat and offering it to Chance. "It will help the swelling
to go down."

Chance gave her a queer look as he took it, and she went to fill a
bowl with water from the pump. Tentatively, he pressed the raw meat to
his face where he'd been kicked and winced.

"You'll appreciate it in a moment," the cook smiled. "It's Liesel's home remedy for everything from a bump to a brawl. It'll lift a bruise right out of the skin. At least, that's what she swears."

"Thanks," Chance said, giving the cook a disbelieving look. His cheek was already feeling a little better, though he suspected it was just in his mind.

"You're more than welcome," Liesel said, coming back with the water. "What about you, Rhett? You alright over there?"

"I'm fine," he piped up from his stool. His attention was caught on a rattrap set in the corner. "Chance stopped them so I could get away," he added without looking away.

"And somehow he still ended up getting caught," Chance pointed out. Rhett's head sank into his shoulders a little more.

"Well, I'm glad they had the mind not to harm you," Liesel said. She set the basin of water on the table and took Chance's hand in hers. "I'd still like to give them a piece of my mind."

Chance couldn't help but chuckle. Liesel's idea of giving someone her mind was going toe to toe in fist-to-cuffs. She was one of the few ladies he knew who fought for sport. Her establishment frequently hosted sparring events where unlucky men could gamble away their weekly earnings over drinks.

True to form, Liesel was typically the first into the circle, and there were few who could hold up against her fortitude.

"Nothing is broken, fortune be counted." She soaked the rag in water and cleaned the caked blood from Chance's knuckles. "One thing you have to admit, we're a resilient breed. Do you have any idea who it was that jumped you?"

"Just a thug and his two goons," Chance said. "I had a run-in with the same guy a few months ago. It was only him back then. I'd thought he was just another local lifter, but after hearing him talk today it sounds like he's a foreigner come to squat."

There were always foreigners coming through Hatteras on account of the trade routes that ran along the coast. It wasn't uncommon for some to linger in the city to collect some coin before boarding a ship to the next town.

Judging by the way the man was dressed, Chance supposed he'd decided to set up a more permanent presence.

"Dirty leech," Liesel cursed. "Well, if he's set up shop nearby there's a good chance he'll make the mistake of coming in here someday. What does he look like?"

Chance tried to picture him clearly "Stout man. A hand shorter than me, perhaps. He wore a green suit with a gentleman's neckerchief. He had thick eyebrows, like caterpillars, and one of the reddest faces I've ever seen."

"And what about the others?"

"I'm pretty sure they were just hired muscle."

"Well, I look forward to meeting this man," Liesel grinned, taking the washbowl away. "How much did you lose?"

"All of it," Rhett sighed.

Chance shot him a look. "Enough to put us behind a week or so, that's all," he corrected. It was a lie, and he guessed Liesel knew it. But, he didn't like others knowing just how deep his misfortunes ran. It only seemed to invite more. "It's just a bit of the wretched luck of the Basin,"

"You're talking about my home," Liesel said, breaking a wedge of cheese and a roll. She gave Rhett half of each. "There's nothing wretched about it."

"Sorry," Chance shrugged, "but I honestly believe it. You can't tell me you don't feel it sometimes. It's like we're destined to watch our lives unravel, and there's nothing we can do about it. We're just being jerked around at the end of a string and made to dance until either fever or famine kills us off."

"No great force is manipulating our lives, Chance," Liesel insisted. She offered him the other half of the roll and cheese and he took it sullenly. Even such a small gesture of charity caused his jaw to clench. "If things go wrong sometimes—"

"Most times," Chance interjected.

"—*sometimes*, it's because they do. That doesn't mean you're being toyed with. It just means you have to change your strategy and come at it again."

"Sounds to me like you're describing bad luck."

"I'm describing life. There's no such thing as luck," Liesel insisted. "This whole luck obsession is unhealthy, thinking the tidewaters bring some ill will or that you can escape it by moving further away. The Basin isn't any worse off than the Spire. Trust me on that."

Chance ate some of the bread and cheese. The truth was, she probably did know—better than most. Liesel hadn't always been a Basin-dweller. She'd been born in the upper tiers of the city to a successful factory owner. She could have enjoyed a lavish living her entire life had she wished it. She'd surprised everyone when she abandoned it all to take up work for herself in the Basin.

"Why did you do it?" Chance asked, curiosity getting the better of him.

"Do what?"

"Leave the Spire."

"Why do you stay in the Basin?" she asked.

Chance gave her an accusing look, and she smiled.

"I left for the same reason anyone would want to leave home; I wanted to be the one in control of my life. And the fashion was changing," she added with a smirk. "It's awfully easy to lose yourself in all that flair and flouncing, and honestly I just never took to it."

Chance hadn't considered her motivations might have been the same as his for wanting to escape. He'd always viewed citizens of the Spire as the ones in control—capable of doing whatever they wanted on a whim. It certainly appeared that way from his vantage point. They had hold on most of the city's resources, occupied the best land, and were born into the right circles. Their opportunities were nearly limitless.

"I wish it was as easy to move up into the Spire as it was to move down," Chance said wistfully.

"It wasn't as easy as you think. There are just as many obstacles moving down as there are up."

Chance doubted her there. Easy might not have been the right word, but there was no way she could convince him that leaving was more difficult than integrating oneself into the meritocracy. Chance had experienced that struggle when he'd nearly climbed the academic ladder years before. That road was marred by dozens of gatekeepers intent on keeping everyone but the truly gifted or well-connected out.

There was a knock on the back door, and Liesel rose to get it.

"Afternoon, Liesel."

The familiar voice of Welch, Liesel's closest friend, caused Chance's shoulders to slump and his eyes to roll. If there was anyone whose company he didn't want to entertain, Welch was near the top of the list.

"Good to see you again, Welch. You can bring that just inside the door here." Liesel directed him inside and pointed to a spot by the wall.

Welch was bent over, shouldering a large block of ice on his back. He held it against him with a wide leather strap looped around its bulk, which he pulled over his shoulder with a tightly wrapped hand. Carefully, he swung the parcel to the side and set it down beside the door with a gentle thump.

Standing straight again, he let out a deep *humph* and stretched himself tall. His back cracking as each of his vertebrate decompressed.

He was a larger man—not puffy as some get when overweight, but certainly stocky. He had a pleasant countenance, though odd to look at. His face was rough and set deeply with wrinkles, one set so deep between his brows that it was difficult to tell if it was a wrinkle or an incision. His hair was a thick bristle from the top of his head to the chin of his beard. It was peppered white, and his jowls jiggled from underneath it when he spoke.

"You wanting it in the cellar?" he asked.

"Yes, eventually," Liesel said. "There's no hurry, unless you have more errands to run."

He shook his head. "No. That's the last."

"Then take a moment to breathe. You've already brought it so far."

"I don't mind the walk," he said. "Keeps my limbs warm and an idle mind turning."

"Just as well, stay and visit a while?" Liesel implored. "I was about to put a kettle of tea on."

Welch noticed Chance and Rhett and his demeanor shifted uncomfortably. "Nah," he said, stuffing his hands into his pockets. "I shouldn't intrude if you've got company."

"Not at all," Liesel insisted. "Malt, mind boiling some water?"

"Sure thing," the cook said, nodding to Welch and taking down a kettle from above the stove.

Welch scratched at his cheek. "What, eh, happened here then?" he asked Chance, pointing at the bruise by his eye.

"It's nothing. Just a bit of bad luck," Chance said. He shot a goading look at Liesel and she shook her head.

"Ah. Perhaps I should wash up quick, if that's alright," Welch said.

"Pump's out back."

"Thank ya, ma'am." He stepped out the door, shutting it tight behind him.

Liesel gave Chance a stern look. "You could be a little kinder to Welch," she said, stepping behind the counter. She picked up a knife and started chopping up some potatoes.

"I didn't say anything!"

"Exactly. Even I felt the cold coming off the shoulder you were giving him."

"I can't help it," Chance shrugged. "He gets under my skin."

"Is it really him getting under your skin, or are you letting yourself get worked up over nothing? He's a pleasant man. Right, Rhett?"

"I like him," Rhett said. Chance hadn't realized, but the boy wasn't sitting at his stool anymore. He was over in the corner crouched down by the rattrap.

"Not the Welch I know," Chance insisted.

"He's not the same man he once was."

"That's what I mean," Chance said. "The old Welch I could stand. Now he's all talk about his new morality or whatever—I can't stand it. If it were up to me, I'd have the old Welch back. At least then I could share a room with him and not feel so uncomfortable."

"Bite your tongue!" Liesel waved the knife in front of her as she spoke, and Chance leaned back a little. "You should feel ashamed of yourself, wishing that kind of ill on another man. You may have known *of* him back then, but I *knew* him. No man should ever have to suffer so deeply as Welch has, and if his new ideologies keep him from suffering like that again then I'll listen to them until the sun goes out. Gladly, even."

"Alright! I take it back," Chance said, putting his hand up in surrender. "I'm just saying, I'm sorry if I can't stand the self-righteous type."

"From where I'm standing, he's not the self-righteous one."

"You think I'm acting self-righteous?"

"I never said acting," Liesel grinned. "All I'm saying is I hear a lot of griping coming from those lips about how unfair life is. If you're unhappy with the way things are, do something about it!"

There was a loud snap from the corner, and everyone looked up to see Rhett frantically tugging at the corner of his coat, which had tripped the spring and was now caught in the rattrap.

"Leave the traps alone," Chance said. "They're Liesel's."

"I didn't mean to," Rhett apologized.

"It's alright," Liesel said. "It was just an accident."

"Don't be so sure," Chance said. "I don't think he likes that your traps kill them."

"Well, it's the unpleasant side of owning a business. Right, Malt?"

"It's either the rats or the grains," the cook agreed.

"I'll set them up again when he's gone," Liesel whispered once Rhett managed to get his coat unstuck. He shuffled back to his stool.

"All I'm saying is if you gave Welch half a chance I bet you'd get along just fine. He's a good man, and he deserves some hard-earned respect after what he's gone through."

"Yeah well, I think I'll stick to avoiding him if that's alright. Everyone's better off that way."

Liesel looked like she might have said more, but Welch came through the door at that moment.

"Am I interrupting again?" he asked.

"Don't worry," Chance said. "We were just about to leave. We've still got to make a trip down to the Exchange before it gets too late."

He set the slab of meat back on the counter and stood to leave.

"Hold on! Before you go—" Liesel stepped into the other room and left them standing where they were.

"So, eh," Welch began. "How've you been, Chance?"

"Fine," Chance sighed, sitting down again.

"Eh, very good. Very good." Welch stroked his beard. "And you, Rhett? How's Ashworth treating you?"

"He's treating me fine."

"Very good. Very good. I wouldn't have expected less." Welch smiled. "And Ashworth? He's doing...?"

"Fine."

"Good. All very good."

Chance poked at the table while Welch rocked on his feet.

"How's the trade these days?"

"Slow," Chance said.

Welch nodded as if he understood, which of course he couldn't. He knew nothing more about alchemy than he did about how little Chance wanted to engage in small talk. Chance did his best to avoid Welch's eyes, focusing instead on the cook as he added his diced meats to a large pot.

"Working on anything interesting?" Welch asked. "I talked to Ashworth a while back. He said you were puzzling a bit over a transmutation?"

Chance bit his tongue. Now Ashworth was telling people what he was working on?

"I asked Ashworth a question about it, that was all. It was just something to break the silence at dinner," Chance lied. "I wouldn't have time to worry about some fool's errand like transmutation anyways. I have a lab to run."

"You might know this already," Welch continued, "but often when I think I put something out of my mind it keeps picking and puzzling over it—sometimes for years even—until, without realizing, the solution is right in front of me and I wonder how I'd done it. The mind is a tenacious thing once it grabs hold of an idea."

"Thanks," Chance said, his voice tired. "I'll remember that."

"Perhaps I could lend my mind to your problem," Welch offered. "I've got thought to spare between work. Maybe you and I can make headway of it together."

"What do you know about alchemy?" Chance snapped.

"Not a lot," Welch shrugged. "But, Ashworth has used me a time to two when he gets stumped. He said I have—now this is what he said, not me—'an intuit's mind'. I always thought that was kind of him to say. Very kind."

"Well, I'd rather work this one out on my own. Thanks for the offer, but no thanks." Chance stood again. "Where did Liesel go? The Exchange is going to close before we get there."

"Keep your pants on," Liesel said, coming back into the room. "You'd think you had an appointment with the electors, you're so tightly wound."

Taking Chance's hand, she placed a stack of banknotes in it.

"No," Chance objected, turning up his hands to refuse the offer. He glanced uncomfortably at Welch.

"Take it," she insisted, "to cover your losses. It's just spare winnings I've set aside. I can do without it."

"I'm not looking for charity."

"Then call it a loan. You can pay me back whenever you have the money."

"I wouldn't be able to come through on it. You know that." Chance donned his coat. "We can get by on our own. Come on, Rhett. Let's get going."

Rhett leapt up from his stool and grabbed his satchel.

"Chance, let me help you," Liesel begged. "I want to help. Let me be some of that good luck you've been looking for."

"You said it yourself," Chance frowned. "There's no such thing as luck."

He retrieved his satchel from the table, and Welch stepped aside so he could pass.

Outside, Chance took a moment to regain himself. His whole body hummed with pent-up frustration. Frustration toward his circumstances. Frustration toward himself. He silently cursed himself from every direction he knew, until his loathing was too much to contain. He lashed out at the bricks with his injured fist, striking its rough surface with all his might.

Looking down at his knuckles, he could see fresh patches of red form underneath Liesel's bandage, yet he couldn't feel the pain. His mind was too numb. He watched with a strange disconnect as the faint red streaks overtook the white fabric, traveling in small channels between his knuckles.

As he stood there, Rhett came hurrying out the door and down the steps, two halves of a sandwich in his hands.

"Liesel said I should take this in case you and I got hungry later," he explained.

"She gave you the money?" he asked, not looking up.

"Huh?"

"Her winnings. She gave them to you?"

Rhett's gaze dropped. "Yes," he said softly.

Chance clenched his fist tighter, a drop of blood falling to the ground.

"It bleeding again?" Rhett looked concerned, but Chance ignored him. He felt no better than the street-side beggars he heard crying out every day. Against all odds, he made a silent promise not to leave his debt to her unsettled.

"Come on then," he said, beginning to walk. "The Exchange is closing."

CHAPTER EIGHT
Introductions

And if we succeed, what then? One thing is surely to give way to another. Can we fully comprehend the weight of what we've accomplished?

— Excerpt from *Mechanarcissism*

Stoddard pulled at his new suit with a tense hand. He'd had Donovan purchase it earlier that morning. It was stiff and clung stubbornly as he moved, tailored after the latest fashion—though notably less trendy. It lacked the flourishing embroidery on the vest and cuffs which had recently become popular, but it would have to do.

Despite his discomfort, he did his best to appear poised else he give off the impression he didn't belong. Squaring his shoulders and stiffening his jaw, he approached the host, who greeted him with a pleasant smile.

"Welcome to the Souit'de Laurue."

"Thank you," Stoddard said, sweeping the room once for Sinclair and his party. The restaurant was filled to capacity, though the space itself wasn't crowded. Servers and busboys slipped between tables carrying large platters of dishes as the patrons chatted in a low drone.

There was no sign of the elector.

"May we check your coat, sir?"

Stoddard allowed a boy to help remove his coat, and was handed a number punched on a ticket stub.

"And will you be dining alone?"

"I have an invitation to dine with Elector Sinclair," Stoddard said, producing his invitation. "Doctor J. Collins Stoddard."

"Of course," the host said. "If you'll come this way, the elector's party has already been shown to the garden terrace."

Stoddard followed the man through the main dining area, admiring the general aesthetic. The tables were laid with clean white linens, with bright floral arrangements placed in the center of each. More plants hung from the ceilings and others still sat shelved along the walls. It gave the atmosphere a natural contrast when juxtaposed with the heavy iron support beams and rich patterned paper which coated the walls.

Much of the lighting was natural, pouring in from large windows along the bayside of the dining room, though he noted that each table had its own hanging electric light—unlit—for the evening hours.

He spotted some more noteworthy figures of the meritocracy, a few lords and their wives amidst other military gentle and business men. Stoddard did his best to walk a little taller, and to greet those who met his eyes as naturally here as he might in his own study. He acknowledged each with a quick, formal nod, which was returned politely.

By the time they'd reached the opposite side of the room he sensed his presence had caused something of a stir in the conversation. It thrilled him to have their attention, after so many long years working in the background, and he felt his confidence bolstered.

His moment had indeed arrived.

But his confidence was quickly challenged as he was led to the patio. The patio floor was entirely made up of glass panes supported by great iron trusses which ran along the underside of the glass and anchored it to the cliff. The host walked on it without the least sign of hesitation, while Stoddard found his steps awkward and uncertain.

"Do not be alarmed by the glass, sir," the host said, noting Stoddard's hesitation. He tapped a foot with force to demonstrate his confidence in the surface. "It is quite safe. And it provides a pleasant view, does it not?"

It was true. The full curvature of the bay's majestic cliffs sprawled before him all the way down to the Basin. The sun shone brightly on the scene, illuminating the bright blue of the water and the colorful gas balloons of the airships which floated inside the bay.

Stoddard couldn't think of a grander view in any part of the city which could rival the one before him. "Indeed," he managed to say. "Though a little overwhelming for those of us who are accustomed to more solid ground."

"Of course," the host smiled. He gestured to a place near the end of the patio. "Your party, sir."

Stoddard saw the small entourage clustered together, chatting under the bowers of a small garden terrace. He caught sight of Elector Sinclair, recognizing him immediately by his black uniform and bright red sash. The man stood as the obvious head of the little company, flourishing tactfully as he spoke—about some important topic no doubt.

For a moment, Stoddard worried that he'd kept them waiting, but it was soon apparent that none were in any real hurry. Sinclair commanded their attention well.

"Doctor J. Collins Stoddard," the host announced as they entered the terrace.

The company turned and Stoddard caught a foot coming up the stairs when he recognized who else was in attendance. He was only just able to recover himself as he was greeted.

"Doctor Stoddard," Sinclair said, dismissing the host with a wave. "Our celebrity of the hour. I'm glad you were able to join us. I imagine your company is in high demand." He removed his cigarette from his lips and offered a hand to Stoddard, who shook it gratefully.

"The pleasure is mine, Elector. I consider myself most fortunate to have received your invitation."

"To be sure," Sinclair grinned. "It is a mutual treat then. Are you acquainted with my other guests? Lord and Lady Worthington? And their daughter, Miss Emmaline?"

Stoddard felt his heart rate rise, and he swallowed hard.

"I have had the fortune of knowing them for some time, actually." He bowed to both Lord and Lady Worthington in turn.

"And me?" Emmaline beamed, stepping forward. "Has it been a good fortune to know me as well?"

Her eyes alighted with a playful mood, and Stoddard quite lost himself in them. Significantly younger than he, she was a dainty thing from crown to hem. Her dimpled cheeks and soft chin gave her a porcelain look.

She was, in his opinion, the most curious creature he'd ever set eyes upon. Or, perhaps, it was the way she drew out emotions he'd quite forgotten he possessed that was the true source of his curiosity.

Whatever the source, he couldn't deny the joy he felt seeing her again after so much time, despite the circumstances of their parting.

"A fortune without compare, Miss Emmaline," he said. He took her gloved hand and kissed it lightly.

Lady Worthington let out a terse sigh.

"And this is my son, Arden," Sinclair said, introducing the even younger lad beside him.

The boy was perhaps in his late teens or early twenties, a full head shorter than Sinclair. He bore all the signs of a youth accustomed to privilege, yet Stoddard detected in his expression and manner of standing that he was an unsure one. He wore a dark uniform, similar to his father's, though it displayed no distinctions or honors of any kind.

Side by side with the elector, he was quite underwhelming.

"Master Arden," Stoddard bowed.

"Overjoyed to finally meet you," the young man said with apparent enthusiasm.

"Haven't we exchanged enough pleasantries for one afternoon?" Lady Worthington asked, interposing herself strategically between Stoddard and her daughter. "I'm positively famished."

"Of course," Sinclair acquiesced. "Shall we?"

He gestured for his guests to take their seats at the table. Mrs. Worthington took Emmaline's arm and led her to her seat. Stoddard followed them, falling in beside Lord Worthington.

"Don't mind her shortness with you," Lord Worthington said in a low voice. "She is an insufferable woman. Always has been, and I fear she always will be. There is no cure for it, I'm afraid."

"Yet, you suffer her so well," Stoddard pointed out.

Worthington chuckled. "It's a husband's solemn duty, else he make the most dreadful misfortune his closest bedmate. You'll know what I mean, one day."

"If fortune favors me."

"Oh, I think it has," Worthington smiled.

Lord Worthington took a seat next to Sinclair and his wife, and Emmaline was directed by her mother to sit beside her. Stoddard was quick to occupy the seat next to her, which prompted another perturbed noise from Lady Worthington. Her husband gave her a severe look, however, which silenced any vocal protest.

Arden took a seat between Stoddard and his father.

At a signal from Sinclair, a small army of servers appeared and soon a diverse spread of seafood and vegetable platters was wheeled out, richly seasoned with spices imported from across the sea.

The aroma teased the senses and made Stoddard's nose twitch. He placed his napkin in his lap as the first dish was placed before him.

"I must say again what an honor it was to receive your invitation," Stoddard said.

"I make it a point to acquaint myself with the more noteworthy figures of the city," Sinclair smiled. "Naturally, I'm as intrigued by the work you did for our good captain as the rest of the world."

"With all the time I've spent in my work, I admit I lose track of the world sometimes."

"Understandable," Sinclair said. "It's better you've been spared the political arena until now, but I believe your days of obscurity are winding down. Your name has been circulating among the meritocracy for some time. Though, I admit, it was at the request of my son that I specifically invited you here today. He's built something of a hobby following your work."

"My father was able to arrange a seat for me in the medical dome," Arden said. "After seeing you work, I knew I had to meet you in person."

"I'm flattered to hear that. I hope you found the experience insightful."

"Yes, I did!"

"My son has a mind to follow in your footsteps. Though time will tell if he's serious or if this is just another fad of his youth."

"My father thinks I'm too flighty in my interests," Arden confessed. "I fear he may be right."

"You'll prove your merit in time," Worthington reassured him.

"Thank you," Arden smiled. "But I find your work, doctor, revolutionary."

"It is a satisfying study," Stoddard agreed. "The field of medicine has no shortage of problems, and clockwork mechanics no lack of possibility. I simply married the two."

"I'm afraid I know very little of your work personally," Sinclair said. "I made an inquiry to my advisers, but it seems very few do."

"It has been a long journey with intermittent success," Stoddard explained. "In its early days I made some attempts to publicize my work, but it's difficult to keep the public eye for long without making significant advances. It's been some time since the public has given me consideration."

"Then by all means, you have our undivided attention," Sinclair said, leaning back into his chair. His hand went to his chin as he eyed Stoddard. "Enlighten us."

It was subtle, but Stoddard saw in Sinclair's eyes a challenge being issued. *Now is your test*, those eyes said. *Prove yourself.*

Stoddard felt his brow grow moist.

"How does it work, exactly?" Arden asked. "The prosthetic. It was disappointing we didn't get to see it in action."

"Your disappointment is shared by all," Stoddard said. "I'm afraid it would be difficult to explain all of its complexities in a single luncheon."

"Give us an idea then," Sinclair smiled. "Dumb it down to layman's terms so that we few poor gentlemen can grasp at it."

Laughter passed between the group.

"Very well," Stoddard acquiesced, setting his knife down and wiping his mouth with his napkin. "I'll do my best. You're familiar with the basic concept of function, Master Arden?"

"I think so," Arden said. "You mean the purpose for which a thing is specifically suited?"

"Precisely," Stoddard affirmed. "In clockwork mechanics, it is function which drives a mechanist. We identify needs around us and work to satisfy them. A businessman sees that he employs too many workers and so discovers a way to streamline his production with a more efficient machine.

"I was first trained as a mechanist, so this was naturally how I approached my work, as a doctor. However, it was when I stood witness to my early mentor as he worked to save our good captain's life during the Great War that I first glimpsed a singular truth. I was impressed with how—quite on its own—the limb which we'd so crudely fashioned became a part of the captain's body.

"Most were willing to call it a miracle and leave it at that. A fluke. However, it opened a notion within my young mind which has become the genesis of all that I've worked to accomplish: when it comes to the human body, function is only a result of form."

"I would have considered function to be paramount," Arden said. "I can't think of anything more complex than the human body with each of its parts."

"True," Stoddard agreed, "But let me illustrate the point. Let us compare the human body to our great city. Like our bodies, Hatteras is comprised of many distinguishable parts. We have streets for transit, shops for commerce, factories for production, and shipyards for trade. Then we have families and great houses, districts and slums. Each of these parts work together to maintain an intricate harmony between them. You may agree so far, elector?"

"I do," Sinclair nodded.

"And if these various parts were placed together by happenstance a governing force would inevitably manifest itself, do you think?"

"I would think so."

"It couldn't exist otherwise!" Stoddard said. "The very nature of it—the city's form—would not allow autonomy between the parts. It was a similar scenario that brought about our meritocracy in its infancy, if I'm not mistaken. And, it is precisely so with the human body. Our parts, with all their functions, invite the intelligence which governs them."

"You mean, our minds," Lord Worthington ventured.

"No..." Stoddard hesitated. "Our mind is just another part of the whole. What I mean is the *intelligence* that both consciously and unconsciously governs each faculty of our bodies. That intelligence is willing to expand if the form invites it, much like the meritocracy expands its influence to the colonies.

"I speculated at first that the body's function need only to be copied and recreated. I sought to replicate the function of a specific joint or limb. However, with each test it proved ineffective. It became necessary to ignore all but the most basic of functions and focus on creating a near-perfect form."

"I'm not sure I follow you," Lord Worthington said. "The *Vultair*, for instance, is my crudest ship—"

"A horrible looking thing," Lady Worthington piped in, capitalizing on the one talking point to which she felt she had some authority.

"—yet she flies surest in the skies. I'd trust her in a gale over any other ship I own. My wife insists I should do something to dress her up a bit, but I see no need to make something pretty if it gets the job done. If anything, trying to beautify her might only slow her down."

"A ship is one thing," Emmaline said, "but Stoddard is talking about a man's arm. It would be unbearable to have something so dreadful attached to you."

"Did you see the apparatus he carried around with him?" Worthington retorted. "Blight of a thing. Makes the *Vultair* look like a prince's galleon."

"I understand your concern," Stoddard said. "However, the issue here is not appearance. The *Vultair* is a worthy vessel, precisely because its form fulfills the measure of its function. It invites a harmony of her parts. In this instance, Lord Worthington, you are correct. But tell me, how is she powered?"

"She's powered by a steam engine in her center hold," Worthington explained. "With two dual-propeller rigs on each wing."

"And you're quite capable of regulating the amount of power delivered to each part?"

"Of course."

"This is a distinction we must make between the animate and in-animate," Stoddard said. "The human body is not something you can power so easily. It requires delicacy. Remember, the good captain's prosthetic did not replace a limb only. We were replicating major functions with such cumbersome materials as brass and iron, not organic tissue. And, like the Vultair, the mechanism needed power.

"At first the mechanists thought to use an external source, yet what could we have used? Certainly not steam! The contraption would have been too cumbersome to bear. Any possibility we contrived inevitably failed to sustain him. It was fortune on our side when his arm merged with our machine quite of its own will."

"See now, that is the thing which intrigues me most," Sinclair interjected. He'd been quiet during much of Stoddard's explanation, watching him intently. "Just how did the captain gain control of the device? I'd had opportunities to speak with Captain Harper on a few occasions, and it always fascinated me. I'd like to have asked him myself if it wasn't such a known taboo to discuss. Can *you* explain it?"

"Even after devoting years to its study, I have only a very preliminary understanding," Stoddard confessed. "What Harper's miracle revealed to us is that it is possible to tap into the body itself to power our mechanics. We knew already that the human body puts off a small amount of electricity, and we made some attempts to use this in our first attempts."

"Are you saying you treated that poor man like a common battery?" Lady Worthington gasped.

"I assure you it's not as invasive as it sounds," Stoddard said. "You'd be surprised how resilient the body is. The problem is that our bodies can only generate a minute amount of electricity."

"Oh," Lady Worthington shook her head and shuddered at the thought. "This is dreadful talk. I can't hear any more of it." She clutched her stomach and put a hand to her brow to steady herself.

"I'm sorry if I put you off from your meal," Stoddard apologized.

"Nonsense," Lord Worthington said. "The man is sparing us any graphic detail. My wife is just being dramatic."

"And you, Emmaline? Am I turning you off?" Stoddard asked.

"Not in the least," she said with perfect grace. "In fact, I find I quite enjoy hearing about your work. It gives me an idea what else has been competing for your attention."

Stoddard's mind stumbled, his thoughts derailing as she gave him a flirtatious wink. He was genuinely confused. What had possessed her to be so forward, in the company of her parents no less?

"I'm sorry the subject put you off," Sinclair said to Lady Worthington, "but I'm afraid I must request your patience a moment more. This is something I must hear. Waiter, perhaps some sherry for the lady?"

One of the servers was quick to deliver a glass, and Lady Worthington sipped it to collect herself.

"Would you continue, doctor?" Sinclair gestured.

"Of course," Stoddard conceded. "Ultimately, my mentor's mechanism was too large. There was no possibility it could function on what little electricity the good captain's body produced. It required a more significant and constant source of energy."

"Yet, it was managed," Sinclair said. "How?"

Stoddard swallowed hard, his words poised on the tip of his tongue. This was the moment when he'd either be hailed as a genius or dismissed as a lunatic. How would they receive his theory? Even to him, it sometimes seemed too strange to admit.

Yet, in his heart he knew his discoveries to be true. Could he convince them of the same?

He glanced toward Emmaline, sitting so perfectly as she was. He inhaled a breath of borrowed confidence.

"Aether," he said. "It was powered by Aether."

"I'm sorry," Lord Worthington said. "What is that?"

Stoddard was into it now. There was no turning back. "It's a theory of mine—an energy possessed by all living things, used throughout history to explain attributes of mankind which were otherwise unexplainable."

"I've heard of it," Arden said. "It was often referenced by alchemists, I think. Used to distinguish a man's spirit energy from other physical elements," he said with a voice of recitation.

"You're well read, Master Arden," Stoddard applauded.

"To a fault," he said, glancing at his father.

"Are you saying that you too don't know what it is?" Sinclair asked.

"Not at all," Stoddard said hurriedly. "To the alchemists it really was just a theory meant to fill in the gaps of their understanding. However, because of our good captain's miracle, I believe I've finally uncovered the true nature of the Aether."

"A power source?" Sinclair ventured.

"And more," Stoddard smiled, his eyes alight. It had been some time since he'd held an audience's attention, and the euphoria was intoxicating. "It's intelligence. Pure, raw intelligence. This is why the prosthetic wasn't just powered when it linked with the captain—it was inhabited. Much like our city might acquire a new colony, expanding its government and harnessing new resources, Harper was able to operate and control the motions of that prosthetic perfectly. Or, as perfectly as the mechanism would allow.

"You see, we'd already determined the electricity produced by the body wouldn't have been enough to power the mechanism. And we knew that whatever source was powering it had also extended the captain's intelligence into the prosthetic, granting him control. Whatever you decide to call it—Aether, intelligence, or spirit—we tapped into it and exposed a remarkable field of possibility."

"And that is what you've been studying all these years," Arden said in awe.

There was a silence among the company as they digested what Stoddard had said.

Sinclair's focus remained on Stoddard. He was leaning back in his seat, stroking his chin. "If this is the case," he said. "I'm finding it difficult to comprehend why your work hasn't gained more attention sooner."

"I'm afraid my theories were not so clearly organized before— when the miracle was still fresh in the public mind. They were only assumptions based on intuition—and flawed ones. It's taken years to be able to share with you what I have just now with any credible amount of certainty."

"I see," Sinclair said.

"So, you created a mechanical extension of a man, not just a prosthetic," Arden said. "Extraordinary!"

"Our understanding is only infantile," Stoddard said, "but it shows signs of great promise."

"It sounds dreadfully barbaric," Lady Worthington said. "I think I see in you a nearly unhealthy obsession as you speak of it."

"I think of it as a stalwart perseverance," Stoddard smiled.

"I think I see it too," Sinclair said. He clapped his hands together slowly, and the rest of the company joined him. "I applaud the dedication you've shown, doctor. I hope my son has taken note of it as well."

Arden nodded, his eyes wide. "Witnessing your work in the dome, it was like watching the creator fashion man anew. But, hearing you explain it now... I'm staring at the creator himself!"

Lady Worthington nearly choked on her food. "Bite your tongue, child! I'm sorry, Elector, but that's blasphemous!"

"Can I help it if mankind is revealing more of the creator's secrets each day?" Arden defended. "It baffles me to think that it was within my own lifetime that Stoddard's work has come about. And now, he works miracles to rival the gods!"

"Master Arden, you've gone too far!" Lady Worthington shrilled. "You have no idea what you're saying. I won't hear another—"

"Hush, woman!"

Lord Worthington barked so suddenly that everyone, including Sinclair, jumped.

"Let the boy speak his mind! These men are discussing progress, if not providence, before your very eyes. Are you so blind, woman? Can you not see it? We need more men like Stoddard who have a mind to dream, not superstitious naysayers yelping at their heels every step of the way. Listen and be taught!"

Lady Worthington's expression sank as the harshness of her husband's words struck her down. Her hurt was only visible for a moment, however, before she adopted the practiced countenance of a lady as she fumbled with her plate.

Indeed, everyone seemed to be focused more intently on their food.

"I'm not feeling well," Lady Worthington said after a moment. "Emmaline, perhaps we shall retire."

She rose from her chair and the men did likewise.

"Lady Worthington, please stay," Sinclair implored. "It was my indulgence which subjected you to these discomforts. Perhaps, we'd best let discussion rest for a moment. Help yourself to another sherry. In fact," he took up his glass from the table. "Let us toast our good captain's memory, for all of his contributions to the city. And our esteemed guest, Doctor Stoddard, in his moment of distinction."

The company all took up their drinks and there was a general murmur of agreement, apart from Lady Worthington who sipped her sherry silently.

Stoddard couldn't help a smile as he drank the toast. The elector's words were exactly what he'd hoped for. He'd been recognized by a leading figure of the meritocracy.

He'd made it.

CHAPTER NINE
The Exchange

I wonder, at times, what we will be required to pay for our ambition. No gods would impart so generously such a gift by magnanimity alone. There must be an exchange.

— Excerpt from *Mechanarcissism*

A nother botch, was it?" the official asked as he waved Chance forward with a meaty hand.

Chance stood in one of the half-dozen lines in the Exchange, a busy courtyard surrounded by large warehouses on three sides. Individual stations had been erected in a row to receive citizens, each with a city official behind a barred window regulating purchases and checking charters.

"Yeah," Chance shrugged, approaching the dusty man. "But what can you do?"

"You could quit," the man burst forth in a blast of laughter. "That's an idea. Save yourself a singed finger or two. You still got them, don't yeh?"

Chance held up his gloved hand, at first only revealing three fingers. The official gave him a queer look, then burst into another round of laughter when Chance held up his other two.

"Heh! You've got it. That was a good one. Almost had me."

Chance forced a smile and swallowed his contempt for the man. He hated city officials, no matter their position. They were gatekeepers, each and every one of them. Behind his laugh, Chance saw only some gentleman cog monitoring his purchases, their greedy hands extended to skim a profit from his hard work. Their regulations made an already difficult life more so, and it was no secret that alchemists were often singled out.

To combat that fact, Chance played the fool.

Under the tutelage of Ashworth, he'd made it a point to trade exclusively with the Exchange near the shipyard. Consistency meant familiarity, and being recognized made it easier to maneuver his way around some of the nit-pickier custom regulations. It irked him to no end, having to entertain, but it kept his visits light and scrutinizing eyes distracted.

It was a small price to pay.

On the other hand, he was gaining reputation for failure. That soured him more than anything. It wasn't what he had in mind when he'd begun his apprenticeship. He'd been useful to Ashworth, though few others would ever see that. It was the lot of an alchemist: even in their moments of glory they were still viewed by society as something lesser.

He handed the official his list of commodities.

"Right. How about your credentials?"

Chance pulled his carrier from under his coat. Laying it open on the counter, he produced his charter identifying him as a free-merchant apprentice.

"All good then," the official said, hardly glancing at it. "Gotta be thorough."

Chance smirked. He was a full partner to Ashworth now, but so long as they worked under the same roof it wasn't worth the hassle to inform the city. Nobody cared enough to come after them about it. It was just one less bureaucratic hurdle to jump through.

"I need twelve measures of phosphorous and aqua fortis, two bottles of thick air, and fifty measures of salt copperas," Chance said.

"Right," the official said, taking the note and jotting something down in a ledger. He handed it to a boy and sent him off to fetch the components from one of the back rooms of the warehouse. "Afraid we don't have any salt copperas, though. You'll have to check back another time."

"What?" Chance asked. "How's that?"

"Asked myself the same thing when I found out. Why not ask your friends? They keep buying out our shipments before we even unload them into the yard. I've had my share of complaints, but I can't do a thing to keep my stock full. And I'm not about to pass up a sure sale."

"Who's buying?"

"Lot of new faces," he said, leafing through his ledger. "But, according to the certificate, they all belong to Gravatts."

That was odd. Salt copperas was nothing more than an additive used to stall reactions within a mixture. It was the very same additive Chance had run short on for his. What could old man Gravatts be working on that he needed so much?

"Any news on what they've been producing?" Chance asked.

"Aye, there is," the official said, tapping his meaty finger on the countertop. He stared at Chance, his expression uncaring.

Chance rolled his eyes and pulled a handful of coins from his pocket, laying them out before him. The official snatched them up in a single motion, depositing them in his own pocket.

"Nothing," he said with a grin, waving his hand in the air as though the word had vanished with Chance's money.

"Nothing? What kind of information is—"

The official gave Chance a knowing look.

"Oh..."

That *was* significant. Gravatts' laboratory was one of the largest in the Basin. His reputation allowed him to do business among some of the higher tiers of society. Of all Chance and Ashworth's competitors, Gravatts was one of the only labs to have obtained a partial customs waiver. Their production paled in comparison.

For Gravatts to slow his production was unusual. But, to have stopped altogether? The news presented quite a riddle.

"Word has it," the official said, "that a while back Gravatts up and sent everyone home with a week's advance in their pockets and told them to come back the following week. No explanation. Nothing."

"What could he be working on?" Chance wondered.

"Not a clue, but he can't keep it up long if you ask me. Either he's got money coming in we don't know about or he's gone entirely mad. Between you and me, I think the latter. Too many fumes over the years. Ah! Here are your components."

The boy came hurrying back and handed over the requested items.

"Thank you," Chance said, paying for them with the notes Liesel had given him. He placed the larger jars into a satchel. The smaller vials he secured in his carrier and tucked it underneath his coat. "You've been a help."

"It's always a pleasure to make an exchange," the official said, tapping his nose twice and waving Chance along. "Next!"

Chance paused near the iron gate, leaning against one of the walls as he waited for Rhett to return from his errand. He watched the people coming and going. They moved about him in a chaotic rhythm that became white noise the longer he watched. Occasionally, a peddler approached him, offering the goods they had on hand.

Chance was quick to turn them away.

The law restricted any unsanctioned trade within the courtyard, but that didn't keep independent sellers from setting up just outside the gates. They shouted at passersby incessantly, assuring whomever would listen that their wares were guaranteed cheaper or of higher quality than anything distributed by the city.

Chance had learned early that those peddlers were more trouble than they were worth. Alchemy was a fickle craft as it was, and it wasn't worth the risk of getting faulty components trying to save a few coins.

His thoughts eventually turned back to Gravatts. He just couldn't fathom what would possess the alchemist to abandon his regular production and dismiss his staff—for any length of time. Perhaps he really had gone mad. The thought wasn't beyond reason.

Or perhaps he was onto something new?

Chance's curiosity was piqued. He had a hard time believing

Gravatts was the type of man who'd develop anything new, but then Chance hadn't paid him much attention. He made a mental note to pay Gravatts' nearest pubs a visit soon to see if he couldn't pry a bit more information out of his men.

"Done!" Rhett popped out from between two larger women looking proud with his satchel. It bulged with foodstuffs and other purchases Chance had entrusted to him.

"Good job. Any money left?" Chance asked.

Rhett held out his hand. He had a few small notes and some loose coins. "You think we could ride in a dirigible still?" he asked.

"Not today."

"But we have enough money."

"But it isn't ours." Chance counted out a few coins and handed them to Rhett. "Go ahead and use that to take a rail back home. I'll be along later tonight."

"Where are you going?"

"I've got some things I have to do." Chance tucked the rest of the coins into his coat pocket and handed Rhett the satchel.

"Why can't I come?"

"Because someone's got to take our things back to the house. And anyway, you'd just slow me down. This is a man's job."

"Now, I know I didn't just hear you refer to yourself as a *man*."

Ponti, one of Chance's friends, came sauntering up. A lumpy rucksack was slung over his shoulder. It jangled and clanked as he walked. Chance was surprised he hadn't heard him approach.

"Don't let him fool you, Rhett. He's a whelp as much as you. Just a head or two bigger." He gave Rhett a wink. "Chance, you shoddy piece of scrap, it's good to see—gadgets, your face is a wreck!" Ponti leaned in so close to Chance's face that the odor of his breath overwhelmed him. "What'd you bump into?"

"None of your business," Chance said, swatting Ponti away. "Just trying to get through a few errands today."

"Doing or done?" Ponti grinned. "Because if you're done, I'm about ready to meet up with a few of the guys. You in?"

Chance thought about Gravatts' men. He wanted to find out what they were about, but the thought of relaxing from the wreck of a day it had been got the better of him. He could always investigate later.

"Sure," Chance agreed. "I could go for something strong right about now."

"Can I come with you?" Rhett asked.

"I don't know, what do you think?" Ponti asked. He took Rhett by the shoulder and jostled him in a rough hold. "Think he's got enough hair on his chest to quaff vice with the worst of us?"

"It's not your type of place, Rhett," Chance explained.

"There you have it. Verdict passed." Ponti pushed Rhett away. "Better luck next time, kid."

Rhett frowned and his lip quivered.

"Hey now, hold up." Ponti swung his rucksack off his shoulder and set it down onto the street with a clatter. He rummaged through the assorted junk before pulling out a tiny toy flying machine and handed it to Rhett.

"Wow!" Rhett said, his eyes lighting up. One of its sides was badly damage, but for the most part it was intact. "For me?"

"Sure, kid."

"Where'd you find that?" Chance asked.

"Came crashing down on me over by Copperfield. Bloody thing nearly clipped my ear clean off it was falling so fast. Anyway, I thought you'd enjoy it. Something to amuse you while we amuse ourselves."

"Thanks!" Rhett said. He cocked his arm back and gave it a toss toward a less congested section of the street. The toy sailed all of two feet before flipping wing over wing and crashing down between Rhett's feet.

"It's going to need some work," Ponti pointed out.

"Go ahead and take it with you," Chance said. "I'll meet up with you later tonight, and maybe we'll see if we can get that thing to fly."

Rhett didn't show any sign that he'd heard them. He'd already scooped up the gizmo and was racing off happily with it. Chance shook his head and smiled as he and Ponti turned down the street toward the bay.

As they walked, Ponti produced a flask from his pocket and tossed it to Chance. "Something to tide you over," he said, "'till we get something a bit stronger. There's a pub down on Balderdash I have to introduce you to."

"Not where the Gaffer's pit used to be?" Chance asked, taking a swig off the watery brew. He handed the flask back to Ponti.

"Same place, though the guy running it now is top shelf. They've done it up a bit, too."

Chance looked skeptical, but followed along. "Since when did you start thinking of Rhett while you're junking?" he asked as Ponti adjusted the sack over his shoulder.

"Never," Ponti said matter-of-factly. "But, I couldn't have the whelp tugging at your heartstrings like that if we were ever going to get a drink. Come on! I lost time fetching you."

CHAPTER TEN
Announcements

Genius? Forerunner? Visionary? Is there a word to accurately describe man's ascension?

— Excerpt from *Mechanarcissism*

"Forgive her," Lord Worthington said, letting out a heavy sigh. "She's a proper lady, but her ignorance can be unbearable."

The men had stepped onto the patio for a moment of privacy away from the ladies. They'd finished their meal, and found the excuse for a smoke sufficient to continue their conversation from earlier.

"I may have spoken a little too loosely," Arden conceded.

"No matter," Sinclair said, taking out a cigarette case and selecting a stick. He offered one to Stoddard, who took it with thanks. "Some have a harder time digesting new ideas than others. I imagine you'll have your work cut out trying to bring us all up to speed, doctor."

"I'll do my best."

"But, it's good to have a moment for more substantive talk," Sinclair said, lighting his cigarette. "My son tributes your work, and rightly so."

"You can't fault the boy for speaking the truth," Lord Worthington said, lighting his pipe and taking a few thick puffs.

"Do you agree with his assessment of your work?" Sinclair asked.

"Master Arden is generous in his praise and he gives me great honors," Stoddard said. "However, there is still much to learn. We have yet to fully grasp the Aether and its possibilities. However, if what we've discovered through this whole ordeal with the good captain is any indication of what is to come then I have high hopes for the future."

"And what would you need," Sinclair asked. "Money? Time?"

"Some time, yes," Stoddard said. "And resources. Up until now I've gotten by in large measure by the generosity of a handful of donors— Harper being the principle donor, naturally."

"And if you had the resources? Where could you see your work a year from now?"

"With the right equipment and more opportunities to test my mechanisms, I expect I could replicate the link reliably and begin testing its capabilities."

"We'll need to see to it then," Sinclair said. "Had I not come with business at hand, I'd like to discuss it more. However, I'm afraid Lord Worthington has been patient enough with me this afternoon and has matters of his own to discuss."

"Cursed corsairs have been harassing the trade routes between our southeastern colonies," Worthington explained. "They've sacked one of my ships already. Over protected airspace, I might add. The spineless viceroys refuse to do anything of their own initiative to uphold their agreements."

"I understand your plight," Sinclair said. Stoddard sensed his exasperation as he took in a deep breath. "I'll do what I can to apply some pressure, but perhaps it would be wise in the meantime to invest in an armed ship of your own to hunt these corsairs. Perhaps you'll have some luck recovering your cargo."

"That would be the worst course of action," Worthington insisted. "As soon as the viceroys saw me policing their skies for them they'd wash their hands of the matter entirely."

Stoddard listened politely to Worthington's take on the corsairs. He had little experience with sky-pirates, the colonies, or the politics that made it all turn. He could only offer the sympathetic nod or comment here and there.

"Congratulations," Arden said to Stoddard as his father and Worthington continued to speak. "I'm sure that was what you were hoping for today."

"Excuse me?"

"Your recognition, from my father. You'll find yourself welcome among most of the meritocracy now, I imagine."

"Thank you," Stoddard said.

"He's yet to recognize me," Arden said, his voice laced with a hint of bitterness. "I'd almost thought he'd forgotten how."

Stoddard was surprised by the young man's openness. But then, he imagined it wasn't easy being the son of such a distinguished figure within the meritocracy. The pressure Arden wrestled with to distinguish himself as his own person must have been intense.

"You'll be recognized in time, I'm sure," Stoddard said. "It's a long road, if my experience is a testament. Nonetheless, it is attainable."

"Yes, well..." Arden shuffled his feet as he watched his father. "I worry about my contribution to the city. I can't ride in my father's shadow forever. It's coming time for me to distinguish myself, but as much as I've tried I haven't found my niche yet.

"Your mechanisms seem so far beyond anything I've ever thought to achieve, and your dedication absolute. For the first time, I'm beginning to believe what my father says about me spreading my talents too thin."

"What seems to be a flaw might actually be your strength," Stoddard offered. "To have entertained so many interests is evidence of an inquisitive mind. That is a more difficult quality to develop than the understanding of any one subject. If I was to consider your ability as a mechanist, I'd suspect great things from you one day."

"My father doesn't seem to think so."

"You're not too different from myself when I was your age."

"You flatter me," Arden said.

"It's true," Stoddard insisted. "If you're interested, perhaps you'd like to look over some of my designs firsthand? I imagine I'll be quite busy in the coming months, but I'd be glad to set aside some time to explain them to you."

"Truly?"

"Of course," Stoddard smiled. "It would be impossible to appreciate their complexity from just one observation in the medical dome. It would be my pleasure."

"I'd be thrilled!" Arden said.

"Then it is done. My office is open to you at your convenience. I'll have my attendant made aware of it."

As the boy fired off a fresh batch of questions, Stoddard grinned inwardly. To have the favor of an elector was a fortune he'd not expected, but to be in confidence with his son was nearing perfection. He suspected it would prove most advantageous to keep the lad close.

"Gentlemen, I'm afraid our brief window of time is nearly run out," Sinclair declared. Apparently, he and Lord Worthington had come to some agreement. Worthington looked considerably less agitated. "The women will wonder why our business has delayed us so long. Shall we return?"

"Of course," Stoddard said.

Sinclair put out his cigarette, and Worthington emptied his pipe.

"Doctor Stoddard," Sinclair said as they began to walk. "If you're able to spare a moment, would you be willing to give a more detailed presentation to myself and the other electors? I have no doubt they'll be interested in your work after I speak with them on your behalf."

"It would be my pleasure."

"It's been too long since your work has been considered among the meritocracy, I think." Sinclair offered his hand to Stoddard, who took it in a firm shake. "I'd like to invest in your work, personally," he added, not letting go of Stoddard's hand. "An initial investment of 100,000 banknotes, which is nothing compared to the sum you may receive after your presentation if you can impress us."

Stoddard stood dazed. "That would... thank you, Elector."

"My pleasure," Sinclair smiled, finally releasing his hand. "I'll be in contact with you in the next few days."

When they'd rejoined the women, servers brought out a fresh

selection of desserts which the company helped themselves to. Lady Worthington appeared to be in better spirits, the effects of the sherry warming her cheeks. The luncheon was running long, and Stoddard wondered when the Sinclair would be required elsewhere, but no one seemed in any particular hurry.

Not wanting to be rude, Stoddard resigned himself to another glass of wine. But, before he could take a drink, his thoughts were interrupted as Lord Worthington rose from his chair and cleared his throat with a deep rumble.

"Excuse me, everyone," he said, tapping his glass. "I feel we were fortunate to be here today. Most fortunate. Not only to have come at the invitation of our beloved elector, but to have with us his esteemed guest, Doctor Stoddard."

There was a general acknowledgment from the rest of the company.

"Perhaps it's not public knowledge, but this is not the first encounter I've had with the doctor," Worthington smiled. "I had the fortune of making his acquaintance when he once—no doubt caught up in a youthful spirit—sought to court my daughter, Emmaline. Do you recall, doctor?"

Stoddard's face flushed. He glanced at Emmaline, but she maintained her calm, collected countenance as though nothing said had surprised her in the least. He wondered how she remained so unfazed in such moments.

"I do recall," he said, trying to mimic Emmaline's cool appearance.

"At the time, there was some concern about his standing in society—our daughter being of an esteemed family and Stoddard yet to prove himself worthy of our fair Emmaline. Given recent events, however, I think it goes without saying that my concerns are no longer pertinent. We are fortunate indeed to witness a man who is offering very real promise to our fair city."

He raised his glass in a toast.

"To the future of your work, doctor."

"To the future of your work," the party repeated, taking up their own glasses.

"And may it always tip fortune toward Hatteras," Sinclair added.

Stoddard swelled with pride as he drank. Even Worthington was laying aside the differences of their past and recognizing him. What more could he have hoped for? A man of control and discipline typically, he allowed himself this moment to celebrate his turn of fortunes and drank deeply.

"And regarding my daughter," Worthington continued. "It's no secret she harbors affections for you still."

Stoddard choked on his wine.

"I suppose it is her nature to nurture youthful affections even after so many years," Worthington continued. "Perhaps she saw in you then what the rest of us only now have begun to see. But, do you still retain the feelings you once disclosed to me so many years ago?"

Stoddard did his best to recover. He'd not expected *that*. He glanced again at Emmaline and thought he could discern a smile hidden behind her gaze, but it was impossible to be sure. Her expression remained cool and practiced.

Whatever course he took now, he was alone choosing it.

"I do," Stoddard admitted.

A curl of a smile appeared at the corner of Emmaline's lip then. That, she could not hide.

"Then I give you two my blessing." Worthington raised his glass again. Lady Worthington made a noise as if to interrupt, but a severe look from her husband silenced her before she could protest. "To a prosperous future," he toasted.

"To a prosperous future," everyone repeated.

Stoddard was in such a dream, he nearly forgot to thank the others offering him their congratulations. Everything was happening so fast. His head was spinning, whether from his turn of fortune or the strength of the wine. The conversation passed like a vague recollection before him.

And through it all, he felt Emmaline's hand on his.

"That was quite impressive," she whispered in his ear, leaning in close.

"I'm glad you thought so," Stoddard said. It was the first time she'd been this close in years. "You'll need to give me a moment to collect myself. This was a little much all at once."

Emmaline offered Stoddard his glass, and he drained it again to calm himself.

"I've never seen you so enamored by the political theater before," Emmaline said. "I thought you disdained it."

"Generally, I do. Today I entertained it out of necessity."

"Well, don't try too hard," she smiled. "It almost looks like you enjoy it."

Just then, the host appeared carrying a letter upon a silver tray. "Excuse me sir," he said, addressing Stoddard. "This missive was delivered for you just now."

"He's busy at the moment," Emmaline said in a humorously bright voice. She held herself close on his arm. "It will have to wait."

"The lady has spoken," Stoddard laughed, and the others shared in it.

"Be careful where that road takes you," Lord Worthington warned. "Give a little and she'll have it all."

"I'm sorry, sir," the host said, "but I was told it was urgent."

"Oh, very well." Stoddard took the envelope with a show of reluctance and opened it.

"Another invitation?" Sinclair ventured.

"Honestly, what could be more important than myself at a time like this?" Emmaline smiled, batting her eyes at him as he read.

Stoddard paid them no mind. His eyes were racing across the letter. A few of the guests passed wary glances in the silence.

"Is everything alright?" Worthington asked.

Stoddard looked up, his gaze not directed toward anyone. His mind was no longer drifting. It had been seized upon—pulled back down to earth with such gravity that his very foundation was cracking.

"I'm sorry," he said, his throat dry despite the abundance of drink. "I'm afraid I'm needed elsewhere."

"What?" Emmaline looked hurt as he released her from his arm and stood to go.

"It can't be helped. Host!" he snapped. "My coat please. Now! I'm sorry, Elector. It honestly cannot be helped."

"Nothing wrong, I hope?" Arden asked.

"I can only assume," Stoddard said, and with that he hurried down the terrace steps and made for the door.

CHAPTER ELEVEN
Poor Company

Easier to keep components separate before you mix them.

— Alchemical Proverb

I t occurred to Chance that what Ponti considered a fine establishment might not be what anyone else would have in mind.

The pub was a shanty, with a worn sign hanging cockeyed from two rusty chains. The windows were warped and tinted green so that only blurred shadows could be seen moving on the other side. As they pulled open the doors, a gaseous slurry of soot, smoke, and booze wafted out into the street.

"Home is where the spirits are," Ponti grinned as they walked in.

The place was packed. Rough looking factory workers and rowdy company contributed to the general roar of debauchery. Along one of the far walls, as removed as could be from the ruckus, Chance and Ponti caught sight of their friends and hurried to join them.

"Look who emerges from his workshop," Serge, the oldest of the group, greeted Chance. He was a thick, muscular man, in his later twenties. A mason by trade, when he clapped Chance on the back it forced the air out of his lungs. "It's been a while since we've seen you. Don't you ever get out anymore?"

"Not if there's work to be done," Chance replied, punching Serge's shoulder with his good hand. It was like punching a wall. "What are you all up to?"

"On a mend," the lad they called Kwame said. He was a foreigner from a colony somewhere beyond Port Elliston, in eastern Pendambu. He worked with Serge as a brick layer since migrating to Hatteras a year before. They called him Kwame because they couldn't pronounce his real name, and it was far too long to remember when inebriated.

A full foot and a half shorter than the rest, he'd perched himself upon a few crates stacked against the wall. "Factory demands hours long and long. There is work to do and few men to do," he explained.

"Didn't expect to hear you complaining," Serge said. "Kwame's happy to have work; don't let him fool you. Wouldn't have been so easy settling in if there wasn't a shortage of hands."

"Don' mean I don' feel. Look!" Kwame pulled his shirt down by his neck and displaying a deep purple bruise across his shoulder. "Mason drop all stack of brick. Don' warn me, and I am half buried!"

"No one cares whether or not you made it through another work-day," Ponti said. He plopped down on one of the chairs and shoved his rucksack underneath. "Who's covering drinks?"

Everyone glanced around the table.

"Kwame?" Ponti pried. "I feel like it was Kwame's turn."

"The guy was nearly buried alive and you're asking him pay for drinks?" Chance asked. "Isn't it about time you covered them?"

"Nah. I got them time before last."

"I thought I had the time before last," Serge said.

"That cheap whiskey is getting to your head. You need to cut back," Ponti smiled. "I'll get it next time. Promise." He crossed his heart. "I swear, you cogs are trying to take advantage of a man's—"

Serge gave Ponti's jaw a swift cuff with an open hand.

"Watch your tongue," he warned him.

"Ehey!" Ponti staggered, rubbing his jaw and shying away from Serge. "Some cogs are bigger than others," he muttered under his breath.

"Well, I've got nowhere to be for a little while," Chance said.

"Kwame, you alright covering today?"

"Ja-nee," Kwame conceded. It wasn't his custom to refuse his friends.

"Atta boy," Ponti laughed, making himself comfortable. "Now this is the place to be! Loud conversation, the greatest girls, and the finest booze you *can't* get your hands on anywhere else in this pious city. Am I right darling?"

He caught one of the server girls by her dress and pulled her against him, jostling her roughly. She forced a laugh as he took one of the bottles from her tray.

"She knows exactly what I'm after when she sees me come through that door," he grinned. "I don't even have to ask anymore."

The girl smiled politely, but managed to slip out of Ponti's grasp and continue with her work.

"I think it's safe to wager someone's going to be pickled before the evening," a man commented as he stepped up to the table, a cigar in his cheek and a bowler tipped assertively over his balding forehead. He wore a colorful gentleman's coat of deep violet with silver stitching along its edges. It was a little worn, however, and its fit didn't quite suit him.

"Indubitably," Ponti grinned.

"That's the spirit I like to see." The man patted Ponti's back. "That's why you're always welcome through those doors. And who are these new friends you've brought me?"

"These unfortunate sods are Serge and Chance. Our foreign looking friend there is Kwame."

"A pleasure to make each of your acquaintances," he said, shaking each of their hands in turn. Chance was startled at how soft the man's hands were.

"But Ponti," he said, "I must disagree with you on one finer point. Unfortunate is not a word we use to describe anyone who comes through my doors. Gentleman, the name is Blake Bracken. But call me Blake, your eager and willing host on any occasion you find yourselves in need. Please, make yourselves at home. I trust you're thirsty. Cherie! A round for my new and esteemed patrons."

"On a house?" Kwame asked.

"Haha! That'd be nice, wouldn't it?" Blake smiled as he pulled up a chair between Ponti and Chance. He laughed, and Chance found himself laughing along with him. He liked Blake.

"I'm a generous man, but not that generous. Now, if you're looking for good conversation, a place to spend your coin, or perhaps just a bit o' friendly companionship, I am more than willing to provide. My establishment is at your disposal, day and night."

"Best man in the city!" Ponti cried and a cheer went up among the nearby patrons. Blake shrugged with a show of humble pride.

Cherie appeared with a round of flagons filled with a thick, porter beer. Serge declined it, but the others helped themselves.

"So what occasion brings you all together today?" Blake asked.

"Just here for a refresher and to exchange the latest news," Serge said.

"Ah, and what is the news you've brought to exchange? Anything interesting?"

"You got idiots on a Spire," Kwame said, drawing a laugh out of the group. Being from a colony, he didn't possess the same inhibitions that some of the locals did when it came to speaking about the meritocracy. His tongue was as loose as a child's. Chance liked him all the more for that reason alone.

"I meant what's *new?*" Blake clarified, triggering another round of laughter.

"Did you hear Maybell is coming back to the city?" Serge mentioned.

"Really? I haven't seen her in months. I thought she'd moved inland permanently," Chance said.

"And who is Maybell?" Blake asked. "Not one of my girls, was she?"

"A girl from our part of the Basin. We grew up with her."

"Funny, I thought I'd made acquaintance with most of the girls near the edge."

"Is that one girl Ponti chase?" Kwame asked.

"No, she's the one that Ponti got!" Ponti boasted. Serge gave him a glare and Ponti shrugged. "What? Aw, you guys need to lighten up a bit. I bet even she's having a good laugh over the whole thing right now."

Serge's face was stern and he gave Chance a look as though he'd reached his limit for the day. He leaned forward and angled himself away from Ponti.

Chance couldn't blame him. Ponti was fun most days, but conversations tended to steer south whenever he was around. He was a fool through and through, but sometimes a fool was exactly what Chance needed in a drinking buddy.

"Do you have anything stiffer?" Chance asked.

"That depends," Blake grinned. "What are you looking for?"

"I'll have what he has." Chance gestured to Ponti and drew out the few coins he had left in his coat pocket.

"Aye, you'd like that wouldn't you?" Ponti grinned, "but this is a euphoria reserved for the truly desperate."

"Is that...?" Chance asked, perking up.

"You bet your sweet bob it is!" Ponti laughed loudly. "Blake here keeps a bottle set aside just for me."

"I don't have the foggiest notion what you're talking about," Blake said, quite stern. "Don't you know there's a ban on the stuff?! To imply that I, a respectable and honest businessman, would dabble in unlawful drink offends me to no end!"

He gave a showy huff and leaned in closer.

"However, if you're of the same temperament as our mutual friend," Blake whispered, "I might be able to produce a bottle or two for the right price."

Chance fingered the coins in his hand, wrestling with himself as he counted what remained. He knew he shouldn't; they needed what they had to pay Liesel back, and to replace Ashworth's hartshorn. And he knew what happened when he indulged. It was a slippery slope. One he hadn't visited for a while.

But, he reasoned, a break would also do him good. They'd already managed to scrounge together most of the supplies they needed for the next batch of deliveries. He'd have the money replaced in a week or so. Maybe sooner if he worked hard enough.

He slipped the coins into Blake's open hand.

"Right," Blake grinned. "Cherie! Special service to this gangly chap. Eh, what was the name again?"

"Chance."

Blake clapped Chance on the back and jostled him in a friendly manner.

"I hope to see you again, Chance. Gentlemen," he said, addressing the group, "I'm afraid I must leave you to your foibles. Do make yourselves familiar and frequent our quaint little home again."

He stepped away and immediately took another man's arm as he came through the door. "Quinn! By Septigonee's fortunes, you've gotten plump."

Cherie delivered Chance a dark tinted bottle without a label.

"You shouldn't drink that," Serge scolded.

"Oh, leave a man his vices," Ponti sighed. "What's the point of life if a man can't enjoy its libations on occasion? The meritocracy enjoys fresh air and sunshine, leave us to simulate their joy."

"Counterfeit pleasures to dilute the spirit," Serge frowned.

"At least they're pleasures," Chance shrugged.

"But don't you see how they're used against us? They dull our minds. Weaken our resolve. It's a means by which the meritocracy holds us at the bottom while they enjoy true freedom on the top."

"Hmm," Chance mused. "I always thought it was the constables doing the holding. I didn't realize it was our half-penny drinks that were arresting us when we started walking too proud."

"You know what I'm getting at," Serge said.

"Yes, he's out to spoil our fun," Ponti said. "For Septigonee's sake, come off it a moment and leave us to wallow in something other than the filth of our streets. Please? Just this once? For your lowly friends?"

He gave Serge the most pitiful eyes he could.

"Fine," Serge threw his hands up into the air. "But mark my words, if things are ever going to change it's going to take sharper minds and resolute hearts, not inebriated fools slow to reason."

"Dully noted," Ponti grinned, and took an extra-long drought from his bottle.

Chance couldn't argue with either side. He knew Serge was right. He'd sat and listened to Serge spout on about his ideas about change many times. In many ways, he had a mind much like the meritocracy—progress driven and given to a dash of entitlement. It was unfortunate his idea of progress was in such stark contrast to theirs or else he might have been able to hoist himself up in society by his passion alone.

As it was, he worked at the brickyard by day and the factories each night, stoking the fires that kept the furnaces burning. It was difficult work, which suited Serge's temperament. He was never one to shy away from difficulty. If anything, it attracted him. He gave all of himself at every moment. Chance admired him for that.

Ponti, on the other hand, was everything Serge wasn't—except well off. They were both Basin-dwellers after all.

"There you are!" called another man who'd just come through the door.

Chance recognized Simon, one of Serge's closer friends. He hobbled over as quickly as he could, which was slower given he walked with a cane. He pulled himself a chair from another table and joined the little group, taking a moment to catch his breath. Kwame passed him his own drink and Simon took a sip.

"Thanks," he said, sliding it back. "Throat was about as rough as gravel."

"What's got you worked up?" Serge asked.

Simon pulled a folded newspaper from inside his coat. Slapping it down on the table, he jabbed a finger at the front-page story. "Read it! Go on!"

The three of them leaned forward together to get a better look at the article he pointed to. The headline read loud and clear:

WAR HERO GIVEN NEW LIFE

They skimmed through it, but Chance had only gone a paragraph in before looking up.

"Harper?"

Simon nodded. "You know of him?"

"Just a little," Chance said. "Ashworth was telling me about him last night, and about how he died."

"Well, he's not dead now," Simon smiled. "I've said it before, you can't keep a tough man down. And that man's one of toughest alive. Even Septigonee's Well couldn't hold him! I bet you Harper met Death on his way down and cuffed him so hard he was sent back for reform."

Chance kept reading, having a hard time believing the words he read. The captain was alive! They were calling it the second miracle.

Catching even the men who performed the operation by surprise, the mechanism designed by Dr. J. Collins Stoddard proved as miraculous as the first that saved Captain Harper's life after his valiant service during the Great War. Details remain obscure, but it can only be anticipated that recent events will draw more eyes to Stoddard's mind-baffling work.

"So… what? They brought him back from the dead?"

Serge rolled his eyes. "They did not."

"You've got the paper. It says it right there," Simon pointed.

"Meritocracy makes pacts with a devil," Kwame said.

"That's to say they aren't devils themselves," Ponti added.

"They didn't goof! The papers just reported it wrong. Here—" Serge pulled the paper over. "It says they '*were too hasty in announcing the captain's death, but the prosthetic exceeded all medical expectations.*' It was premature reporting, that's all."

"That's complete poppycock," Ponti laughed. "It's a publicity stunt. They're trying to sell more papers."

"The Nightingale is a respectable newspaper," Simon defended.

"You're kidding me, right?" Ponti said. "I've never read any paper out of Hatteras that wasn't above spinning tales out of its bu—."

"So, what then? He came to after the fact?" Chance asked.

"That's what it sounds like."

"Poppycock," Ponti repeated. "You can't trust the paper. I doubt he's alive at all."

Simon groaned.

"Hear me out," Ponti said, leaning forward. He pointed to the end of the article. "'*Captain Harper was unavailable for comment.*' He's probably still on some slab somewhere. Nobody ever sees these old veterans anymore, so no one will think the wiser if he doesn't make an appearance, right? They just need to keep his name alive to take care of some agenda behind the scenes. Tie up some lose ends. Sign over his family fortune and whatnot."

"You're just being stupid now," Serge said.

"You watch!" Ponti said. "In a month, when they're good and done with him, you'll be reading about his relapse and some gentleman is gonna walk away fat and easy with his fortune."

Chance shrugged, only half listening. He was thinking about his conversation with Ashworth, and wondering where exactly his mentor had gone that night.

"Oh gods, what is she doing here?" Ponti's expression turned to one of absolute disgust. Chance followed his eyes.

Sitting at the bar was a woman in a heavy purple dress with fancy black-lace trimmings. It was exceptionally fine, for the establishment. Her bright blond curls bounced as she laughed, juggling the attention of the men doting on her. It wasn't difficult to see why she had the attention of so many men; she stood out from the other girls.

Leave it to Margarete to upstage everyone.

"Well, there goes the reputation of this place," Ponti mourned. He slumped forward dejectedly. "Seriously, why does she always have to ruin the best this miserable city has to offer?"

"She hasn't done anything yet," Serge pointed out. "How do you know she's going to ruin it?"

"Trust me," Ponti said, pounding his finger on the table. "She—ru-ins—every—thing—she—touches." Each word came out forced and dripping with bitterness.

"Do I now?" Margarete asked, walking up behind him.

"Oh, gods above." Ponti hugged his bottle, as if she might snatch it away from him at any moment.

"Hello boys," she beamed.

"Hello Margarete," they all said, with varied levels of enthusiasm.

"What's gotten you all into such a bunch?" she asked, leaning against Ponti's chair, which only made him cringe more. She didn't seem to mind. In fact, Chance saw a twinkle in her eyes as she did so.

"They're just sour," Chance said.

"Oh, poor dears. What's got you all stressed out, sourpuss?"

"Nothing a moment's privacy wouldn't remedy," Ponti muttered.

"Be courteous," Serge warned. "There's a lady present."

"A lady?" Ponti gave him a look. "Have you met her?"

"It's alright, darling. I was on my way out anyway. Thought I'd just come and ruffle this one's feathers a bit." She stroked Ponti's cheek with a gloved hand and he recoiled under it. "Perhaps I'll find the rest of you later in more pleasant company?"

She turned and caught Chance's eyes. Making a motion ever so slight, she left. Chance wasn't sure if anyone else had noticed. Despite himself, he couldn't hold back a smile.

"Did you feel it?" Ponti asked. "That horrid, nasty air that settled while she was here?"

"Her perfume?"

"Nah, something worse. It's like she walked through a—where are you going?" he asked as Chance stood up from the table.

"Just remembered I have somewhere I've got to be."

"What? Where?"

"When fortune favors you, it's not polite to question her," Chance grinned. He took his bottle and slid the newspaper back to Simon. "Thanks for that."

"You can't honestly tell me you're giving up our company for that tart?"

"No," Chance said. "I'm giving it up for that lady."

CHAPTER TWELVE
Mundane Dreams

Not everyone can admire what an alchemist attempts with their craft. Not everyone can rub two cents together either.

— Alchemical Proverb

Back in Chance's workshop, Margarete carefully pulled her dress up over her head and hung it up on a hook on the wall. It billowed out like a bell, taking up a corner of the tiny room. Unlike a true lady's gown, this one was designed for quick changes. Margarete always said it was worth not needing a lady's maid.

Standing around in nothing but her undergarments might have been odd when they first began meeting, but she was beyond feeling uncomfortable about things like that. And Chance had grown comfortable with her as well.

Besides, she couldn't risk ruining her dress.

"How's it coming along?" she asked, peering over Chance's shoulder.

"Just a minute or two and it'll be ready."

Chance worked steadily, combining a few substances in a wide-brimmed bottle. Margarete took the moment to soak her hair in the basin of water he'd brought in from the kitchen.

"Is it new?" he asked, motioning to the dress. He couldn't remember if he'd seen her wear it before. For someone from the Basin, Margarete owned a lot of dresses.

"Oh, yes," she said, combing the water through her curls with her fingers. "It was a gift."

Chance shook the bottle vigorously for a few seconds before pouring the mixture into a large bowl. Selecting a few components from his shelves, he ground them down to a powder with his mortar and pestle. The mixture smelled faintly of lavender. When it was ground fine enough he added it to the bowl, stirring until it was the consistency of a thin, wet paste.

"It's ready," he said, carrying the bowl to where Margarete sat. Leaning to the side, she let her hair drape down where he could reach it and he set about applying the paste with a brush.

"Maybelle had her baby," Margarete said from under her hair.

"Oh? How's she doing?"

"She had us worried for a while, but she's recovering."

"She going to keep it?" Chance asked.

"That's up to her."

"She seems too young to care for a child on her own."

"She's not on her own," Margarete insisted. "And she didn't have a say in how young she was. If she wants to raise her baby, then she has every right to. She has a place at least. I've already seen to that."

Chance nodded, not pressing the subject. Margarete was awfully protective of her girls, as she thought of them—young women, like her, who were forced too young onto the streets. Margarete knew all too well their future prospects, and so she'd taken to looking after as many as she could. She'd even purchased a brothel and converted it into a home. It didn't do any favors for her reputation in the city since some of her girls still chose the working lifestyle, but she did what she could for them.

He'd never asked directly, but Chance was certain her money came from the many acquaintances she'd made on the Spire in her younger years—whether they'd been eager to make a contribution or not.

Once the paste was evenly distributed through her hair she held it away from her neck, letting the compounds set in. "Honestly, what would I do without you?" she asked with a smile.

"You'd get by just fine," Chance assured her. "It's only a coloring."

"Yes, but one I can trust. Not everyone is as careful as you are. Some of the other girls have gotten serious burns when they tried to get one."

"That's because they're going to hacks who don't know their craft. There are safer ways if they're willing to take the time."

"That's why I'm glad I have you."

"It's nothing," Chance shrugged. He leaned back on his stool. "It's about all I'm good for."

"Oh, don't tell me you're going to be a sourpuss tonight too?"

Chance almost protested, but when he looked at her—the way she sat with her hair draped to the side—he didn't feel much like arguing. "No," he smiled. "But don't you think this is all a little... routine?"

"Of course," she said. "We have a standing appointment."

"You know what I mean. Sometimes I wish there was something more to do than just... dye hair."

"Would you like to dye my eyebrows?" she teased. "That would be new."

"Funny," Chance chuckled. "I don't know. Didn't you ever think to leave Hatteras? Start a new life somewhere?"

"I did start a new life," she said. "This one."

"But people here know you from before. Wouldn't it have been easier to leave that all behind and go somewhere else? Start somewhere with a clean slate?"

Her eyes flashed with mock-offense. "Why Chance, you're not trying to get rid of me, are you?"

"No," he said. "I just wonder. Sometimes I feel so bottled up here, and you... Liesel... anyone who's had a chance to leave and hasn't baffle me. I can't figure out why you chose to stay."

"Where would I have gone?" Margarete asked. "I've made Hatteras my home. I've got my girls here."

"You don't owe them anything."

Margarete rolled her eyes. "And where would you go? What would you do if the opportunity came along?"

"I'd take it!" Chance said, snatching at the air as though the opportunity were literally before him.

"You wouldn't miss your friends? Or your work?"

"If any of my friends took the first ship out of the Basin, I wouldn't begrudge them a backwards glance. I'd wish them the best of luck and follow just as soon as I could."

"I think you'd have more difficulty leaving than you admit."

"Not the way I see it. I'd set out for Port Elliston—maybe further. Work as a shipmate on a dirigible to pay my way. Simon used to do that, before his leg went bad. It wouldn't take me but a few months and I'd be free to set foot anywhere I wanted."

"And when you finally reached wherever it is you're going?" Margarette asked. "What would you do then?"

"I'd visit every pub I could, build up my contacts in the city and redefine myself. It wouldn't matter one iota if I were an alchemist or from the Basin. There, I'd be a new me—a me I had a say in becoming."

"So, what's keeping you? It sounds like you've got a plan."

"No," Chance frowned. "Just a dream."

He poured a pitcher of water through Margarete's hair to rinse out the paste. There in her white petticoat, her hair draped to the side, she looked serene. It was a privileged view few got to see of her.

When her hair was rinsed, she stood and patted it dry with a towel while Chance set the dishes aside.

"Don't you ever tidy up?" she asked, looking at the messes piled up on nearly every surface. It wasn't just dishes, there were books and instruments everywhere.

"I'm an alchemist," Chance said. "It's our nature to work with messes."

"But do you have to live in one? I'm amazed you get anything done at all." She picked up a bottle which held a clumpy mixture. "What is this for?"

"A pox treatment."

"It looks like moldy cheese in water."

"Smells like it too," Chance grinned.

She crinkled her nose, set it down, and picked up another. This one was mostly transparent, like dirty water with a thick film on the bottom. "And this?"

"That's a catalyst."

"A catalyst for what?"

"For a specific reaction."

"What reaction?"

"A reaction."

"Like turning lead to gold?" she pried.

Chance grinned. "Something like that. Look," he said, taking the vial. He shook it furiously for a few seconds and held it up in the light. They both watched as the mixture nearly solidified into a marbled green.

"That's it?"

"Yeah. Why?"

"I don't know. I thought it would be more... impressive."

"Just because it doesn't glow or explode doesn't mean it isn't impressive. As it is, I wouldn't trade this vial for a hundred banknotes if I was offered it."

"A thousand?" she toyed.

Chance shook his head.

"Is this part of your secret project then?"

"Yes." He gripped the vial in his hands. It gave off heat from the reaction. "It's the furthest I've been able to get so far."

"I'll never understand your work," she said.

He placed the vial on the shelf again. "Then why do you keep asking me about it?"

Margarete laughed, and took a seat on the only empty portion of the couch. Chance watched her stretch herself out slowly. "I like to hear you talk about your dreams—to see you excited."

"They're only dreams," Chance dismissed. "Dozens before me have wasted their lives away chasing after lost secrets of alchemy. I'll more than likely do the same."

"So why do you keep trying?"

"Because..."

Chance struggled to find the words to explain how he felt. There was a part of him that truly believed it was hopeless, just as another believed he could defy the odds. He couldn't count the nights he'd found rest only after hours of troubled thoughts of the future. It's uncertainty loomed more menacingly every day, wrapping itself around him like an unwanted blanket.

And yet something compelled him on. To try, again and again. All the while, the conflict raged on inside—sometimes dangerously close to the surface.

"...I believe it's possible," he finally said. "And it's not like anyone gave me a worthwhile alternative. I figure if I'm destined to waste away my life, at least I'll waste away pursuing something I chose."

"What a truly doleful dreamer you are," Margarete teased.

"Only on my good days."

He joined her on the couch, clearing it of his papers and books and positioning himself against the armrest. Margarete crawled over and leaned herself against him.

"I wouldn't have you any other way," she said.

They laid like that for a while as her hair dried, Margarete drifting off to sleep and Chance lost in his thoughts. He found he thought best when she was there, and so his mind wandered through passages he'd read earlier that week, trying to bridge connections between them. It was like trying to pull threads across miles, often they'd break or become so tangled he'd have to start over from the beginning.

Yet, with each success, he became more hopeful he'd work out the next.

Tonight, however, no new or profound thoughts formed. The alchemist he'd been reading was a shoddy one and had taken to peddling false concoctions later in life. Chance had hoped some of his earlier work might have held more integrity, but it was apparent he'd been a charlatan from the beginning.

Chance ran his fingers through Margarete's hair, combing it out and enjoying the faint scent of perfume. There were few women with locks like Margarete's. The dye lightened her hair, but it didn't strip it completely of her natural color. It would have been a sin, he thought, to tamper too much with something already so near perfection.

Perhaps an hour passed before she stirred again, looking up with sleepy eyes.

"You're beautiful when you're sleeping," Chance said.

Margarete rolled over so she faced him and smiled her rare smile—one without fanfare or tease—before she buried herself against him again. Some of the curl was already coming back into her hair.

"You think I'm beautiful?" she asked.

"Of course."

"You're the only one I've heard say that who I believed. You almost make me believe it too." Her expression became sad, and she rolled onto her back again. Chance felt her sigh. "Where were you ten years ago?"

Chance remembered exactly where he was. "Wasting time in a school somewhere," he shrugged.

"I bet you looked handsome in your uniform."

"It never suited me."

"I never got to go to school."

"It wasn't anything special," Chance explained. "Just a lot of cogs telling you where to go and what to think."

The topic was disrupting Chance's dream. He stood up carefully, leaving Margarete on the couch, and went to his cupboards. He wasn't looking for anything in particular, but he rummaged through some of the mess to busy himself.

"Still," Margarete said wistfully, sitting up. "I would have liked to learn some things in a school, I think." She smiled, though her eyes were moist. "Life might have been kinder, you know?"

Chance returned to the couch and sat down beside her, wrapping her in an embrace. He held her there for a moment, a quiet understanding passing between them. It was still surreal how a woman so much older, and with such a strong exterior, would turn so soft in his presence.

Without her walls, Margarete was a rare pearl. Selfishly, he hoped she'd always stay that way—that the dream would last forever.

Eventually, however, Margarete made to stand.

"Don't go yet," Chance pleaded.

"I should. My girls will need me tonight," she said. "And besides, if I stay too long we might cause more of a scandal than we already do."

Chance watched as she slipped back into her dress. She smoothed down the front, tugging at the laces until it fit just right.

"I don't care what people think of me," Chance said as she retrieved her purse and checked herself in the mirror.

Placing a hand on his cheek, she tilted her head and looked into his eyes. "Yes, you do. We all do. But it's nice, isn't it? The moments we forget? Thank you for the dye."

"Margarete," Chance said as she was going out. She stopped in the doorway. "You *are* beautiful."

"I know," she glowed.

CHAPTER THIRTEEN
Investigations

*An hour in a book can save you a lifetime of
disasters repeated.*

— Alchemical Proverb

Stoddard stepped down from the carriage with Donovan close behind. He moved at a quick, agitated clip, forcing the man to break into an awkward jog to keep up. Ever since he'd received the letter, Stoddard just couldn't move fast enough.

"I forgot to mention, we received a request earlier from a Master Arden," Donovan said as they entered the morgue. "He mentioned you'd given him permission to come speak with you, but I wasn't certain."

"Yes," Stoddard remembered. He'd forgotten all about the boy since his luncheon the day before. "Inform him I'll meet with him at his convenience, but after I've had time to sort through this mess. But don't use that word—mess."

"Yes, sir. Shall I just call it what everyone else is?"

Stoddard cringed. The city had already taken to calling it the second miracle. He nodded, but made no effort to look pleased.

"You don't think it was a miracle?" Donovan asked.

"The miracle will be if we're able to get to the bottom of whatever *actually* happened."

They approached the desk where a young woman greeted them. "Good morning, Doctor Stoddard," she said in a pleasing voice. "It's so good to see you again. How can I help you?"

"I need the records for Captain Harper," Stoddard said. "All of them."

The girl hesitated a second, but nodded before retreating into the back room.

"Sir, if I may," Donovan said. "Don't you think you're being overly concerned about all of this? Isn't fortune turning in your favor?"

"I never trust things out of my control," Stoddard explained. "No matter how favorable they may seem."

He glanced down and noticed the visitor's board behind the desk. Picking it up, he leafed through it to the day Harper's body was brought in. "As expected," he sighed.

"Sir?"

"It's empty." Stoddard handed the board to Donovan. "Not a single visitor from the time he was brought in to the time he was discovered."

"You expected someone?"

"No," he said. "Not necessarily."

But then he paused. There had been someone that night. They'd passed him on the steps. He'd been walking as though he were about to enter, but he'd paused when they'd come out.

"The record has been tampered with."

"Sir?"

"Do you remember a man that night, as we were getting into the carriage?" Stoddard asked. "An elderly gentleman with a heavy coat?"

"I don't recall anyone."

"Of course you don't," Stoddard frowned. He closed his eyes, rummaging through his memory, trying to conjure an image of the man.

He was... frail, his face sunken with both age and... illness.

He could see it. He could hear the stranger's labored breath on his way up the steps.

"It's possible there were no visitors that day," Donovan suggested, but Stoddard hissed at him to be silent.

Odd for a sickly man to be wandering alone in the rain so late. He closed his eyes again, beckoning the memory.

He wore a heavy coat. It hung loose on him, old and tawdry. And it had... pockets. Many pockets. The collar was turned up close against his neck to shield his face...

His face.

Stoddard focused harder.

The man's eyes, nose, lips, and even his expression of apprehension and fear materialized in Stoddard's mind.

"There you are," he whispered to himself.

"Here are the recor—" The girl stopped short when she saw Stoddard holding the visitor's log."—the records for Captain Harper," she finished. She set down the documents before Stoddard and smiled as pleasantly as she could. "Was there something you were looking for specifically?"

"No, thank you," Stoddard said. "Just being thorough." He took the papers and flipped through them.

"If I might say, it was amazing what you were able to do for Captain Harper."

"Mmm," he murmured. "I amaze even myself it seems."

As he'd feared, the documents proved useless. No records had been kept in the midst of excitement which might have provided him any insight to the morning when Harper had been discovered.

But Stoddard wasn't about to let the facts evade him.

"It's interesting to me," Stoddard noted, "that besides my assistant and myself it shows here there were no visitors to the morgue the night the captain's body was brought in. And," he glanced at the woman's tag, "what good fortune. It seems you were the same attendant that night as well. Ambre, is it? I remember you, now that I think of it. Tell me, there was a man that night. We met on the steps as I was on my way out, but I see no entry in your log that he was here."

"A lot of people pass by our building," she said. "There was no one after you."

"Interesting," Stoddard said. "He seemed quite intent on coming in before we'd gone."

"He must have gone on when you left."

"Did you observe anything of interest during your shift?"

"No," Ambre said quickly.

Too quickly, Stoddard perceived. "Nothing at all?" he asked.

"I mean, nothing more than usual," she tried to clarify. "I mean, it's quiet here. Not a lot of people come and go. Besides the bodies, I mean."

"No, I don't expect you get many visitors to a morgue so late in the evening." He set the logbook down on the countertop. "You didn't observe anything strange about Harper's body in particular?"

"No, doctor. It was next shift when he was discovered."

"Curious," he said as he focused again on the file, leafing through a few more papers.

"What is?" she asked.

"Curious how these reports don't match up, Miss Ambre," Stoddard said, snapping the folder shut. His smile vanished and was replaced with a sneer. "Curious that *none* of this makes *any* sense to me. That from the moment I last observed the body of the captain—and I assure you, miss, he was just a body then—to the moment he was discovered alive the next morning there wasn't a single thing out of place.

"Stranger yet," he continued, "considering the pooling of blood and the bruising of the skin which is typical of the recently deceased, is that a body would reanimate after such a long period of time. And yet, Captain Harper walks, eats, and talks this very moment, the very picture of health, and he has no such bruises or pooling. How do we explain that, miss? Can you shed any light on any of this?"

"I couldn't say." Ambre's head sunk low.

"You know," he laughed, "I don't believe I'm aware of a single instance throughout all of medical history when such a remarkable scenario has played out so naturally as this."

"A testament to your work," Ambre ventured weakly. She was shaking with the effort to stand.

"Yes... that's what everyone is saying," Stoddard frowned. "Do you know why I practice clockwork mechanics, Miss Ambre?"

She shook her head.

"Because there is consistency in it. Reliability. It functions precisely as its designer intends it to. Yet, here it seems to have taken on a function of its own. It's quite *unbelievable*, wouldn't you agree?"

Ambre fidgeted. "Yes, doctor."

"I thought you might. Well, you have been most unhelpful, Miss Ambre," Stoddard said, emphasizing her name one last time. "I'll be keeping these records for a time. Please make a note of that fact for those who will relieve you."

Tossing the file into his briefcase, Dr. Stoddard snapped it shut and bid a final farewell to Miss Ambre.

CHAPTER FOURTEEN
Ashworth's Summons

All things are frustrating before they are understood.

— Alchemical Proverb

"Chance?" Rhett said, poking gingerly at Chance's shoulder.

Chance stirred begrudgingly under his blanket and mumbled something unintelligible before turning over on the couch.

"Chance!"

"Rhett," he groaned. "If you want to make it to the end of your apprenticeship you better not be here when I open my eyes."

"But you promised!" Rhett urged. "You said we'd get to fix my flying machine today."

Chance cracked his eyes open, blinking in the light that spilled through the window. It struck him like glass dust and he squeezed them shut to dispel the crusty morning haze. An empty bottle fell out of his blanket, clattering on the floor as it rolled away.

Goodness did his head ache.

"Shouldn't you be helping Ashworth?" he mumbled.

"He isn't here."

Chance rocked up into a sitting position on the side of the couch.

"You have your regular chores. Why not get to those?"

"I already did them."

"Really?" Chance cast him a doubtful look.

"Some of them," Rhett confessed.

"Well then, finish the rest. Ashworth will be back in a while and he'll have something else for you to do."

"But..." Rhett's pep was failing.

Chance's eyes narrowed. "What are you trying to get out of, Rhett?"

"Ashworth said that we were going to clean the laboratory today. I thought if you had something for me to do then..."

Chance smiled despite his hangover. Now things were beginning to make sense. "Ashworth would have to do it all by himself," he concluded.

"No," Rhett insisted, folding his arms. "We could do it another day."

Chance smiled despite the pain in his head. There would be no appeasing the boy now that he'd gotten his hopes up. He'd be altogether useless until he was satisfied.

"Alright," Chance conceded. "Go grab your machine and we'll take a look at it before Ashworth gets back. But, once he does, you're his for the rest of the day."

They set up in the kitchen, leaving the door open to enjoy the fresh air coming in. As they set about removing each piece it became clear the flying machine was more complicated than it appeared. Inside were a series of tiny gears and levers which needed to be synchronized, or it'd throw off everything when the wings caught the breeze.

Soon, without realizing it, an hour had passed. And then two. They stripped and reassembled the contraption time and time again. It didn't help that Rhett got bored and distracted himself playing with the pieces. It made keeping track of what went where a real headache. Every so often, Chance sent Rhett off to fetch a tool he needed. Soon they'd nearly relocated the entire toolshed.

"Where did that lever go? And where in this forsaken world did this come from?" Chance fumed, holding a tiny screw in his fingers as he examined the underbelly of the machine.

"I dunn'o," Rhett sighed, poking at his rat. He was at his limit.

"Would you run and grab me the box of scrap from my workshop? It should be by the sink."

"Where?"

"Never mind," Chance said, getting up. "I'll get it."

He needed the stretch. His legs were almost asleep and he shook them out as he walked. Unsurprisingly, the scrap wasn't where it should have been. He turned the place upside down, shuffling the mess around from one place to another. After a few minutes, he stood exasperated in the middle of the room.

"That's it," he conceded. "I'm cleaning you before the week is out."

Finally, after he'd turned over most of the room, he spotted the box nestled under the corner of his couch and snatched it up.

"Find it?" Rhett asked when he returned.

"Yeah." Chance selected a tiny gear and tested the fit to the piece he'd been missing.

"Those came while you were out," Rhett said, pointing to a crate of tinctures in the corner.

"Want to put them in Ashworth's lab for me?" Chance asked.

"They're too heavy."

"Then how did you bring them inside?" Chance asked. Then he noticed the scratches across the floor. Sure enough, they led all the way down the hallway. "Never mind. I've got it."

He picked up the crate and carried it to Ashworth's laboratory. Rhett was right, it was almost too heavy even for Chance. Carefully turning the doorknob so as not to lose the crate, he opened the door and set the supplies down by Ashworth's workbench.

The lab was definitely in need of a thorough cleaning. It wasn't cluttered like Chance's, but the residues and spills from countless years had collected so that there were few surfaces that didn't have some substance caked to them.

He was about to leave when he noticed one of Ashworth's notebooks on the ground, its pages crinkled underneath. He picked it up and tried to straighten them out a bit.

Despite himself, he couldn't resist giving the text a glance while he held it. He wasn't worried about reading something he wasn't supposed to. Like many alchemist's notebooks, large portions of each page were written in cypher. Alchemist spent years during their apprenticeships developing their own unique cypher to safeguard their research from prying eyes.

Thieving secrets wasn't exactly a common practice anymore, but the cyphers were still used. It was just one of the unwritten rules: alchemists dealt in secrets.

He glanced over Ashworth's cypher, looking for any similarities he'd inherited when he'd devised his own. There were some common symbols, but he couldn't remember if he'd copied Ashworth for those or not.

He did find one mark though—a precede. It symbolized the section was written out of order and that the rest of the passage was found earlier in the notebook. Flipping through, he tried to locate the connected passage. It was difficult, since he didn't know how the mark would pair itself. He assumed it would mimic the pen strokes, but after a few minutes he gave up trying. Ashworth's cypher had been developed over a lifetime. He wouldn't crack it at a glance.

He set the notebook down on the workbench and bumped square into Ashworth as he turned to go. His sudden appearance gave Chance a shock and he let out a cry of alarm.

"Ashworth!"

Ashworth looked a little shaken as well. He recovered quickly, however, looking a little amused by it. His eyes fell on the notebook.

"Your orders came just now," Chance tried to explain. "I was just putting the crate in your laboratory for you."

"And to do that, you felt you needed to peruse my journal?" Ashworth asked.

"It was lying on the floor. I didn't read anything impor… what's wrong with your arm?" Chance looked with concern at the bandage wrapped around the length of Ashworth's forearm.

"This?" Ashworth asked, as though he were only then noticing it. "Oh, this is nothing. Just a scratch."

"What happened?" Chance asked. "And where have you been? Rhett and I were worried about you. You didn't even leave a note."

"I'm sorry about that," Ashworth said, "but it couldn't be helped. Something came up and I've been quite busy. By the look of things on the table out there it looks like you have been too."

"It's just a toy Ponti found for Rhett. I'm helping him fix it," Chance shrugged. "I replaced your hartshorn."

"Hmm?"

"The hartshorn." Chance pointed to a case by Ashworth's components. "I purchased some to replace what I took last week."

"Oh, yes. I'd forgotten all about that," he said, fetching it off the shelf. He turned the box over in his hands a few times.

"You heard about Captain Harper then?" Chance asked, trying to sound casual.

"Yes," Ashworth smiled, returning the box to the shelf. "Remarkable, isn't it?"

"It's the only thing anyone wants to talk about down at the pub. Well, except Serge. He's a bit put off by the rumors going around."

"Rumors?"

"About how he came back to life," Chance explained. "Everyone's speculating about what happened. I think I agree with Serge though."

"And what does Serge think?"

"He's convinced that the papers got it wrong—that Harper was never really dead in the first place."

"Oh, no," Ashworth said. "I assure you he was quite dead."

His eyes were twinkling, and Chance was getting frustrated.

"Okay," Chance said, abandoning his act. "What is it? What do you know? And where in Septigonee's Well have you been?"

Ashworth couldn't contain the amusement in his eyes. He pulled a letter from his pocket and handed it to Chance. It was sealed with wax and bound in a ribbon.

"What is this?"

"Open it," Ashworth urged.

Chance broke the seal and began reading. It took only a few lines before his brow furrowed. It wasn't a letter at all. It was a summons—to a secret meeting of alchemists the following night. He glanced up at Ashworth.

"Rhett may need to finish the flying machine on his own," Ashworth beamed.

CHAPTER FIFTEEN
A Secret Meeting

*Fate pulls an invisible thread between those who are destined to
meet. Best try not to tangle them.*

— Alchemical Proverb

For the next twenty-four hours, Chance was alive with curiosity. Ashworth wouldn't say anything about where he'd been or about the upcoming meeting—except that it regarded Captain Harper and involved the local alchemists.

Chance didn't know what to think; he wasn't used to Ashworth being so secretive. Generally, he bore everything out in the open. Chance appreciated that about him. In Hatteras, everyone had something up their sleeve, and it was refreshing to know there was at least one man who went against the grain of expectation.

That was, until this past week.

The whole affair frustrated Chance, like a splinter at the tip of his finger. But, he resigned himself to bite his tongue and be patient until the meeting. While he waited, he finished his orders and even took to rearranging his workshop to pass the time faster. It gave him something else to fuss over.

Rhett was in a particularly grumpy mood since he'd been told he couldn't come to the meeting with them. He'd spent the day off somewhere by himself with his flying machine. It still wouldn't fly, but he wouldn't ask Chance for help anymore.

When Ashworth finally came and fetched him late that evening, Chance's workshop was cleaner than it had been in months. The two of them donned their coats in the dark and left the workshop with few words.

Rhett was already asleep, so there was no need to inform him they were going. According to Ashworth, he was too young to be in the thick of things just yet.

They headed southwest through Cheapside into Browbank, then crossed the canal that separated Browbank and Garret Town. It wasn't a town so much as a small sub-district. Hatteras might have been a single city, but sections of it had formed internal communities on their own initiative. Many born in Hatteras identified themselves exclusively by these sub-districts. They almost forgot the rest of the city even existed.

Garret Town was one of the more coordinated sub-districts, a little ways inland from the Basin. They'd installed electric lanterns themselves, and maintained them on weekly rotations. The light afforded evening travelers safer passage during the night.

After a half-hour or so, Ashworth paused on a street corner, raising a hand to signal Chance to wait. They were in an industrial district, its street lined by larger workshops and small businesses. Ashworth kept glancing up and down the streets as though looking for something or someone.

"Are we there?" Chance asked.

"Nearly," Ashworth said. He pointed to one of the shops a little ways down the street. "Wait here a few minutes while I go inside, then follow me in. Can you do that?"

"Sure I can. But why?"

"For the sake of appearances," Ashworth said. "Can't have a group converging all at once. Might draw unwanted attention. Okay, here I go."

With a nod, he was off across the street. Chance watched him go at a brisk walk, summoning a casual air, before entering a small gate which led back into some alley alongside one of the shops.

Leaning up against the brick wall, Chance patiently waited as he had been instructed. Some loose newspaper drifted slowly across the sidewalk at his feet, and he kicked it away. He didn't want to see another article about Captain Harper.

Since the first announcement, the papers and gossip mill had only grown louder. And yet, despite all of the noise, Harper still hadn't made an appearance. At the bottom of every news story was the same line: *unavailable for comment.*

After a few more minutes, Chance spat on the ground and hustled across the street to the gate where Ashworth had vanished. It was a fairly large business on a corner lot. Glancing up at the doorpost, he caught sight of alchemical symbols on their sign.

At least he knew they were alchemists. He squinted to read it.

FOXX AND KELLER
VOLATILE COMMODITIES

The names were familiar, which eased Chance's anxiety. Ashworth had a good relationship with Keller.

Ignoring the door, he walked around through the alley. It opened up to an alcove where a heavy set of double iron doors leaned against the building. A man Chance didn't recognize, with a thick beard and belly, stood vigil by the doors. His arms were folded rigidly across his barreled chest.

When he saw Chance approach, he lifted one of the heavy doors and ushered him inside.

Chance crept down a steep set of stairs, ducking to avoid bumping his head against the cramped ceiling. A coal chute ran down along the stairwell's side, forcing him to bend awkwardly as he stepped. The air was thick with the smell of coal and slag.

At the bottom, the stairway opened into a furnace room. It wasn't large, but it was cleared enough so that a small group of men could gather, sitting comfortably on what stools and surfaces they could find.

Ashworth was chatting with a few of the other men, and excused himself when he saw Chance.

"Why don't you take a seat?" he said. "It may be a minute until everyone arrives."

"Who's all coming?"

"Oh, everyone," Ashworth smiled.

"Is that all?" Chance asked. He was still not amused by all the secrecy.

He found himself a stool and dragged it to the back by the unlit furnace. From there he could get a good read on everyone present. He recognized the owners of the shop, Foxx and Keller. They were standing at the front of the room speaking with Ashworth, their expressions serious.

The two looked as if they could have been brothers, but there was no family relation. Keller had been raised in Hatteras his whole life while Foxx came from a country across the sea. Chance couldn't recall which.

From what he'd gleaned from conversation, they partnered up when Foxx shipped himself across the sea and took up residence in Hatteras. Foxx wasn't an alchemist by trade, but his overseas connections helped Keller expand his operation and gain a foothold in foreign trade.

As their sign stated, they specialized in combustibles.

Gravatts was there. The unpleasant miser was reclined in the most cushioned seat in the room, next to Yoon and Sager. They were considered two of the more successful alchemists locally, so naturally Gravatts would gravitate to them. Chance rolled his eyes; he'd never liked the man's sense of self-importance.

Keefer was there also, an indistinct, middle-aged man who worked with curatives. He dozed toward the back, among a few other men Chance didn't recognize. Chance was appraising them when Liesel appeared on the steps, with Welch close behind. She spotted Chance right away and came over.

"Mind if we join you?" she asked.

Chance moved over to make room. He avoided Welch's eyes and pretended not to hear his greeting, but Welch didn't seem to take offense. Instead, he found a chair and brought it over for Liesel.

"Wait," Chance said, realization striking him. "Why are you two here? I thought this was for alchemists only?"

"It was Welch who received the invitation," Liesel explained. "I'm just here for moral support. I hope that's alright with everyone."

She winked at him, and Chance couldn't understand why.

He was about to ask, but the heavy doors of the chute slammed shut and the burly man came down to join the gathering.

"Any idea what this is about?" Liesel asked.

"Not sure. I think it has something to do with Captain Harper though?"

"Oh."

"Excuse me!" Ashworth waved his hands to gather the attention of the room. "If everyone could find a seat please, we'll get started without further delay."

The guests finished their conversations with rushed whispers before the last of them shuffled to find a place to sit. A few took to leaning against the walls, chairs being limited.

"Thank you all for coming tonight," Ashworth began, once they'd settled. "I understand meeting like this is a bit untoward, but your response and patience is most appreciated. It's not often we see so many of us gathered under one roof.

"You represent the top minds of our craft, so I feel it's only appropriate that you be made aware of what has transpired in the past few days, since I am certain the effects will be felt widely by all here."

"If this is some gloating session, I really don't have a stomach for it tonight," said a little man sitting atop one of the taller stools in the front. Chance recognized the little windbag as Estrada. He must have overlooked him as he'd come in, which was easy to do considering the little man's stature.

"I assure you, what we have to say will be of benefit to everyone here."

"Doubtful," Estrada mumbled.

"By now," Ashworth continued, ignoring Estrada, "I'm sure you're all familiar with the events surrounding Captain Harper's death, as it has been reported in the papers?"

"Do you think we're deaf?" Estrada said. "Of course we are. Any ninny with half a wit is familiar with it."

"What is your problem?" Liesel snapped. "Keep your trap shut if you can't be decent. I make it a point not to be in the same room as you, and if I'm going to have to make an exception tonight I won't sit and listen to you carry on like you tend to do."

Estrada's face turned a mix of red and purple, but he held his tongue.

"You were saying, Ashworth?"

"Thank you," Ashworth continued. "The papers have been quite exuberant in proclaiming the 'miracle' which has transpired, but I'm curious if any of you have heard much as to exactly *how* it occurred?"

"I don't know," said one of the men Chance didn't recognize.

"People on the streets have been speculating ever since we first heard," Keefer said.

"The new mechanism," Yoon called out.

"That's the general consensus," Sager said, agreeing with Yoon. "They'd finished the operation after he died, and the heart took in the end."

"Yes... the heart took," Ashworth mused. "Tell me, have any of you ever before heard of a mechanism reviving someone after death? Even hours after?"

"I admit it surprised me," Liesel said. "But then I don't know much about clockwork mechanics."

"It's possible," Welch said, taking her hand and giving it a squeeze. "Most anything is possible."

"Ah, Welch. I hadn't seen you in the back," Ashworth said. "You've spent some time studying clockwork mechanisms. What are your thoughts?"

"Doctor Stoddard has built quite the reputation among mechanists over the years," Welch explained. "It doesn't seem thinkable, but, if it was, he'd probably be the one to do it."

"We aren't even sure Harper was dead," Keefer pointed out.

"I assure you, he was," Ashworth said.

"How would you know?" Estrada questioned. It was obvious he

was straining to hold back his temper. He glanced in Liesel's direction to see if she would interrupt him, but she remained silent. "What makes you so sure?"

"Because I visited the captain that night in the morgue."

Chance's head snapped upward. His suspicions had been correct. A few of the men exchanged quick whispers.

"Why?" Sager asked.

"More importantly, why are we caring?" Estrada added. "Does anyone else wonder what this has to do with any of us?"

"Make your point, Ashworth," Keller said, stepping up beside him. He gave Estrada a stern look.

"Alright," Ashworth said, regaining himself. "I called you here not to discuss the success of a clockwork mechanism. As I said, the captain was dead that night for what I estimate to be six or seven hours before I got there. As you recalled from the papers, he died just before the surgery was completed and so his surgeon finished the procedure and pronounced him dead."

"There is documented evidence proving this fact," Gravatts interjected. Chance was a little surprised he was offering support in Ashworth's defense.

"Doctor Stoddard was sufficiently thorough in his reports so that there is no doubting it. This brings me to the purpose of our meeting tonight. When I arrived at the morgue that evening, I administered to the captain a serum of which the existence of only a select few in this room are aware—and of which you all will soon be made so.

"Gentleman, and lady," he added, looking toward Liesel. "It was alchemy which reanimated the captain, not any clockwork device."

"You're out of your mind, old man," Estrada chided.

"Just listen to what the man has to say," Keller implored.

"No, you all listen to me," Estrada said, standing up from his stool. It was an ineffective move, because he was nearly as short standing as he was sitting.

"What Ashworth is telling us is insanity. Forget the captain's recovery; Ashworth has admitted to tampering with the body of one of Hatteras's most important figures in the past century. Never mind if what you did is the reason he's alive or not. Do you think that will matter when they arrest you for your tampering?"

"He saved a man's life," Liesel said.

"You don't know that!" Estrada sputtered. "And so what if he saved him? Even if that's true, they'll never give credit to an alchemist. That would be as bad as admitting a tinkerer invented the gear."

He shot Welch a nasty glance.

"I don't know how you got it into your head that you're going to pull me into this with you, Ashworth, or why—but you can forget it! And if any of you have a head on your shoulders you'll turn your back on this whole mess with me before he goes on another minute!"

He looked expectantly from face to face, but the company remained silent. None seemed to heed the man's rant. Their expressions were pensive as they gave Ashworth's announcement thought.

The red in Estrada's face deepened, and his gaze became viperous, but after a moment he crawled back onto his stool and fell back into silence.

"He's right though," Keefer pointed out. "They've already claimed credit for what was done. It is a missed opportunity. We haven't gained anything."

"I got a friend back," Ashworth said defensively.

"If I remember correctly, he wasn't much of a friend to alchemists," Sager said. "He's half the reason we're where we are today. I think of him every time I pay one of those ridiculous tariffs!"

There was a general muttering of agreement among the others.

"No, he wasn't fond of us then," Ashworth said. "But a man can change, given the right catalyst. It's my belief he will be the key in turning over a new leaf for us. He will be our voice where we've had none. A voice on the Spire itself!"

Estrada laughed loudly.

"Is that so?" he said. "I always thought you a bit over-trusting, but now I'm thinking you've gone senile. I haven't seen a lick of evidence to suggest that he's even noticed your little act of heroism. Who says he will? Eh?"

"I do," said a gruff voice from the back of the room.

Chance jumped, and the whole group spun around. He'd thought he'd been the only one there, but emerging from between the furnaces was a man—or half a man. He wore a coat in military style: slate grey and double-breasted, the top few golden buttons left undone, leaving the top of his shirt and chest uncovered.

Whether this was for comfort or simply a necessity for fit was unclear. Regardless, the jacket couldn't conceal the prosthetic of his right arm. A metallic casing encompassed his shoulder with delicate supports and grips reaching across his chest.

As the man stepped closer, Chance felt the warmth rush out of him. He saw how the metal sank into the man's flesh—fastening, no doubt, to the bone itself. As he stepped forward, the noise of whirling gears and the faint hiss of valves depressurizing silenced all other sounds within the room.

With a brass fashioned hand, the figure adjusted the hang of his coat.

"Gentlemen, and lady," Ashworth added as he extended a hand toward the new guest. "I'd like you to meet the man of whom we were just speaking: Captain Willard Harper."

CHAPTER SIXTEEN
Tea and Gossip

Where there's smoke, there's likely to be a fire. Hopefully one you meant to start.

— Alchemical Proverb

I'm so sorry that Willard wasn't able to be here with us," Lady Harper said, resting a tray of tea and cookies on the coffee table. She and Stoddard were in one of the sitting rooms of the Harper estate—a two-story manor which afforded a modest distance from its neighbors and a lush garden enclosure. It was quite the luxury within the crowded city, but such were the privileges of living on the Spire.

The sitting room was decorated with a variety of bright floral patterns on most everything. The wallpaper was an interlocking weave of pink hibiscus buds, while the rug and furniture were decorated with hydrangea and roses, respectively.

Stoddard thought the combination god-awful.

Lady Harper passed him a cup, and he took it politely before setting it down on the table. He didn't intend to stay long if Harper had already stepped out.

"Don't let it trouble you," he said. "I only meant to check up with him about his recovery. No doubt he had some urgent matter to attend to?"

"Well, I wish he'd have taken your visit more seriously," Lady Harper said, "considering what he's been through."

"I hope nothing is wrong."

"Oh goodness, no. Nothing is wrong." She sat down across from him. "He just needed to step out for a moment."

"Should we expect him back soon?"

"I honestly couldn't say," she shrugged. "I'm not sure where he was off to. I hope it isn't bad for his health for him to be out," she added, concern welling up in her voice.

"No, I shouldn't think so," Stoddard assured her. "As long as he isn't overexerting himself. I'm surprised to hear he's up and about so soon."

"Well, that is a testament to how well your practice has come along, Doctor. Willard hasn't been out of the hospital a week, and he's more active than I've ever seen him. It took him months before he was moving after his first operation, and even then I would hardly say he was active."

"Harper's good fortune continues to astonish us all," Stoddard said. He had difficulty controlling the tenor of his voice.

"It's a modern miracle," she said proudly, taking no notice. "I'll be sure to share it with everyone I meet with. You'll be the toast of the city if I have any influence. And, as you know by now, I have no small amount of influence among the women of this city."

Stoddard rolled his eyes. Her influence wasn't half as important as she tried to hint. She was a socialite philanthropist, tolerated by the meritocracy for the sake of her husband. Her sphere of influence was limited to those ladies and wives who attended her quaint tea parties and discussed causes they had no real knowledge of. Among such company, it was easy to fool herself into significance.

"Now, if I could only get him to spend more time with me," she smiled. "That would be another miracle. He's entertained more guests this week than I can count."

"I'm sure many will be seeking audience with your husband in the coming weeks. He's caused quite the sensation."

"Like a biscuit in tea," she said. Stoddard wasn't sure he knew what she meant by that. "But it's so unlike him. You knew what he was like before."

"I'm afraid we kept most of our interactions to matters of business."

"That's just his way," she said. "Or was his way. Honestly, he's felt like a different person. It's taken some getting used to. He used to have such a routine. He would get ever so cross when it was interrupted. But now, if I bring him his paper he refuses it, preferring a walk. I have Anne prepare his favorite meals and he won't touch them, preferring to work."

"He isn't eating?"

"I'm sure he is. He just won't stop to sit down and have a decent meal with me. Is that typical?"

Stoddard rubbed his brow. He had a feeling it wasn't the meal that turned away the captain's appetite. "I don't think it's anything to be alarmed about," he said. "Perhaps he's working through things. It's a rare thing for a man to come so near to death during his life, and the captain has done so twice."

"Perhaps," she said pensively. "But, I'm not as alarmed about his meals as I am what he's been... saying. Yesterday, I tried stopping him before he went out, to remind him of our visit with Lady Tulk that afternoon and he told me he didn't have time for—honestly, it upsets me to repeat it—keeping up our 'superficial friendships.' I couldn't believe what I was hearing!"

Stoddard tried to express an appropriate amount of disapproval. It appeared the captain shared a similar opinion of his wife as the rest of the capitol.

"I can see how that would be upsetting," he forced himself to say. "I'm afraid I have little experience to lend on the matter, however, having never married. I'm a mechanist, not a counselor."

"Oh, that reminds me!" she said, practically bouncing in her seat. "Congratulations on your recent engagement, doctor."

"Thank you."

"I remember when you and Emmaline were first considered a

match. How old was she at the time? Fourteen, was it? Difficult to recall, it's been so many years. She was such a dainty thing. And still is. My friends and I thought it a fine match; we knew you'd prove yourself in time. Your work had already shown such promise. I'm glad Lord Worthington has come around."

"As am I," Stoddard admitted. It had been only a week since they'd announced their engagement, but the time had escaped him. With so much happening, and all at once, he felt like he'd hardly had a moment with Emmaline.

Yet, she'd affirmed it again when he'd gone to see her after the luncheon. Her affections for him had endured the years—as had his for her.

"Well, I'm afraid I should be going," Stoddard said. If nothing more could be expected of Harper today he didn't intend to waste what time he had. "Emmaline will be expecting me."

"Oh, you won't stay longer?" Lady Harper asked. She looked positively distressed by the interruption. "I haven't gotten to tell you what Willard said about it when I told him."

"I'm sure I'll have a chance to hear it from the source in the near future," Stoddard assured her. He was making to rise when she reached out and clasped his hand in hers.

"And he's made comments about your work too," she added quickly.

Stoddard's brow raised. She was trying to bait him in order to prolong their meeting. It wouldn't do for her reputation if a guest left prematurely. And what surprised Stoddard more was that it worked. She'd set the hook in just the right spot.

"My work?" he asked.

"I overhear him with his guests, and I hope you don't take this as ingratitude on my part because it certainly is not," she explained. "But, he's *criticizing* it."

Stoddard spine stiffened, and he felt a twitch in his cheek. "I see," he managed to say. "And what exactly has he said?"

"Well," she began, sitting back with a look of satisfaction at holding him longer. "He seems to be under the impression it wasn't you who saved him at all! I told him how ridiculous that was. All one has to do is look at his heart to know he has your craftsmanship to thank for it still beating. Yet, he still denies it."

"Perhaps he's confused," Stoddard said. "He may be feeling the effects of the surgery after all. I'm curious, who has he been complaining about me to?"

"Oh, nobody of importance," she assured him. "I'm certain they're not members of high society. From the way they're dressed, I believe they were alchemists. Even if he didn't tell me where he was going this afternoon, I suspect he's with them again. That's something else I wanted to speak to you about. Are you certain you've given him strong enough medicines for the pain?"

"I was confident in my prescription, yes. He's seeking remedies from alchemists?"

"What else would he have to do with alchemists?"

That was a good question. One Stoddard intended to ask him personally. The image of the man in the coat surfaced in Stoddard's mind again. *The pockets*, he thought. *Is that who you are?*

"Maybe I'll talk with him about it again when he comes back," Lady Harper suggested.

"Yes," Stoddard agreed. "And perhaps I'll be more persistent in obtaining a meeting with him in the future."

"I hope you will. Who knows what they might peddle on him in his discomfort? I'd be much more at rest knowing he wasn't going to that lot for his remedies."

"Or at all," Stoddard agreed, taking up his tea from the table.

CHAPTER SEVENTEEN
The Plan

Best not to let others witness your surprise, lest they be the wiser about your accidents.

— Alchemical Proverb

Who the hell?"

"This is Captain Harper," Ashworth repeated. "I thought any questions you had or rumors you'd heard could best be put to rest by the man around whom they revolve."

The captain approached the front of the room with a slow gait, leaning heavily on his right side as he eyed those whose gazes were fixed upon him. The winding and ticking of many working gears hidden inside his metallic arm accompanied each of his movements.

It surprised Chance how old the captain appeared. Though he assumed Harper and Ashworth were close in age, the captain's face bore the signs more glaringly. He was grizzly and unkempt, apart from his immaculate uniform. His grey hair was trimmed in a flattop, patches of hair straying wildly from a few stubborn cowlicks.

But his eyes bore an intensity Ashworth's had somewhere lost, and when their gazes met, Chance had to look away.

A heaviness permeated the room as the alchemists gave one another troubled glances. It was as though an apparition walked in their midst. Chance couldn't be sure what he was feeling, whether awe or fear or a blend of both.

Without resistance, Harper walked to Ashworth's side.

"Thank you, Charles," he said, his voice raspy and strained. It emanated from deep inside of him, and his entire body flexed with each labored breath. Again, the whirling of gears was heard.

It was strange for Chance to hear Ashworth called by his first name, adding to the surrealism of the moment

"Perhaps I'll start," Harper began when no one made any attempts to speak. "Yes. I died."

There was an audible out-breath across the room.

"How?" Keefer asked, the first to overcome his stupor.

"Heart failure. Or a mechanical failure. Both apply in my instance, I suppose," Harper explained. "Years ago, I served in the war. While deployed abroad, I sustained a life-threatening injury—shrapnel through the chest and arm."

Harper pulled down the collar of his shirt to expose his shoulder more clearly—or what was left of it. No one could miss the metal fixtures which comprised much of his shoulder.

"Splendid work," Chance heard Welch whisper in quiet admiration. "Phenomenal work."

"They did what they could to restore what I lost, but those older parts didn't prove the test of time. A clock pumping my heart was too old to sustain me any longer, and it was in their attempt to rebuild it that they lost me. I suppose you could say that I *expired*."

"How dreadful," Liesel said.

"What was it like? I mean... "Welch fidgeted on his stool, "...dying."

Harper made a face as though a pang shot through his left side. "It's not easy lying there, being torn apart and pieced back together. I'm not going to lie—it was agony."

"What? You were conscious while they worked on you?" Liesel looked shocked.

"Certainly, he wasn't," Keefer insisted.

"Impossible," Estrada scoffed. "No man could have endured that without being sedated."

"They had me heavily sedated during the procedure," Harper said, "but I felt it. Like thousands of tiny clamps under the tissue being tugged and twisted. I knew they were losing me. It was as though my heart were being wound tighter and tighter, until finally something snapped and I was hurled in every direction at once.

"For those few moments, I had no sense of myself. I felt I was spinning—or my mind was. I say a moment, but really I couldn't be sure how long."

"But you were still conscious?" Sager asked.

"I believe I was."

"Impossible," Estrada said again.

"Yet, here we meet, master alchemist." Harper opened his arms wide, gesturing to Estrada. "Evidence to the contrary."

"Improbable then," Estrada muttered.

"Hush," Liesel hissed. "Let him speak."

"That's it, more or less," Harper said. "Ashworth is the man to fill you in from there. However long I was lost, I came back to myself when I woke and found myself packed away like a sardine in one of those iron lockers in the morgue. It was quite the scene," he grinned. "Nearly gave the young woman working that night a heart attack."

"I can't be certain why we would take your word for any of this," Estrada began. "Some offense intended, Captain, but this sounds like an old man's delusions under sedation. I've heard more believable stories from drunks after their frolics. You expect us to believe this? This is just another old man's feeble attempt to advance his own fame on an account of dumb luck. For all we know, you two planned this from the start, hoping to gain some final glimmer of fame before you 'expired,' as you called it. Is that right?"

"Estrada," Keller said sternly.

"Here's a story for you," he continued. "An old kook went to meddle where he had no business. He found a man pronounced dead prematurely by his doctors, and he fed him lies about how he'd brought him back from the dead."

"Estrada, please!" Ashworth said.

"And then, once they'd begun believing their own silk themselves, they called a meeting to ensure that everyone else be dragged down their deluded ploy."

He spat the last few words with venom.

"That's it!"

Liesel rose from her chair and lunged toward Estrada. He was so caught off-guard that her fist caught him upside the head, spinning him like a top before he fell backwards onto the floor. Everyone was too stunned by her suddenness to react. Estrada's eyes went wide as she overturned the stool he'd been sitting on and seized hold of him by the collar.

"Get her off me!" he cried, flailing wildly to try and escape her grasp as she dragged him toward the door. "She's gonna kill me! Someone!"

"Enough!" shouted Ashworth. "Liesel, let him go!"

Liesel reluctantly released Estrada, shoving him away so that he stumbled to keep his footing. Most of the room had risen to their feet, a few of the men taking a step or two away from Liesel.

Estrada fumed, and he touched his cheek gingerly. "If you dare touch me again you—"

Liesel shot him a glance that communicated he wasn't out of danger yet, and he stopped himself.

"Take your seats!" Ashworth shouted. The whole room jumped at the sound of his voice. It wasn't common for Ashworth to bark, and everyone quickly returned to their seats—everyone except Estrada, who opted for a wall on the furthest side of the room.

Chance just smiled, he'd heard Ashworth's voice enough over the years to read when Ashworth was actually at his tipping point. He was only just beginning.

"Goodness, what has brewed in all of you tonight? I bring a man who could be the key to redeeming our livelihood and here you are quarreling like schoolchildren. I invited you here because I thought you were capable of handling yourselves with some amount of dignity. Was I wrong?"

Silence passed uncomfortably between them.

"Does anyone have anything constructive to contribute?" Foxx asked, trying to restore some order.

"What now?" Chance spoke up from the back of the room. Heads turned in his direction. "I think we'd all like to know what you plan to do now."

"He's already begun doing a great many things for us," Ashworth explained. "Our greatest handicap is our lack of a voice on the Spire. There was a time—some of us may still remember—when an alchemist was regarded as a valued member of society. Innovators by nature, we were recognized as some of the greatest minds behind medicine with our curatives, industry with our combustibles, and we were among the greatest dreamers with our transmutations."

"The Philosopher's Stone!" Gravatts cried out.

"Lead to gold," Foxx grinned.

"Aether," Yoon whispered with reverence.

"Yes," Ashworth said, nodding to each of the men. "The three greatest pursuits of our trade. Dreams we all admire, but have never seen realized... until now."

"Then it is Aether? You've created Aether?" Welch asked, quite animated.

Chance looked between Welch and Ashworth. Was he right? Had Ashworth been developing Aether?

"It is," Ashworth smiled. "Or the spark of it, at least. It's not stable enough to sustain itself, but we've developed a spark powerful enough revitalize it."

"I never thought—" Yoon put his hand to his mouth.

"In the past, such a moment as this would have been shouted from the rooftops. It would have been broadcast from the tip of the Spire to the shores of the Basin. However, we've been reduced to rags—disparaged and dispirited as gears and machinery occupy the minds of the city. It's been a long while since alchemists have had any recognition in Hatteras. But now, we have a miracle in our hands and a voice once again."

"And that will be my honor," Harper said. "I'll take your words to the ears of those who can do something with them. I've already begun speaking with my closest acquaintances among the meritocracy. I can't guarantee change will be quick or effortless, but I know these men well. I know what motivates some and compels others. I promise you, I'll see this through until you're given the credit and support you need to reestablish yourselves and take up your great pursuits again."

There was a cheer from a few of the alchemists.

"Correct me if I'm wrong, Captain," Sager said, "but it was *your* signature on each of those legislations which put us in this plight."

"That is true," Harper admitted.

"Then why now? I'm not trying to undermine you here, but this is a bit much to swallow all at once. Why the sudden change of heart?"

Harper let out a heavy sigh.

"I've spent the better part of my life pushing legislation to expand clockwork mechanics. I've always considered it a lifesaving craft. Given my experience, was there any other way I could have seen it?"

He tapped the metal casing of his shoulder.

"It sustained my life after the war, and those of many more who served alongside me. We were more than willing to give what we could to support the minds that made our preservation possible.

"But now, after so many years, this cold appendage is a sore to me—a hollow memory of what I once possessed. The life I gained was hardly a life. Waking every day to the weight of this... blight." He looked at his arm as if it weren't a part of him at all. "It's a canker wrapped in a fancy tin can."

"But it's remarkable!" Welch argued. He rose from his chair and turned, facing those near him. "It's beautiful. It is! Can't you see it? You're the last man I thought would slight your own miracle."

"Welch, please."

"He's ungrateful!"

"Welch!" Ashworth snapped. Chance heard the edge now.

Liesel took Welch's arm and directed him to sit down again, the two of them speaking for a moment in hushed tones.

"I don't take offense for saying what you feel, Master Welch," Harper continued. "But understand that it is one thing to admire this gift from a distance and another to carry it with you—carry it so close you can't tell where you end and where it begins."

His arm moved again, weaving back and forth to demonstrate the intricate control he had over it. Chance couldn't get used to the sound.

"At first, I was too busy celebrating the fact that I was alive," Harper reflected. "But over time I felt the heaviness, deeper than I can explain. As if a weight were pulling against me every moment of every day. No rest. No relief. I slept, but upon waking I felt as though I'd been working through the night. A lifetime of that wears on a man's soul."

"But your name is still there on every piece of legislation the meritocracy has passed promoting clockwork mechanics," Sager said, "and simultaneously burying our craft."

"The mechanists came to me with their propositions, yes. Every time they wanted to pass another law or approve another project they sought me out for my support."

"And you gave it to them," Yoon said.

"I'm afraid in recent years I've consented more out of desperation than any nobler motive. I kept hoping they'd find a way to improve what they'd done. But, I hoped in vain. The dreams of the clockwork mechanists have developed the same hollowness to me now as this arm has."

"And what Willard has not explained to you is what is most disconcerting about all of this," Ashworth said. "There are others just as interested in the Aether as we are. After our conversations, Willard and I are concerned they'll try to—I'm not sure how to say it—harvest it. Harvest the spirit of a man."

"You can't be serious," Yoon said.

"You're even losing me a bit on this one, Ashworth," Sager agreed. "That's not possible. Otherwise some alchemist would have thought of it ages ago. It's not like you can just open a tap and fill a cup with the stuff."

"Actually," Harper grinned, though his expression was grave, "that's exactly what we think they've done. Only the cup... well, it's not exactly a cup."

The captain he held up his clenched brass fist.

"I know the difference between what they accomplished with this," he tapped the metal casing of his arm, "and what Charles accomplished the night he brought me back with his spark. *I* am the difference."

"So, what you're saying is... you're on our side now?" Sager said.

"Yes, master alchemist, I'm on your side."

"And what happens now? I mean, what's next?" Yoon asked.

"We need to let others know what has happened," Ashworth said. "This is too important to keep hidden. Only the present company knows about the Aether spark, and even fewer know the details of its creation. The people of the city have been deceived into believing it was Doctor Stoddard's mechanism which saved the captain."

"Stoddard and the other mechanists will use that misunderstanding to their advantage," Harper added. "I guarantee new petitions to the capitol are already being written up and sponsorships are being granted. We will first need to correct what's falsely been concluded about my recovery. We can contact the papers and have them give the true account of what happened."

"How would that help us?" Estrada said. "The papers are just a puppet-theater for the cogs on the Spire. There is no way in the depths that they'll print anything which might upset things. Not before it was hushed by the meritocracy."

"I'm afraid on this point I have to agree with Estrada," Sager said.

"So, what do we do?"

Nobody moved for a while as they contemplated their predicament.

"We give them a demonstration," Chance said, the many similar conversations he'd had with Serge coming to mind.

Everyone's eyes turned to him.

"We hold a demonstration, or a rally, or something. It will attract enough attention the papers will have to report on it," Chance explained. "If we have enough people there then the meritocracy won't be quick enough to stop it. The people will hear the truth from the source, and the capitol will be forced to respond."

"The meritocracy will never let you organize a demonstration," Estrada said.

"Then we don't tell them. We keep it secret."

"How do we attract the public if we can't announce it?" Keefer asked. "This can't just be a street-corner meeting if it's going to gain any traction."

"Maybe we disguise it? Or at least hide our real intentions until it's too late for the authorities to stop us?" Sager suggested.

"How would we do that?"

"We could hold it in the Exchange," Gravatts suggested.

"Great idea!"

"No, it isn't," Keller frowned. "There are officials all over the Exchange. They've got that place so tightly watched they'd stop us as soon as they realized what we were doing."

"What about at a plaza?" Ashworth said.

"We still don't even know how we're going to disguise it."

"We could use a holiday," Yoon suggested. "People would already be brought together, and we could just set up a place to speak."

"Why not on Septigonee's Day?" Chance said. "That's not too far away, and we'd be guaranteed a crowd."

"That's not a bad idea," Keller said.

"Got a fair sense of irony to it," Foxx agreed. "Fortunes turning and everything."

"It wouldn't be difficult to find a place to set up and address the people," Sager added.

"A rally it is then!" Ashworth affirmed. "On Septigonee's Day. That gives us two weeks to set things in motion."

"We'll need more than just a crowd," Keller pointed out. "If this is going to be lasting, we'll need some support already. A few well-placed members of the meritocracy who are sympathetic to our cause would keep the capitol from trying to sweep this under the rug."

"I'll do what I can to win over some supporters," Harper said. "I may have accumulated some rust over the years, but I still have some sway with the gentleman of the meritocracy. I should be able to bring a few friends over by then."

"Good. What else do we need?"

The rest of the night was spent in a spirit of animation, making preparations and dividing up tasks between those present. Chance felt a thrill rushing through their little company, as though a great energy was surging beneath them, lifting their cause.

The tides truly were preparing to turn. He felt it.

Even Estrada had a few comments to contribute that were less noxious than usual.

PART II

CHAPTER EIGHTEEN
A View From Above

*Be careful not to breath too deeply the thick air.
Or for too long.*

— Alchemical Proverb

In the weeks that followed, Chance found himself unable to stay
still. Indeed, since their secret meeting, all the alchemists were a
bustle of industrious energy. Ashworth's place hosted visitors daily, some alchemists, others affiliates of the meritocracy, and others still
Chance didn't know.

Ashworth entertained each guest, occasionally accompanied by
Harper, who was still maintaining a measure of secrecy at their rec-
ommendation. It wouldn't have done to have him make appearances
prematurely.

Chance went about his regular tasks gladly, hardly stressing over the
little inconveniences which usually soured his mood. They seemed so
trivial now. He even took on Ashworth's more mundane chores without
protest.

This was the first time since Chance could remember when he genuinely had something to look forward to. Things were happening, and
he felt the anticipation building. It was only a matter of days until the

rest of the world felt it too.

It was as though all of them were sitting on a powder keg, and the suspense was almost too much to bear.

The day before the event, Chance arose bright and early. He got himself ready, finished a few odd orders, and rushed inside and up the winding stairs to Rhett's attic in a sprint.

Bursting through the door, he gave Rhett a start. The boy was sitting in the middle of the floor, a large collection of glass vials and flasks spread out before him in clusters of similar contents. He was busy affixing fresh labels on each vial with a brush dipped in thin glue.

It was clear, however, the glue had gotten the better of him as it dripped and ran down the brush onto his fingers.

"Come on, Rhett," Chance said. "Hurry and put that stuff away. We've got an appointment."

"With who?"

"With whom," Chance corrected, more to tease the boy than to educate him. "And what do you care? It's a reason to put off your chores. Now come on! Or I'll leave without you."

Rhett didn't argue. He set the glue down on the newspaper he'd laid out, but, despite his best efforts, he had trouble letting go of the brush.

Chance smiled in good humor.

"Maybe fifteen minutes then."

When Rhett finished separating his fingers and washing the glue off his hands—a process that took considerable time and a bit of help from Chance—the two of them set off toward the bay. Chance carried a pack, which he had to adjust periodically so it didn't poke his back.

It was a particularly pleasant day, a steady wind blowing fresh and warm from the sea. Chance breathed it in deep. Since the meeting it seemed everything had grown more pleasant. Not even the closeness of the derelict streets could sway Chance's mood.

It was incredible what the right prospects could do to perspective.

After a brief walk, Chance stopped underneath a small platform. It looked much like a railway terminal might, except much smaller. It was only a single platform, raised above the ground perhaps twenty feet, but with no tracks. Instead, there were thick posts where ropes could be anchored.

"Where are we going?" Rhett asked.

"You'll see," Chance smiled back at him. "Keep up, slowpoke!"

Grasping the railing, Chance climbed the steps two and three at a time, with Rhett scrambling after him. Rhett did his best, but by the time he was at the top of the stairs he was out of breath, as was Chance. They both took a moment to breathe.

"What are we doing here?" Rhett asked.

"Waiting."

"For what?"

"That." Chance pointed toward the end of the street.

Turning a tight corner, a small wood dinghy floated toward them, suspended by a faded balloon. Rhett stared at it for a second, perplexed. But then his face lit up, and he looked wide-eyed at Chance.

"Is that for us?"

"Sure is." Chance couldn't hold back a smile. "You didn't think I'd forgotten, did you?"

Rhett gaped, at a loss for words as he watched the dinghy navigate between the buildings and come abreast the platform. With a skillful turn of the helm, the pilot maneuvered the dinghy so it came to rest a foot off the edge.

Simon stepped up out of the dinghy, balancing on the lip with a practiced lightness in his good foot for such an unsteady surface.

"Right on time," Chance called to his friend.

"That's how we like it. You coming aboard?" Simon asked Rhett, offering a hand to the boy.

Rhett beamed from ear to ear as he bobbed his head and took Simon's hand. He was lifted carefully from the platform and dropped safely into the vessel. Chance grasped the tie-downs and clambered in as well.

"All's aboard and clear to sail," Simon shouted, though the tiny vessel was small enough he needn't raise his voice.

By appearance, one might have doubted the craft's airworthiness. The main balloon was clearly disproportionate to what would normally be required to lift a vessel, even one this small. However, as Chance climbed on he noticed thick bags secured to the bow, straining against their anchors. He ventured a guess they were filled with thick air—an alchemical compound which altered the buoyancy of air to nearly eight or nine times its natural state.

With a few of those, it wasn't so impossible.

"Right. On we go then," the pilot called.

He lifted a flume by his feet and the propellers behind him lurched into action, receiving a flow of heated air from the ship's underbelly furnace. Rhett teetered backwards as the ship began to rise, but was steadied by Simon before he took a tumble.

"Hold onto something if you ain't got legs for the sky yet, little master," the pilot chuckled.

"You'll get used to it in a moment," Simon assured him. "But until then, best to keep a hand in the ropes."

Rhett did as was suggested, threading his arm through a few of the ropes as he glanced over the edge of the vessel as far as he safely could.

The world moved swiftly below them, the buildings like the rocks that bordered a riverbed and the air an invisible current that carried them away. Chance watched Rhett's face as he gazed wide-eyed down on the streets he was all too familiar with.

Their world looked quite different from above.

"Thanks again for putting this together," Chance said to Simon.

"It's my pleasure. Honestly, I was feeling a bit too grounded myself. Would have done it soon anyway, or else I'm liable to lose my flight legs. Plus, I have a meeting over in the factory district. I'll just have him drop me there when we're done."

"What meeting?"

"Oh, just one of Serge's meetings. You know," Simon said. "I think he has it in his head to help the factory workers organize a union."

"Good luck with that," Chance said. "The owners get a whiff a union is forming and they'll turn the lot of them out and replace them with a fresh batch of desperates before you can strike a match."

"Maybe," Simon shrugged. "But then I don't work in the factories, so it's not my decision to make. Every man has a right to work out his own destiny."

Chance couldn't argue there, but he thought Serge a little too eager to stir up trouble. It was one thing for Serge to walk that road himself, but he was liable to drag quite a few lives down with him if he wasn't careful.

"So, who's the pilot?" Chance asked, changing the subject. He kept his voice low, though the man seemed preoccupied enough maneuvering the narrow streets that he wasn't paying them much mind.

"Peter Barlow," Simon said. "One of the most daring men I've ever had the fortune of flying with. Met him back when I was serving overseas in the militia. Now he runs his own ferry."

"An old friend then?"

"I wouldn't say that," Simon smiled. "But a good man. I'd trust him with my life."

That was good to hear, because as the vessel carried on it was steadily gaining speed. Chance gripped the ropes tighter as Barlow spun the helm and the dinghy rounded a tight corner. The contents of Chance's stomach lurched, and he felt a tingle move upwards into his throat.

He sat down before it got the better of him.

Rhett didn't seem to mind the pace they were setting. He kept leaning over the edge, his face sometimes only feet from the buildings they passed. They raced by swiftly, but occasionally the passengers caught a glimpse through the windows at businessmen, clerks, families, and others' lives. Privileged glimpses completely foreign to them.

Rhett waved as he passed, and those inside peered at him queerly.

They were climbing, hovering beside the upper levels of the taller buildings. From the looks of it, they were heading toward the bay. Chance welcomed that idea. Though Barlow was proving his skill, Chance didn't know how much more weaving he could take.

"What do these marks mean?" Rhett asked, pointing over the bow at some strange characters written on the side of the dinghy. Chance joined him and glanced at the characters. 'Mauriel,' it read. But he couldn't be sure what language the other characters were derived from. A colony language? Ungarra, perhaps?

"That's the ship's name," Barlow said. "Every ship needs a name.

It's bad luck to sail without one."

"And the characters around it?" Chance asked.

"They're from an old Ungarran proverb," Barlow explained. Chance smiled inwardly at his correct guess. "Loosely translated, it means 'a treasure loath to lose.'"

"Barlow and I spent a few summers in Ungarra during our service overseas," Simon said. "Godforsaken desert."

"A garden oasis," Barlow corrected with a smile.

"As you might guess, we had very different experiences."

"And who's Mauriel?" Chance asked.

"My one true love," Barlow said, his voice softer and his eyes steady ahead.

Chance didn't pry. Instead, he watched Rhett's boyish excitement. He missed the days when such simple joys held so much wonder.

"Why don't we fly higher?" Rhett asked.

"Because, little master, there are bigger ships than us in the open skies. Great airships with their thick metal edges. Wouldn't want to get clipped by one of them out over the bay, now would you?"

"Can't you just fly around them?"

"Mauriel may be agile in the sky, but she's certainly not the fastest. The bigger vessels are brutes. They wouldn't even notice we were there if they came upon us. No, I take my chances with the streets, even if it does take a little while longer to get where we're going."

"We don't mind," Chance said. He leaned back against the wood to steal a bit of rest. "As long as we get there."

Rhett leaned out a bit further, craning his neck as he tried to catch a glimpse of the airships Barlow was talking about. The balloon proved a tough barrier, however, and Rhett huffed in frustration.

After watching him strain a while, Barlow gave a thick laugh. "Alright, little master. We'll take a peek up top. For your sake." He opened the flume a bit more and the dinghy lurched forward as the propellers picked up even more speed.

"Simon, would you give us a bit more lift?"

Simon twisted a lever on what looked like a large thurible that hung below the skirt of the main balloon and the vessel climbed. He added a bit more fuel and left the chutes open as he took a seat again.

They climbed steadily now, and soon they breached the upper limits of the city, the expanse of the bay opening up on them like a burst bubble.

Seeing the world around them, Chance understood why Barlow had been hesitant. The skies weren't just crowded, they were swarming. It was easy to forget when walking through the streets, but, between the ships coming and going from both the shipyard on the bay and the platforms throughout the city, the air lanes were a mess of chaos.

Barlow removed his hat and hung it on a peg beside him as he craned his neck around, keeping his eyes peeled for other ships. They sped forward, like a dart through the sky. Rhett gasped as he looked around him. The ships appeared to move in tiny currents, clusters falling in behind one another as a string of them moved inland, and then another as they traveled seaward.

Some moved with no predictable pattern at all, and Chance did not envy Barlow as he struggled to anticipate their movements.

What caught their attention more than anything was the great warships. They counted eight massive ships with heavy plating and many-handed crews, hovering near the cliffs below the Spire. As he looked, Chance realized they were being outfitted. Not with cargo, but with decorations. With Septigonee's Day nearing, they were being prepared with great white drapes and ribbons along their bows. The balloons which held them up were similarly draped in large swaths of golden fabric.

It was odd, seeing something exude a spirit both awe-inspiring and intimidating.

One of the ships was not clustered with the others, however. It came up fast behind them, passing not a hundred yards away, going out toward the sea with none of the decorative trimmings. Its massive frame blocked out the sun as it overshadowed their small dinghy.

"Probably off to join the armada," Simon offered, guessing at Chance's thoughts. "Interesting they have so few of them here for the celebrations this year. Usually they bring in twenty ships or more. Must be having more trouble with the colonies."

"The colonies are the least of their worries," Barlow said. "Selaria's the one they're worried about."

"Why would they be worried about them?" Chance asked. Hatteras had a peace accord with Selaria ever since they'd beaten them back in the Great War all those years ago—the same war in which Harper had earned his distinctions. From what Chance gathered, Selaria had been perfectly compliant ever since.

"Because they're massing a fleet off the coast of Madura—as rumor has it."

"They've broken the treaty?"

"Well, I don't think so. Not technically. I don't think they've done anything but relocate their fleet, but you can imagine how uncomfortable it is for trade ships to pass by them."

"Why would they do that?"

"Likely a show of force," Simon ventured. "Selaria is tired of being overlooked. Perhaps they're trying to flex their muscles a bit. Get Hatteras's attention. It's sending a message, that's for sure," he chuckled. "I've already had requests come my way from Hatteras. They're forming a temporary militia. Seems they're going to make a statement in return."

"Give it a week, and Hatteras will scare them back into their ports," Barlow said. "Hopefully it doesn't cast too much of a shadow on the festivities."

He turned the helm over and they glided smoothly beside the great warship. Chance saw the crews working the deck. He couldn't imagine what it would be like to face off with a ship that size.

This particular vessel had two cannons at opposite ends, each mounted on a pivot. For an airship like that, even with a large portion of their hull dedicated to thick air compartments, weight was still an issue. But then, all it took was a well-placed scatter shot through one of those compartments to stop a ship in its tracks.

Two trained guns were plenty to do the job.

Barlow peeled away from the warship and sped out over the open bay. Chance shook off the heavy feeling that had come over him being so near the warship and tried to think of something else.

"Hey, Rhett," he said as he dropped his pack on the deck and pulled out Rhett's flying contraption. Rhett couldn't contain his excitement at the sight of it. "What do you say to sending her off on her maiden voyage?"

"Can we?"

"You're not going to get another chance like this for a while."

"But we might lose it," Rhett said, looking at the waters below them.

"You've already seen what Barlow can do with his ship," Simon said. "He'll snatch it up again before it ever touches land."

"Go for it," Chance urged.

Rhett snatched the contraption from Chance's hand and was about to cock it back when Barlow cried out.

"Hold boy! Didn't you hear a thing I said before? You got to name her before you send her off like that. It's bad luck to sail without a proper name."

Chance laughed. "We're not the best when it comes to naming things."

"Even so," Simon warned. "Best to appease the captain. He's mighty superstitious about things like this, and for good reason. Omens. He reads them like a map."

"A map of the sky," Barlow said. "And none more accurate has man ever made."

"But what should I call it?" Rhett asked.

"Whatever you feel she is to you."

Rhett looked at the contraption a moment. "I think I'll call her... *Spirit.*"

"A fine name," Barlow nodded with approval.

"Hand her here," Simon said. He took the toy and used his knife to etch the name into the side. "There. Now she's got a name."

"Alright," Chance said. "Let's see it fly!"

Rhett climbed up the dinghy's side, a hand secure in the rigging and the other holding the flying contraption. He gave it one last check to be sure the wings and tail were straight and leveled it off over the bow.

"All clear to launch!" Barlow belted.

Rhett thrust his arm forward and released.

The flying machine sailed forward steadily, its wings cutting through the air as smooth as a gull. They watched it with fascination as it caught a gentle swell and curved slightly until it was flying parallel to them.

Barlow tracked it skillfully.

"It's flying!" Rhett shouted. "Chance, look! It's flying!"

Rhett's eyes were wide and his toothy smile could not be restrained. Again, Chance couldn't hold back a smile of his own. There was something inspiring about a boy who could smile like that.

But, Rhett's smile faded, until it was replaced by a look of pure distress. The flying machine was veering off to the right—cruising straight for the warship!

Chance jumped up from his seat.

"It's going to crash!" Rhett cried out.

"Can we try and get to it?" Chance asked.

"No good," Barlow said, tilting the helm a little, but not enough to pursue. His eyes were on the warship. "We come up on her too quickly and I'm afraid what she might do to us. Best we can do is hope it catches another swell and misses her."

They held their breaths, eyes glued to the tiny flying machine, but there was no saving it. It flew true and struck the warship's plated hull with a crack. Rhett let out a sob and the four of them watched helplessly as the *Spirit* plummeted into the bay.

CHAPTER NINETEEN
Desperate Measures

Right? What is right? There can be nothing more right than unhindered progress!

— Excerpt from *Mechanarcissism*

A storm had blown in from the bay, blanketing everything in a dark screen as it chased away the sun. Even the Spire was caught in its gloomy atmosphere. The sound of thick, heavy droplets striking on rooftops sustained a metal timbre, as though many voices were arguing just beyond the walls.

Stoddard leaned against the window in his study, pressed up close enough that the cold coming off the glass chilled his forehead while he listened to the otherworldly conversation.

He favored this space. The drapes gave him a sense of privacy, even from his work. He could think clearer, watching the comings and goings of the city below him. He thought often of moving his desk here, but each time he resisted the idea. This space was sacred to him, and he feared disturbing it with his constant presence. And so, for now, he simply let his mind run like the rain down the glass—slowly sinking as it clung to some transparent pain.

"Doctor," Arden said, looking up from Stoddard's desk. Stoddard turned his head slightly. The young man was reading over a passage from one of the many journals Stoddard had kept over years. "I'm not sure I'm making sense of this."

Stoddard stepped away from the window. "What exactly isn't making sense?"

"All of it." Arden leaned back into the chair with a sigh. "I don't understand half of what you're referencing, and when I do I end up spinning around in circles again."

"I warned you it would be a challenge," Stoddard said. Walking by his bookshelf, he pulled a thick volume and laid it down over the journal. "Why don't you begin with this? If you wish to make sense of it, you'll need to study both mechanics and medicine simultaneously. Read from the best books, and once you understand how we came to where we are, perhaps I can show you where we might go from here."

"That could take a long time," Arden sighed.

"Undoubtedly it will," Stoddard agreed. "But, unless you have something of greater importance with which to occupy your time, I recommend spending it on an endeavor with promise."

Arden nodded reluctantly and opened the book, starting from the beginning.

Stoddard smiled. The boy was perhaps a little undisciplined, but he wasn't lazy. It was only a matter of anchoring his mind to a task or purpose. If he could conquer his wandering mind, Stoddard expected the boy would see his endeavor through to the end.

There was a light knock on the door, and Donovan let himself in.

"I have the news prints you requested, sir."

"Set them on the desk there," Stoddard said. "I'll get to them in a moment."

Donovan hesitated as he approached the desk; a wealth of reports and newspapers were piled high across it, in some places dangerously close to overlapping. But, he managed to find a space for the news prints and set them down carefully.

"I also have your informant's report here," Donovan said.

Stoddard nodded. "Perhaps it would be best if you continued your reading in the comfort of your own home, Master Arden?"

"That might be a good idea. May I?" he asked, holding up the book.

"It's yours as long as you need," Stoddard assured him. "And if that one doesn't deter you, I have another I'd like to recommend when you're finished."

"I'll try not to lose heart," Arden said. "Thank you." He gathered up his coat and saw himself out, closing the door behind him.

When he was gone, Donovan handed the report to Stoddard who took a seat as he opened it. His eyes swept briefly over the piles. At times, he felt like his whole life had become a sum of all the forms and reports which passed through his office.

How dull and lackluster it all was.

For a moment, he allowed his mind to wander to days when he'd spent more time in a workshop designing and perfecting his mechanisms than he did keeping up with protocol and politics. It had only been a short while, a little over a week, yet the demands to be present at social functions and entertain public figures had left him little time to do what he truly longed for.

But, that was the way it had to be. Every piece must be in order if the whole was to function. Procedure followed exactly. Directions clear. Their execution meticulous. It was a tenant Stoddard had committed to in all aspects of his life—more in recent years than ever before. It was the defining attribute of a civil society.

Until a single cog comes loose, he thought.

"He still won't meet with me?" Stoddard asked as he read.

"I'm afraid not, sir. At least, he hasn't responded to your invitations as of yet. We've sent him several telegrams by personal carrier, but I'm afraid they've been unable to persuade him of its urgency."

"Then nothing is improved. If he won't meet with me by now, he won't meet with me at all."

The week spent trying to track the captain down had been a nightmare. With members from the capitol looking to expand Stoddard's work, he needed Harper's endorsement. At the very least he needed to see the man for a medical evaluation.

Yet, Harper remained aloof.

Stoddard let out a long, labored sigh. "These days are beginning to wear on me, Donovan. He's undermining me. And intentionally!"

"It might appear that way, sir."

"Might?" Stoddard stared hard at the reports. A week he had kept a man trailing Harper, and he had received nothing but disturbing news. His copious time spent in the Basin districts was enough to cause alarm, but his apparent association with alchemists left Stoddard unsettled.

What business did he have with that lot? Stoddard couldn't be sure. The easy answer was that Harper was in pain, and therefore seeking relief through their cheap narcotics. But that answer wasn't sitting well with Stoddard.

Taking a notebook from his pocket, he flipped to a marked page and glanced over a set of notes he'd jotted down before.

> *Mechanism's design flawless. Operation executed perfectly.*
> *Yet, captain dies.*
> *Tapping Aether after death impossible; too weak a link.*
> *No Aether, therefore no power to the mechanism.*
> *Yet, mechanism functioned?*

Somehow, beyond all probable expectation, it had functioned after the captain was dead. How? The question perplexed him greatly. But more than that, another matter pressed upon his mind.

He scribbled a new series of notes.

> *Harper won't see me; meeting with alchemists.*
> *Pain?*
> *Something else?*

Of what was happening behind closed doors, Stoddard couldn't be sure. But the captain's association with the alchemists coincided with another bit of news which had also reached his ears. News he couldn't ignore.

> *Alchemists' success?*

He penned the last line with a sneer. Rumor had surfaced from the crevices of the city—the faintest whispers—that it was the alchemists who were responsible for Harper's revival. He'd not been able to confirm the rumors himself, but his informant swore by them. And with the captain's recent actions, Stoddard was prone to trust his man.

It was the worst scenario Stoddard could have imagined, playing out right before his eyes. He rubbed his brow. "Who put these things into his head? You know he's meeting with an elector this afternoon?"

"I didn't, sir."

"Do you look at these reports? Do you even know what's going on under your nose?" Stoddard threw the folder across the desk, the papers scattering.

Donovan shifted uncomfortably.

"He's preparing to criticize fifteen years of legislation—fifteen years of my work! I never expected he'd devise some reason to withdraw his endorsement. It could shake my whole industry."

"It appears that way," Donovan agreed.

"He endorsed the bills that made my work possible! I didn't hear him complaining when the capitol permitted us to test the mechanism! You realize if he keeps on like this everything we've done will come under scrutiny?"

"You think he would be capable of halting your work?"

"No," Stoddard said firmly. "But he could impede it. He could cast doubt where doubt isn't needed. What we need most is trust—trust enough to permit us to step further than anyone has been compelled to step. The timing is undeniable. All events of the last century have pointed to this moment—to my work."

"If providence is with you, sir, then I hardly think one man could undermine you."

"Yes," Stoddard said, eying his assistant. "*If.* Funny that word crept into this very conversation. You think the citizens of this city will be more believing than you, Donovan?"

There was another knock at the door, and Stoddard waved Donovan to answer it.

"Lieutenant Vanzeal, sir," Donovan announced, allowing a uniformed officer into the room. He wore the typical military suit of Hatteras, except for the red cape draped over his left shoulder, signifying his status as a gentleman duelist.

"Ah, Lieutenant." Stoddard rose to greet the man, shaking his hand firmly. "I'm glad that you could meet with me."

"I came as soon as I received your missive," Vanzeal said. "Your message was… alarming."

"Not without just cause, I assure you. That will be all for now, Donovan."

"I should take my leave, sir?" Donovan asked.

"Could I have meant something else?"

Donovan nodded and stepped out of the room, closing the doors behind him.

"I'll try to keep this visit brief," Stoddard said. "I'm sure your time is precious."

"We serve the gentlemen of the meritocracy, Doctor," Vanzeal said. "And as Elector Sinclair has given you his endorsement, I am at your disposal."

"Let me come straight to the point then," Stoddard said. "It's about this whole business with Captain Harper. It's sparked a great deal of commotion recently."

Stoddard walked back to the nook by the window, and Vanzeal followed him.

"I've heard things, Lieutenant," Stoddard said with an air of gravity. "And I felt it my duty to bring them to your attention. I believe there is a plot developing that might undermine the meritocracy, and I have reason to believe the free-merchant alchemists are at the heart of it."

"That is a serious accusation," Vanzeal frowned. "How did you come upon such an idea?"

"I've had an informant working for some days now to uncover it. Forgive me for not having come to you earlier, but I had to be certain of his reliability myself. His findings are all here." Stoddard gestured to the table. "You're more than welcome to examine them. Though, if I may, I will summarize their contents for you."

The lieutenant brushed his cape away so that it fell back over his shoulder. Leaning over the desk, he began reading through the report.

"Why would you take such an interest in free-merchants?" he asked. "They seem a bit below you, I would think, to warrant the attention of a gentleman of your newfound reputation."

"Because they're using my work to do it!" Stoddard couldn't help the passion in his voice from getting away from him.

"You're aware of the events surrounding Captain Harper?" he asked rhetorically. "I myself can't explain how such a phenomenon occurred, and that is exactly the fact which the alchemists are exploiting. With no clear explanation, they've circulated a rumor that it was they, and not I, who revived the captain!"

"Plenty of militia pups have boasted to be better swordsmen than myself," Vanzeal said. "But, I've proven they're filled with nothing more than hot air. Surely a few alchemists can't bring your success into question."

"If it was them alone I wouldn't be concerned," Stoddard said. "But they've managed to confuse Harper into believing their story. He's the one perpetuating it even as we speak. I'm certain of it."

"Captain Harper?" Vanzeal eyed Stoddard. "I find it difficult to believe he'd mingle with Basin-dwellers."

"The evidence is already gathered for you."

Stoddard pulled a document from the pile and handed it to him. Vanzeal took it reluctantly.

"Whatever their method, whether narcotic or otherwise, it's clear they've influenced his judgment. I don't have to explain what risk there is in their having hold on a man of Harper's significance. I have it on good authority that they intend to reveal this false claim publicly. The captain is going to speak to the people and tell them that alchemists saved his life!"

"I see the reason for your distress, Doctor," Vanzeal said. "But why? What do they hope to gain from this?"

"What does every man hope to gain?" Stoddard asked. "Power! Influence! Wealth! It's in their nature. Bred into their very craft. They know their hour is nearly spent, and they're seeking to leech off of anything that can buy them another day. They're desperate, Lieutenant.

And desperate men do desperate things to survive."

"Pardon my asking," Vanzeal said, "but can you not prove it was you who saved his life?"

"That isn't the issue here," Stoddard snapped.

He saw the displeasure in Vanzeal's face, being spoken to so curtly, but Stoddard's passion carried him away.

"What matters is that they are making wild claims. When the captain speaks, he'll infect the masses with the suspicion that those within the meritocracy are ignorant of what is going on under their very noses.

"He'll seek to return favor to the alchemists when we know—we know—that they're charlatans. Lead to gold? I'd like to see evidence of them once producing a single bar from that endeavor. The philosopher's stone? Who among them bears the sign of unnatural youth? Can you name me one?"

"I see your point," Vanzeal nodded stiffly.

"And the Aether! They're fools if they ever thought they cou—"

Stoddard paused as if struck by a blow, and he grew quiet. Turning, he stroked his chin and sat back down in his chair.

"Are you alright, Doctor?"

"Unless it was Aether," he whispered to himself. "Is that what you did?"

"Doctor?"

Stoddard came back to the moment. His eyes held a different glint now—and, for a brief moment, a half-smile crept across his face. But he concealed it, focusing again on the matter at hand.

"I'm greatly concerned that Captain Harper is not in his right mind," Stoddard said as he turned back toward Vanzeal. "I fear that he's been influenced by unsanctioned narcotics prescribed by vagrant alchemists. He's there nearly every day, in their shops and residences as I'm sure you'll confirm when you make your own investigation. I fear that he's about to do something very rash. Something which could produce in the populous a state of civil unrest."

He spoke the last words with deliberation.

"And what, exactly, is it that you would like us to do about them?" Vanzeal asked.

Stoddard grinned despite himself. Protocol be damned.

CHAPTER TWENTY
Septigonee's Day

And the gods—if there be any gods beside ourselves—remained silent as the works of our hands emerged. Their indifference gifted us the freedom to seek these favors of our own initiative.

— Excerpt from *Mechanarcissism*

Despite having slept on his laboratory couch, Chance awoke feeling particularly well-rested. He couldn't remember dreaming, but, if he had, the dreams had put him in a remarkably good mood. He sprang from his couch and donned his shirt and vest, tripping over his chair and knocking over a few components on his desk.

It was only seven thirty, but he already heard early sounds of celebration throughout the city. Splashing water on his face, he paused to look at himself in the mirror.

"Today, your luck is changing," he said to his reflection. Grabbing his alchemical case, he hurried out his workshop.

The weather was still cloudy from the storm which had blown through, the early morning sun catching the clouds in brilliant fashion as it rose over the bay. The dramatic light only enhanced Chance's mood.

He felt it in his bones. Septigonee's cursed tides were turning for sure.

Inside, he found Rhett still in his nightclothes, munching on some fruit. He couldn't see it, but he suspected Rhett's rat was enjoying a portion in his lap. Chance gave the boy's hair a rough tousle and tossed himself into the empty chair.

"Hey!" Rhett protested.

"Is Ashworth here?" Chance asked.

"He left already, I think."

"But the rally isn't until this afternoon. Did he go to see Harper?"

"I don't know," Rhett shrugged. "He was gone before I came downstairs."

"Did he leave a note?"

Rhett just shrugged again and focused on his food.

"Well," Chance said, selecting an apple for himself. "Let's you and I not linger too long then. He'll probably need help setting up."

"Gravatts said he was gonna help him with it."

"But Gravatts is an old man. They'll still need some help."

"Fine," Rhett sighed.

"What's got you all bent out of shape?"

"Nothing."

"You still sulking about that flying machine?"

Rhett looked further into his lap.

"Those things happen," Chance tried to explain. "You can't expect everything to last."

"I only got to fly it once," Rhett sulked.

"Hey," Chance gave the boy a friendly nudge. "It's Septigonee's Day. The tides are turned, and that could mean your fortunes too. How about you and I forget about your flying machine and go have some fun today?"

"But, I thought you said we needed to help Ashworth to set up."

"Now you're going to fight me on it?" Chance smiled. "It's not like it would be the first time we left our chores undone. How about we take the morning to enjoy the celebration? Then we'll meet up to give them a final hand. How's that sound?"

Rhett thought it over, petting the rat under the table.

"And who knows," Chance added, "perhaps another kid will lose his flying machine."

Rhett smiled. "Alright," he said.

"Did you name him yet?" Chance asked, pointing to the rat.

"Not yet."

"Why not? You didn't have any trouble coming up with a name for your flying machine."

"That's different," Rhett insisted. "I keep trying, but I can't figure it out."

"There's nothing to figure out. It's a name."

"But what if he's already got one?"

"He's a rat, Rhett. You found him on the street. I don't think anyone's thought to name him before now."

Rhett looked down at the creature. It nibbled at the bottom of his shirt. "I think he has a name."

"Why don't you give him a new one," Chance suggested, taking a bite of his apple. "New life, new name?"

"But he might like his old one."

Chance grinned around the apple in his mouth. "Alright. He's your rat. Do what you will with it. But right now, you need to get changed."

While Rhett got ready upstairs, Chance finished his breakfast and fetched the morning-edition papers from the porch. Ashworth paid some of the newsboys a bit extra to bring them by before they took to the streets to peddle the rest. They hid them behind the bush to keep them from being swiped.

He didn't bother glancing through the papers; he had a feeling tomorrow's was going to be a tad more interesting.

When Rhett returned, Chance locked up the house and the two of them made their way toward the central road that wound through the city. It was long and serpentine, stretching from the very top of the Spire all the way down to the water's edge of the Basin. It was an important feature, not only for its general usefulness, but for its history.

According to city legend, it was the very same path the girl, Septigonee, had run when she fled from her betrothed the night before her marriage. It was a story every child in Hatteras grew up with, about the very earliest years of the city.

Septigonee was a daughter of a founding family trapped in an arranged marriage to a man of high status, but lacking in honor. Her betrothed had appeared drunk one night on her doorstep and demanded to be let in. When she wouldn't admit him, he broke the door down to get at her. In her fright, Septigonee fled her home on the Spire and ran until she came to the edge of the Basin. There at the water's edge, as he was about to seize her, she cast herself into the dark waters and drowned in the violent surf.

It was her death that had cursed the Basin's waters and brought ill fortune to anyone who dwelt near them—a cursed luck which turned only once every year, on the anniversary of that dreaded flight.

In honor, the city was decorated in traditional wedding decor. White drapes hung out of windows and garlands of gold and silver were strung up everywhere Chance and Rhett went. People dressed in their best wedding attire, though often with costlier garnishing and accentuated styles. They wandered in masks and flouted the highest status they could imitate—even the Basin-dwellers.

When they weren't preening about and making a show of themselves, most citizens spent the day shopping at vendors who set up temporary stalls and carts in the streets to tempt new business. Others made new acquaintances or sought out old friends.

But the real activity of the day was that of business. Contracts were signed, risks taken, ventures planned, and partnerships formed and severed— all with the belief that the day's good fortune would bless their enterprise in the coming year.

Chance had no such business at hand today, not for a few hours at least. So, he and Rhett took to wandering as they enjoyed the commotion of the streets, making their way into the nicer districts as they climbed the road toward the Spire.

The constables were notably lax when it came to enforcing the segregation laws, so as not to tempt any ill fortune of their own. Vagrants and vagabonds from the Basin were tolerated even so far as the Spire.

Chance and Rhett were just crossing the channel that bordered the Spire when a familiar voice caught their attention.

"Well, didn't you just go all out?"

A woman behind a great feathered mask approached, waving a fan and leaning suggestively toward them with an elusive smile. "You look so... festive, I almost didn't recognize you."

"I didn't recognize you either," Chance said. "Until you smiled."

The woman laughed. Pulling back the mask, Margarete shook out her curls and gave Chance a wink.

"Wow," Rhett gasped.

As was her talent, Margarete stood out, even among all the pomp around her. She was wearing one of the whitest dresses Chance had ever seen. It was cut like a wedding dress and embellished with golds and silvers, like the decorations around the city. Chance bet she needed help getting in and out of that one.

"Thank you," she beamed. "And how are you today, Rhett?"

"Fine, thanks."

"Where are you two off to?"

"Just wandering," Chance said. "Thought we'd explore the Spire a bit. Rhett doesn't get to see it all that often."

"I saw it yesterday!" he said excitedly. "From the dinghy!"

"That's not the same as actually being there," Chance pointed out.

"Sounds like fun," Margarete said. "But, you can't just wander the Spire dressed like that."

"What's wrong with the way we're dressed?" Chance asked. He liked to think he looked respectable, for an alchemist. Sure, his clothes were a bit worn and faded, and he didn't have the fanciest vest, but a vest he did have.

"I know what you two need," she grinned. "Cravats!"

Rhett perked up. "I'd like a cravat!"

"You don't even know what a cravat is," Chance laughed. "We don't need anything. We're fine as we are."

"You're going to turn down a face like that?" Margarete teased, taking Rhett in her arms and mimicking his look of dejection. "What a dull boy you are, Chance. What harm would it do? It's a festival!"

"What would he even do with one?" Chance asked, a little more abrasively than he intended. Margarete pursed her lips.

"Enjoy it?" she suggested. "Just because you've got no sense of style doesn't mean Rhett should have to suffer. But, if you won't get him a decent cravat, then I will." She walked to a nearby vendor and exchanged a little money for a cream-colored cravat from his wares and offered it to Rhett.

She winked at Chance while Rhett handled the new fabric.

"It's so soft," he said, rubbing the fabric against his cheek.

"You don't even know how to tie it," Chance said.

"Why don't you show him?" Margarete nudged.

Chance frowned and folded his arms. "It's his cravat. He should figure it out himself."

"Of course," Margarete smirked. "Here, Rhett. Let me help you."

She wrapped the fabric around his neck and tied it with a loose twist, as was the current fashion of young gentlemen. She tucked the rest into his vest.

"There you are. Our little gentleman alchemist."

Rhett practically glowed with joy.

"He looks ridiculous," Chance muttered under his breath, but Rhett wasn't listening.

"Perhaps. But then, isn't that the point?" Margarete stepped past Chance, running a hand along his cheek. "Do me a favor, will you? Try and let yourself have some fun today. For me?"

Chance nodded stiffly.

"Alright then. I'll leave you two to it. Rhett, don't let this sourpuss get to you, okay?"

Rhett nodded, and then kept nodding as he enjoyed the rub of the fabric against his neck.

As Chance watched, he couldn't help but smile. Margarete was right. He was letting little things bother him. He couldn't help how he felt about the meritocracy and their ridiculous fashions, but he could ignore them for a day.

And if he was to enjoy himself, Chance knew exactly where to go. A little further along, he led Rhett away from the main road and into one of the side streets.

"Where are we going now?" Rhett asked.

"Just taking advantage of an opportunity," Chance said. "Keep quiet and follow my lead. Let's put that cravat to good use."

They meandered through the neighboring streets where the pomp was somewhat less grand. Here there were fewer vendors. Men and women knelt around games of cards, dice, cockfights, and any other street-worthy game which could coax a wager out of a crowd.

Here the hopefuls gathered, convinced that today of all days their luck could change.

Chance strolled among them, listening to the wagers and surveying faces. Some were betting low, only pocket change, and these he passed by. But a few were playing higher stakes. He watched two games' final pots rise into the hundreds.

At these he lingered, studying the players, his hopes tickled.

A younger gentleman made a wager well beyond the current pot, and the dealer accepted it gladly. Chance could see where this hand would go. The young man was in far over his head. Chance wasn't too concerned for him, however. He was likely some gentleman's son from the Spire, out for an afternoon of amusement squandering a small portion of his family's fortune.

Their type was always welcome in the street games. Encouraged, even.

For most of the participants, the game was the key. It was a matter of skill. They believed that if they played through the day they had a fair chance to come out on top, walking away with a small profit. But that was just playing the odds—the same odds that kept most on the bottom.

That wasn't how Chance played. It wasn't about the game or the odds. It was about a person's pride—their willingness to bet, and bet high. One sudden burst of luck.

The lad lost his hand, cursing lightly as the winner gathered the pot to himself and assigned a man who was standing nearby to go with the young man to retrieve the rest of what he owed.

"Have room for one more?" Chance asked, leaning into the circle.

The man gave him a slow, appraising look.

"Aye," he said. "But not for just anyone. This is a high stakes game.

If you doubt your purse, why don't you try a pauper street somewhere down in the Basin? They'll let just about anyone play."

The company chuckled.

"I'd rather play against you," Chance said. He looked the man square in the eyes, unblinking. The man had a gentlemanly look about him, but without the character to match. A manservant, Chance guessed. His narrow features converged to a point just below the nose. Even his eyes were squeezed together.

He looked back, the indifference in his face shifting.

"You know the game?"

Chance nodded.

"You have enough to wager?"

Chance nodded again.

"Fine." He gestured to the open spot. "Open purse. We want to know what you're betting with."

"Didn't I just see you take a blind wager a moment ago?"

"From Timberman's son, yes. I'd let him bet his entire inheritance if I wasn't afraid his father would lock me up for it. Him I know, and he always comes through. You're a different story, stranger. I don't trust just any guttersnipe."

He scooped up the dice from the ground, and Chance took his seat.

"I can't argue with you there. It's an awful risk to take someone at their word alone. But, we businessmen shouldn't miss out on an opportunity to profit just because our coffers can't fit in a purse."

"Businessman?" The dealer looked doubtful.

"Handle fifty-nine separate contracts personally, with goods going out to each of them weekly."

"In the Basin?"

"With my trade, the Basin provides an advantageous locality to my clients and the shipyard," Chance explained.

"And what exactly is your trade?"

"Free-merchant."

"That doesn't tell me much," the man said. "Could just be a fancy way of saying you're a desperate man."

"Or it could mean I'm pulling in profit enough to maintain my own license, with enough to spare that I can enjoy a generous wager in my spare time."

The man rotated the dice in his hand a few times, thinking it over. Chance kept his expression cool, suppressing his eagerness. His eyes remained fixed on the man's. If he was going to be permitted to play, he had to appear confident, and a little smug.

"And you want to play with uncapped stakes? On your word alone?"

"On a businessman's word," Chance said. "And even if I lose, I'm sure you've got means to secure any loose debts which might come up. But don't you worry," he said, picking up the dice from the man's hands. "I'm not about to run."

"No... you won't," the man said. He scratched at his chin. "If you don't come up with what you owe when you lose—well, let's just say you'd need more than a father like Timberman to keep me off you. We understand each other?"

"Absolutely," Chance grinned.

CHAPTER TWENTY-ONE
An Unlikely Reunion

Can we be blamed for our curiosity? For our mortal audacity?
Man must evolve to survive. It's in our nature to climb. What
heights could we attain given none of our corporeal bounds?

— Excerpt from *Mechanarcissism*

"Gizmo!" Chance leapt into the air, pumping his fists as he did a little jig. "The tides really have turned today!"

The circle of men glared as he pulled the pile of coins and banknotes toward himself.

"Might want to keep your trap shut about it," the man running the game snapped. "It's not good manners to win gracelessly."

Chance couldn't hold in a snicker. "Sorry boys, but when you've had luck as bad as mine you can't help celebrate when a better hand is dealt. You can't fault someone for taking advantage of Septigonee's Day."

"Still, you make it unpleasant to play for the rest of us."

"You've still got deep pockets," Chance laughed. "Not a reason in the world for you to be bent out of shape."

"It's useless," another player said. "You can't teach slag manners. Leave him be."

Chance's expression grew stern. "What did you call me?"

"What you are," the player glared back. His eyes were beady and dark in his plump face.

Chance appraised him a moment, gauging just how close he might be to doing something about his losses. He still held the dice, and Chance saw a desire burning behind those beady eyes to teach him a lesson. He was expecting Chance's luck to run out eventually, and Chance was willing to bet he thought it would be soon.

"I'll tell you what," he said. "I'll give you a chance to win it all back. Double or nothing on one roll."

The man's eyebrow raised. Chance was sitting on a little over two hundred banknotes. The wager was good.

"Well, gents? What do you say?" Chance asked. "You gonna put me in my place? Is my luck about to run out?"

The man with the narrow features bit on something in his mouth and spit it on the ground as he considered Chance's proposal.

"Alright," he said. "Double or nothing. And why not match the game to its wager, shall we? Doubles to come up, or you're bust."

Chance kept his expression unfazed, but the hairs on his neck rose a little. The switch lessened his odds significantly. The rest of the group seemed to take heart with the terms, however, a few of them fetching fresh notes from their pockets to get in on the wager.

This could prove very profitable indeed.

"Alright," Chance agreed. "Doubles. I suppose we'll see who Septigonee favors more." He took the dice. "If anyone else wants their money back, now's your opportunity."

Three of the men matched their losses, tossing their wagers in the middle, and soon Chance was looking over a small fortune.

"Now," he grinned, "about your money."

"You won! You won!" Rhett said, bouncing in circles around Chance as they walked back to the main street. The coins in Rhett's pockets jingled as he danced, making a ruckus and turning heads.

Chance smiled. *Let them look*, he thought. This wasn't just a show of wealth, this was fortune's turning.

"I can't believe you won!"

"There was no way I could lose," Chance boasted. "The guy had arrogance dripping out of his ears. He was overdue for a loss."

"He looked scary to me."

"They all try to be, but if you look them in the eyes most of them are just cowards in fancy clothes."

They passed by a pastry cart, and Rhett tipped his head up as he breathed in the sweet confectionery aromas.

"Do you want one?" Chance asked.

"No. I was just enjoying the smell."

"Pick one. My treat."

"Really?"

"Sure," Chance said, counting out a few notes from his now over-stuffed purse. "We're going to have to spend this somewhere."

He brushed Rhett's head and motioned to the vendor for two of the frosted pastries. Rhett chose one with an orange and cinnamon glaze. He held it delicately between his hands.

Chance smiled inwardly as he watched Rhett bite into such a treat for the first time. The boy's eyes lit up, and, though he tried to savor it, much of the glaze ended up on his chin and cheeks. Chance sampled his and couldn't blame Rhett—it was sweeter than anything they were used to eating.

"It's amazing!" Rhett exclaimed. His feet did a little jig as he polished it off and licked at his fingertips.

"For the next few days, you and I are living like we own the Spire," Chance laughed. "Have you eaten any real food yet?"

Rhett shook his head.

"We should probably get something more filling into you or that pastry is going to make you sick."

"But shouldn't we be getting back?" Rhett asked. He looked up at the sun, which was now high in the sky.

"We'll grab something along the way. There's probably a—"

"You! There he is! Right there!" a voice shouted.

Chance looked back over his shoulder and caught sight of the narrow-eyed man gesturing at him, a constable standing at his side.

Chance cursed. "Time to run!"

Rhett looked bewildered as the two men started toward them. "But you won."

"Like that ever mattered. We've overstayed our welcome. Let's go!"

Chance tossed his pastry and grabbed Rhett's shoulder—pulling him into motion. They bolted for the end of the street, the constable's whistle sounding behind them. Chance turned into a larger crowd, weaving between the people. If they were lucky, he figured they could lose them in a crowd somewhe—

An arm shot out and seized Chance's collar, bringing him to a sudden halt.

Chance twisted to try and free himself, but the grip was vice-like. Looking up, his heart sank in his chest. The man wore a slate grey military uniform, and a red cape hung over his left shoulder—the uniform of a duelist.

His fortune had run out.

Rhett hesitated a few feet away, not sure if he should stay with Chance or continue to flee.

"Hold, boy!" the duelist commanded. Rhett turned to stone where he was, and the duelist signaled to the constable approaching that he'd apprehended the runner.

"We did nothing wrong! You have—" Chance stopped as he looked, unbelieving, into the duelist's face. "Ringgold?"

Chance was stunned. His friend from youth stood before him dressed in the uniform of a gentleman duelist. He was older, but still possessed the familiar features Chance knew.

"By Septigone's misfortunes," Ringgold whispered, equally dumbstruck as he recognized his detainee. The constable and man were approaching, and Ringgold gave Chance a look as if to keep quiet.

"That's him," the man said, pointing with his lean finger. "Lock him up! Run him out! But get my money first," he added.

"Hold, sir." Ringgold held his hand up to stop the constable from trying to take him. "What is your accusation of this man?"

"Little thief cheated a respectable game and walked away with our money," the man spat.

"Is that so?" Ringgold asked, turning to Chance. "Is this man's claim founded?"

"I didn't cheat," Chance explained. "He just can't stand the thought that he isn't as clever as he thinks."

"He's a liar!"

"Hold, man!" Ringgold's voice startled the gambler to silence, and his grip on Chance's collar tightened. "You expect to employ the law to settle your gambling losses? As far as I'm concerned, this is a private matter, and should have been handled as such.

"As it is, you've caused a public commotion as well as occupied the valuable time of not only a city constable, but myself. See that you take greater precautions next time with your wagers is all I can say."

"But our money!" the man protested.

"Is of little consequence to the law," Ringgold said flatly. "And, therefore, little consequence to me. I am, however, disturbed by the unrest which this little scrap has inspired. This is Septigonee's Day, and this type of behavior invites ill fortune. You'll both be fined for disruption of the peace."

The man clenched his jaw, but resisted saying anything more. It wasn't wise to argue with a duelist.

"Constable, see to it that man is properly charged. And you," Ringgold said, jostling Chance. "I think you'd be better off where you came from. I'll escort you back to the Basin where you belong."

Chance allowed himself to be led away, with Rhett trailing along behind them. The narrow-eyed man glared daggers at them as they walked, but there was no way he was going to argue further.

Chance cast him a subtle smile which left him steaming.

A duelist, Chance wondered as he was led away. *How the blazes did Ringgold manage that?*

There were few distinctions which could rival it. The duelists were the very elect of the military—the symbols of regency and law with their bright capes and golden rapiers hanging at their hips.

And somehow, Ringgold had made the cut.

When they were a ways off, Ringgold stopped and released Chance from his grip. "Not a minute after I see you and you've already got me playing watchdog again? Goodness, Chance, don't you think I've got better things to do?" he scolded.

Chance looked uncertainly at his friend. Was he serious? But then he caught the glimmer in Ringgold's eye, and the two of them clasped hands firmly together as they embraced.

"I can't believe it," Ringgold said, patting Chance on the back. "This is a reunion I'd never expected. What are you doing here?"

"What do you mean what am I doing here? What are you doing here?" Chance asked. "I thought you were stationed in Madura or somewhere exotic."

"My tours overseas concluded more than a year ago," Ringgold explained. "I'm stationed in the city indefinitely."

"I never thought I'd say this," Chance said, "but I've never seen you looking so smart. And that's saying something."

"The uniform gives me away, does it?" Ringgold smiled. "It's not quite what I imagined when I started out, but it seems they've found a use for my talents."

"A gentleman duelist, of all things." Chance stepped back and gave Ringgold a respectful clap. "I see you traded in for a bigger sword. Still trying too hard to impress the ladies, are you?"

"And you're still ignoring them," Ringgold retorted. "Is that vest meant to make you look fuller? Because I suspect you're just as twiggish now as you were before." He gave Chance's collar a playful tug.

Chance grinned. Even after so many years their wits were still readied at one another.

"What are you up to these days? You're not still apprenticed to the apothecary, are you?" Ringgold asked.

"Alchemist," Chance clarified. "Yeah, I'm still with him. I entered a full partnership this past year. We've even taken on another apprentice. He's right there."

He pointed to Rhett, who was standing awkwardly a ways off looking positively puzzled.

"I see," Ringgold said, catching sight of Rhett. "How fortunate for him."

Chance felt a stab of annoyance as he sensed Ringgold's critical eye on him again. He heard in Ringgold's voice the same distaste for his chosen life as he had all those years before, and it scorned him.

Ringgold didn't know what he'd been through. He couldn't begin to comprehend the struggle Chance had endured to make it even as far as he'd come. Not like Ringgold, whose life was a fine wine—chilled and served in a golden goblet.

All the while, Chance had been left to lap in the gutters like a dog. The familiar feelings of envy rose in his stomach.

"What about you?" Chance asked, turning the subject away from himself. "I take it you're more than a fancy ornament from your stripes. What are you, a general or something?"

"Sergeant, actually," Ringgold clarified. "Don't go trying to fluff me up more than I need to be. It's difficult as it is to stay modest."

"The prodigy's curse I suppose," Chance said with an air of annoyance.

"And the prodigal's envy it seems." Ringgold eyed Chance. "You're not sore with me for earning a few stripes, are you? Envy is a poor badge to wear."

"Not at all," Chance assured him. "Fortune has to favor someone. Why not you? You two have become so acquainted over the years."

Why was it so difficult to speak to Ringgold? He should have been happy to see his old friend, and here they were making jabs and uncovering old sores. Yet, the sting came bubbling up out of him so forcefully Chance couldn't contain it.

"So, have you met anyone since school?" Ringgold asked, trying to change the subject.

"I don't have time to meet people. I've got a living to make."

Ringgold cast Chance an uncomfortable glance. "Have I offended you somehow?"

"Of course not," Chance said, feigning indifference. He felt his cheek twitching. "You have to be around long enough to offend someone."

"So, that's what this is about? You're still upset that I left and you stayed behind?" Ringgold said. "Septigonee's misfortunes, Chance, that was years ago!"

"I'm aware of how long it's been."

"For what it's worth, I'm sorry for leaving you."

"Not necessary," Chance dismissed.

"Still, I'm sorry."

There was a long silence.

"Well," Ringgold said. "This wasn't how I imagined our reunion going." .

"Maybe we're just rusty," Chance suggested.

At that, Ringgold laughed. Chance laughed a little too.

"I've got an idea," Chance said. "I know a pub not too far from here. How about we get a few drinks in us and loosen the rust a bit? Come on. The first round is on me."

Chance jingled the purse he had won from the game earlier, but Ringgold hesitated. He looked over his shoulder, and Chance became aware that there were two other duelists standing stiffly nearby. Looking around, he spotted three more.

"Afraid I can't at the moment," Ringgold apologized. "I'm technically out on assignment. Your little scuffle only gave me reason to pause. I should be continuing along."

"Why is the guard out?" Chance asked.

"Just a precaution," Ringgold said, waving the soldiers on ahead. "It's standard procedure when a crowd of this size gathers."

Chance didn't know if he completely believed that. He'd seen other gatherings as large or larger unattended by military personnel. It was odd to see duelists out in numbers not accompanying members of the meritocracy. They should have been attending social events somewhere, not monitoring the masses.

"It was good seeing you, Chance," Ringgold said. "We should meet up soon for those drinks though. Where are you located these days?"

"Down on Caber Street, in the Basin."

Ringgold nodded. "I'll look you up when I have a free moment." He embraced Chance again and turned down the street. Another duelist joined up with him as they hurried to catch up to the rest.

"Who was that?" Rhett asked, approaching after the duelists were out of sight.

"I don't really know," Chance admitted.

CHAPTER TWENTY-TWO
The Rally

Life is made in many moments, but often remembered
by one alone.

— Alchemical Proverb

When Chance and Rhett arrived at the plaza where they'd agreed to meet the other alchemists, Chance still felt shaken from his encounter with Ringgold. He walked distractedly, and Rhett had had to correct him a few times when he almost walked down a wrong street. But they'd made it, and Chance tried his best to push his feelings to the back of his mind.

He spotted Ashworth beside a makeshift stage amidst the market. It had been erected earlier by a troupe of local performers who'd been gracious enough to share the space with Ashworth, so long as he waited until the conclusion of the troupe's performance of *The Well, O' Well* before he made his announcement.

"Sorry we're late," Chance apologized.

"Quite alright," Ashworth said. "We had more than enough hands this morning. The troupe was particularly accommodating. I think they are under the impression we're partly responsible for the size of their audience."

"Jokes on them." Chance chuckled.

"How was the rest of the festival?"

"It was neat!" Rhett piped up, tugging proudly at his cravat. "Margarete got me this."

"It looks quite smart," Ashworth smiled.

"There are so many people here," Chance observed, glancing at the crowd.

Ashworth nodded. "More than I expected. I knew this troupe had a reputation, but I didn't think they'd draw a crowd like this."

"That's to our fortune then," Chance smiled.

He noticed Ashworth was wringing his hat in his hands and shifting uncomfortably on his feet.

"Relax, Ashworth. You look like you're standing over a lit burner the way you're fidgeting."

"Ah, so I am." Ashworth chuckled as he tried to still himself. He leaned in close to Chance. "I'm just a little on edge knowing at any moment one of these constables could seize me for my meddling."

"You're going to be alright," Chance assured him. "Nobody knows anything about that yet, and when they do Harper's testimony will have already explained everything. Your little break-in will be overlooked. For all we know, the city might give you a medal."

"Really?" Rhett asked.

"No," Ashworth said sternly. "I don't want a medal. And I didn't break in."

"But you weren't supposed to be there," Chance grinned.

Ashworth let out a huff. The play was nearing the end of its third act, when Septigonee's ghost would persuade another maiden not to make the same mistake she did. It was a serious moment, though Chance thought the costuming—with its exaggeration of the gentleman's style—made it a little ridiculous.

He took the opportunity to look for the other alchemists.

He spotted a few gathered together on the other side of the stage. Keller and Sager stood together, with Estrada perched a few paces away. He must have been standing on a box or Chance doubted he would have seen him.

Gravatts seemed to be enjoying the performance from within the audience itself. And he saw Liesel and Welch near the fountain.

"I don't see Foxx or Yoon," Chance mentioned.

"They'll be here," Ashworth assured him.

Chance frowned. *They had better hurry if they're going to make it before the announcement*, he thought.

"Is everything alright?" Harper's voice came from behind a curtain draped behind the stage. He'd been hiding there most of the morning. They didn't want people to recognize him too early.

"Just fine," Ashworth assured him. "How are you holding up?"

Harper peeked out from his hiding place. "I'm fine," he said. "Not long now?"

"Not long at all." Ashworth clasped his friend's good hand. "Chance, you and Rhett best find a good spot to watch before the play finishes. This will be history in the making!" His chest swelled as he said it.

"That it will be," Harper said, and he and Ashworth stepped behind the stage to prepare themselves.

"Come on, Rhett," Chance said. "Let's try over by the fountain."

He led Rhett through the crowd until they reached the plaza's fountain, where they could get a good view of the whole market. It was difficult to push their way through the mass of people.

Again, Chance found himself surprised by the sheer number gathered. He estimated a couple hundred filled the plaza. It was difficult to tell with the festival costuming, but it appeared there were men and women from all levels of society.

It was just the turnout they'd hoped for.

The play ended, with a dramatic wedding ceremony and the merging of two lovers' fortunes. The audience applauded as the performers bowed once, twice, and a third time. Chance felt himself getting eager.

Hurry up and get off the stage already.

Finally, they took their fourth and final bow and retreated behind the curtain, and Ashworth stepped up on stage. The audience continued their applause, assuming him to be a part of the troupe.

"Ladies and gentlemen," Ashworth began, clearing his throat to give time for the crowd to quiet down. "Citizens of this great city. We welcome you to this assembly of the common people—to this open forum on this blessed day, when all walks of life revel in their common bond."

The members of the audience cast each other glances, not quite understanding what Ashworth was getting at. Those nearer the front began to listen more intently, curiosity drawing them in.

"Chance, I can't see," Rhett complained.

"Here, climb up on my shoulders," Chance offered. He knelt down and Rhett clambered onto his shoulders. The boy was heavier than he expected. Chance clenched his teeth and tried to keep him stable.

"It is not by coincidence that we meet today," Ashworth continued, "but by a greater design. I've long anticipated this day, the day when I could share with you one of the most profound successes this city has seen since its birth—a breakthrough unmatched in all of history.

"As is the heritage of all great discoveries, we have been challenged in our experimentation, undergoing much trial and error. Yet, through perseverance we have unlocked a mystery that will revolutionize the very fabric from which our great city is fashioned. It will have a profound impact on the citizens of Hatteras, as it has had a profound impact on the man we gather to hear from today—for it is this discovery which allows him to be with us."

There was a general murmur through the crowd. Chance feared Ashworth was losing himself in the moment.

Enough with the theatrics, Ashworth. Come out with it already!

"You've read the papers. By now you know all about the recent miracle surrounding our Good Captain Harper. Stories have been shared and gossip exchanged, but the figure around whom this miraculous event has taken place has remained unavailable to comment on his own miracle...until now."

Pride gleamed in Ashworth's eyes as he spoke, and Chance couldn't help but smile. For as long as he'd known him, Ashworth had worked diligently in the background, slaving to help those around him with little to no recognition. He was glowing in his words.

Go ahead, Chance conceded. *You deserve your moment in the spotlight.*

"It is with great exhilaration that I now introduce the man to whom this miracle belongs, to give his own account of what transpired, and set straight the details which were so grossly misrepresented these past few weeks. I turn the time over to my dear friend, Captain Willard Harper."

The crowd was at attention as Harper emerged from behind the curtains and exchanged places with Ashworth at the podium.

The crowd's reaction was strange and uncertain. Some applauded and cheered, but it would die quite suddenly in parts of the crowd, replaced by whispered conversations as people pointed to his mechanical arm. He'd left it exposed so that everyone could get a clear look at it. The sun reflected off its metallic surfaces as he came forward.

Chance thought he heard some hecklers somewhere among the crowd too, which he thought a bit odd.

"My fellow citizens of Hatteras," Harper began. "Comrades of our beautiful city. I stand before you today as a man..."

Chance was only half listening. Someone was definitely shouting. He tried to see exactly where the commotion was coming from.

"Hey," Rhett said as he was turned away from the stage. "What are you doing?"

Chance didn't answer. The crowd was making it difficult to see clearly, but he thought he saw people jostling one another left of the stage. Glancing up, he saw Ashworth was similarly distracted by the commotion.

"Rhett, can you see what that is?"

"What *what* is?"

"The people over—"

Something was happening. He saw the crowd shifting, a man in a heavy trench coat pushing his way toward the stage. Ashworth noticed him too.

"Rhett, I need you to climb down," Chance said urgently. He tried to hurry Rhett off his shoulders.

"What? Why? He just started talking," Rhett protested. Other people were noticing the commotion as well. Harper paused in his introduction.

"Rhett, get down!"

The moment slowed in Chance's mind, and all sound seemed to fall away. It was as though he stood in the middle of a bubble, spectating as the world around him turned in slow motion. Chance saw the man reach the front of the stage. Saw him reach into his coat and draw out a device. He raised it high over his head.

Harper's expression turned to horror.

Then the stage erupted in flames.

CHAPTER TWENTY-THREE
The Powder Keg

I still recall that first moment, when I glimpsed the beauty of my accomplishment. Had I then acknowledged the dread which strove to warn me of what could become my undoing.

— Excerpt from *Mechanarcissism*

The explosion knocked Chance to the ground as the stage under Harper tore apart from the inside out, casting debris high into the air. Women screamed and men cried out as splinters of wood rained down upon them. Chance curled up and covered his head with his hands to avoid being pelted by the debris.

Someone kicked him in the face as a man stumbled over him in panic. Everyone was scrambling, and another foot compressed his stomach.

Lifting himself to his feet, Chance scanned the area. Most of the people were fleeing away from the stage, and a few around him were holding bleeding wounds. Others were being pushed to the ground and trampled in the chaos.

A few lying nearer the stage weren't moving at all.

Rhett! The thought struck Chance like the man's foot. *Where's Rhett?*

He searched frantically through the moving figures, shoving his weight back against those who pressed up against him as they fled. He couldn't see where Rhett had fallen.

From somewhere distant he heard whistles blowing. The constables were arriving.

"Rhett," Chance called out. "Rhett!"

He caught a glimpse of the boy, crumpled face-down on the ground. People were tramping over him without a thought.

"Curse it, all, get off him!" Chance shouted as he shoved a man away from the boy, toppling him. He knelt over Rhett. The boy was unconscious, his face peppered with tiny cuts and his hand twisted under him at an odd angle. Part of his cravat was soaked with blood against his neck.

Shouting for strength, Chance lifted Rhett into his arms and moved with the flow of the crowd. He couldn't fight them while carrying Rhett, so he let the mass direct him.

What is happening? he wondered, his mind racing. *And where is Ashworth?*

He glanced back toward the stage. He saw bodies strewn across it among flames and broken wood.

Please don't let one of them be his.

From the sides, he saw red capes sweeping in. The duelists. They formed a perimeter near the stage with the constables on the scene. He thought he spotted Ringgold among them. Chance never thought he'd say it, but for the first time in his life he was glad to see them.

Someone collided into him again, and he nearly dropped Rhett as he stumbled to recover. He had to find somewhere safe, away from the crowd. It was thinning near the center of the plaza, and Chance pushed until he was by the lip of the fountain.

Setting Rhett down at the water's edge, he checked the boy. Rhett was cut up, and he had a nasty bump above his ear. A piece of the stage must have struck him, Chance concluded.

He lifted the cravat and winced. There was a deep cut just under Rhett's chin. Chance readjusted the cravat and pressed it against the wound to stop the bleeding.

"Chance!" he heard someone call. It was Liesel. She limped toward him, clutching her side. Welch was on her arm.

"Liesel, what happened to you?"

"Had a run in with one of the guard," Welch said, not taking his eyes away from Liesel's wound.

"What?" Chance looked at her dumbstruck. "What happened?"

"Tried to arrest me for suspicion or some nonsense, but I gave him more than he bargained for." She smiled and gave Chance a wink, but he saw a red patch of blood where her hand rested.

What is happening?

"Welch, I need a favor," Chance said. "I need you to get Rhett out of here."

"Sure," Welch said, only reluctantly redirecting his focus. "What's the matter with him?"

"Knocked down by the blast. He's got a cut under his chin. He was trampled when everyone started running."

"I've got him." Welch lifted Rhett from the fountain's edge.

"We'll take him back to my place," Liesel said. "He'll be fine there." She grimaced and turned to go.

"You sure you're alright?" Chance asked.

"We'll be fine," she assured him. "What about you?"

"I've got to make sure Ashworth's alright."

"Be careful," Welch said, giving the stage a wary glance.

"And don't let the guard stop you," Liesel warned. "I don't think they're here to help."

She and Welch began a slow walk toward one of the side streets. Chance watched them go until they'd cleared the plaza before setting off in a sprint for the stage. They'd be alright. Welch was a resourceful man—as much as Chance resisted admitting it—and Liesel was a tough girl. She hadn't earned her reputation for nothing.

With the crowd clearing, Chance got a good look at the damage the explosion had caused. Parts of the stage still burned, and the fire had spread to one of the nearby buildings. Men were busy setting up a fire line to bucket water from the fountain to douse the flame before it consumed the whole structure.

Chance ducked into the group of men fighting the blaze as he worked to get closer to the stage. Two duelists stood guard over a line of men lying prone nearby. Most weren't injured, but had their hands bound behind their backs. Chance spotted Sager and Gravatts among them.

Guards still apprehended others.

Come on Ashworth, where are you?

A bucket was thrust into his arms and Chance half-heartedly passed it to the next man. His focus was on the stage. There had been more injured than he'd expected. Perhaps thirty or more, by his estimate. And then, huddled underneath the lip of the stage, he spotted Ashworth.

Dropping a full bucket, Chance dashed to join Ashworth, sliding on his knees to duck into the hiding spot.

"Ashworth! Are you okay? You can't stay here. They'll find you," he warned. "Where is Harper?"

"He's dead," Ashworth shrugged. He said it so matter-of-factly that Chance felt chills run down his spine. It was then that he noticed the fragments of a brass hand cradled in Ashworth's lap.

"We have to get you out of here," Chance urged. He noticed Ashworth's sleeve had been completely burned away. The exposed skin was red and blistered.

"They killed him. Oh, gods! They killed him!" Ashworth was suddenly taken in a fit of sobs, his hand covering his mouth. "How could they kill him?"

Chance suspected Ashworth was in shock.

"There's nothing we can do about it now. Come on. We have to get away from here."

He grabbed Ashworth's shoulder and tried to raise him to his feet.

"They're going to kill us too." Ashworth's voice was calm again—resolved. It sent a second chill down Chance's spine with how quickly his tone had changed. Ashworth spoke as though it wasn't just a probability, but as if it were already happening.

"Not if I have anything to say about it," Chance said, to reassure himself more than anyone else. He removed Ashworth's coat and tossed it under the lip of the stage, then lifted the alchemy case from around Ashworth's waist and slung it over his shoulder.

"They killed him," Ashworth continued to mutter. "They'll come for me next. And then you."

"Ashworth, listen to me," Chance said, grasping the front of Ashworth's shirt and forcing him to face him. Ashworth's eyes were wide and unfocused. "He's gone," Chance said, shaking Ashworth when he tried to protest. "He's gone! You can't do anything about that. Not yet. But, I promise we will. Ashworth, we *will* do something about it."

Ashworth nodded slowly.

"Listen," Chance said, selecting a vial from his carrier and dumping its contents into his hands. He patted it liberally on Ashworth's injured arm. "I need you to run now. See that side street over there? You run to it and don't look back until you're home. Got it?"

Ashworth mumbled, and Chance gave him a firm shake.

"You got it?" Chance urged. "I need to know you understand me."

Ashworth nodded again.

"Alright then," Chance said, letting go of him. He didn't feel too assured, but there wasn't anything more he could do then. He glanced around the edge of the stage. A pair of constables were apprehending yet another man.

"Now!" Chance pushed Ashworth forward. "Run now!"

Ashworth stood and ran toward the street Chance had indicated. His steps fell unevenly, but he was moving. That was enough for Chance.

One of the nearby duelists called out as he spotted Ashworth's flight. "Hey you! Stop! I said sto—*ugh!*"

Chance barreled into the duelist with all his weight as he passed by, knocking the wind out of him as they tumbled to the ground. The duelist's sword clattered against the brick road. A few other guards called out and hurried to assist their comrade.

Chance scrambled to his feet. Now, it was his turn to run.

Choosing a side street in the opposite direction of Ashworth's, Chance sprinted across the square. It was nearly clear now, save for the wounded and those few who had stayed behind to mourn the dead. Chance leapt over an abandoned body and between another two guards trying to cut off his retreat.

A third leapt out at him from a small group—another duelist—but Chance pulled a vial from Ashworth's carrier and chucked it at him. The duelist swept his arm in a wide circle and shielded himself from the vial with his cape. It bought Chance enough time to sidestep him and turn down one of the side streets.

He couldn't resist a laugh, but caught his breath as a constable lunged for him. He seized Chance by the hair, dragging him back painfully. Chance let out a cry, then leaned back despite the pain and raised his foot into the man's abdomen. The constable let go with a grunt, and Chance kept on, sprinting as fast as he could down the street.

Outside of the plaza, it was easier to evade his pursuers. The streets were built narrow, only wide enough for carriages to squeeze past one another, and the roads took unorthodox twists as they mimicked the surface of the cliffs.

After a few tight turns, Chance ducked behind some steps coming down off a residence and tried to catch his breath. It came in short fits. He wheezed heavily, clutching at the wall for support. He wasn't used to running so fast, and it felt as though his lungs were being squeezed in a press—winding like rough gears in his chest.

Is this the feeling Harper was talking about at the meeting? he wondered.

He couldn't be certain if he was still being followed, but he couldn't go further. He was seized by a violent fit of coughing, though he tried desperately to control himself. If a constable was still chasing him his hiding spot would be compromised for sure.

But, none came, and Chance thanked his fortune.

After a few minutes of labored breathing, Chance was able to collect himself enough to stop coughing. He slumped down exhausted in the corner and rested his head against the dirty stone, mouth open to draw in as much air as he could.

What just happened?

He kept asking himself the question over and over, the events running through his head in rapid succession. It didn't make sense. Who would try and sabotage their rally? Who else even knew about it?

And what was the guard doing? Why weren't they helping those who had been wounded in the blast? They seemed intent only on making arrests.

A nagging thought surfaced in the back of Chance's mind—they had been seizing, almost exclusively, those who resembled alchemists.

He thought again of his friend and their peculiar reunion earlier.

"Ringgold... what were you doing here?"

Rising from his hiding spot, Chance stepped into the street and fell in with a few others moving away from the plaza. For now, he needed to make it home. With any luck, the others would have made it out as well.

CHAPTER TWENTY-FOUR
Ringgold's Warning

I must admit, I was a little surprised by the outcome myself.

— Excerpt from *Mechanarcissism*

Neither Chance nor Ashworth spoke much that evening. They sat at their table in a state of quiet shock, the silence passing tangibly between them—or perhaps through them—as they mulled the horrid day over.

They'd made it back safely. The guard hadn't given much chase beyond the plaza. They seemed to be satisfied with those they'd been able to snag near the stage. No word had come of how many in their company had been arrested, but Chance feared the worst.

Rhett was resting in his room. He was alright, though shaken. The cut under his neck was more superficial than it had first appeared, but his wrist was broken. Afraid to take him to a hospital, they'd splinted the break themselves and given him something to lessen the pain.

Liesel had offered to stay and keep a vigil with him after she'd cleaned her own wound, which was also fortunately shallow. Chance hadn't objected. Rhett didn't seem to want Chance near him since Chance had dropped him in the plaza.

Chance fidgeted as a multitude of questions whirled in his head. But he couldn't concentrate on them. Every sound, from the groan of the boards to the way Ashworth's breath leaked out of him, irritated Chance. He couldn't understand how Ashworth sat there so calmly. He wanted nothing more than for the silence to break.

"Care for another cup?" Chance offered as he stood.

"What? Oh, yes. Thank you," Ashworth said, handing his cup to Chance. He'd only drunk it down about half-way, but it had obviously gone cold. Chance poured it out and retrieved a fresh cup for him.

Ashworth stared at its contents when it was returned to him, swirling it around in the cup. "You don't happen to have anything stronger, do you?"

Chance was surprised by the request, but produced a small metal flask from his pocket.

"It isn't anything fancy."

"The worse the better," Ashworth said with a forced smile. "It's not meant for a celebration."

He poured a bit into his cup and offered it back to Chance.

"Nah," Chance said. "You keep it."

"I can't believe he's gone," Ashworth said. "You know, when I administered the spark I half-expected it not to work. But when it did... gods above, I thought we had something."

He took a sip and winced. Chance imagined the mixture wasn't quite what he'd expected. Nevertheless, he kept on drinking.

"That wasn't our first test, mind you," he continued. Now that the silence had been broken, he talked like he was warding it off. "I don't know if I mentioned that to you before."

Chance shook his head and took his seat at the table again. "There's a lot you didn't mention before."

"Willard must have been the tenth person we'd tried the serum on. We started locally—victims of illness or disease mostly—but that didn't last long. In its first stages the serum was too... aggressive. It burned out the victim's body within a matter of minutes. It was too shocking for the families to witness for us to continue."

"How did I not hear about this?" Chance asked. "All this was going on right under my nose, and you didn't think to tell me about it? Or to include me?"

"I'd tried to steer you in that direction a few times. Why do you think I kept trying to get you to befriend Welch?"

"Welch knew about this?" Chance said, louder than he'd intended.

"Not exactly," Ashworth admitted. "But, he worked out a few of the problems we'd encountered along the way—without even realizing what it was we were trying to do."

Chance sat dumbfounded. "I can't believe *Welch* was in on it."

"A part of it," Ashworth clarified. "We kept our circle small for a reason."

"And you didn't think you could trust me with it?"

"I'm sorry about that, Chance," Ashworth said, his voice breaking. He placed a hand on Chance's arm. "I should have brought you in sooner. Especially when I decided to take you on as a full partner, but I didn't know how."

"How about 'Hey Chance, want to work on developing a secret compound with me?' That might have worked."

"I didn't want to tie you to an enterprise that seemed destined to fail."

"So instead, you left me to struggle on my own?"

Ashworth frowned, his brow furrowed as he watched Chance sulk. Rising from the table, he stepped out of the room, only to return a moment later carrying a bound folder made out of two thin wood panels.

He set it down in front of Chance.

"What is this?"

"Your invitation," Ashworth said. "I'm sorry it's a little late, but that's a summary of the research I've conducted during the development of the Aether spark. I was writing it out in layman's terms so that others might have an idea what we'd accomplished."

Chance leafed through the first few pages. Even simplified, it wasn't easy material to follow.

"I wonder what Welch would have to say about you explaining away all his psudo-spiritualism?" Chance mused as he read.

"The Aether isn't spirit," Ashworth said. "At least, not in the way most men think of spirit. How do I explain this?" Ashworth stroked his chin. "It's a reaction—a constant, ever-changing reaction. It reacts with nearly everything that it comes in contact with and changes its nature according to the elements surrounding it. It's just so fine an element we have difficulty perceiving the reaction. But, rest assured, it's there. It's working in each of us right now."

Chance read on, his interest piqued.

"I'd be interested to hear what you think."

"I suppose I could look it over."

"I'd appreciate that," Ashworth smiled.

"And Ashworth..."

"Hmm?"

"I am sorry about Harper."

Ashworth nodded solemnly. "At the very least, we were able to say goodbye the way we should have. Do you know he forgave me? Before I could say anything about our grudge, he forgave me. Unconditionally. I'd never expected that." He shook his head and stared at the table. "I suppose that's one good thing that came from all of this."

They heard Rhett's bedroom door close, and Liesel descended the stairs.

"How's the boy doing?" Ashworth asked, as she came to join them.

"He'll be alright," she assured them. "Still a bit stunned, I think. I finally got him to relax enough to sleep."

"Glad someone was able to," Chance said. "He wouldn't let me touch him. I think he blames me for losing his rat."

"He'll get over it once he's had a little time to recover," she said. "In the meantime, any idea what happens now?"

"Nothing," Ashworth said.

"We can't just do nothing," Chance said. "What about those who were arrested? They were alchemists. Are we just going to forget about them?"

"What can we do? Even if we tried, we wouldn't be able to help. They likely made the arrests to keep up an image of control for the public. They'll let them go after things settle down a bit. Our interfering would only add to the problem," Ashworth said.

"But—"

"I think Ashworth is right," Liesel interjected. "If we show up they'll have us in a cell with the rest of them."

"Then what do we do?" Chance protested. "I can't just sit here waiting."

"Of course not," Ashworth said. "We'll listen. We'll help support the families of those who were arrested. And you'll be busy with my research while Rhett recovers."

Chance paused. "Wait. What do you mean?"

"They know I'm involved," Ashworth sighed. "I announced it publicly when I introduced Willard today. I can only expect a visit from the guard in the next few days. They'll almost certainly arrest me."

"For what? You were as much a target of whoever set off that bomb as he was!"

"For anything they want. All they need is an excuse." Ashworth sipped his coffee.

"But Harper lived!" Chance struck the table with a clenched fist. "Without you he'd have stayed on that slab. You're a hero! The proof is there."

"But our support isn't," Ashworth said matter-of-factly. "So, all I can do is wait for the inquisition to arrive." He swirled his drink in his cup. "I was counting on Willard's testimony."

"But, that doesn't mean you have to be here when they come for you," Liesel said. "You can stay at my place until things calm down. We've got a room in the cellar all ready for you."

Ashworth chuckled weakly. "I appreciate it, but I'm too old to go into hiding. I'd rather confront the problem at hand. And if there are men trying to stop what we're doing, what better way to meet them face-to-face than to be here when they come knocking? If any amount of fortune still favors us, the truth will be on our side."

"Since when has fortune ever favored us?" Chance snapped.

"A time or two," Ashworth smiled. "For example, fortune sent you to me, Chance, when I needed you the most. You've been nothing but a trove of good fortune to an old man near the end of his usefulness. And, as a token to show I've always had trust in your abilities, you'll find all of my research and properties in your name. See? Look there."

He pointed to the bottom of the folder he'd handed Chance. Sure enough, hidden in the corner was a mark—Chance's mark!

Chance was taken aback.

"A precaution, in case something was ever to happen to me," Ashworth explained. "You didn't think I took you on as a partner just to collect rent on the work shed, did you?"

Chance was about to say something when there was a sudden knock at the door. Everyone tensed as they looked to one another.

"Are you expecting someone?" Liesel asked, hopeful.

"Not that I know of," Ashworth said. "Unless..."

"That can't be them already, could it?" Chance asked. He stood up and stepped into the threshold to the entryway. "Perhaps it's another alchemist?"

"Let me get it," Liesel said, rising. "If something is wrong, you two slip out the back. I'll stall them."

"What about Rhett?"

The knock sounded more urgently.

"We'll have to pray they don't think anything of him," Ashworth said. "If they ask, he's not apprenticed to me."

"Alright, stay out of sight," Liesel said, waving them aside. Chance followed her to the hallway, listening intently.

Liesel opened the door.

"What do you want?" Chance heard her say.

"Is this Ashworth's residence?"

"He's not here."

"Is Chance here?"

Chance peeked around the doorway and recognized the man standing before Liesel. He felt his stomach climb into his throat. Without realizing what he was doing, he marched forward and pushed his way past Liesel.

"Chance! I was hoping you'd b—"

Chance struck Ringgold across the face with a clenched fist and sent him stumbling backwards down the stairs.

"How dare you!" Chance yelled. Liesel tried to hold him back, but

Chance pulled away from her. "Out on assignment? You rotten sell-out!"

He swung again, and Ringgold retreated down the path.

"I can explain," Ringgold said.

"Explain what? How you sold your soul to the devils on the Spire? Watchdog? Try hellhound!"

"If you'd just listen!" Ringgold pleaded.

"What's going on?" Ashworth was at the door. Recognizing Ringgold's uniform, he too pushed past Liesel. "What business do you have here?"

"You here to arrest us?" Chance spat.

"No," Ringgold insisted. He cupped his nose, a fresh pool of blood forming in his hand. "I'm here to warn you!"

"Of what?"

Ringgold straightened up and wiped his nose on a handkerchief from his pocket. "Can I speak with Chance, please?" He let out a heavy breath. "Alone?"

"If you have something to say you say it here," Liesel said. "You're not taking him away. He had nothing to do with it."

"It's okay," Chance said. His eyes were fixed upon Ringgold's. "Why don't you two go check on Rhett?"

"Are you sure?" Ashworth glanced nervously between the two of them.

Chance felt like he could take another swing at Ringgold, but he swallowed the urge.

"I'll be alright," he said.

"Very well," Ashworth said. He gestured to Liesel to return inside with him.

"We'll be in earshot," Liesel promised as they closed the door.

A long silence passed between them, and Ringgold continued to mop up his nose. Neither seemed to know where to begin.

"I'm sorry about what happened today," Ringgold said finally.

"The only people I want to hear that from are those responsible for it," Chance said bitterly. "What happened, Ringgold?"

"I can't talk about it."

"You can't talk about it?"

"I don't know."

"What do you mean you don't know? What were you doing there?"

"I told you…" Ringgold began.

"I know, standard procedure or some slag like that, right? I saw you there, dragging away those men and women."

"I was following orders." Ringgold said. "I'm a soldier. That's what I do."

"And what were your orders, exactly? Apprehend as many alchemists as you could?"

"What?"

"The people you arrested—the guard was targeting alchemists."

"I find that hard to believe," Ringgold said defensively.

Chance gave Ringgold an incriminating look.

"Well of course we arrested alchemists," he admitted. "Who do you think set off the blast? We have eyewitnesses who described the man who attacked the stage—some of them from our own guard. He fit the description of an alchemist."

"And what makes you think that? Had on a long coat, did he? A little too much dirt on his face and a couple extra pockets?"

"No," Ringgold spat in disgust. "It wasn't that. Come on, you're smarter than this, Chance. The flask bomb? The extra explosives under the stage? You can't honestly tell me we have no reason to suspect an alchemist was behind it. We had to respond to the present threat, and it was pretty clear what that was."

"Perhaps you don't realize it, but we're not the only ones out there who could make a bomb," Chance said. "Who's to say some nut-job out there didn't get their hands on some explosives? Or what about your precious meritocracy? Do they merit any suspicion, or are they exempt? They're just as capable of an attack like this, and, from where I stand, they seem to have the most the gain from it. But no, you lay hands on the lowest of us the first opportunity you get."

"Still trying to play the martyr, I see," Ringgold said.

"Why would I need to do that? We've got one of those already," Chance said. "You've met him, haven't' you? His name was Captain

Willard Harper."

Ringgold shifted uncomfortably.

"You think we'd sabotage our own enterprise? Our one advocate on the Spire?"

"I can't pretend to know what they'd do," Ringgold said.

"What is that supposed to mean?"

"Enough!" Ringgold shouted. "Please. This isn't why I came."

"Then why did you come?"

"To warn you, Chance!" Ringgold pleaded. "Whoever was actually behind the bombing, the city guard suspects *you*. Ashworth is a key suspect, and with you as his partner that means you're suspect too."

"And what do you think? Am I suspect?" Chance asked.

Ringgold gave Chance a weakened glance.

"Sounds like you've already decided."

"No, I haven't. But they have." Ringgold rubbed his brow in frustration. "You have to believe me. Why else would I have come here right now? I'm putting myself at risk trying to warn you. You have to distance yourself from Ashworth."

"Not going to happen."

"Hell is going to come down upon him, and he'll bring it upon you as well."

"We're ready for it," Chance said. "Perhaps you were too busy to notice, but Ashworth has been there for me all these years. He's the reason I've made it as far as I have. I'm not about to abandon him. That's not my way."

Ringgold pulled at his hair. "Why do you always insist on being such a fool?"

"I'm not the one in costume," Chance countered.

Ringgold face contorted with frustration, and he shouted into the sky. Turning about, he marched down the path and up the street.

Chance watched him go. His head was light and his thoughts bounced about his mind in a frenzy. Yet, even as he took pride in watching his old friend retreat, he was left unsettled by Ringgold's words. He couldn't help feeling that Ringgold was right about one thing.

Hell was coming.

CHAPTER TWENTY-FIVE
Night Terrors

If you want something great, you must risk something
great... and sacrifice something great.

— Alchemical Proverb

That night, Chance slept in his workshop. He usually did when things were troubling him. It was easier to think in his own space, and he suspected Rhett wouldn't have welcomed him into their shared room anyway. The boy needed space of his own to process things.

Chance stretched out on the sofa, his legs draped over the armrest as he clutched a blanket around his middle. His other arm gripped Ashworth's folder close to his chest. He'd tried to read through it when sleep was difficult, but he kept drifting off mid-read.

Sleep was fitful. Not a moment after drifting off he'd be set upon by horrid dreams filled with harsh voices and flames. Everywhere there was confusion as he floundered about, seeking something—but he didn't know what.

And always in the end, was Harper's face locked in his last frightened stare. No matter where Chance fled Harper's face would not leave him, drawing ever closer until Chance felt he would be pulled into those terrified eyes.

Chance started from his sleep, sucking in air as if he'd not breathed before. The folder fell to the ground, its pages scattering wildly. He touched his forehead. It was wet with perspiration, and there was a nasty kink in his neck.

Sitting up, he untangled himself from the blanket and rubbed his arm to dispel its numbness. Retrieving his watch from the chair, he checked the time by the moonlight coming through the window. It took him a while for his eyes to adjust, but he could see it wasn't much past midnight.

Will this night never end?

He slumped over and rested his head over his knees—his arms hanging so the back of his knuckles pressed against the rough wooden floor planks. He wondered if any of the others were resting.

After a few moments, he set the watch back on the chair. On occasions such as this, being an alchemist had its advantages. Rising groggily, he went to his shelves and rummaged in the poor light for a few components to mix a sleep aid.

He'd just finished and was about to drink it down when the sound of breaking glass chimed in the night. He paused, craning his head to listen. It sounded as if it had come from the house. He set his mixture down and went to the door, cracking it slightly.

The lights were still on, casting a weak glow into the courtyard. Was Ashworth still awake? He heard more noise from the house.

Pulling the blanket across his shoulders, he stepped outside. Even with the walkway blocking the breeze from the bay, the night's chill pricked Chance's exposed skin and the hairs on the back of his neck stood on end. The air came in thick and heavy. There would be another storm in a day or two. He could sense it.

He made for the house, hoping Ashworth hadn't partaken too liberally of his flask. It was a rare thing for Ashworth to reach such a low, but there had been a time or two since Chance came under his roof when he'd seen Ashworth surrender control to the bottle.

Chance didn't doubt losing Harper a second time might drive him to it again.

He noticed the potted herbs Rhett had been working on still strewn about the patio. He had yet to finish hanging them. And after his spook at the rally it was even less likely he'd get to them. But they couldn't be left in the cold if they were going to be salvaged. Chance made a mental note to take care of them himself, and to go through and make sure the rest of Rhett's chores were—

Chance dropped to the ground.

Coming around the corner of the house were two soldiers. Even in the dark, their signature red capes were plainly visible. Duelists. They moved guardedly, and Chance was able to scurry back into the shadows of the retaining wall before they spotted him.

"Check the greenhouse," he heard one say.

The soldier entered the walkway and crept to Chance's workshop, stumbling over a few of the discarded plants.

Ashworth had been right. They'd come for him first.

Chance held his breath, then risked leaping over the wall. Neither seemed to notice, and he crawled back behind the bushes that grew along the house.

The second soldier stood guard at the back door, but his focus was on something through the window. Chance heard voices coming from inside and cursed under his breath. They'd already gotten to Ashworth.

He couldn't just sit idly by. He had to do something. Rising to his feet, Chance removed his blanket and held it before him like a snare. He could hear the other soldier rummaging through his workshop.

And I just cleaned it up!

Chance crept toward the soldier, his bare toes gripping the cold cobblestone, until he was just behind him.

"Hey," Chance whispered.

The soldier spun around so quickly that Chance was nearly caught off guard himself. His hand had already gone for his sword, but Chance threw the blanket over him and seized him in a bear-hug before he could draw the blade fully.

Chance struggled against the man's strength, but the soldier was too much for him. The blade came free, and Chance ducked back as it swung wildly over his head. The soldier ripped the blanket off just as Chance grabbed a spade from the ground. He swung as hard as he could, and the spade connected across the soldier's head.

The man fell to the ground in a graceless heap.

Chance crouched low, listening if anyone had heard the scuffle. The voices inside and the sound of rummaging from his workshop could still be heard. No one seemed to have noticed the scuffle. He pulled the soldier over to the side of the house and rested him up against the wall.

"Why don't you just wait here a moment?" Chance said. He took the man's sword and tossed it into one of the bushes. "You won't need that."

Chance crept up underneath one of the windows. He could make out perhaps a half-dozen voices inside. Rising up slowly, he risked a peek.

There, kneeling in the middle of the kitchen were Rhett and Ashworth. Their hands were bound and their mouths gagged with cloth. Around them stood a half-dozen red-caped soldiers. Chance noticed the decoration of their uniform was different than the man he'd grappled with.

Ducking back down, he took a moment to think over the situation. Ambushing a single soldier was one thing, but how was he going to take on five?

Somewhere in the distance, an explosion echoed through the city. It made the window shake, and Chance craned his head in the direction it had come.

What is going on? Chance wondered. *Would this miserable day never end?*

He crouched down against the wall again. He needed a plan. Something to thin them out and give Ashworth and Rhett a chance to get away. He thumped an open palm against his head.

"Think, Chance," he told himself. "Think."

He remembered the rain gutter alongside the house. It led close enough to one of the upstairs windows. With any luck, he could weasel his way in, and from there...

The feeling caught Chance in the gut before he registered just what was wrong, and he felt his shoulders sink on their own accord. He sighed in unconscious acknowledgment; the workshop had grown quiet.

He was turning around to look when the pommel of a sword caught him across the side of his head and everything went dark.

CHAPTER TWENTY-SIX
Flames in the Night

What chaos I have caused. What lives I've laid aside in my
pursuit. Each name and face has become its own eternal haunt.

— Excerpt from Mechanarcissism

C hance came to his senses slowly, his head throbbing where he'd been struck. He tried to lift himself from the floor, but his arms were tied behind his back and his legs bound. Blinking, he looked around him. He was in the kitchen, surrounded by soldiers.

Ashworth was next to him. He gave Chance a look of concern, but Chance shook his head. He would be alright. Rhett sat quietly, staring wide-eyed at... nothing. His gaze was fixed on a point beyond all that was happening around him.

Chance risked a glance at the soldiers. They appeared to be waiting on something. One of the men stood where the table had been, reading from what Chance recognized as one of Ashworth's many notebooks. He had a severe look as he surveyed its pages. From the stripes on the exposed sleeve of his uniform Chance discerned he was a man of rank.

One of the soldiers whispered something to leader, and he nodded before closing the book. His eyes fell on the three of them. At his signal, another soldier pulled the gag from Ashworth's mouth.

"You're the one they call Ashworth?" he asked.

"That is my name," Ashworth replied. "And who are you that we have the pleasure of hosting you and your friends this evening?"

"I'll be asking the questions."

"Yes, but it would make answering them much easier if I knew who was asking them." Ashworth met the man's glare with calm reserve.

"Lieutenant Vanzeal," he said finally.

"I wish I could offer you a seat, Vanzeal, but you've overturned most of the furniture already."

"You've been making enemies, Ashworth," Vanzeal said, ignoring Ashworth's grim humor. "And not the kind you should like to attract, I swear to you."

"Why don't you just tell us what you're here for, and dispense with your theatrics?"

Vanzeal sneered. "You think this a performance?"

He gestured to one of his guard, and Ashworth was delivered a rough kick from behind. Ashworth fell face-first on the floor, unable to catch himself.

"I swear to you that it is not."

Ashworth rose up again with difficulty. His lip was bleeding, but he held back any evidence he was in pain as he looked into Vanzeal's eyes. "You still haven't answered my question," he said calmly.

Vanzeal frown deepened. He didn't appear to admire Ashworth's resolution. "We have some questions to put to you," he said.

"Does it usually take a break-in for your guard to get answers to a few questions?"

"Consider yourself under investigation."

"I'm honored."

Vanzeal nodded to another soldier, who stepped up and read from an official-looking document.

"Charles Ashworth, you are suspected of being in connection with recent events surrounding the late Captain Willard K. Harper and are subsequently charged with, but not limited to, the following: interfering in matters of the meritocracy, tampering with government property..."

Ashworth chuckled at that. "He was considered property?"

"...inciting subversion against the meritocracy among the citizens of Hatteras, and lastly, the death of the now late Captain Willard K. Harper."

At the last one, Ashworth's expression fell.

"I did not kill Willard Harper. Where is your evidence?"

"It is not my responsibility to educate you," Vanzeal said, stepping forward. "Only to make an example of you. To be completely transparent, I really have no interest in these charges. What I'm more interested in is just how you came to be tied up in all of this in the first place. If you were able to educate me, we might dispense with the less pleasant aspects of my employ and be on our way."

"What do you mean?"

"Names," Vanzeal said sharply. "I want the names of every associate you've had in connection with the development of this 'Aether spark.'"

He held up the notebook and pointed at the page where he'd been reading, as though it contained exactly what he was referencing, though Chance was fairly certain there was no mention of the spark in that particular notebook. Ashworth would never have been so careless with his secrets.

Which means someone squealed, Chance realized.

"Why?" Ashworth asked. "So you can hunt them down? Accuse them of crimes they haven't committed? Even had I any help, as a man of honor I wouldn't turn them over to you. As a man of honor yourself, how could you ask such a thing of me?"

"Honor?" Vanzeal chuckled. "Oh no, my poor old man. I hadn't taken you for an idealist. How refreshing a find in such a dismal part of this city. But, surprises aside, you're looking at this the wrong way. You see, I have no interest in honor. That, perhaps, is why I'm the one here in your home and not some other. I suggest you dispose of any preconception that I am restrained by any of the rules you hope to hide behind. One way or another, you'll tell us what we need to know."

"Your threats mean nothing to me."

"Who did you work with?" Vanzeal asked, more severely.

"I worked alone."

"We both know that's a lie."

"It's the truth."

"Is it?" Vanzeal frowned. "And what of these two? Your apprentices. They know nothing of your work?"

Chance glanced at Ashworth.

"Nothing," Ashworth said resolutely.

"You're sure about that?" Vanzeal grinned. He signaled again and a soldier seized Rhett's arm, dragging him across the floor and away from Ashworth. Chance struggled against his bonds, but another soldier shoved him back.

"What are you doing?" Ashworth asked.

"Making threats," Vanzeal said. "I thought we'd already come to that understanding. Or was I unclear?"

Rhett was lifted to his feet and positioned next to Vanzeal. It was haunting how unresponsive the boy was to what was happening around him. His eyes remained locked in their distant stare.

"This is your apprentice, is it?" Vanzeal asked. "Seems like a nice boy. Innocent. Not yet fully aware of how cruel the world can be."

"He's wise enough to recognize your kind," Ashworth said.

"Is that so? I'm glad to hear it." He knelt down to Rhett's level, forcing Rhett to look at him. "Is that true? Do you know what kind of man I am?"

Rhett stayed silent, his jaw rigid and eyes fixed on a spot on the wall.

"How did you get this?" Vanzeal asked, touching the bandage on the side of Rhett's neck. The boy flinched.

"He doesn't know anything," Ashworth insisted.

Vanzeal flashed Ashworth a look as he seized the boy by the neck and pressed his thumb down on the bandage. Rhett let out a whimper.

"I said he doesn't know anything!"

"Then who does?" Vanzeal demanded.

"No one knows; it was my secret!"

"You expect me to believe that?" Vanzeal jerked Rhett's neck forcefully, and Rhett cried out in pain. "Who did you work with?"

Chance writhed against his bindings and strained to shout through his gag. White-hot rage rose up inside him, and he felt every desire to tear Vanzeal to pieces for what he was doing.

"Enough!"

The whole room froze. Ashworth was standing. He may have been old, but in that moment Chance had never seen him more imposing. He was the embodiment of resolve as he stared down Vanzeal. Vanzeal's grip loosened under that stare.

"You call yourself a gentleman?" Ashworth asked. "A man of merit? It takes more than brute strength to demonstrate power. You *are* transparent, Vanzeal. Hollow, straight through. Anyone can play the villain, and you have taken that path of least resistance. If that be the case, then I am proud to be resistance in your path. You're nothing more than a common thug hiding behind the favors of more cowardly men than you."

Vanzeal's gaze was cold. His lip twitched as he tried to summon words to rebut Ashworth's, but he was at a loss.

Chance grinned. It was satisfying to see the man shamed. He doubted Vanzeal had had many men stand up to him in such a bold way.

Vanzeal's hatred seethed from behind his eyes, and before anyone realized what had happened his sword flashed from its sheath with the sound of spring and gear.

Ashworth fell backward against the wall and gasped for air as his collar turned red. Pitifully, he slumped down to the floor.

"Gather everything from his laboratory," Vanzeal barked as he sheathed his blade and thrust Rhett away. "Every notebook, ledger, and receipt. We take it all."

His men seemed as alarmed as Chance, but they were roused to action at Vanzeal's words. They disappeared into the laboratory and soon began emerging with piles of Ashworth's records.

Chance hardly noticed their movements. His eyes were locked with Ashworth's, watching him struggle for breath. Tears came to Ashworth's wizened face as he looked to Chance and Rhett. He tried to say something, but the words wouldn't come.

Finally, his head bowed forward, and he was still.

Chance couldn't believe what was happening. He glanced at Rhett, whose expression was now one of stark terror. How would he recover from this? Chance wondered. How could he himself?

"What of the apprentices?" one of the soldiers asked. The men were about finished with the laboratory. Vanzeal looked at Chance and Rhett as he pulled on his gloves.

"As long as we've got the man's research, they're unnecessary. Leave them."

Chance focused all his anger on Vanzeal. It seethed through his wet eyes, directing every known curse toward the man. Vanzeal seemed amused when he saw it. His lips turned up in a half-smile.

"Burn it," he ordered.

The soldiers emerged from the house, arms full of the evidence they'd seized. Vanzeal marched down the steps from the front door and was met at the bottom by Ringgold.

"Sir," Ringgold greeted.

"Sergeant Ringgold. A fire has started in the house. Maintain your perimeter guard and see to it that it doesn't spread to any of the neighboring buildings. I'll have my men alert the fire brigade."

"What about those still inside?" Ringgold asked.

"My men are all accounted for," Vanzeal said with a businesslike air as he pulled on his gloves. "There is no one inside."

"But I thought—"

"Sergeant," Vanzeal snapped. "There is *no one* inside that building. Now, you've just received an order to maintain your perimeter, and nothing more. I suggest you see to that."

"Yes, sir."

Ringgold stood straighter, unable to entirely hide his concern. Vanzeal peered at him sideways before signaling for his company to follow him. Ringgold's jaw clenched as tightly as his fists as he watched the first curls of smoke issue forth from the windows.

The flames were already climbing the walls and smoke billowed thick overhead. Chance and Rhett shuffled as best they could down the tight hallway. It was difficult with their bindings, but they managed to crawl into Ashworth's laboratory and Chance kicked the door closed behind them.

It wasn't going to hold back the flames for long; the place was a tinderbox. But, perhaps, it would buy him time to loose their restraints.

In the corner of the room lay the body of their mutt, a wound at the base of her neck where she'd been stabbed. The sight of it both infuriated and sickened Chance. If fortune favored him and they survived, he swore to himself he'd see Vanzeal pay.

He wrestled for a while with the gag around his mouth, rubbing it against the floor until it came loose. He sucked in what clean air he could. It wouldn't be long before the house was full of smoke.

Crawling to the table, Chance kicked against its leg.

"Rhett!" he shouted. Rhett looked at him despite his obvious fear. "Rhett, help me!"

He gave the table leg another furious kick, and it came loose some. Rhett seemed to understand what Chance was trying to do. He shuffled to the other leg and began kicking. After a few seconds, the legs broke and the table fell forward.

It crashed on the ground, spreading its contents across the floor. Chance rummaged through, looking for something sharp enough to cut his bindings.

The best he could find was a large magnifier. Stomping on the glass with his heel, he shattered it and grasped one of the larger pieces. With the edge, he dug at his bindings.

The room was getting hot. Smoke seeped through the cracks in the door and flame came through the top, licking the ceiling eagerly.

"Rhett! Get back."

Rhett shuffled away from the door, pressing himself up against the broken table. His eyes were fused open, unable to look away from the horror that was clawing for them. Chance worked harder with the glass, scratching at the stubborn cords until his palm bled.

The flames caught the curtains near the door and quickly spread to the bookshelves. Chance threw the shard of glass away and seized another with what he hoped was a better edge, but still it wouldn't cut.

The flames crept across the shelves around them, the compounds catching fire and making small explosions. The flames turned a rainbow of colors, releasing thicker plumes of tinted smoke.

The realization flashed across Chance's mind that this was how he was going to die. Of all the vices he'd been criticized of, none of them had managed to do him in. Yet these men—strangers in uniform—had condemned him to this hellish end.

He let out a laugh in the face of his misfortune and dropped the shard of glass.

"Rhett," he yelled in as humorous a voice as he could muster. "Rhett, remember the potted plants? You never did get to hanging them, did you?"

Rhett looked at him like he was crazy, but he did look at him.

"I'm glad you didn't waste your time with them," Chance said. "Would have been an awfully poor use of the day."

It was all he could do. He couldn't shield Rhett from the fear, but he could distract him. At least for a moment or two before the end.

A piece of the ceiling fell, crashing nearby and sending a spray of embers into the air. Chance felt them sprinkle his back, and he rolled to put them out. This was it. He shuffled up next to Rhett as another ceiling piece fell, this time on Ashworth's reading chair. It caught flame almost instantly.

"Close your eyes, Rhett," Chance said. "Don't look at it." He grasped Rhett's hand, and the boy clenched his eyes closed. Chance did the same.

The two of them listened to the room fall apart around them. The crackling and combustion of chemicals sounded otherworldly. He heard laughter, and voices.

At least there would be company in hell.

But suddenly, Chance felt a hand on his shoulder, and he opened his eyes in surprise. Kneeling over him was Ringgold, singed some by the flames, but shielding himself with his cape. Oddly, it hadn't caught fire.

Drawing his blade, Ringgold cut Chance's bonds before moving on to Rhett.

"What's wrong with him?" Ringgold asked.

"He's in shock," Chance said. He was in shock himself as he watched Ringgold check the boy. "How did you get here?"

"Through the back. And that's our way out," Ringgold cut Rhett's bonds. "Help me with him!" They lifted Rhett into Ringgold's arms, and he draped his cape over the boy. "Through the kitchen," he instructed.

"It's engulfed! We should go out the—"

"The guard will seize you as you leave. There's no one guarding the back. Now go!"

He shoved Chance forward, and Chance dove through the flames. It was difficult with the pieces of burning wall and ceiling now littering the floor, but they stumbled through.

In the hall, the heat was nearly unbearable. The air and smoke burned Chance's lungs, and he tried to hold his breath through it. The flames licked at their arms and legs as they ran until they made it to the back door.

Before he left, Chance glanced where Ashworth's body lay. Flames had engulfed the area, and debris from the ceiling had buried the body. Chance's felt the pull on his heart at the sight. It was a poor burial for such a man.

"What are you waiting for?" Ringgold shouted impatiently.

Chance grimaced, then with a solid kick he burst the door open and the three of them spilled out into the courtyard. Ringgold set Rhett down on the ground. They patted their singed clothing, taking in full breaths of cool, fresh air.

"You can't linger here. Someone may still come," Ringgold said between breaths. "Leave while you can." He stood up and pulled his cape across the more singed portion of his uniform.

"Hold on," Chance said, rising to his feet. A thought had come to him. He hurried into his workshop and grabbed his carrier and what other necessities were readily visible. Ashworth's notes were still strewn across the floor, and he scooped up as many pages as he could, stuffing them into his carrier.

When he returned, Ringgold had managed to get Rhett to stand, though he was still coughing violently.

"Are you good?" Ringgold asked Chance.

"We'll be alright."

"Then go, Chance." Ringgold put his hand on his shoulder. His eyes were pained. "I'm sorry for all of this."

Chance stared at his friend with a mix of emotions. Ringgold had saved them, but he'd also been one of the men responsible for what had happened tonight—for Ashworth's death. He found it difficult to meet Ringgold's gaze. So many thoughts and questions ran through his mind, yet, despite how desperately he wanted to voice them, he couldn't find the words.

"You don't need to say anything," Ringgold assured him.

Chance nodded reluctantly and led Rhett away from the house. He heard the sound of bells as the fire brigade approached. Clambering over the retaining wall, Chance looked one last time at the place he'd called home all these years. It was eerie, set in the dancing red flames.

And there, silhouetted against it all, stood Ringgold in his uniform.

CHAPTER TWENTY-SEVEN
The Informant

Don't be overzealous in your scheming.
Fate schemes far better.

— Alchemical Proverb

S toddard sat at his desk, fidgeting with his pen. It hovered impatiently over a fresh page intended for a missive to Elector Sinclair. He'd been milling over what to say for half an hour, but his mind wouldn't apply itself to this particular task. Not while he awaited news about the raids.

They were underway that very moment. He imagined the great minds which had been tucked away forgotten in the underbelly of the city, now rediscovered and collected.

Tomorrow, he would have quite the team at his disposal.

He'd already dismissed Donovan. There was no need to include him in the more sensitive details of tonight's activities. He would fill him in as necessary, but no more. The less he knew the better.

As much as Stoddard resisted admitting it, there was a certain thrill to the past few days—a powerful sense of influence he'd not anticipated. Where before he'd been a quiet and studious man, he had been thrust into an entirely new world in which swift action and bold decisiveness were rewarded.

What was more incredible was that he felt himself a major piece already. He'd established himself as naturally as Sinclair's own son. Perhaps more so.

A faint knock sounded at the door, and Stoddard straightened.

"Come in," he called. The door opened and in hobbled one of the most unpleasant looking men Stoddard had ever had the misfortune to meet. He was bent forward, draped in a tawdry coat. He walked with a pitiful limp caused by a visibly withered leg.

"Oh," Stoddard frowned. "It's you, Mr. Skaggs."

"Just Skaggs, if you don't mind," the man said as he closed the door behind him and approached the desk. "Not a real fan of all your formalities, you might expect. Seem a bit hollow, don't you think?"

"Very well. Have a seat. Would you care for some tea?"

"No, I wouldn't," Skaggs said. "How about you and I ignore the kindly gestures as well? The less time you keep me the sooner you can stop pinching that nose of yours, and I can get back to my miserable self."

"Very well," Stoddard consented. "Business then."

"Where's my payment?"

Stoddard retrieved a small wallet from his desk and slid it across the table. Skaggs snatched it up and leafed through its contents, fingering the edges of the notes in quick succession.

"Oh, now that's a sight I've been missing something terrible," he sang. "Shame about that poor fellow and the flask bomb though. Don't expect his share would end up in my cut, would it?"

"I'm only paying you what we agreed on," Stoddard said. "Nothing more."

"Ehh, I suppose a man like yourself needs something to stuff his pillows with. What poor sod did you get to perform the grisly deed?"

"One only slightly more desperate than yourself."

"And what'd you tell him to get him to do it, I wonder? Tell me, because it's been tickling me all day..." Skaggs leaned in close over the table, and Stoddard recoiled at his proximity. "Did you even tell him about the other explosives?"

Stoddard's expression remained unchanged.

"Thought not." Skaggs leaned back and let out a raspy chuckle. "I had you figured. I knew I did. Right from the first moment we met I says to myself, 'there's a man to watch out for.' Just like me, you're not above getting your hands dirty."

"The only thing we have in common, Mr. Skaggs, is where our interests intersect at the point of your employ."

"What? It make you uncomfortable to admit it?" Skaggs grinned. "Oh, there's no denying it, Doctor. There are no clean hands here."

"You're taking liberties with your tongue," Stoddard growled. "I suggest you remember what your place is, and don't overestimate our relationship. There are hundreds of your kind willing to do what you do."

"Perhaps," Skaggs shrugged. "But can they deliver? It's hard to know just looking at a man, isn't it? First impressions aren't always what they seem, especially when the right pressure's applied? Am I right?"

"Most are too sold on the idea of self-preservation, you see, and likely to prove a liability come a problem. But not me," he said shaking his head. "Me, I can't sink no lower than this, so what have I got to hold onto? I've a reputation, don't I? I deliver on it, don't I? And my reputation, as filthy as it is to men like you, is still a reputation. So, don't go try and get all high and mighty with me, Doctor. You hired me, so here I am."

Stoddard clenched his jaw. Taking a letter from the desk, he tossed it to Skaggs. "Your next assignment then."

"Oh? There's another?" Skaggs's eyebrows arched as he picked up the envelope. "I thought you'd be looking for the first opportunity to sweep me under that rug of yours."

"Believe me, I am," Stoddard said. "But, I have another task I'd like you to perform—one that will require a larger investment of time, and your increased discretion."

"The doctor loosens the leash? Now, that's an interesting turn of events," Skaggs mused. He slipped the wallet into his dusty coat and sat himself down on Stoddard's desk, lifting his withered leg up on the corner to rest it as he read.

Stoddard's temple pulsed as he glared at the leg, but he said nothing.

"It's a list of names," Skaggs said. "What do you have in mind for me then?"

"I need you to come into the trust of any free-merchant alchemists you come in contact with. Those are the names I've managed to collect so far, but I want you on the street pulling any information you can about any significant work being done."

"Alchemists again is it? Why might a mechanist like yourself have such an interest in them, I wonder?" Skaggs asked.

"That's for me to understand, and for you not to concern yourself with."

Skaggs scratched his chest as he thought the offer over. "It might take a while to ingratiate myself into the likes of their company. Lot of conversations. Lot of time. And time's a precious commodity, Doctor. Difficult to trade. Difficult to place a real value on. Now I've got some, but how to know what to exchange it for..."

"Price is the least of my concerns," Stoddard said. "You'll have enough for your drunken frolics for months to come."

"Won't that be nice?" Skaggs grinned condescendingly. "So kind of you."

"Provide me useful information and I'll double what you've got in your pocket now."

"Do you know what the problem with money is?" Skaggs asked, rising from his perch and circling the table. "Once you've got some, it loses its novelty. I've already enough here to enjoy my little life of foibles for some time. Well, as much as I can enjoy them as I am."

He patted his bum leg.

"You're asking a hefty chunk of my time. Not to mention more risk. People aren't too keen when you go snooping around into their secrets. Why wouldn't I just cut my losses and enjoy myself as I am?"

"Is there something you're trying to get at, Mr. Skaggs?" Stoddard asked, tapping his pen. "Or do you just enjoy wasting my time?"

Skaggs stroked the patchy stubble of his cheek. "I want a leg. A new one. And not just some piece of scrap you throw together. I want what that old captain had—all the bells and whistles and what have you."

"You're in no position to negotiate with me!" Stoddard shouted.

"Oh, but I am!" Skaggs barked back, rising up to match Stoddard's boldness. "I'm a man who's seen the little game you've been playing—how low you're willing to stoop to get what you want. I've seen the blood on your hands. That don't give me some position to negotiate?"

Stoddard tightened his grip around his pen. The tip cut through the paper and the ink bled through in a small patch around the point.

"Listen here," Skaggs continued. "I've spent my life trying to escape the infernal pain of my leg. But it doesn't matter how much I drink, it's only pissed away in the end. I wake each and every morning with this blight of a limb dragging along behind me!"

He pulled up his trouser leg to show the wither more clearly. There was little evidence of muscle under the skin, and the curve of the bone bent outward.

Stoddard gazed long at the man. He didn't like people making demands on him, but Skaggs had been useful in uncovering the alchemist's plots. They were known for their secrecy, and yet Skaggs had penetrated their shroud—in a matter of days, at that. Stoddard wasn't ready to discard him entirely.

Not yet.

"That's quite the expense," Stoddard said, setting down his pen.

"No, it isn't. Not for you. High and holy mechanist. Miracle worker that you are. You benefit from this as much as I do. You're living for the chance to cut into a man, build on him and what—just like the good captain. I see it in your eyes, turning over in your mind. You're already thinking of what you could do with me."

Or to you, Stoddard brooded.

"You presume too much," he said.

"I see an opportunity for you and I to profit off each other," Skaggs insisted. "And if I'm never going to see another one like this I'd be a slagged fool to settle for anything less. Besides, if I don't deliver, you're not out a bit in the end. It's service for service rendered."

Stoddard pressed his fingers together as he rolled the arrangement over in his mind. He despised the man; the way he spoke drove through

Stoddard in a way that left him feeling as though his mind were exposed. Skaggs was certainly no ally. It wouldn't take much, Stoddard imagined, for Skaggs to turn on him. A better prospect was all he'd need.

It was best to keep someone like Skaggs close.

"Done," Stoddard said finally.

"Done," Skaggs repeated, and grinned an unrestrained grin. "Now, which of these poor sods is first on my list of friends to be?"

CHAPTER TWENTY-EIGHT
The Aftermath

*Fortune, in both her guises, is a fickle mistress. Don't hold
either too close to the heart.*

— Alchemical Proverb

C hance and Rhett hurried through the streets, avoiding the main roads and keeping to the shadows as best they could. The moon wasn't high, and the night played tricks on their vision. Shapes of men rose up and faded around them with every step. It was all Chance could do to keep Rhett from crying out whenever they were spooked. It was all he could do not to cry out himself.

They moved aimlessly through the dark, running from the dread which stalked close behind them. In time, their wits returned and Chance was able to set his mind on the one place he knew he and Rhett might be received.

Liesel's.

It was the safest place he could think of. He hated the thought he might bring the dangers which followed him onto her doorstep, but he didn't know what else to do. He needed help, and he knew she would understand.

Fortunately, there were very few people out. The two of them hustled across the open street and slipped into the back alley which ran alongside the Pub & Brawl. Even just entering the familiar alley brought relief, and Chance breathed deeply again after what felt like hours. He glanced up and down the alley to be sure they weren't being observed, then knocked.

The door opened immediately and there stood Liesel, still in the same clothes.

"Chance?" She looked surprised, and then her expression fell. "Oh, no..."

"Sorry," Chance began. "I didn't know where else to go."

"Of course," she said, collecting herself. She ushered them inside and shut the door, latching it behind them.

She wasn't alone. Simon and Welch were both there, sitting at the table. Welch had an odd assortment of parts and pieces laid out before him, and was tinkering with some gizmo. Simon sat with a tall glass in his hand.

Serge was there too, standing rigidly by the wash bin.

As Chance and Rhett entered, all three straightened up and cast each other quick looks of concern.

"Why don't you two have a seat?" Liesel told Chance and Rhett, fetching each a stool.

"What happened?" Serge asked.

"They came," Chance said. "Just like Ashworth said they would."

"Who came?" Simon asked.

"The guard. They burned the laboratory—with us inside. We were barely able to make it out alive."

"What of Ashworth?" Welch asked, concern welling up in his voice.

Chance shook his head, and their expressions fell.

"I'm sorry," Chance said. "I'm probably wrong putting you all at risk right now, but I didn't know where else to go."

"Don't you be sorry. This is the best place you could have come," Liesel assured him. "Just look at the state you're in."

For the first time, Chance became aware of his condition as he looked down at his shaking hands. Patches of skin were red and blistered, and he wasn't without a few cuts and scratches. Rhett was in a similar state.

"We'll have to take care of this before we do anything else," Liesel said. "You two have a seat. Simon, fill a bowl with some water, will you?"

Simon did as he was asked.

Chance pulled his stool up to the table while Liesel checked Rhett. Welch remained quiet where he sat, even more absorbed in his gizmo.

"What's kept you all up tonight?" Chance asked.

"It's been an eventful night for everyone it seems," Serge said.

Chance was about to ask what he meant when Liesel concluded her examination.

"Rhett, I'd say you're one of the luckiest boys I know. Just a few bumps and scratches. I'm going to have Simon here clean you up a bit, and we'll have you back to your chipper self in no time."

She led him over to a stool by Welch, and Simon brought over the bowl and a fresh rag. She handed Rhett a piece of stick candy to suck on as Simon began working, then turned her attention to Chance.

"Now, let's see to your arm."

Chance cringed as Liesel carefully removed the charred fragments of his sleeve.

"This is becoming a common thing," Chance said, "you patching me up like this."

"I've dealt with more than my share of injuries in my lifetime. I don't mind." She pressed a cold, wet rag lightly against his skin. Chance clenched his teeth. "Sorry," she said.

Chance opened his carrier and handed her a flask.

"Use this," he said. "It will help with the pain."

Liesel uncorked the flask and soaked the rag in the mixture before reapplying it to the burn. It stung for a moment, but the pain dulled some.

"Do you have any idea who was behind it?" she asked.

"I'm not sure. It was a whole company of duelists who raided the workshop, so there's no doubt it was someone from the Spire. The lieutenant's name was Vanzeal."

He didn't mention Ringgold.

Liesel frowned. "I don't recognize the name. Simon? What about you?"

He shook his head. "Never heard of him. But it wouldn't take me long to find out who he is, if he's anyone of consequence."

"I think that would be a good idea," Liesel said. "It's likely they're connected."

"What's connected?" Chance asked, and Liesel glanced at Serge. "What's happened?"

"Your laboratory wasn't the only one attacked tonight," Serge said. "Keller & Foxx were hit only an hour ago."

"Gentleman duelists," Welch chimed in. "Just like your place."

"Are they alright?"

Liesel hesitated.

"They killed Keller," Simon said. "Apparently he put up a pretty good fight when they entered his shop. Blew up most of the street before they finally got him. We're not sure what became of Foxx."

Chance sat stunned. He'd never pegged Keller for the fighting type. He leaned on the table and pulled at his hair. "This is insanity."

"No," Welch said "It isn't. There's logic in it."

"And what is that?"

Welch sighed and turned back to his gizmo. "I don't know yet."

Chance rolled his eyes. "I don't suppose there's more where that came from?" he asked, pointing to Simon's glass.

"I've got something, sure." Liesel went to the cupboard. "What would you like?"

"Just bring them all," Chance said.

Surprisingly, she did, and without lecture. She produced glasses for Welch and Serge, too. Welch declined, but Chance poured himself a glass with a bit from each bottle. They all gave him a queer look.

"What?" he said. He capped the last bottle and swirled the mixture before taking a gulp. It raked his esophagus with a fury.

"You sure that's a good idea?" Simon asked.

"I never mix reason with my drinks," Chance said, shuddering as he shook off the drink's unpleasantness. "And as Ashworth once said, this isn't meant for celebration."

"I suppose this means the business with the Aether is through," Liesel said, pouring herself a glass.

Chance grimaced. A knot tightened in his stomach, and it wasn't just the alcohol. It was the familiar feeling of being beat. He was sick of that feeling. Hiding in a bar, drinking to help ward off the pain of another failure. It was cowardly.

When had he become such a coward?

A vivid image of his academic board came to his mind—standing there as they read his expulsion. He'd said nothing as it happened. He'd given no defense for himself. Just walked out when they'd dismissed him.

Why hadn't he said something? Yelled at them? Cursed them to Septigonee's Well for how quickly they'd turned him out on the street?

And now, the same thing was happening again. He was being turned out and left to salvage the scraps of his life. And just as before, he was expected to fail.

But he hadn't. He was still fighting. He'd been knocked down, but he wasn't about to roll over. He gulped down another mouthful of his mixture, his eyes watering as he shook it off. He had nothing to lose.

"No, it isn't," he said resolutely.

Everyone looked up at him. Even Rhett, who'd been staring blankly at his stick candy as it grew sticky in his hand.

"They've done this before," Chance explained. "They've tried to take my life from me. Destroyed my prospects. Stripped me of any friend I had and left me to fend for myself in the gutters. I won't let them do it again. They may have taken my home... they may have taken my work... but Ashworth's work is still here."

He held up the wooden folder Ashworth had given him.

"Ashworth's work on the Aether spark was his life, and as long as it's alive then Ashworth isn't gone. They may have killed him, but I won't let them pick his bones for their profit. This is Ashworth's work, and I'm going to see it through."

"Well, if this wasn't a war before, it certainly is now," Serge said, looking animated.

"Not now," Simon warned.

"You heard him," Serge said. "This is a cause worth fighting for."

"Against whom? We don't even know who did this."

"Yes, we do," Serge insisted. "The meritocracy—"

"Yes, but *who* in the meritocracy?"

"All of them! They're all guilty!" Serge bellowed.

Simon rolled his eyes.

"I'm not one to back down from a fight if it shows its face," Liesel said, "but I'm also not for picking one with someone I don't know anything about. Half of a fight is sizing up your opponent before you get into the ring. I agree with Simon, now is not the time."

"The fight has begun already. Whether you want it or not, it's come," Serge protested. "And they're the ones who started it."

"We're just a few Basin-dwellers," Simon shrugged. "There's not a lot we can do."

"Maybe not us here alone, no," Serge admitted. "But, what if we had twenty more? Fifty? A hundred? What if every Basin-dweller finally stood up and said they'd had enough?"

"It'll never happen," Simon frowned. "It's basic survival instinct. Everyone's looking out for themselves and their own."

"But, tonight is just the kind of thing we could use to spur people from their apathy. Help them recognize that it's not just about a shop or two burning. This is about every injustice we've been forced to endure from the meritocracy."

"It's not enough," Simon said. "Someday it might be, if we're desperate enough, but it's not enough right now."

"We can't just sit it out!" Serge ranted. "Not forever."

"But right now, we have to," Liesel said.

"Why? Why can't we fight back?"

"Because they'd obliterate us," Simon said. His voice shook. "They'd seize us the moment we stuck our heads out, and we'd spend the rest of our lives wasting away in the Steep before they gave us a second thought. Well intentioned as you are, Serge, we can't win this one. I've been on their side of the line before and seen it play out countless times. They're hoping we'll rise up to fight. They're goading us so that they can destroy us."

"But they can't pretend that what happened to Keller—what was done to Ashworth—was legal!"

"They'll say it was an accident," Liesel shrugged.

"We know it wasn't," Serge insisted. "The bombing at the rally. The raids. They're connected. The duelist's involvement proves that."

"But we have no idea who exactly is behind all of it." Simon said. "Whoever it is, they've kept out of the spotlight."

"Hold on," Chance said. A thought flashed across his mind. "Maybe they haven't."

"What?"

"Maybe they've been in the spotlight this whole time. We just didn't realize who we were looking at."

Chance rushed out of the room and returned bearing one of the newspapers from the bar. Flipping it open to one of the latest accounts of Captain Harper, he jabbed a finger at one of the names.

"Right there."

Liesel craned her head to get a better look. "Stoddard?"

"His name comes up in every article they publish about the captain," Chance explained. "I bet you anything he's tied up in all of this mess."

"He's a scientist, not a gentleman of the meritocracy," Simon said, stepping forward to read over Liesel's shoulder. "He wouldn't be able to order the duelists around like we saw tonight."

"I didn't say I know how he's involved," Chance said. "And honestly, I don't really care. He's the best lead we have to finding out what's going on."

"But you can't be sure."

"Did they have proof Ashworth was guilty?" Chance asked. "What about Keller? If they can hunt their leads down based on a few assumptions and loose connections, then I will chase this one."

"He's right," Serge said.

"So, what are you going to do?" Liesel asked. "You don't know anything about him. You don't even know where he is."

"I'll figure it out."

"Even if you do, you can't just show up at his door. The people involved are going to be just as intent on finding you as they were Ashworth. They know you were his partner."

"Perhaps Margarete could do some uncovering for me," Chance proposed. "She knows her way around the meritocracy better than anyone. It wouldn't take her long to find out about him."

"You'd put her in harm's way?" Liesel asked.

"I'm not going to force her," Chance said. "I'm not forcing anyone to join me on this. This was Ashworth's unfinished work, and now," Chance swallowed hard, "it's passed on to me. Not anyone else. Margarete loved Ashworth as much as I did. She can make the decision for herself."

There was a moment's pause as the small group considered Chance.

"I still have a few connections in the navy from my militia days," Simon offered. "Perhaps I can figure out who's been directing the duelists. They're not exactly military breed anymore, but maybe someone knows something."

"Alright, see what you can find out," Chance said. He was getting excited. It wasn't much, but having a start was something.

"And that's it?" Serge said. "We're just going to snoop? What about action?" He slammed his fist on the table.

"Serge," Chance said. "I know how much you want this to be about your little movement, but this is about our friends and what happened here tonight. It's not some bandwagon movement to hitch yours to."

"But what about—" Serge protested.

"He's right," Liesel affirmed, cutting Serge off. "It's not everyone's fight. Not yet. We need information. We can't go running off halfcocked."

Serge looked like he was going to say something more, but Simon took him by the shoulder and drew him out into the hallway. They conversed privately, Serge gesturing wildly while Simon talked what Chance could only assume was reason.

While they spoke, Chance took another vial from his carrier and applied a thick salve to his arm. Liesel helped him wrap it in a fresh bandage.

He didn't like the idea of using others, especially asking Margarete to spy on the meritocracy. It was clear that anyone who might be suspected of knowing anything concerning the Aether spark was in very real danger, but he didn't know what else he could do.

He understood what Serge felt; Chance didn't like waiting around for something to happen either. But, like Simon had said, until they had a clearer idea of what they were up against they couldn't do much.

Chance picked up Ashworth's folder and flipped it open.

"Is that it?" Welch asked. "The recipe for the Aether spark?"

"No," Chance sighed. "Just some notes Ashworth gave me."

"About the Aether spark?"

Chance nodded. "But they're incomplete. His notebooks were taken by the duelists, so I'm not even sure I can reproduce it. I need to figure out who was working on this with him."

Then something dawned on Chance's mind, and he felt foolish. Ashworth and Welch were close friends. He'd almost begged Chance to go to Welch before. Why not now?

"Welch... you worked on this with him, didn't you?"

Welch shrugged. "I think so. I'm not sure with what part exactly. Ashworth never told me what he was working on. Only shared bits of whatever was puzzling him at the time."

Chance cursed silently. Welch really was one of the most useless people he'd ever met.

He thought about who else he'd heard Ashworth speak about. He couldn't remember anyone specifically, but Ashworth had said that those who'd helped him would be at their secret meeting. Thinking back, Chance pictured the room again and where everyone was sitting. He remembered Keller hanging around Ashworth throughout the night—even coming to Ashworth's defense during Estrada's outbursts.

But Keller was dead, and Foxx was unaccounted for. For all he knew, that was as dead an end as any. However, it was another lead, and Chance knew he couldn't be stingy with the leads he had.

He needed to find Foxx.

It was clear when Serge reentered the room he wasn't content with the general decision, but he didn't push it further. Instead, he poured himself a drink, mumbling under his breath.

He was about to take a sip when there was an urgent knock at the back door. Everyone jumped, and Rhett, who had been quiet the whole meeting, let out one of the most disturbing sounds Chance had ever heard—like a squeak.

The pounding continued until Liesel unbolted the door and cracked it. There stood a man Chance didn't recognize. His breaths came in heaves, and he leaned heavy on the doorpost.

"It's burning," he said. "Gravatt's place is burning!"

"Are they alright?" Liesel asked.

"I'm not sure. I didn't dare get too close, not with all the soldiers up and down the street like they were."

Serge slammed his glass down on the table and cursed. "Let's go then. Maybe there's still time to help."

He and Simon donned their coats and hurried out the door.

"I'll come with you," Chance called after them.

"You shouldn't be out right now," Liesel insisted. "What if someone recognizes you?"

"I'd rather be out trying to help than waiting for more bad news."

Liesel looked conflicted, but Chance saw her waver. "Fine," she said, though it obviously wasn't sitting well with her. She grabbed her coat from the peg by the door. "We'll all go."

"Welch, will you watch Rhett?" Chance asked.

"Sure I will."

"Thanks. I owe you one."

Chance donned his carrier and their little entourage slipped out the door and hurried down the street toward Gravatt's, hoping beyond hope this was the last ill news that would reach them that night.

CHAPTER TWENTY-NINE
Only Need One

Just try to bar progress and you'll discover, quite acutely, how unwaveringly fate rolls forth. There's no sitting still when we feel the clock tick.

— Excerpt from *Mechanarcissism*

"Is it much further?" Stoddard asked as he followed the warden down a staircase into the bowels of the prison.

The Steep, as it was known, was carved into the cliffs below the Spire and housed the worst of society's rejects. A single, long stairway below the capitol acted as the main entrance.

Stoddard's back ached from the cramped descent. "I don't think I can take much more of these stairs," he complained. "How much further?"

"Not far now," the warden said. "It's better than the seaside entrance, mind me. Those swells are tough to make, even with a good team to row ya. Likely to end up on the rocks. I'd brave these steps any day over that. Mind them here, though. They're a bit damp."

The descent was abrupt, twisting through tight tunnels of rough-hewn stone. The further they ventured, the more claustrophobic Stoddard became. Hatteras was a crowded city, but this place was tomb-like and put him in a grave mood.

The warden held a small gas lamp to light their way, and Stoddard had to keep close to watch his feet. The man reeked of decomposing earth, blended with heavily soiled cloth. Stoddard tucked his chin into his neck as he walked, answering the man's incessant and mundane commentary with short grunts to minimize his breaths.

"As I was saying, I've been there a few times, what with my father being the boiler-man and all. I says to any man, Pendambu is the most beautiful of all the colonies I ever set eyes on. And, I don't mind going nose-to-nose with any man who argues with me about that. Trees as tall as buildings, they have, with thick palms you could wrap a man in. Their buildings ain't but a hut compared to the one's we've built here in Hatteras, o' course. I never seen anywhere builds like we do."

He thumped his chest heartily, and Stoddard turned to avoid breathing in the cloud of soil which was knocked loose from the man's shirt.

"And the food," he continued. "Stews and rice that can cook a man's innards before he realized what he's eating. The lads and I made sport of it whenever in port. Spoon for spoon, just like a drinking game.

"Shame though, I never did set my foot on land myself. Always had to stay on the ship. Was for the better, I suppose. Nothing but filthy barbarians the lot of them. I wonder to myself sometimes, why is it that the very worst of people get the best of things? I wonder it often, I do."

Stoddard doubted the man had ever considered what the land looked like before Hatteras had been built up. Likely it looked much like Pendambu sounded, a beautiful coastal point with its cove a safe harbor leading up into the luscious gardens of the terraced cliffs.

Industry marred the land, and this Stoddard accepted as a worthy consequence. It may not have been as appeasing to the uneducated eye, but Stoddard appreciated the beauty of what man had created—the satisfying mark of progress.

Perhaps that was the price of enlightened man; there was no innocence in paradise.

"Bah. Just Septigonee's luck, I figure," the warden dismissed. "Who am I to think after more than I've been given?" He spat at the ground and hit the wall, the thick mucus turning Stoddard's already weak stomach.

"Ah, Vanzeal!" Stoddard said with great relief as he and the warden turned a corner at the bottom of the steps and came face-to-face with the lieutenant.

He stood in a space only slightly larger than the stairway, where perhaps a half-dozen men could have gathered uncomfortably around the small table. He was accompanied by another duelist of his company, and Stoddard and the warden greeted them in turn.

"I was worried I wouldn't get the opportunity to speak to you tonight," Stoddard said.

"I was instructed to remain until you arrived," Vanzeal said. He didn't seem keen about his post, but he'd remained nonetheless. Stoddard decided it best to be brief and to the point.

"Where are the prisoners being held?" he asked.

"They'll all be just there. Behind those doors." The warden gestured down the corridor to a few of the nearby cells.

"I'd like to speak to the man, Ashworth, if I can."

"Ashworth?" the warden asked, glancing over his ledger. "No record of anyone here by that name. Unless he goes by another?"

Stoddard frowned, looking unsure. "There's a mistake then. Ashworth should be here. Vanzeal?"

"I'm afraid he's right," Vanzeal said matter-of-factly. "Ashworth isn't here."

"Then, where is he?"

"Dead," Vanzeal sneered. "The fool resisted arrest and ended up burning down his whole laboratory, with him and his apprentices still inside. A tragedy, of course, but what's done is done."

Stoddard was beside himself.

"And how, then, am I supposed to question him about his work?" he asked. "He was the entire reason your services were called upon! Sinclair assured me you were the man for the job, and you... you've completely botched the one task assigned to you. I've never heard of such... incompetence!"

"Excuse me?" Vanzeal said. His voice had gone from moderate disinterest to cold intensity. He straightened, his eyes growing brighter as he squared off with Stoddard.

"The fact is," Stoddard continued, bordering hysteria. "Without putting too fine a point on it, you've single handedly destroyed the very thing I sent you to secure! And quite possibly crippled the work Sinclair employed you to safeguard."

"We seized all of his records and journals," Vanzeal said. "Any information you were looking for will be among them."

"I don't think you've grasped the gravity of the situation," Stoddard's voice rose in his throat. "My work—my life's work—hung on the edge of a knife these past twenty-four hours, and you very well may have destroyed it all. When Sinclair hears about this—"

"Let me stop you there before you go on," Vanzeal said, stepping forward so quickly and so close that Stoddard stumbled back against the wall. "Let us get something *perfectly* clear. I don't work for you, Doctor. I work for Elector Sinclair—and he knows how I work. I've been in his favor for years, and no probationary gentleman-hopeful like yourself has a prayer of disrupting that. If I were you, I'd look to your own affairs. They'll be the ones in question after tonight, not mine.

"Now, I have something to say to you on a personal note," Vanzeal continued. "I don't care in the least what your opinion of me or my men is. You are inconsequential, and after this meeting I won't consider you again. However, I'll give you some friendly advice—you've been noticed, and like a schoolboy in his father's cellar you've drunk in that moment deeply. Be careful you don't let it go to your head. This game can be far more costly than I think you realize."

Vanzeal donned his gloves and saluted the warden.

"I'll have my men deliver the evidence we seized to your office," he said to Stoddard, not looking at him. "After that, I consider my duties fulfilled." He ruffled his cape, and, with a gesture to his second, stormed out.

The warden looked concerned, but did not dare say anything.

Stoddard was pained. He was furious with Vanzeal, and suddenly quite terrified of the prospect of facing Sinclair. After tonight, what did he have to offer? He'd gambled and come up with a poor hand.

Yet, it was still possible there were others who knew something about Ashworth's work with the Aether—partners, associates and the like. There was only one way to find out.

"Are you alright, sir?" the warden asked. "You don't look so well."

Stoddard had turned white, and not from the cold or smell, but he snapped out of his thoughts. "Was anyone else imprisoned from Vanzeal's raids?" he asked.

"A few, yes. And we still have the lot they seized off the streets after the bombing yesterday afternoon."

"Let me see them."

"Certainly." The warden beckoned Stoddard to follow, leading him to one of the barred iron doors. There was nothing more than a slit in it the width of a man's eyes. "Mind you keep your distance. They're a sorry lot, but we don't want to risk them trying anything rash while you're in there."

He untied a string of keys from his belt, unlocked the door, and pulled the heavy bolt back with a resonating clang.

"Away from the door!" he barked through the slit, then swung it open.

Stoddard entered the room behind the warden, its occupants pulling away as they did. Surveying their faces, he had the impression this lot wasn't the type who was going to try anything. These were common citizens, not criminals. Their every characteristic testified of the fact.

"I'm looking for information regarding Captain Harper," he said. "Does anyone have any information regarding what happened yesterday? Or of events concerning him these past few weeks?"

"Speak up if you do," the warden said. "This might be your one chance to gain some favor back with a gentleman before judgment."

There was silence in the group. Stoddard half-expected as much. Vanzeal's abilities proved less than satisfactory once again.

"What of the man Ashworth? He was a free-merchant from the Basin District. Anyone know anything of him?"

Again, there was silence, but one of the men glanced up when Stoddard mentioned the name. Stoddard narrowed his eyes at the man.

"You have something to say?"

The man nodded his head. "Yes. I knew him."

"Quiet!" another from the group hissed. The warden stepped forward and swung his club at the man, beating him back until he was clinging to the wall.

"How?" Stoddard asked the first, ignoring the interruption.

"He was an alchemist, like myself. We were competitors, but in different parts of the district."

Stoddard approached the man and knelt down in front of him. "And you have information on him? What he produced? What he was working on?"

"I think so," the man said. "I'm not sure what you want to know, but I know enough about him that I can guess at why you're interested."

"And why is that?"

"The Aether spark," he said in a low voice.

Stoddard's whole body came alive again with the words. So, there *were* others who knew.

"What's your name?" he asked.

"Gravatts," the man said.

"And what do you know about this Aether spark?"

"A bit, I think. I wasn't part of its development, but I allowed Ashworth to rent space in my laboratory from time to time. And I helped him get through customs when he needed something he couldn't purchase."

"How did you do that?"

"I've special connections within the city."

"And why would a businessman like yourself assist a competitor? What did you gain from it?"

"It didn't put me out any," Gravatts explained. "It was a simple investment, and, had things worked out, I'd have had a share in the payout. I'd have been stupid not to do it."

"Is that all you know then?" Stoddard asked. "His shopping list?"

"No," Gravatts hurried. "I was there at his secret meetings—when he organized the rally."

"Can you identify who else was at those meetings?"

"Sure I can. There was Keffer, Yoon, Keller, Foxx. All alchemists from th—"

"All names we're already aware of," Stoddard lied. He needed to appear a step ahead. Keep the man desperate.

Gravatts swallowed hard. "Sager was there." He gestured to the man who'd been beat. "And Liesel and Welch. They aren't alchemists, but they were close to Ashworth. She owns a pub. And his apprentices, Chance and Rhett. They were there, too. They'd know more, I'm sure of it."

Stoddard sighed. Those leads had already been snuffed out. Vanzeal had seen to that. They were nothing more than charred remains under a heap of rubble.

"None of this is useful or new information," Stoddard said. "Unless you know about the Aether itself I'm afraid I'm losing interest in you."

"Well, I..." Gravatts stuttered as he tried to think of something valuable to share.

"Of course," Stoddard frowned. He turned to the man who'd been beaten. "I don't suppose you have anything you'd like to share, do you?"

Sager stayed quiet, though he cast a look at Gravatts which could pierce flesh. Stoddard rose again and returned to the hallway, with Gravatts' pleadings following him out.

The warden bolted the door behind them.

"Warden, I wonder if you'd be willing to see what other information you can get from that man. It's possible he does know something that could be useful."

"Certainly," the warden said. "We're keeping them another week or so. I'll give him special attention."

"You're planning to release them already?"

"Of course. No need to hold the lot of them. Got orders to clear out as many prisoners as we can now that Selaria is getting bolder. There's been rumors of war, and if that happens then we'll have more bodies than we can hold. Besides, it's pretty clear this lot is innocent. We only need one, after all."

"One?"

The warden took a few steps further down the corridor and pulled a slit back on one of the doors. Stoddard hesitated, but at the urging of the warden he peered in.

Curled up in a corner of a solitary room sat a tiny man. He was bent low over his knees, his arms resting on the floor dejectedly. His eyes were red and his cheeks glistened as he let out the occasional sniffle.

"We only need one to keep the peace," the warden explained. "We'll have the papers print his confession when we release the others, and then he'll be forgotten."

"Who is he?" Stoddard asked.

"Who cares?" the warden shrugged. "The sorriest of the lot they dragged in. Pitiful, isn't he?"

Stoddard watched as the tiny man wiped his nose on his shoulder, then rested his head on it before closing his eyes.

"Yes," Stoddard agreed. He stepped away from the door. Something sat unsettled in his stomach.

The warden eyed him. "You sure you're alright?"

"I need to go."

"I'll see you out," the warden offered.

"No," Stoddard said, perhaps a little too vehemently. "I mean... I know my way back. I just need some space to think. Thank you, Warden."

He seized one of the extra lamps from the table and began the cramped climb back to the surface. The atmosphere of the place was getting to him, the walls were too close for comfort. And that man in isolation...

Stoddard picked up his pace until he was almost sprinting for the surface.

CHAPTER THIRTY
Sifting Through the Wreckage

When working with fire, it's best to have some insurance.

— Alchemical Proverb

Chance wandered through the burned-out building that had once been Foxx and Keller's Volatile Commodities. What had been a busy laboratory now resembled nothing more than the charred remains of a cooled furnace. He walked solemnly among the ruins, grave under the weight of the awful, lingering silence.

Everywhere lay evidence of the skirmish. Walls lay torn open from what Chance could only conclude was Keller's last stand. Portions of the building still stood, however, despite the damage. Its heavy beams supported the skeletal frame of the rooms, through which Chance could see a starless sky.

Once the fires had cooled, the city had conducted what they deemed a 'thorough investigation' and pronounced the structure condemned. Oddly, no squatters had taken up residence in the abandoned space yet. Perhaps the tragedy was still too near, the proximity to death more uncomfortable than the streets.

Whatever the reason, Chance found much of the place undisturbed. He hoped there might be some clue left behind—a page or two of research, perhaps, spared from the ravenous inferno. Anything that might give him some direction.

Climbing a set of metal stairs, he stepped carefully between collapse and debris, kicking loose pieces aside. He would stop and stoop over a pile of rubble to pick out the blackened cover of a ledger or notebook. Too often the pages were burnt and nondescript, and he tossed them aside and continued on.

As much as he hated to admit it, his search was turning up scrap.

Clearing a spot for himself, Chance sat on an overturned door and rested his head on a crumbling wall. He hadn't slept well all week. He'd grown used to being an outcast growing up, but he'd never been a fugitive. Always he feared eyes upon him. Every moment he anticipated soldiers in red capes leaping from the shadows, flashing their clockwork blades and dragging him away to the Steep.

And, whenever his mind turned to them, he thought of Ringgold.

He hadn't heard anything more from or of him—whether he was alright or if he'd been found out for helping them escape the fire. Chance hoped Ringgold was okay, but then he wished every curse he could muster to come down on his old friend's head as images of the red flames danced before his mind.

Just as quickly, he'd hate himself for thinking that way.

One thing he'd decided on, however: he had no desire to see Ringgold ever again.

Perhaps he was being ungrateful. Ringgold had risked his life rescuing them from the fire. But, he'd also been part of the group who lit the fire in the first place. Whatever debt would have been owed his old friend was negated, in Chance's mind.

As he sat there on the door, bouncing back and forth between his feelings, his gaze caught the corner of a charred bookshelf. The wood was withered and frail, but behind one of the shelves he saw the exposed corner of something metal. Chance crawled over and flipped the bookshelf over with a strained grunt. Sure enough, a small lockbox was attached to the underside of one of the shelves.

The lock itself didn't look too thick. Tearing a pipe from one of the walls, Chance swung at the lock with all of his might. His strike missed, carving out a chunk of wood in the bookshelf. He tried again, this time delivering a blow to the box itself, but to little effect.

After a few minutes of swinging, he struck the lock squarely, cracking it open with a distinct metallic ping. Tossing the pipe aside, Chance knelt and opened the box. Inside, he found some loose leaves of paper, a notebook, a brass tube of rich red lipstick, and a ring.

Strange, he thought as he sorted through it. He set the rest aside and examined the notebook. It was bound in thick leather with a locked brass band across the front—similar to Chance's alchemical notebook.

He wanted to try and open it then and there, even thinking of trying his luck with the pipe again. He decided against it, however, considering the state of the lockbox. Instead, he would ask Liesel, or perhaps Welch, if they had a way to open it without causing damage when he visited them next.

He was just tucking the notebook away in his carrier when he was interrupted by a voice behind him.

"What are you doing here?" a man not much bigger than Chance asked. He stood in the doorway, surprise in his eyes. From his apparel, Chance decided he was just another vulture there to pick the bones of the dead.

"Just having a look around," Chance said, closing his carrier and turning toward the man.

"This is Foxx and Keller's private property," the man said. "Anything here belongs to them."

"Don't worry," Chance shrugged, kicking a board aside and sorting through another pile. "I doubt either of them will mind anymore."

"It's still their property."

"They're dead. Their remains are scattered around this building somewhere. If you're lucky, maybe you'll find them."

"I'm not here to sort through their stuff. I was employed by Foxx and Keller to safeguard their property."

"I believe you when you say you worked for them," Chance said. "But, I don't believe for a second you're here on goodwill. They're dead. I hate to break it to you, but that means whatever job they gave you is obsolete."

"I don't care." He seemed upset. "I'm still supposed to—"

The man caught sight of the open lockbox and lost his voice. A look of concern flashed across his face for a fraction of a second before he regained his composure, but Chance noticed. This man was no ordinary vulture. He was there with as much intent as Chance was.

"You're not just here to guard property, are you?" Chance asked, rising slowly. "What is it? What are you looking for?"

"Nothing," the man said. He took a step into the room, and Chance slid his carrier into his coat.

"You're lying," Chance said. "You know how I know?"

They circled one another, stepping carefully over debris as they sought out sure footing. The man watched him, the tension winding tighter with each passing second.

Chance smiled. "Because we're both telling the same lie."

The man reached into his breast pocket, and Chance was barely able to close the distance before he produced a wheel lock pistol. Chance collided with the man and the gun fired into the crumbling ceiling.

The two of them stumbled backwards over the debris as Chance scrambled to wrest the gun away. He managed to wriggle it out of the man's fingers and toss it aside. It fell amongst the rubble.

Chance tried to pin the man's hands, but he flailed so wildly Chance couldn't maintain his grip. The man managed to turn himself over and seized a pile of loose ash, thrusting it into Chance's face as he pushed him away.

Chance snapped his eyes closed, but he was too slow. The dry ash raked at them, and the man squirmed out from under him. Scrambling to his feet, he fled across and out of the room.

Chance knelt there, blinking the ash out of his eyes. He caught sight of the pistol and seized it as he rose to give chase.

At the stairwell, he caught up to the man turning the corner on the lower platform. Chance leapt and landed on him, sending the two rolling the rest of the way down. They came to rest at the bottom of the stairs, sprawled in an unceremonious heap.

Both of them were slow to recover. Chance felt the many tiny aches from the impacts down the hard metal stairs, but he managed to push himself up off the ground. Crawling on the man again, he seized his arm and held his own against the man's throat.

"Who sent you?" Chance shouted. "Tell me, or I swear they're going to find you stuffed in that lockbox come morning!"

"Please," the man choked. "I'm just a hired hand."

"Fancy pistol for an errand boy," Chance said, waving the wheel lock in his hand. "Who're you working for?"

"I can't say."

"Tell me!" Chance pressed harder into the man's throat. He coughed as he fought to speak.

"Foxx—" he gasped, "and... Keller."

"Liar!" Chance pressed harder. "Foxx and Keller are dead."

"Not... Foxx," the man coughed. Chance eased up on the pressure and the man sucked in air.

"What do you mean, not Foxx?" Chance asked. "He's still alive?"

"Yes. He's in hiding. That's why he sent me. He wanted Keller's notebook. I need to get it back to him before it's too late. He's leaving tonight!"

"How do I know you're telling the truth?"

The man pulled a slip from his pocket, and Chance seized it. "It's a receipt, for a ship out of Hatteras. He had me purchase it for him earlier today. It's his ticket out of here."

Chance looked over the receipt. Sure enough, the ticket was for that evening, made out to a Mr. Smith. Chance wasn't certain the man's story was true. But then, Chance had little else to go off of.

It was enough. Chance released him, and the man stood up slowly, nursing the bruises on his throat.

Even with the good news, Chance was frustrated. He'd thought he'd met with the face of his enemy, not some hired hand. But, his hopes were vain. Whoever else was after the Aether spark, Chance still had no sure leads.

Yet, there was a small light to follow. If Foxx was still alive, then the secrets of the Aether spark weren't entirely lost. Not yet.

"You said he's skipping town?"

The man nodded, glancing at his watch.

"Where is he now?"

"Why should I tell you?" the man asked.

Chance raised the gun and leveled it at the man's heart. "Because I'm getting impatient."

CHAPTER THIRTY-ONE
Tracking a Foxx

When the winds blow, some take to ground while others raise
fresh sails.

— Alchemical Proverb

Chance raced down the street, his coat flapping behind him. Foxx was skipping town, but there was still time—still hope to find help with Ashworth's research—and Chance wasn't about to lose the opportunity.

Turning a corner, he caught sight of the platform the hired man had described. There, pacing between the iron buttresses at the top, was the figure of a man. Chance sprinted to the platform, climbing the spiral stairs three at a time as he pulled himself up the railing. At the top, he doubled over, short of breath, but he didn't allow himself time to recover.

"Foxx!" he called out.

The man slowed to a stop, hesitating before he turned around and considered who was calling out to him. He looked tired, his eyes heavy and bloodshot, his hair wild and ungreased. He stood with a slump in his back and his arms hung low at his sides.

Chance gulped down air.

"You have a message for me, boy?" Foxx asked.

"Foxx..." Chance struggled to speak around his gasps. "It's me. Chance?"

Foxx didn't appear to recognize him.

"Ashworth's apprentice?" he tried. "I need to talk to you about Keller. About why they came after him."

Foxx's head bowed, and he glanced out over the platform. "How did you know to find me here?"

"This." Chance held up the notebook and the other articles from the lockbox, and Foxx's eyes widened. "I think you and I had the same idea tonight."

Foxx advanced. "May I?" he asked, holding out a hand.

Chance obliged, and handed them over.

Crouching down against one of the support beams, Foxx studied the ring and lipstick in his hands. He chuckled weakly before pocketing them. He produced a key on a chain around his neck and, with a twist, the lock across the notebook clicked open. He flipped through the first few pages slowly. His eyes were intense as they searched—for what, Chance didn't know.

"Useless," he said after a few minutes. He closed the book and set it down beside him. "Keller guarded his secrets in life; it seems he'll keep them forever in death."

"Foxx, I need to talk to you," Chance said.

"Be my guest," Foxx said, gesturing to the spot next to him. "I'm not going anywhere just now." His head lolled back against the pillar, and he gave Chance a stare. "You know, apart from that man I sent back to fetch this, I haven't spoken to anyone for a week? Bloody pain, being dead. I suppose he was the one who told you where I was?"

Chance nodded.

"I thought as much," he said, to the air as much as to Chance. "This is why most partnerships are so bloody pointless. No matter how much you want to, you never can count on the other party to come through on their end of the bargain."

Chance frowned. Since they'd first been introduced early in his apprenticeship, he'd always viewed Foxx with admiration. He was a charismatic figure with a pleasant wit that could make any situation feel lighter than it was. But, the man before him now resembled very little of the Foxx Chance esteemed.

"Foxx," Chance said. "Foxx, what are you doing?"

"Right now?" He shrugged. "Running. I'm supposed to be dead. I have a reputation to uphold."

"But you're not dead."

"I *am* Keller's partner, in life and in death. I'm doomed to share his same fate."

"That's why I need to speak to you. You were Keller's partner."

"I am Keller's partner!" Foxx turned on Chance with such energy and passion that Chance jumped.

"You are," Chance corrected himself.

"Partners in life... and partners in death." Fox squeezed his eyes shut, and Chance saw tears forming on their edges.

"That's what I need to ask you about. I need to know more about your work with the Aether spark."

"It wasn't my work."

"But you were with Keller. You must know something about how it was created?"

"Not a lick. Not a single iota." He clasped his hands together nervously. "It's his work. His genius. I'm afraid all I've ever amounted to was an investor." He held out his hands helplessly and shrugged. "It's all I ever was."

"But I need to find out how they did it," Chance said desperately. "There has to be something he left behind—some clue we could follow to recreate it."

"Anything left of his work is right there," Foxx gestured to the notebook. "But I'm sure you already know that it's written in gibberish. Only Keller would be able to understand what he wrote."

Chance knelt and picked up the notebook. He didn't bother looking inside. He knew what he'd find.

"Look, I know what it's like to survive a friend," Chance said. "I'm feeling the same loss. But, how can you turn your back on them so quickly? He's your partner. How can you ignore what was going to be

Keller's greatest work?"

Foxx choked back tears as his eyes grew redder.

"Because," he managed to say. "I'm a coward. I know I don't look it, but that's what I am. Keller was the quiet visionary, and perhaps without me he might not have had the success he did, but without him I'm just hollow noise—a charlatan. I've got nothing of myself."

"But his work is still here," Chance tapped the notebook with his finger. "His dream is still alive right here. And so is Ashworth's. If we try, maybe we can figure it out. Maybe we can fix this."

"I'm sorry," Foxx said. "I'm sorry, I just can't risk it."

Chance stared dumbfounded at the man sitting before him. His frustration boiled inside him until it was a steady anger. The pressure built inside his chest until he feared it might tear him apart.

He loathed Foxx.

But then, the anger seeped out of him as quickly as it had come. He knew it wasn't Foxx's fault. He was running from what he considered a failed enterprise. Septigonee knew, if Chance had the opportunity to leave all of this mess behind he would. He couldn't hold it against the man.

Chance took a seat beside Foxx, setting the notebook down again. "So that's the end of it then? Just like that?"

"Just like that," Foxx repeated.

"Every single time," Chance sighed. "It's like fate isn't satisfied with just destroying me, she wants to see me break first."

Foxx nodded. "She's a cruel lady, fate."

"We were almost there, too. We had a ticket out and into..." Chance gestured to the city around them. "Something else."

Chance and Foxx sat for a few minutes in silence. Chance felt his emotions writhing inside him—a potent blend of desire for vengeance and a wish to simply roll over and give up. He wanted to cast himself over the edge of the platform and into the sea, and let the waters bury him in their depths. He'd thought about it before, and sitting above the waves now he felt the thought tugging at his will.

Chance forced himself to look away from the waters. In the distance, he saw the lights of a small dirigible moving in their direction. Its lamps cast a soft, warm glow through the dark.

"Is that for you?" Chance asked.

"Yes."

"Where will you go next?"

"I thought of going to Selaria originally, but that cursed barricade has discouraged most ships from passing that way. Perhaps I'll try Pendambu. It's plenty far. It doesn't really matter to me as long as it's beyond the memory of this place. Somewhere I can start over again."

Chance scowled. How nice it must be to have the option of starting over, to skip town and begin a new life. If Chance had that liberty, he'd choose a country landlocked on all sides without a city within a hundred kilometers. He'd live his life without a thought or care, and no one to account to or for.

The image of Ashworth's face interrupted the daydream, his eyes full of... it wasn't fright. They were heavy, full of sorrow and longing. They were pleading.

Foxx picked up the notebook and rose to his feet, brushing off the dust from his trousers and dabbing his eyes on his sleeves.

"I suppose it's time," he said.

Indeed, the dirigible was only a stone's throw out now. It maneuvered sideways as it came abreast the platform. A man in flight garb hailed the platform.

"Which of you is Smith?" he shouted over the noise of the propellers, cupping his hand beside his mouth to direct his voice.

"I am," Foxx called back. The man cast a rope out of the ship and Foxx caught it. Looping it over one of the anchor posts, he helped pull the dirigible in against the platform.

"I have orders to take you to the *Versai*," the pilot said once the propellers had quieted. "You ready?"

Chance glanced toward the ports that lined the Spire. Somewhere up there, amidst the massive airships, was docked the *Versai*, probably finishing its final preparations for the long journey.

"Any luggage?" the pilot asked.

Foxx handed over his case and bag. As he was preparing to climb on, he hesitated.

"Chance, was it?" he asked.

Chance nodded.

"You've lost as much as I have this past week. Perhaps... well, there would be room for you on the *Versai* if you wanted to get away. I could use a traveling companion. You carry my bags and I'll pay your way to whatever port you want to put in at. I'm convinced that this city really is cursed."

Chance's heart beat faster at the offer. He didn't have much on him, but he could certainly make it on his few possessions. He had a few banknotes he'd sewn into his coat, but it was unlikely Foxx was about to rough it, even in hiding. For a moment, Chance saw himself in his daydream free and happy.

And then there was Ashworth's face again. Those eyes. Pleading.

"I can't," Chance heard himself say. "Someone has to take care of Rhett. And someone needs to carry on their work. Ashworth and Keller were onto something important. I owe Ashworth for everything he did for me. I owe him this. You understand, don't you?"

"You're a braver man than I am," Foxx said, a glimpse of a smile crossing his face. "You know, you sounded a little like Keller just then. He would have sided with you in a moment like this. But... I'm afraid I'm a lesser man in many ways."

He boarded the dirigible, and Chance let a breath out. He was turning to leave when Foxx stopped him.

"Chance!" Foxx called him back. "Wait there."

After a few words with the pilot, he stepped off the ship and took the key from around his neck. With apparent difficulty, he handed it to Chance along with Keller's notebook.

"He told me to destroy it if anything ever happened to him. Obviously, I didn't have the opportunity until now, but if you're going to try and finish his work you'll need somewhere to start. Perhaps you'll find a way to make sense of it."

"Thanks," Chance said. He flipped through the notebook. As expected, the marks inside were gibberish. He was going to have his work cut out for him trying to decipher it.

"And take this as well," he said, handing Chance a billfold.

Chance opened it and looked disbelievingly at Foxx. There was more money there than he'd seen at any point in his life—enough to take any number of ships out of Hatteras. Enough to begin again.

"My last contribution to Keller's work," Foxx said. "Just promise me you'll finish what he began. He would want that, I think. I'm just... well, I'm just not the right man for the job."

"I'll see it through," Chance promised.

Foxx nodded, and after a moment's hesitation he boarded the ship again. The pilot cranked a lever and the propellers gave a lurch. The airship pulled away slowly, but picked up speed as it ferried upward toward the Spire in the direction it had come.

Foxx gave Chance a solemn salute as it went, and Chance returned it.

In the silence that followed, Chance watched the dirigible fade into the distance, soaking in a feeling he couldn't quite identify.

As he descended the stairs, he watched the people passing by. He listened to the dull drum of the factories and machine shops, and breathed in their sooty air.

He held the notebook close, imagining if Ashworth was alive how he would be smiling—and then smiled thinking how he'd have reminded them not to be fools with it all.

Confidence. That was what he felt.

PART III

CHAPTER THIRTY-TWO
A Garden Party

Had I read the warning signs, I might have ventured to guess what all of this would mean what lay at stake if I saw it through. Yet, who among us can resist so tempting a lure?

— Excerpt from *Mechanarcissism*

"This whole business with Selaria has gotten out of hand, if you ask me," Gentleman Carthus grumbled. "It is an entirely belligerent ordeal."

Stoddard sat amongst a small cluster of chairs outside of Elector Sinclair's estate. He and a company of other invited guests lounged under shaded boughs. They watched the other garden party guests with detached interest as they bobbed here and there across the lawn.

With the warm days of summer fading, Sinclair had decided to host yet another social gathering. And, as Sinclair was Stoddard's distinguished patron, Stoddard was pressed to attend. He'd attended so many of them throughout the spring and summer that he'd completely lost count, in part for their number and in part for the redundancy which he experienced with each.

Emmaline sat beside him, enjoying herself among the present company. Stoddard shared little of her enthusiasm. He had found the fresh air to be momentarily diverting, yet the conversation had grown stale;

he'd heard variations of it before. And would again.

"They have no place interposing themselves into our business with the colonies," Carthus concluded.

"I don't know," Merryfield ventured. "I think I understand their trying to get our attention so desperately. If I recall, it was we who imposed some rather harsh restrictions after the war. I for one wouldn't want to live long under such impositions."

Stoddard had to give Merryfield credit where credit was due; he'd been persistent in reinforcing their association in the past few months. Though Stoddard had always thought the man a bit daft, he'd proven exceptional prowess ingratiating himself into influential circles when opportunity arose. He was a socialite of the subtlest kind.

"Count yourself fortunate that you don't," Carthus said. "It is a privilege hard won."

"Do they truly intend a war, do you think?" Emmaline asked.

"There have been no direct engagements," Sinclair affirmed. "But, they continue to refuse to relocate their fleet outside of our trade routes."

"How else are we supposed to interpret their actions but as hostile?" Carthus asked. "Camping half of their bloody fleet in the middle of the sea is an act of aggression—I don't care what excuse they make for it. They're growing too bold. If you ask me, I say it's high time we reminded them who it was that won the Great War."

"If it comes to a confrontation, rest assured our armada stands prepared to quell it," Vanzeal said. "It wouldn't last a day."

Stoddard couldn't help frowning at Vanzeal's hubris. He'd seen firsthand Vanzeal's incompetence.

Vanzeal caught his eyes for a second, and they exchanged glares. Their encounters had only grown colder with the passing months. While Sinclair did not often require their company simultaneously, they were not immune to the occasional shared event. Stoddard made it a point to keep their conversations to a minimum.

"I assure you, the situation is not so dire as it's been made to sound," Sinclair said. "At its worst, they likely wish to have the terms of their treaties reconsidered. Our ambassadors are in contact with their government as we speak, and have clear instruction how to negotiate a withdrawal."

"And in the meantime, what becomes of Madura?" Carthus said. His voice denoted an acute impatience. "I haven't been able to get a ship to her for nine weeks because of that cursed blockade, and, from what I hear, Madura is growing all too comfortable with their detachment. What are we doing about it?"

He looked expectantly at Sinclair.

"I agree, it is cowardly of them to use Selaria's blockade as an excuse to grow lax in their obligations to the city," Sinclair said.

"It's all planned out," Carthus said. "Madura is not just taking advantage of an opportunity; Selaria is *creating* one for them. They should be dealt with swiftly before they get too much of a head on them and other colonies get the same idea. From what I hear, Sorrento isn't far behind."

"Of course, they'll have to be dealt with. Don't you think the electors realize that? The question is how."

"Selaria and Madura would not be so foolish as to goad a real conflict from Hatteras," Sinclair insisted. "They haven't the forces, even together. Confrontation could not be their intent."

"Then I say give them confrontation!" Carthus said. "Let them feel the force behind our military, and send them back to their ports with their tails between their legs."

"Their intentions are still unclear," Sinclair said. "Once our ambassadors return we'll know better what they're hoping to gain from all of this."

"And all the while, our commerce suffers," Carthus fumed.

"They're only trying to assert their individuality," Arden said. "I don't see what's so outrageous. Isn't that what we encourage here in Hatteras?"

Stoddard couldn't help a smile. Ever since he'd begun working alongside Arden he'd observed a growing eagerness to resist the common thought, which tickled Stoddard. For the son of an elector, Arden had a rebellious streak.

"That is the privilege afforded to citizens of Hatteras," Carthus

AETHER SPARK · 287

explained. "Not barbarians across the sea."

"There is a fine line between demonstrating one's individuality and asserting one's independence," Sinclair added. "Independence is the product of the vain fool's imagination. We, all of us, exist in a state of dependency; that goes for ourselves and the colonies who swear loyalty to us. To believe—or go so far as to act—as though we could exist independent of established society is renegade."

"And must be quelled!" Carthus said.

"In its proper order," Sinclair concluded.

"Perhaps someone simply needs to go there and talk some sense to them," Lady Merryfield suggested.

"My dear, that is precisely what we're doing," her husband said.

"But have you met one of them?" Carthus said. "They're not exactly the most sensible breed. Miss Emmaline should know, I'd think. Doesn't your father do business in Madura as well?"

"He does," Emmaline said.

"And how has this little show of Selaria's affected his trade?"

"It's been dreadful. He comes home almost every night with more news of misfortune about his fleet. His airships can avoid the blockade without too much difficulty, but his ships have had to round Port Elliston to avoid it, which is a dreadful inconvenience traveling so near Pendambu. The islands near Pendambu are riddled with pirates you know."

The others gasped at the mention of pirates, but Stoddard sensed it was more for show than real surprise. The topic was entertaining. That was all.

"Oh, it's been terrible," Emmaline continued, taking her cue. "Why, just last week we received news that another of my father's ships was chased down by pirates on its way home."

"Oh, dear! How awful!"

"It seems there is nowhere that's safe," Carthus said. "Apart from our own blessed harbors."

"Father is incensed about it. The colonies won't do anything to hunt down pirates, so he's had to commission ships to hunt them down himself. "

"Is there no end to the trouble brewing overseas?" Carthus fumed.

"It's almost as though it were fashionable to cause mischief these days," Merryfield laughed. "I might take it up myself had I the disposition, just to see what the attraction is. Fortunately, we have men like Vanzeal and the guard here to right it for us."

"At your disposal always," Vanzeal said. The company of duelists standing in attendance each bowed in a humble salute.

"Well, I feel better already," Merryfield beamed, helping himself to another sandwich.

"I only hope they sort this out quickly," Carthus grumbled. "If it weren't for their exquisite textiles, I'd say just let the colonies have their way and go. However, my wife would have a fit should we ever lose their mercantile."

Stoddard felt his head bob and he caught himself, glancing around to see whether anyone had noticed his lull. Try as he might, his interest in the conversation was wearing thin.

What had been intended as a luncheon had evolved into tea, a game of stoolball, and yet another round of tea. And they were *still* mingling. Still prating on with the same inane conversations. The whole event was a bore, and Stoddard's heels itched to escape.

How he longed to be back in his workshop. He still had much to do if he was ever to get to the bottom of Ashworth's research. Every invitation he was forced to entertain delayed his progress.

He'd devised a plan to compare the records Ashworth had kept of his incoming components with the concoctions he sent out, hoping to discern a more complete ingredient list for the Aether spark.

This had proven a difficult task, even after hiring a pair of alchemists to help him understand each component's use. Often the records were incomplete, and there was no way of being certain if Ashworth had left particular components off the books. Gravatts had mentioned he'd helped Ashworth cut corners.

He glanced toward Sinclair, gauging his attitude. Events overseas occupied his focus for now, but Stoddard knew he would run out of time if he had nothing to show for his work soon. The steel trap was closing in on him.

Sinclair looked his way and Stoddard diverted his eyes to Emmaline, feigning interest in her story. He'd heard it repeated at a half-dozen other gatherings. What did she find so appealing about repeating it again?

"Oh, it's horrible the tales that come back. The *Paulina* was defenseless when she was set upon by three other ships! They could hardly raise an alarm before she was sunk and the whole crew lost. Not a single survivor."

"Terrible," Merryfield said solemnly.

"Disgraceful."

"If it were my call," Carthus said, "I'd say we purge the colony and send our own citizens to inhabit it. Establish some finer breeding abroad."

"I'm afraid it's not that easy," Sinclair said. "But, I assure you, we're looking into every possible solution. Your wife will still have her dresses in years to come."

"The true sign the world remains in balance," Carthus smiled.

"But enough for now," Sinclair said. "It's not good to remain so long on such heavy topics. It's obviously wearing on the women. We could do with a diversion."

"Perhaps your duelists would be willing to entertain us with a demonstration?" Lady Merryfield suggested. "Like that time at Timberman's?"

"Oh, please do!" Emmaline said, clapping giddily.

"I'm sure most of the guests have already seen the trick," Vanzeal said.

"Nonsense, and if they have there's no harm in once more."

"It's quite diverting," Emmaline smiled. "Please show us."

"Very well," Vanzeal conceded. "Ringgold, perhaps you would do the honors?"

One of the duelists standing at attention bowed his acknowledgment and stepped forward. "Is there a young woman who possesses a handkerchief she'd be willing to part with?" he asked.

Emmaline was quick to produce hers and handed it over delicately.

"You've heard it said that swordsmanship is more than a skill," Ringgold began, pushing his cape over his shoulder and freeing up his arm. "It is an art, filled with flair..." He waved the handkerchief dramatically in the air, then, with a motion, it vanished in his palm. "...and deception."

The little company clapped approvingly at his trick.

"But above these, it is an art sustained by honor." He drew his sword, its straight edge gleaming in the sun as he held it high in a soldier's salute. "The same principle upon which our great city was founded."

From his other hand he produced the handkerchief again and waved it before the group. Stoddard, however, noticed his thumb press forward a small lever on the hilt of his blade.

He was pricked with intrigue, and he leaned in for what he knew was coming.

"To master any art, it takes years of practice and dedication. Patience. Discernment. Decisiveness. All of these must be employed when facing a foe, even one so delicate as a handkerchief."

He grinned as the little company laughed politely.

"But above all of this... is timing."

There was the sound of springs and gears as the complex mechanism within the hilt activated. The blade became a blur as he slashed three times through the air in what time a normal man might have swung once, and the severed handkerchief fell to the ground gently, like four wounded feathers.

Their company applauded politely, and Ringgold bowed low just as another call for tea was heard across the lawn. Each of the husbands rose stiffly and took the arms of their wives as they retired to the house. Stoddard dutifully took Emmaline's arm, but as they crossed the lawn his eyes lingered on the duelist as he reset the mechanism within his blade and sheathed it once again.

CHAPTER THIRTY-THREE
A Grisly Ordeal

It's the nature of a meritocracy, while one life rises out of obscurity another must descend. Attention is a fickle favor to keep.

— Excerpt from *Mechanarcissism*

C an I help you, sir?" the server asked.

Stoddard rested his hands on the counter of the bar, tapping its surface anxiously. "You're not serving anything stronger than tea, are you?"

"Yes, sir. What will you have?"

"A gin and tonic."

The server reached beneath the counter and fetched up a bottle, glass, and a small icebox.

"Doctor Stoddard, I presume?"

Stoddard turned to see the duelist from earlier step forward. "I am," he said.

"Sergeant Ringgold, at your service," Ringgold said, bowing low with a flourish. "I've heard a great deal about you—of your work for our Good Captain Harper. When I saw you earlier I knew I couldn't pass up this opportunity to meet you in person."

"Of course," Stoddard said, taking Ringgold's hand. "I remember."

"You're something of a legend among us mechanists," Ringgold said. He tapped the hilt of his sword.

Stoddard nodded, though his mind was preoccupied. Sinclair stood a ways off, conversing closely with Vanzeal. About what, Stoddard wondered with agitation.

"I hope you don't think me presumptuous in observing that you're not enjoying yourself."

"What makes you think so?" Stoddard asked. He took his drink from the bartender and strained it through his lips, the ice numbing them.

"Forgive me, but we duelists spend years learning how to read people. Your every movement expresses a desire to escape from this place. Except your face. You have quite the look of determination to remain. May I ask why?"

"I am here attending Elector Sinclair."

"Ah," Ringgold said, as though he understood perfectly. "Not your first invitation, I take it?"

Stoddard didn't acknowledge the question.

"Well, perhaps I have overstretched my liberties. I should leave you to rejoin your—"

"No," Stoddard said, downing his drink. "It's alright. I'm just a little distracted at the moment."

"So, how are you enjoying our party?"

"To be honest, you're the first person today apart from the bartender who has made any attempt at a real conversation." He returned the glass and gestured for another. "Everyone else seems to only tolerate me."

"Yes, well," Ringgold smiled, "the meritocracy is not known for their generously cheerful demeanor. Too many ulterior motives bumping up against each other. But tell me, what is yours?"

"Mine?"

"Your motive for being here. I don't know if I've ever encountered anyone that doesn't have some hidden objective. Some secret enterprise they hope to obtain."

Stoddard gave the sergeant a once over. Who was this duelist that he felt bold enough to speak so forwardly? What was *his* motive in initiating such a conversation? He was considerably young to be so confident in his speech.

Suspicion welled inside Stoddard.

"I'm not certain I should say," he said.

"And there you've learned the first rule of survival on the Spire—keep things close to the chest," Ringgold said. "But, may I share with you a second?"

Stoddard nodded.

"Make friends. There's no hope of remaining in this social arena without them. It's all about connections. Building a network of contacts you can rely on. Making yourself indispensable. A man is only as great as the friends he keeps. Trust me when I say that most of the people here are only so because of their connections—else they'd have been swept from the Spire long ago."

"And you think me soon to follow them?" Stoddard took some offense at the implication. "I'm still here. Am I not?"

"Yes, but why are you not there?" Ringgold gestured to where Sinclair conversed with Vanzeal. "You are, I must point out, an outlier. You've gained recognition for your work, so merit has opened up a brief window of opportunity. Unfortunately, merit isn't what keeps a man in this sort of company. Not for long."

"What does?"

"Maneuvering."

Stoddard eyed Ringgold carefully. He got the feeling Ringgold knew more about him than he was divulging. Again, he wondered for what purpose he'd attracted his interest.

"Why tell me this?" Stoddard asked.

"Because I believe every man deserves a sporting chance. Those who aren't bred for this sort of game tend to find themselves overwhelmed, as I thought you might be just now."

"It's not so overwhelming as you suppose," Stoddard insisted. "And I'm not so devoid of friends as you suggest. I attend at the elector's invitation. He's graciously taken me under his wing."

"Ah," Ringgold smiled. "Your ambition is admirable."

Stoddard felt mocked. "What do you mean?"

"I mean that you've selected a rather difficult first contact. Or was it you who selected him?"

"As a matter of fact," Stoddard said with some pride, "it was Sinclair who sought me out."

"Then forgive me, I worry for you even more."

At that moment Vanzeal concluded his conversation with Sinclair and bowed low as he departed. He passed Stoddard with his companion, casting Stoddard a hard look. But he walked on without any formal acknowledgment.

"Yes, I worry for you a great deal," Ringgold said watching Vanzeal go.

"You seem to be favored in his company."

"I am assigned to Vanzeal for a time, yes. Perhaps I've shown promise in the interim. But, my association is by assignment only, and will end. And none too soon."

The way he said it pricked Stoddard. He was just about to ask what he'd meant when a disturbance on the lawn interrupted them. A man had barged into the garden, trailing two servants who looked desperate in their attempts to hold him back.

"Get your hands off me! I must have an audience with Sinclair. Let go!"

He struck a manservant with his cane and the servants recoiled as he turned again toward the gathering.

"Sinclair! I have words for you!"

"Contain yourself, Woirhayes! You are not welcome here anymore." Vanzeal had appeared again, stepping forward to block the man's path. Even in his hysteria, Woirhayes paused before Vanzeal's imposing presence.

"I will not be so easily dismissed," Woirhayes insisted. "My family has been in good standing with the city for generations. Their sweat and blood has tempered the steel of the buildings you call home!"

"The contribution your family has made to Hatteras is not the matter in dispute," Sinclair said, stepping forth. "What is in dispute is *your* contribution, Mr. Woirhayes. And, as is evidenced by your manners here today, they are only further deserving of scrutiny."

"I am a Lord!" Woirhayes shouted.

"Silence!" Sinclair barked, the first time Stoddard had heard such a tone from him. "We will have no more of your protests here. You disturb my guests."

"I'll not be silenced, not until the slight done to my family's honor is righted, or I die of shame."

"You very well could," Vanzeal growled.

"You... damn you to Septigonee's Well, Sinclair. Elector you may be, but a colder more unpleasant man I've never had the dishonor of knowing. You hold men's lives cheap, and it will one day be a price to be reckoned."

"Enough!" Arden stepped forward. "You will not dishonor my father!"

"Stay, Arden!" Sinclair commanded.

Arden halted, his fists clenched as he strained against his will, but he obeyed his father and stepped down.

"Gentlemen, remove this man from the grounds. See to it that he is not permitted to enter again."

"Do not touch me." Woirhayes struggled, swinging his cane at the men who approached him. It took two to distract him as a third seized the cane from behind.

"I will not be dismissed! Sinclair! Sinclair!" he shouted.

But, Sinclair had already turned his back and was enjoying his tea as though the whole affair had never occurred.

"Sinclair! I challenge you! For my honor's sake, I challenge you!"

The men who carried Woirhayes stopped, hesitating as they turned back to see Sinclair's response. Sinclair stood quite unfazed, taking a few sips of his tea.

"Did you hear me?" Woirhayes shouted again, though he need not have with the silence which had fallen on the garden. "You will right the wrongs you have done to my family's name or else settle this in blood!"

"I heard you," Sinclair said. He set his cup down in its saucer and handed it off to one of the servants. Turning around, he locked eyes with Woirhayes. "Are you certain this is the course you wish to take?"

"What choice have you left me? Mine and my posterity's wellbeing are forfeit by an ill spoken word from your lips. I'll see your tongue removed before I let this indignation go unanswered."

"Think carefully before you commit yourself to such a course," Sinclair warned.

"I've chosen my course! Now, how do you answer?"

Sinclair eyed the man with distaste. Stoddard's eyes darted between the two men. The hate which rose from Woirhayes collided violently with the cold in Sinclair's demeanor. Never had Stoddard witnessed such a contest of wills as in that moment.

"I accept."

"I offer my services as your stand-in." Vanzeal spoke the words without missing a beat, and he stepped forward between Sinclair and Woirhayes.

"This," Sinclair grinned, "I also accept." He turned his back to the whole affair and took up his tea again.

"Of all the cowards," Woirhayes fumed. "Will you not face me yourself?"

"The elector has accepted me as his stand-in," Vanzeal said. "According to the gentleman's rules of engagement, your dispute is now with me. Seek for yourself a suitable stand-in or else we commence with the duel. Unless, of course, you're not actually bound by the gentleman's rules?"

Woirhayes' face flushed as Vanzeal spoke. It was his one avenue to escape, to avoid the contest to come. Vanzeal was a dangerous man, and Stoddard did not envy Woirhayes' position.

Woirhayes looked at the other duelists standing nearby, his eyes searching for a sympathetic face—but none were to be found.

"It seems you find yourself disadvantaged, Woirhayes. Does no one here wish to fight for your honor as you do?" Vanzeal laughed, and his men laughed with him. Few others seemed to feel the humor in the moment, however. "Come man, be bold and take fate into your own hands."

"Very well," Woirhayes said. He twisted his cane and drew out a simple, straight-edged saber.

"Attend me," Vanzeal commanded. A soldier from his company approached as Vanzeal unclasped his cape and handed it off. Ringgold and a few of the others requested that the servants usher the ladies from the garden, and the audience waned to a few men only.

Emmaline protested as one of the servants offered to direct her to the parlor room. "Why should I be sent away?" she said. "Surely this unpleasantness can be handled in private. They should be the ones to go."

"We don't get a say in what happens," Stoddard said. "It would be best if you went with the others."

"Then come with me," she pleaded.

"I cannot. I'm attending to Sinclair. He would be insulted if I abandoned him now."

"Then I'll attend you," she winked.

"No," Stoddard insisted. "This is no place for a woman, and now is not the time to argue. I'm trying to secure us a future, and a place among the meritocracy. To do so, we must attend to Sinclair's desires."

Emmaline frowned. He saw the color rising in her cheeks, but he had no time to explain himself. She'd have to understand and trust his judgment.

"I'll come find you when all is over," he promised.

"Don't bother," Emmaline snapped, and she huffed off, following the procession of guests.

Stoddard watched her as she went, frustrated by her shortsightedness. She would see in time how crucial this moment was, how delicately their future hung in the balance. He couldn't afford a moment's neglect.

Woirhayes and Vanzeal were readying themselves, clearing a space in which their confrontation would commence. The men in attendance circled around, conversing in whispered tones. As Stoddard stepped forward to join the group he overheard the general prediction of the duel.

Woirhayes was not a popular choice.

Vanzeal drew his sword, the steel blade gleaming in the sun. Stoddard noticed that its design was different from Ringgold's. Where Ringgold's had been a simple straight edge, Vanzeal's weapon was curved and had three locked hinges in the blade itself. Its hilt wrapped around the base with a series of twisting gears and springs, like a clamp. He saluted Sinclair with it before stepping the traditional distance from his foe.

"You're dancing in a world you don't belong," Vanzeal said.

"My family has been a part of this city for more than three generations," Woirhayes said. "I've more of a right to be here than some military hopeful like you."

"We'll see."

One of the gentlemen present stepped forward to moderate the duel.

"A challenge has been issued," he said in an official tone. "Let all who stand by as witnesses seal the outcome of this confrontation with their testimonies, and let none dispute it. Gentlemen, stand ready!"

Twisting a dial in the hilt of his saber, Vanzeal lowered his blade and squared off with Woirhayes. His face communicated a hard confidence, and his eyes glimmered with a hint of pleasure.

Woirhayes shuffled and turned himself sideways, his sword point extended toward Sinclair's chest.

"To the death!" the moderator shouted, and the duel commenced.

There was an uneasy moment as the two men stood unmoved. For a second, Stoddard wondered if they'd missed their cue to begin, but the look in their eyes communicated otherwise. Stoddard glanced toward Sinclair who watched expressionless as Woirhayes shifted back and forth on his feet, finding his footing.

"A pity," Ringgold whispered, stepping up beside Stoddard.

"What is?"

"To duel, one must be able to read the fight from beginning to end even before blades are drawn. It's the nature of our weapons," he said, patting the curious hilt of his own rapier. "The timing of the advantage."

"Does Woirhayes not have a chance?"

"Vanzeal is an expert duelist, but more than that his intuition is honed to precision. The mechanisms of our blades are designed so that the wielder can set the timing of his advantage. A truly skilled duelist will time his advantage so carefully that the mechanism springs at exactly the opportune moment. Spring it too soon, and the mechanism may not penetrate your opponent's defenses. Spring too late, however, and the opponent might gain the advantage before you."

He sighed. "Here, I'm afraid the duel is already decided."

Stoddard looked at Ringgold, then to Vanzeal and Woirhayes. Vanzeal had yet to move. He stared at Woirhayes with cold eyes. Woirhayes was sweating, but he kept his eyes locked with Vanzeal's.

And then Stoddard saw it. Had he not been trying to read the moment, as Ringgold had suggested, he might have missed it altogether.

The corner of Vanzeal's lip curled up in a sneer.

It happened quickly. Vanzeal blinked, and Woirhayes saw his opportunity. Lunging forward, he struck with all his might—the point of his blade driving for Vanzeal's heart.

But the point never found its mark. The sound of springs and hinges coincided perfectly with Vanzeal's counter step, and Woirhayes' blade pierced empty air.

Woirhayes stood stunned, Vanzeal's saber buried a few inches into his back. He let out a desperate groan before falling forward, lifeless.

Vanzeal drew out his blade and wiped it on a cloth. "It is done," he announced.

"See here, all of you," Sinclair said, gesturing to the body. "A reasonable man would have seen the opportunity to remake himself, and not given in to unbridled passions of the moment. Remove him. And let's be done with these grisly affairs for the afternoon, shall we? Someone fetch the women."

Two servants scooped up Woirhayes' body, moving him out of sight while another went to announce the duel concluded. Stoddard watched as they carried the body away and cleaned the blood, fighting a queasiness in his stomach.

"Are you alright?" Ringgold asked.

"I'll be fine," Stoddard insisted. "I just need a moment."

"I take it this is your first time witnessing a duel?"

Stoddard nodded and dabbed his brow.

"It's natural to be unnerved. There's nothing beautiful about such a death."

"Coming from a duelist, that surprises me. I imagine you've dispatched a man or more yourself?"

"I've seen enough die to know it's not something men should grow accustomed to. And yet... we do." He frowned on the company before him. "One final word of advice if you'll permit me, Doctor?"

"Yes?" Stoddard asked.

"The day you stop feeling for another man's life, get yourself out of politics."

Stoddard was about to respond when Sinclair summoned him, and he was taken up with the rest of the group in a quest to find some fresh air.

CHAPTER THIRTY-FOUR
Working with Scrap

How often we fail to acknowledge the role our failures played in life. What might we have obtained had our course continued undisturbed? And what might we have missed?

— Excerpt from *Mechanarcissism*

"Wake up!" Rhett shouted into Chance's ear, shaking his shoulder. "Chance, wake up!"

Chance groaned and rolled over, his elbow bumping into the leg of his desk so hard that it sent chills up his arm. He cradled it against him to calm the pain as a few of the containers on the desk rolled off the edge. Rhett managed to catch the glass vials before they shattered.

"What do you want, Rhett?" Chance asked groggily. He realized he was laying on the floor. The light through the window seared his eyes, and he kept his head down to shield them. "What time is it?"

"Noon. You looked like you were..."

"Like I was what?" Chance asked, sitting up and grasping his head. It ached violently, and glancing at the empty bottles beside him he remembered why.

"You looked like you had a bad night," Rhett finished.

"How about a bad life?"

"What?"

"Don't worry about it," Chance said. He used the desk to pull himself to his feet. They were in one of Margarete's empty rooms, a loft at the top of the stairs, crammed with all his laboratory equipment, a chair, and a single bed.

They'd moved his laboratory almost a month before, when Ponti's place had been found out.

Everything was a mess, from his equipment to the remains of food left untouched to rot. Chance had reached a new disregard for cleanliness, but that was what happened when one was living in spare corners and working with scrap.

"What were you making?" Rhett asked, his nose turning up at the smell. One of the burners was still on, the contents of its cauldron burnt black as char. It reeked of sulfur.

"Nothing," Chance said, switching off the burner. "Just testing a compound."

Rhett picked up Keller's open notebook; it was full of notes tucked into the pages. Chance had been recording what he hoped was the first real step in decoding the cipher in the past few months. It had proven one of the most difficult undertakings Chance had ever faced. Keller's cipher was even more elaborate than Ashworth's, with few similarities to Chance's.

Rhett flipped through the pages curiously, staring at the symbols. Chance had been doing the same thing for months now. He didn't expect Rhett was about to make any more headway than he had. But, he let the boy look. There was no harm in that.

Chance dipped a rag in his wash bin and wiped his face. The cool water helped ease his aches, and he let out a weighty breath. It was getting harder every day to get himself going in the morning. As Rhett had pointed out, he was making a habit of skipping morning altogether.

"Did you get those supplies I asked for?" he asked.

"Most of them." Rhett pointed to a few satchels by the door. "They're rationing the Exchange more every day."

"Greedy cogs," Chance cursed. "What's their excuse this time?"

"They say it's because of the colonies making trouble."

"Can't blame them for wanting to defect. They're just as sick as we are of having the meritocracy breathing down their necks." He tossed the rag back in the wash bin. "Doesn't matter. We'll find another way."

"How? We've used up almost all of Foxx's money."

"Let me worry about that, why don't you?" Chance said.

They'd certainly burned through Foxx's investment quicker than Chance had anticipated. It hadn't helped when their first lab was seized by the city. Fortunately, they'd all been away when the raid came, but Ponti's place was out of play.

It alerted them to a new realization: whomever was after the Aether spark wasn't playing around. They were after him. Somehow, they knew he'd survived the fire. Chance had had to withdraw almost entirely from the public eye to keep safe.

Rhett took care of most of the errands, which left Chance ample time to worry over Ashworth's work. He'd had a difficult time starting over a second time, especially with the conflicts breaking out across the sea making commodities harder to come by. The timing wasn't ideal.

Lately, he'd hardly had resources enough to experiment. Sure, there were other ways to get by if they were resourceful. They still had some friends sympathetic to their plight, and there were places both within and without the city with parts to spare if one knew where to look—but it didn't make it any easier.

Rhett certainly had stepped up. He'd seemed to grow three years in a few short months. He was almost unrecognizable from the timid little boy he'd been, with a new decisiveness. Chance wondered where he'd picked it up.

"Where have you been?" Chance asked.

"Nowhere," Rhett said. "Just over at Welch's place."

Chance gave a shudder of annoyance. "You and him are getting along pretty well it seems."

"He's interesting."

"Yeah? Well, don't let him fill your head with too much of his pseudo-spiritual nonsense. You're unbearable as it is. I don't know if I could handle it."

"I'll try not to," Rhett smiled.

Chance grabbed his boots from one of the chairs.

"The recruiters tried to stop me again," Rhett said.

"Yeah? What did you say?"

"Nothing. Like you told me."

"Good."

"What if..." Rhett began. "What if I did sign up to go?"

"Why would you do that?" Chance asked. "You're like, ten years old. War isn't for boys."

"I'm eleven," Rhett said defensively.

"Yeah?" He'd honestly forgotten. "Well, you don't know the first thing about fighting. Or what this whole scrap with the colonies is really about. You want to be some militia pawn in their hands?"

"Simon was in the militia. He doesn't think it's so bad."

"Simon," Chance said, lacing up his boots, "tries to scrounge together a living just like you and I. If he's willing to sacrifice his freedom to do that then that's something he'll have to square with someday. But you and I, we're better than that. We're our own agents. Whatever shots we've got to take, we're the ones who call them. You got that?"

"Yeah." Rhett nodded. "What are we doing today?"

"I'm going to go visit the scrapyards to see if I can't scrape together some more equipment for the lab. You can do whatever you'd like."

Rhett frowned, but didn't protest. He'd stopped arguing with Chance these days. Instead, he picked up his bag from the floor and went to the stairs. "Oh! Margarete wanted to talk to you."

Chance winced. "She say what about?"

"No. But, she seems awfully upset. She tried to hide it, but I could tell."

Chance swallowed hard.

"Are you going to talk to her?"

"Yeah, I'll talk to her," Chance said.

"Now?"

"I'll talk to her!" he repeated.

"Just being helpful," Rhett said as he descended the stairs.

The noise from the girls below drifted through the open door. Chance heard them making a fuss over Rhett. They loved him, perhaps because he was still harmless. But not Chance. Despite their efforts to make him feel welcome, he could tell they weren't altogether comfortable with his being there.

Even Margarete seemed to be second guessing her decision to let him stay.

Chance collected his coat and the carrier he'd fashioned to replace his old on. He checked one last time to be sure he hadn't left any burners on. Ignoring the door, he opened the window and scrambled out as quietly as he could. Clutching onto one of the gutter drains which ran down the side of the building, he clambered down, dropping to the street and slinking away before anyone noticed.

Chance hurried across the tracks, careful to keep his balance as he made his way through the train yard. He'd gotten his foot caught once between the tracks when he was a young boy, and the memory of that experience gave him reason to exercise more caution than he typically did.

A train passed by slowly and he waited for it to go. The yard was filled with cars and boxes, tucked away here and there to be retrieved later when they were needed. A large train was in a dock, unloading what looked like carts of old scrap.

When the track was clear, Chance ran by some unused boxcars, popping his head in a few as he passed. Most were vacant, but after a few minutes searching he spotted what he'd been looking for.

There, in one of the open cars, lay Ponti. He was leaned up against his signature sack of junk, sleeping away the day. Chance banged his hands on the wooden floor and called to him.

"Time to get up!"

Ponti started with a jolt, but rolled back over on his sack when he saw who it was. "Blast it, a man's got to sleep. Leave me alone."

"Not this time. We've got work to do."

"What makes you think I haven't got things of my own to do today?"

"The fact that you had time to spend with one of Margarete's girls last night," Chance said, climbing into the boxcar. Ponti looked up at him, blinking away his sleepiness.

"Who said I did any such thing?"

"We had an agreement, Ponti."

"Yeah?" Ponti looked indignant. "Well, I don't remember us saying anything about whether one of them found their way to me."

"You leave her girls alone," Chance warned. "I mean it."

"Since when do you care for a bunch of—"

"You'll leave them alone!"

Ponti recoiled. Chance wasn't usually so short with him, even in his foibles. But he recovered quickly, stretching himself out on his sack.

"Whatever you say," he said with an air of dismissal. "You're the boss, it seems."

"Good. Now, seeing as I'm the one who's going to have to face Margarete when I get back, you're going to help me with a little errand today."

Chance's tone was no nonsense.

"Alright!" Ponti fumed, throwing up his hands in surrender. "Mangy slag. I swear, she wasn't worth it." He said the last part under his breath as he rose from his resting place and shouldered his sack. He cleared his throat and spat.

"So, what've you got me doing today?"

Chance smiled. "Junking."

It was about an hour by train to reach the scrapyard. The two of them managed to steal away on an empty flatcar without too much difficulty. Ponti remained in a sour mood the whole way, complaining constantly and pointing out the trouble they could get themselves into.

Chance let Ponti's attitude wash over him without response. Instead, he let his mind puzzle over the compounds he'd worked on the night before. For months he'd been working with the hints he could glean from Keller's and Ashworth's notebooks.

The rest he had to discern from trial and error.

At one point, he'd thought he'd been making real progress, but had ultimately come to a dead end when the mixture turned volatile and ate through the cauldron he'd been heating it in. He just couldn't get the compounds to react the way they should.

He wished silently Ashworth was still there to talk to. He'd always had a more patient mind in the face of failure. What Chance wouldn't have given for one more kitchen conversation.

When they arrived, Chance wiped his eyes, and he and Ponti hopped off the train just before it pulled into the station. They made their way down the tracks until they came to a small supply shed.

A tall metal fence, perhaps a dozen feet high, blocked their way into the scrapyard, but they weren't deterred. Chance followed Ponti down the fence until they came to a ribbon wrapped around one of the posts. Ponti pushed on the fence. It opened easily on cleverly disguised hinges, and the two of them slipped in unnoticed.

The scrapyard was busier than normal. A few workers were milling about near the depot, preparing to load up another shipment of scrap back to Hatteras.

Ponti looked nervously at Chance.

"Not sure why Hatteras got themselves such an interest in junk all of a sudden," he said. "I haven't done nothing to bother them, and they go put me out of business in a single day."

"It's because of the blockade," Chance said, watching the men work. "They can't keep the factories going without it. They're salvaging what they can, wherever they can."

"Then scrap that pretty Spire of theirs. They've got plenty and more to share if they need it so badly."

Chance rolled his eyes. He couldn't imagine any gentleman parting with their fine china or fancy watches just to smelt another gun or two.

Pulling a list of items he needed from his coat, the two of them set to it. It was challenging work, sorting through the colossal piles of trash and scrap, collecting pieces which might do in a pinch. A broken valve. A curved plate of metal. Anything that might resist high temperatures or store compounds was useful.

Chance couldn't afford to be picky. Much of what he was able to collect wasn't ideal, but with some tampering he could make it work. Again, he thought Welch might be a good one to ask for help, being a tinkerer and all, but he shook the idea off.

They moved carefully, always mindful to avoid the men who were working the piles. A few times they were forced to abandon their search as city men came by with their carts, but the yard was large enough that Chance and Ponti could always find another unoccupied section.

It was a slow, tedious search. The sun beat down on them mercilessly. Ponti voiced complaints at every opportunity. Despite being a junker by trade, he wasn't accustomed to keeping at any single task for long—and he made sure Chance was aware of it.

"How much of this scrap are you looking to collect?" he asked for the hundredth time as they paused for a rest. "You can't possibly have enough room for all of this back at Margarete's."

"We need as much as we can get." Chance tossed another bent metal strip into his sack as Ponti let out a groan. "Don't worry," Chance assured him. "I think we've gathered enough for today. We can call it."

Ponti let out a sigh of relief and tossed a pair of worn boots aside. "About bloody time. Not that I don't like risking my life for a bunch of junk. How about a drink after all this rummaging, when we get back? It would do me finely."

"Sure," Chance shrugged. "And if we hurry, perhaps we won't have to walk the whole way." He pointed to the depot where an engine was just linking up with a fresh load. "That's our ride."

"What?! What are we still scrapping for then?" Ponti grumbled, shouldering his pack. "If we miss it, it's your fault."

"Quit complaining," Chance said, passing him as he ran with his own sack. "Hurry!"

The two of them hustled back to the hole in the fence and fed their sacks through. They hurried across the tracks as quickly as they could, their awkward parcels weighing them down. The train was pulling out just as they reached it.

"You see an open one?" Ponti called.

Chance scanned the boxcars. "There," he said, pointing to a cracked door. "Hurry up!"

They ran alongside the cars as the train picked up speed. As the boxcar came up beside them Chance hurled his sack up onto the open platform and leapt on. Ponti came up close behind, swinging his sack and scurrying onboard just as the train pulled away.

"That could have been a long walk," Ponti said, setting up a comfortable spot beside the door with his sack and laying himself out. "So, tell me, how goes this little enterprise of yours? Any headway yet? Or you still chasing your tail?"

"A little progress, I think," Chance said. "The notebook is still the key, and the thing giving me the most trouble. I've been able to figure some of it out by running my own tests, but it's slow progress—and costly."

"I know what it costs," Ponti said, chuckling weakly. He looked out the boxcar.

"Ponti, you know I'm sorry about what happened to your place. I never meant for my troubles to spill into yours."

"Doesn't matter. Can't change what happened now," Ponti shrugged.

Chance sat down at the edge of the boxcar, his legs dangling out of the door, the ground racing by underneath them.

"You know, if I manage to figure this out then we'll all have a share in it. You as well, for what you did for us when Rhett and I were out a place."

Ponti raised his hand to silence Chance's words.

"Don't do that," he said. "Don't promise me something you don't have. I made the mistake of being drawn into your little enterprise by those promises before, and it cost me almost everything. I won't let you do it again."

"I'm just trying to make things right."

"Then you do that, but keep your promises to yourself."

Chance let it go and focused instead on the landscape outside. The train moved at an easy clip, the countryside passing lazily on. The sun was approaching the horizon, its rays casting faint reds and golds.

Chance watched it sink, soaking in the openness of the space. It had been some time since he'd seen a sunset that grand. He would have to remember to bring Rhett out sometime. It was so easy to get trapped in the cramped city; it would do the boy good to see there was room still to stretch.

In a short while, Chance's thoughts drifted into dreams as the moving scenery and the gentle rumble of the train lulled both him and Ponti to sleep.

CHAPTER THIRTY-FIVE
Manufactured Chaos

It's only a matter of a few degrees and a simmer becomes a boil.

— Alchemical Proverb

The train gave a shudder and stirred Chance from his dreams. He blinked the sleep from his eyes, and stretched his sore legs. Ponti was there, as always, leaned up against his sack of junk. Chance couldn't understand how he slept like that, night after night. Ponti's backbone must be as twisted as the junk he carried.

Chance rubbed his arms. It was getting colder, and with the sun gone the wind from the train chilled his skin. The boxcar shuddered again, reverberating offbeat to the jostling of the tracks.

Chance stood up and grasped the edge of the door while he looked out of the car. The wind rushed past him, whipping his hair and clothes. They were moving slower now that they were within the city limits, passing through the factory districts.

Coming up on a tunnel, Chance stepped back as the darkness overtook him and watched electric lights flash by like a flickering picture show. They left streaks of light in his eyes that lingered even when he shut them.

When they emerged from the other side, Chance had to blink to refocus before he could believe what he saw.

One of the factories was in flames, casting a bright orange glow on the surrounding street. The flames licked the air from broken windows as people gathered in the streets around it.

Chance stood mystified, watching the scene unfold before him. The boxcar trembled again and entered another tunnel. Chance stepped back inside and shook Ponti awake.

"We there yet?" Ponti asked. He rubbed his eyes and looked out of the car as they emerged from the other side of the tunnel. He too caught sight of the blazing factory just before they turned and it was lost from sight. "What was that?" he asked.

"Trouble," Chance said. He donned his coat and checked to make sure his carrier was secure. "I need you to see this stuff makes its way back to Margarete's. Can you do that?"

"Why me? She'll have my head if I show up there again."

Chance smirked. "I knew you'd made a visit last night. Just get this to my lab. Rhett will give you a hand."

He tossed Ponti his sack and inched closer to the edge of the train.

"And where are you off to?"

"To see what's going on."

Chance waited until there was a clear patch of dirt before he kicked his legs over the side and leapt from the boxcar.

He landed rougher than he'd meant to, losing his footing as he tumbled down the slope of the tracks. He stopped in a heap of dirt among some tufts of grass. Rising to his feet, he brushed himself off and checked his carrier to be sure nothing had broken, then hurried toward the crowds.

It was clear the whole factory district was in distress. Chance raced down the streets, assessing the scene. Many of the buildings were ablaze on the adjacent streets, and he saw scuffles here and there between figures in the dark.

On one street, he met with a dead end where a human barricade had formed. Constables held the line, repelling the crowds who jeered as they ran by.

Chance seized the arm of a passing man.

"What is going on?" he asked. The man stared at him as though he were daft.

"Can't you tell? Whole place is gone mad."

"Why?" Chance asked. "What happened?"

"Factories have been shut down. Not enough work. When the workers tried to make a stand, they were fired upon. Whole place has lost their minds over it."

Chance let the man go and watched others run by. They were ducked low in the commotion, but it wasn't fear he saw in their eyes. These people were *angry*.

But they weren't united. They were turning on each other. People were fighting in the streets, businesses were being looted. All the while, the constables' lines stood their distance.

Why weren't they restoring the peace? Chance wondered. Then it dawned on him. They were waiting for the fight to go out of the crowd before they moved in.

It was like the man said, everyone had lost their minds.

Chance hurried in the direction of Liesel's pub. It was possible she'd be dealing with some of the backlash, being nearer the factory district. Fortunately, the madness died down as he neared her place. Yet, the sound from the factories carried through the night, and Chance thought he heard the occasional report of gunfire.

Chance banged a fist against Liesel's front door.

"Liesel?" he called out. "You there? Liesel, open up!"

The door opened suddenly and Liesel stood with a rifle over her shoulder and Welch with a pistol at the ready.

Chance stepped back in surprise. "Were you planning on shooting me?" he asked.

They didn't take time to answer before they pulled him inside.

"What's gotten into you?" Chance asked, but he fell silent as he saw the room. It was full to capacity with men and women. Most carried a gun, but a few gripped hammers and spades tightly in their hands. They looked at Chance with tense curiosity.

"Never can be too careful, night like this," Welch said, latching the door as he shut it again, only then lowering his pistol.

"We didn't know who was banging on the door so late," Liesel explained. "Could have been a mob for all we knew. Or worse."

"Who is this?" A man Chance didn't recognize had stepped forward, casting him an unpleasant look.

"Don't worry," Liesel explained. "He's a friend."

"I see no token," the man said, his eyes wandering over Chance's outfit.

"He's with me," Liesel insisted, focusing on Chance again. "What are you doing here? This isn't a good night to be out."

"I was coming back from the scrapyards on one of the rails when I saw the chaos. I was worried you might be dealing with trouble of your own, so I came to see if you were alright."

"Oh, we're dealing with it alright," Liesel said.

The others in the room stared at Chance, and the hairs on the back of his neck rose. "Who're all these people?" he asked.

"You really shouldn't have come tonight," Liesel frowned. "Welch, will you explain this to the others?"

Welch nodded, and Liesel hurried through the room to the back, grasping her rifle tightly. Chance followed, feeling crowded out as he walked through the looks everyone was giving him.

In the backroom, Liesel laid her rifle on the table and got herself a drink.

"Liesel, what is going on here? Who are all those people?"

"Resistance."

"What?"

"They're resistance fighters," she explained. "We were preparing to step in and help the factory workers, but the whole thing has fallen apart. We were hoping for an opportunity to lend a hand, but there's just no one to lend a hand to."

"You're..." Chance blinked, dumbfounded. "You're part of a resistance?"

"In a word, yes."

"Welch too?"

Liesel nodded.

Chance felt like he'd been hit with the butt end of her rifle. He had a sudden flashback to the moment when Ashworth had first told him about developing the Aether spark and how out of the loop he'd felt then.

This had much the same effect.

"How did I not know about this?" he asked.

"You've got your own worries," Liesel explained. "We didn't want to add to them. And we're better off the fewer people who are aware a resistance is even organized, which is what's going to give us grief tonight. There's a room full of men and women through that door who aren't too comfortable with the idea that you've seen them organized like this."

"You know I won't say anything."

"I know that, but they don't. Everyone is capable of crazy in moments like these," she said. "It's best if you stay here for a while, until we can settle any reservations they might have about you."

Chance shrugged. "I've got nowhere else to be."

"Good, then why don't you help me with dinner? We're going to have quite a few mouths to feed."

"How long are you planning on them staying?"

"We don't want anyone to suspect there was a gathering here, so we'll filter them out one at a time over the next day or so. Why don't you go upstairs and call Rhett down so he can give us a hand?"

"Wait, Rhett's here?" Chance's brow creased, and he felt his cheeks grow warm. "*Rhett's* in on it?"

"Chance," Liesel said, setting down the bowl she'd taken from the cupboard. "Don't take it personally. You know Rhett's been spending more time with Welch. He figured it out on his own. And it's done him good, I think, having something to be a part of."

"He's helping me," Chance insisted. "He's *my* apprentice."

"Yes, but how often do you have him do more than the grocery shopping? Actually have him work with you?"

Chance couldn't answer.

"Trust me, he needs this." She fetched some fresh vegetables and laid them out on the table.

Chance stepped back and leaned against the counter. He'd missed everything ever since he'd inherited Ashworth's work. He'd been so pre-occupied with figuring out Keller's cipher he hadn't noticed what was happening right under his nose.

There was a knock on the front door and a commotion from the front room. Liesel seized her rifle, and Chance stepped back from the doorway as two figures came through, carrying a third.

"What happened?" Liesel asked.

"Shot," one of the men said. "They collapsed on us. Just like that. All hell broke loose."

"Serge!" Chance cried, recognizing who they carried. He stepped forward. "Serge, are you alright?"

Serge didn't respond. His head lolled back and forth as he cringed with pain. He was muttering nonsense and staring wide-eyed at the ceiling.

"He's in shock," the man said. "We tried to take him back to a safe house, but he wasn't gonna make it. We thought you might—"

"I'll do what I can," Liesel said. "Clear the table. Someone get me a basin of warm water. Chance, grab some cloths from the cupboard there."

Everyone scrambled to their tasks as they laid Serge out on the table, the vegetables dumped unceremoniously on the floor. Chance collected what clean cloths he could find from the cupboards and brought them to Liesel. Carefully she lifted Serge's shirt and removed a make-shift bandage.

Fresh blood spilled onto the table from a bullet wound just below his hip. Chance watched, horrified, as it dripped from the table onto the floor.

"Can you help him?" one of the men asked.

"There's no exit wound," Liesel said. "Hopefully means he hasn't bled out too much. We'll need to find the bullet and stop the bleeding before he loses too much more. Welch!"

Welch ran into the room.

"Welch, get your tools. See if you can sterilize them. We're going to have to retrieve the bullet." She looked up at Chance. "Do you have anything we could use to stop infection? Or numb the pain?"

"I've got a few things. They weren't meant for this, but they might help. If you give me some time I may be able to prepare something better."

"We may not have much time to spare, but do what you can."

Chance pulled his carrier from his coat and flipped it open. He selected one of the vials and handed it to the man holding Serge's head. "If he gets difficult," he explained.

Welch returned from the other room with his tools and knelt by the oven. Swinging the door open, he heated each before handing them off to Liesel.

"Thank you," she said, laying out the instruments and selecting one she could use. Chance watched in horror as she turned Serge onto his side and began her search.

Shaking his head, Chance focused on his task. He cleared a space by the wash bin and laid open his carrier, rummaging through its contents.

"Can I help?" Welch asked over his shoulder.

Chance hesitated, scrunching his eyes in reluctance. But Liesel's words surfaced in his mind. She was right; he didn't have to do everything on his own. And Serge needed whatever help he could get.

"Help me find something to heat this compound?"

Welch nodded, turning over the kitchen in search of a suitable vessel. Chance glanced over his shoulder at his friend. Serge seized up in pain as Liesel dug for the bullet. One of the men was trying to feed him the tonic while the other held him steady, but Serge was giving them trouble.

Just hold on, Chance prayed.

CHAPTER THIRTY-SIX
The Unwelcomed Truth

*Fortune comes to those bold enough to seek it. And, then again,
sometimes she doesn't.*

— Alchemical Proverb

C hance stepped through the doorway, tired and aching. The
front room was still crowded. People had been slipping out
slowly throughout the night, but now it was morning. The rest
would have to be more discrete.

He took a seat on one of the stools at the bar and reached behind
it to grab himself a drink. The bottle came up half-full, so he decided
to forgo a glass.

"Is Serge alright?" Simon asked, joining Chance at the bar. He'd
arrived sometime in the night, along with Kwame and a few others.
Apparently, everyone had ties in one way or another to the Resistance.

Everyone, except Chance.

"Liesel did what she could for him. The bullet nicked the bone in
his hip," Chance explained. "She managed to retrieve it and some of the
fragments, but we'll have to wait and see how he recovers. Right now,
infection is what we're most worried about."

"He should be to a doctor," Kwame suggested.

"Yeah, well it would be a little suspicious if he showed up at a hospital after tonight with a gun wound, wouldn't it? They'd arrest him the moment they were done with him."

"But it could kill him," Kwame said adamantly.

"I gave him an antiseptic, and I trust Liesel's skill. I don't know what more a hospital could do for him."

Kwame was obviously unsatisfied, but he said no more about it. Instead, he stepped behind the counter and retrieved a glass from the bar. He tipped it to Chance, and Chance begrudgingly filled it from his bottle.

Simon fetched another glass. "An odd night," he said.

"Yes, it was," Chance agreed. "Who would have thought things would have escalated like that?"

"All for none and none," Kwame said.

"I wouldn't say that," Simon said. "It proved there is still some fight in the factory workers, if nothing else. That'll make the meritocracy hesitate the next time they try something like last night."

"What good it do?" Kwame asked, his accent coming out thick. "Workers tear 'emselves in two before a real fight start? You fed up as my people in Pendambu? Ready and to fight? Nee! You do no more and kick under a ground."

"It's too big," Simon pointed out. "You can't fight something this big. Not with force."

"What to do then?" Kwame asked. "Roll over and let a meritocracy trample me and you?"

"The only thing to do is confront them face-to-face. Meet them on their ground—in politics."

"But my people got no voice in politics!"

"Which is exactly why their rebellion will fail," Simon said so matter-of-factly that Kwame stared, dumbfounded. The rest of the company felt the sting of Simon's words too, and the atmosphere shifted uncomfortably.

"What do you know?" Kwame said. "You a mercenary. You fight men like me, many and many for a few wages. What do you know of my home? You are not one of us!"

"He didn't mean it," Chance said, trying to cover for Simon and ease Kwame's growing temper.

"I meant every word," Simon said, immovable. "If it bothers you, then I invite you to prove me wrong. What I've said is the closest I can discern to the truth. You're right. I've seen conflicts before. Dozens of them. Rebellions. Wars. Massacres. All of it. I've been on the side of the institution, felt the surge of power behind me as I held ground against revolutionaries like us. I'm telling you, we can't beat them."

"Nee! How do you say that? You know nothing!" Kwame's voice shook and he overturned his stool. "Pendambu readies now to fight Hatteras. They ready and sacrifice *everything!*"

"I'm sorry," Simon said, "but they very well might. You organize yourselves together and tell yourself these things will bring about some great change, but nothing new will come of it—even if you succeed. Nothing changes through force, only the faces of your tyrants and the hands which bear the blood."

"No one as cruel as meritocracy!"

"If you stick around long enough," Simon said, "you may just see how wrong you are."

The little band shuffled uncomfortably. Simon's words cut deep, and Chance could see their resolve injured. Kwame held his tongue with obvious difficulty. Finally, he turned away and pushed his way into the back room.

"For a member of the Resistance, you sure do talk some unpopular ideas," Chance whispered as he gazed around the room. The atmosphere had grown grave, and many of the men were looking at Simon with evident distaste.

"They know my loyalties," Simon said. "And they know my views. Everyone resists in their own way. No man can fault me for wanting to resist where I think it will do the most good."

"Still. You shouldn't say that type of thing around desperate men. It's likely we'll find you in a gutter after this."

"They'll do no such thing. Look at them," he said, pointing to the present company. "They're not soldiers. And they're not murderers. They're just a band of hopefuls caught in a current. The only one here

I'd fear is Serge."

Chance looked surprised.

"Why do you say that? I thought you and Serge were close."

"Out of all the men I've encountered since joining this little Resistance, Serge is the only one I've seen who has the look of conversion—true conversion—in his eyes. I saw it a few times, quelling foreign revolutionaries. Those kinds of men hold the passion," Simon said. "There's no telling to what end they'll go for their cause."

"But you think they'll fail?"

"I think there's a chance they'll start something. Perhaps they will change things someday. But, the way they're going about it, I'm worried what they will sacrifice in the process."

Simon bowed his head and sighed.

"Things like this are never so clean as we like to hope. They'll set a precedence with how they go about it, and I worry they won't be able to stop what they begin."

"What if there is no other way?"

"There is always another way. If we're not so blind we'll see it. I've tried to open Serge's eyes to alternatives he could take. Men like Serge are dangerous if left out of check," Simon explained. "I'm his check."

Chance shook his head. He felt like a toddler discovering the world for the first time again.

Liesel came out of the back and had a quick, whispered conversation with one of the men. At a signal, he and most of the others departed, perhaps to hide out in the storeroom as she opened the pub for the day.

She caught Chance's eye and joined him at the bar.

"It'll be a few weeks before he's standing again, but I think Serge will recover."

"I'm glad to hear it," Simon said.

Are you? Chance wondered, in light of their conversation.

"At least we know our division is quick to assemble," Liesel smiled. "Less than thirty minutes and we had most everyone here. I didn't see Faulkin though. We may want to check and see what kept him away."

"I'll check in on him this afternoon," Simon offered.

Who else was Simon assigned to keep in check? If Serge, then maybe Kwame? Liesel? The other alchemists?

Perhaps Chance himself?

"How are you holding up?" Liesel asked Chance. "Sorry about the reception earlier."

"Makes sense," Chance said. "I'm not exactly a frequent anymore."

"You alright?" she asked, picking up the tone in his voice. "You sound upset."

"It's just..." Chance was having difficulty finding the words. "I'm away for a few months, trying to sort out Ashworth's work, and I hardly recognize anyone anymore. Everyone seems to have changed on me."

"We're still the same," Liesel assured him.

"No," Chance said. "You're not. No one is. Even Rhett is a different person than the boy I knew before I inherited this whole mess." He watched Rhett across the room looking at some gizmo with Welch. "I don't know what I'm saying. I guess I just don't feel as at home here as I used to."

"Of course you're at home," Liesel insisted. "You're always welcome."

"Just not here?" Chance gestured toward the back where the rest of the Resistance was hiding. "Gods above, I don't know anything anymore."

"What's the matter, Chance?" Liesel asked. "What's wrong?"

What was wrong? Chance didn't know where to begin. He thought of telling her about the cipher. How he'd made no progress—absolutely *no* progress—in the past months. He thought of telling her about the pain he felt in his gut with every passing failure. About how difficult it was to rise out of bed knowing what awaited him.

About how lonely he felt.

"Nothing," he insisted. "I probably don't have any reason to be mad right now, but I am. Just... leave me alone."

He stood up and made for the door.

"Chance!" Liesel tried to stop him, but Simon held her back as Chance pushed his way through the doors.

"Let the boy go," he heard Simon say. "It's been a long night. He just needs a moment."

In the street, Chance wiped the edges of his eyes on his sleeve, realizing he still held the bottle in his hand. Liesel wouldn't mind him taking it. He took a deep swig and kept walking.

"I am alone," he said aloud.

CHAPTER THIRTY-SEVEN
Cruel Revelations

*Gradually, I watched an interest become an obsession—and
soon there existed no diversion strong enough to pull me from it.*

— Excerpt from *Mechanarcissism*

Stoddard poured over the collection of documents that lay across
his desk: the texts that Vanzeal had seized from Ashworth's laboratory. Months had transpired, yet he always found himself coming back to them.

No more were they organized into neat piles or webs of thought,
as they had been when he'd begun. Instead, his study was filled with
loose leaves which lay spread about the room. He'd combed through
them again and again, looking for any clue as to what the alchemists
had uncovered.

All the search had turned up was a single name and an indecipherable notebook.

He held the book, turning it over in his hand. He didn't bother
looking inside it anymore. He knew he'd find only gibberish. Yet, the
notebook taunted him. Somewhere between its pages, hidden in all the
nonsense, were the answers he so desperately sought.

Then there was the mark which appeared on the corner. It appeared on each of Ashworth's notebooks, and many of his documents. But it wasn't Ashworth's mark. It was the same mark beside the name that appeared on the deed to his laboratory—Chance.

He'd confirmed the name of Ashworth's apprentice when Skaggs had turned up his suspected whereabouts, but they'd botched their timing and found nothing but a makeshift lab.

But it told Stoddard one thing, the apprentice was still working. Whether he was just setting up his own shop or continuing his mentor's work, Stoddard couldn't know. It was clear he'd been closest to Ashworth. If anyone knew anything about the Aether spark, it would have been him.

But they'd lost him again.

Stoddard muttered a curse to himself.

Arden looked up from his chair in the corner where he'd been reading. "Is everything alright?" he asked.

"I'm fine," Stoddard assured him.

"The notebook again?"

"Just a problem to be solved, nothing more." Stoddard placed the notebook back in the drawer. "And, as with all problems, time is an asset. How go your studies?"

"I'm intrigued by your assertion that energy exists within the body—beyond that of a simple electrical pulse. If it's as fine an energy as you suggest, I wonder how you're able to detect it at all."

"It's difficult, but not so imperceptible as you might think. You see evidence of it every day."

"Where?"

"Let us say we were to take an ordinary rat and cut off that rat's tail. Immediately we observe that the tail is no longer a part of the rat, yet it will twitch for a time even after being severed. Now, after the tail has ceased moving, what if we ran an electrical current through it? Could we expect the tail to twitch again?"

"I would think so."

"But, only sporadically, and not in response to any intelligent command from the rat or ourselves."

"Of course not."

"So then, we can observe there is something more than electricity at work in our motor functions," Stoddard concluded. "Perhaps it doesn't hold up in this instance so well, but when Harper was able to manipulate a completely foreign mechanism it affirmed the true nature of intelligence to me. Unlike the application of electricity alone, intelligence yields not only power, but *control.*"

"I suppose so... but electricity is energy. Energy that can be created and applied."

"And I believe intelligence is a similar energy," Stoddard said.

"But, by that claim, you would also have to assert that intelligence is governed by similar laws and principles."

"That is correct."

"But intelligence cannot be transferred from one object to another."

"Can't it?" Stoddard asked. "Isn't that what has been happening just now, as you've been studying my research? Between me and you as we've explored this particular question? Intelligence is transferred every day in our interactions, though in a subtler way."

"But..."

Arden was perplexed, his face twisted in concentration, and Stoddard couldn't help but smile. For all of Sinclair's criticisms of his son's lack of focus, Stoddard had never encountered a more determined and methodical pupil.

"I see how intelligence can be shared," Arden said as he pieced it together. "However, if intelligence were governed by laws of energy then it would follow that intelligence could be transferred completely between two beings? I've never heard of such a case before."

"The fact that something has not been done before by no means limits its possibility," Stoddard assured him. "If one's vision is great enough."

There was a knock at the door and Donovan entered.

"Sir, there is a man here who says you are expecting him. A duelist by the name of Ringgold? I wasn't aware you'd sent for him, so I thought I'd check with you first."

"I did send for him," Stoddard said. "It's a private matter. Send him in."

"Should I go then?" Arden asked.

"Yes, it's probably best you do. You're welcome to take that volume with you if you'd like."

"I think I will," Arden said, collecting his things and a few of the books he'd been referencing. "I'd like to talk to you more about this idea about transferring intelligence. I find the idea fascinating."

"Of course," Stoddard nodded. He found he enjoyed the time working with Arden more than any of his interactions amongst the meritocracy. Master Arden was a youth after Stoddard's own likeness—inquisitive, and an audacious visionary.

Ringgold entered the room as Arden stepped out. They exchanged quick pleasantries, and Ringgold closed the door behind him.

"That was Sinclair's boy, wasn't it?" Ringgold asked.

"It was."

"You've nestled up close to the elector these past few months. I have to give you credit, you're managing better than I'd expected."

"I'll take that as a compliment," Stoddard said. "Can I get you something to drink?"

"No," Ringgold declined. "But thank you."

"Sergeant, let me get straight to the point. What you said to me at the garden party... it has been distressing me a great deal these past few days."

"You have a persistent memory," Ringgold said. "I'd all but forgotten."

Stoddard turned toward him directly. "Dispense with the intangible conversation, Sergeant. I implore you. It's too much for me to manage at this moment. You were forward with me before—please, be so now." He leaned up against the windowsill and sighed. "Why do you worry for me?"

"Tell me," Ringgold said, joining Stoddard by the window. "What do you know of Lieutenant Vanzeal?"

"He's a skilled duelist, in Sinclair's service and confidence."

"And what do you think of him?" Ringgold asked. "Be honest."

"He's a brazen snake, whose incompetence rivals only his pride. I'd consider myself fortunate if I never cross him again."

"He and Sinclair," Ringgold said, "they're men fashioned from the same cloth."

"I find that hard to believe," Stoddard frowned. "Sinclair is far more collected than Vanzeal could ever hope to be."

"Politics teach men to hide their true natures, or change them altogether. I'm not sure if you're aware, but Sinclair was once a duelist, like Vanzeal. He was lieutenant of the same company, in fact, before he entered the political arena. And, let me assure you, he's more lethal as a politician than he ever was with a sword."

"But Sinclair has been nothing but supportive—"

"To whom?" Ringgold asked. "You? And why do you think that is? What could he hope to gain from your enterprise?"

Stoddard thought back on his first conversation with Sinclair. How he'd been less interested in Harper than he had been in the possibilities of Stoddard's work. He'd wanted to know to what extent Stoddard had pushed his tests. Whether it was solely medical reconstruction... or more.

The spark.

The realization sent a shiver though Stoddard. Sinclair was hoping he could replicate the alchemist's spark.

"There's little doubt there is value in your friendship," Ringgold continued. "Something about your enterprise from which he hopes to benefit. What you should be asking yourself is just how long will what you have retain its value?"

Stoddard's stomach sank. He felt suddenly very small.

"And here is where I approach you with *my* motive," Ringgold said, growing very serious. "About six months ago my company was ordered to join with Vanzeal's as part of a raid on an alchemist's laboratory in the Basin District—a Mr. Charles Ashworth."

Stoddard looked up at Ringgold, unable to hide his recognition of the name.

"During the raid a number of documents were seized by Vanzeal's company and the alchemist was killed. Similar raids were conducted that night on other laboratories, with more documents seized and lives taken.

"Another raid was conducted a fortnight ago in the same district on a suspected laboratory. No one was present during the time of the raid, but, once again, all documents were ordered seized."

Ringgold stepped closer to Stoddard.

"What interests me about all of this is that for each of these raids the orders have been delivered at the request of Elector Sinclair. And in each order, your name has been mentioned as the recipient of those documents."

He glanced around the room at the strewn papers, and Stoddard swallowed hard. The evidence was against him.

"Tell me, Doctor," Ringgold said, his voice a growl. "What is your interest in the alchemists?"

"Nothing," Stoddard said weakly. He didn't want to talk anymore. He didn't want to think. His prospects were coming down around him.

"If that is the case," Ringgold persisted, "then I demand to know why my company is being employed for nothing." He took another step forward until Stoddard was backed against the windowpane. "Why men are dying for *nothing*. I'm sworn to serve the city and the meritocracy that governs it, but that does not mean that against my conscience must I follow orders from men seeking after their own gain—not at the expense of the citizens of Hatteras. So, I ask you again, what is your interest in the alchemists?"

"They're..." Stoddard fumbled.

He'd been disarmed by Ringgold's forwardness, and his guard had been stripped. He was cornered, with nowhere to flee. Could he trust him? Could he be as honest as Ringgold appeared to be?

"I'm..." he began. His brow dripped with perspiration. "I'm a fraud."

He surprised even himself saying it, but it was the truth. Ringgold too was obviously stunned by his declaration.

"What do you mean?" he asked.

"The miracle. It wasn't me. I never revived Harper. Oh, gods above," Stoddard cried. "You're the only one I've confided this to. The most I was able to accomplish was reconstructing the mechanism. I never thought to revive someone after death. If it were left to my work alone, he'd have remained nothing more than a corpse."

Now that he'd said it, he couldn't hold back the words.

"But, if it wasn't your mechanism that brought him back to life, then what was it?" Ringgold asked.

"I'm not certain. I believe that the alchemists know—that they were involved somehow. If I'm correct, then I need to find it out at all costs before Sinclair and the others realize..."

He swallowed hard.

Ringgold turned and paced the floor. "And for this you're willing to kill," he whispered.

"No," Stoddard said, standing up from the windowsill. "I never meant to kill. I never—"

He clenched his jaw and fists. He had meant to kill. Once. In desperation he'd ordered the life of the man he'd been credited for saving.

"You've blood on your hands I don't think you can wash off," Ringgold said coldly. "And you're still out for blood? Forgive me, but I've misread you all along, Doctor."

Ringgold turned and strode toward the door. Stoddard leapt in front of him, barring his way.

"Let me pass," Ringgold warned. "I don't associate myself with murderers."

"What has happened has happened. I know that," Stoddard pleaded. "I regret what I've done and what it's caused. I do. Every part of me feels the weight of it. But if I'm going to fix it—"

"You mean if you're going to save your own skin," Ringgold corrected.

"Can you fault a man his final throes for survival?"

"I can't help you," Ringgold said, pushing past Stoddard. "My loyalty is to the welfare of the city and her citizens, not to those who seek to abuse their powers."

"I'm not the only one who knows about the alchemists," Stoddard called after him, and Ringgold hesitated in the doorway. "You said it yourself: Vanzeal was there during the raids. He was ordered to secure the documents, to arrest Ashworth so I could question him about his work. That was the arrangement through Sinclair. I swear. It was never my desire to have Ashworth killed."

"Can I honestly believe what you're telling me is the truth?"

"There's one thing I know for sure," Stoddard said. "If I'm found out, and Sinclair discovers me a fraud, he'll have Vanzeal pick up where I've left off. He'll track down the alchemists in his own way. I'm no saint; I know this. But you and I both know Vanzeal. I ask you to gauge which is worse."

Ringgold stood rigid, weighing Stoddard's words.

"Help me find them," Stoddard pleaded. "Help me discover the truth of the captain's miracle. Perhaps then we can fix all of this. Perhaps we'll save more lives than my own."

"Some things cannot be fixed," Ringgold said.

"That doesn't mean we shouldn't try, right?"

Ringgold paused in the doorway for a moment, weighing Stoddard's words in his mind. "I can't help you," he sighed, and closed the door behind him.

Stoddard strength ebbed out of his limbs, and he slumped to the floor. He would need more than a miracle to recover from this.

CHAPTER THIRTY-EIGHT
A Friendly Gesture

*Had I not been so blind, I might have seen the toll it was taking
on me. Or the effects it would have on those near me.*

— Excerpt from *Mechanarcissism*

I t was late afternoon when Chance finally made it home—if Margarete's loft could be considered home. He'd taken the long way along the bay to try and walk off his sour mood, but he couldn't shake it.

Everyone had a secret. Ashworth. Liesel. Welch. Rhett. All of them! Should he have expected anything else? After all, he had his own. Perhaps that was what was getting to him; he'd never thought to suspect any of them. Somehow, he'd convinced himself that among his circle of friends all things were open.

How wrong he'd been.

He was tired. Tired of everyone and their half-truths. He'd been apprenticed to Ashworth for seven years and hadn't the slightest clue he'd been developing the Aether spark. And how long had he known Liesel, Simon, or Kwame? Had they been a part of their Resistance the whole time?

He didn't feel like he knew any of his friends anymore.

Chance was about to scramble up the gutter again when the door opened and Margarete stepped outside. She'd obviously been watching for him, and the look she gave him made it clear why.

He wasn't about to avoid this conversation.

"You know there are perfectly functional stairs you're welcome to use," she smiled, though Chance didn't feel the warmth he usually did. "Why don't you come on in? We have some catching up to do."

She turned back inside, leaving the door open behind her. Chance's shoulders slumped, but he abandoned the gutter and followed.

The place was quieter than usual. Chance couldn't remember a moment since he'd arrived when there wasn't a cluster of women talking freely and laughing loudly. It had become something of a pleasant backdrop to contrast the gravity of the world beyond their walls. When he entered now, however, he was greeted by silence and the sound of Margarete's footfalls down the hall.

"Come on to the back," she urged, and Chance followed her to a communal room full of boxed storage and furniture arranged to provide as much sitting room as possible for the space.

"Take a seat," she said.

"I know what this is about," Chance said, finding himself a sturdy box to perch on. "It's about Ponti, right?"

"And other things."

"Look, I'm sorry he's come around. I've tried to keep him away, but he's not exactly the type of guy you can order around."

"So that's what he meant when he came by last night when he said you'd sent him." She gave Chance a teasing look.

"Okay, I did send him last night to drop off a few things of mine, but that was it. I swear."

"Huh," Margarete smirked. "I'm not worried about last night. It gave me an opportunity to boot him good for skulking around earlier."

"Wait? So, you aren't upset?"

"No," she said.

"Then what's all this about?" He waved his hands in the air.

"All what?"

"Your stern look just now and leading me back here like this,"

Chance said. "And where is everyone?"

"How should I know?" she shrugged. "My girls do as they please. No one's stopping them, and I certainly don't keep tabs on them every waking moment. I have my own matters to take care of."

Chance didn't know what else to say, so he occupied himself with poking at the lip of the box.

"Actually, I wanted to ask how *you* are doing," she said.

Chance kept his gaze down.

"How are you doing, Chance?"

"I'm fine," he shrugged.

"Are you?"

"Why wouldn't I be? I'm dandy. I'm chipper even!"

Margarete sighed and took a seat across from him on one of the couches. "I was talking to Rhett," she said. "He worries about you."

"I'm surprised he has the time. He's awfully busy these days."

"I worry about you, too," she said. "You're not your usual self. I should know more than anyone."

Chance stood up, his arms out to the sides. "Take a good look. I'm still the same mangy rat as always."

"That's not what I see," Margarete said, undisrupted by his outburst. "I see the young man whose eyes are bigger than his body. I see the dreamer who used to sit with me and share all the ways he planned to change the world with his work.

"But lately I've seen less and less of him. Ever since..." She paused and Chance felt the mood shift. "...you just haven't been the same, Chance."

Chance bit his lip. He missed that part of him, too. He felt the divide, between who he was and that overlooked piece. How long had it been since he'd even looked at his own work?

He had been tampering with transmutations, trying to figure out how to turn lead into gold. He remembered fighting to find moments between his other tasks to work out the problem, scrounging together a little extra money to run his experiments and sifting through every book he could find.

Somehow, those days seemed sweeter to him now.

AETHER SPARK • 335

"I think you might do with a break," Margarete said. "I know you have nothing but the best intentions trying to finish Ashworth's work, but I worry about the effect it's having on you."

"Someone has to do it."

"Do they really?"

"Of course!" Chance snapped. "This was Ashworth's life work, and he left it to me. No one else can finish what he started. Without it, Ashworth is dead."

"Chance." Margarete's voice grew soft as silk. "Ashworth is *gone*. I can't believe that he'd have wanted you to lose yourself over what he started."

"Do you think I wanted this?" Chance asked. "I wish every day that Ashworth had never developed that cursed spark! I wish we were back in our lab together working on nothing more interesting than foot creams and primers.

"But, that's not how it's played out. Even if I wanted to turn back, there's nowhere left to turn back to. This is the hand fate has dealt me. I can't just abandon it now; it's all that's left."

Margarete rose and put her hand on Chance's shoulder. He thought to pull away, but didn't. Her touch was comforting, and for a moment he let it calm the heat which simmered beneath his skin.

"It should have been me," he mumbled. "I should have been the one to die, not Ashworth. If he were here he might know how to salvage this mess, but I don't. I've tried, but nothing makes any sense to me. I still have no idea what the Aether spark really is, or how to create it. I don't even know how to know if I'm on the right road to finding out."

Margarete pulled Chance close, and he went limp in her embrace, his emotions rising up in him so strongly that his body shook with effort to restrain them.

"It should have been me," he repeated.

"Nonsense," Margarete said. "You can't blame yourself for what happened to Ashworth. He knew the risks he was taking. Even if it didn't go how he planned, that doesn't mean all is lost. You're forgetting; you were one of his projects too. I think he'd be proud to know you're still out there trying to do good."

"And bringing misfortune everywhere I go." Chance pulled away. "I'm nothing like Ashworth. He would never have let so much ruin come upon his friends. He never would have hurt so many with his work."

"But he did," Margarete said.

Chance shot her a glare.

"I know you don't want to think of it," she continued, "but whether he intended to or not, his work has hurt others. It's hurt you."

"I'm fine," Chance insisted.

"No, you're not. I know what you've been up to. You're not just working on the spark..." She swallowed hard as her emotions rose into her face. "Rhett told me what you've been mixing."

Chance's cheek twitched. Ever since the raid on Ponti's place, he'd wrestled with the increased paranoia as he felt the guard closing in around him. He'd fallen back into old habits, mixing a cheap narcotic to ease his anxieties.

"Rhett should keep his mouth shut," he hissed.

"Is it true?" she asked. "Are you drugging yourself?

"What's it to anyone what I do with my own time?"

"It matters to me," she said. "Chance, it could kill you!"

"Then it might as well get to it sooner than later," he snapped. "Save everyone some time and misery." He pushed his way past her and trudged for the door.

"You don't mean that," she said. "You don't really mean that."

Chance paused. Margarete's eyes were wet. He saw plainly the pain he was causing her. She didn't deserve this. None of them deserved any of this.

Which only added to his guilt.

"More than you can know," he said. "Maybe you're right, Margarete. Maybe I have changed."

"Chance!" she called after him as he hustled down the hall. But he ignored her. Throwing the door open, he ran as fast as he could. He needed to get away.

CHAPTER THIRTY-NINE
A Chance Encounter

Try something new. And if that doesn't work,
try something else.

— Alchemical Proverb

Skaggs cursed bitterly as he limped his way down the crowded street. The uneven paving, the jostling passersby, the loose fit of his left shoe—it didn't matter. He cursed everything. He had no lack of curses in his repertoire.

But above all, he cursed the blackened depths for his blighted leg.

He'd been at it for months, dredging the pits of society and scouring the most forgotten nooks for any scrap of information which might satisfy his employer's incessant hounding.

He'd had a spot of luck when he'd caught wind that Ashworth's apprentices were still alive, but that trail had gone cold the moment he'd turned over the information. One botched raid and months of his time were wasted.

The list Stoddard had provided had proven rubbish. None of the alchemists he'd suggested were working on anything of real significance. They were too busy scrounging together their own meager existences to be preoccupied with anything as grandiose as the Aether spark.

More disappointing, he'd learned firsthand that many of the alchemists—including ones he'd turned to for remedies to treat his leg—were nothing more than fakes. Fortunately, that revelation had been soothed some by the sheer number he found who dealt in narcotics.

Skaggs had spent much of his search painless.

But today, the pain was back in force. With every step, the bone in his leg panged with a fire that twisted his stomach and emptied its contents into his throat. He needed relief, but where he was going he knew he couldn't expect much.

Stopping momentarily outside the Pub & Brawl, Skaggs tightened the rag which held his flimsy brace against his leg. Leveling his eyes, he gave the doors a deliberate push and hobbled through with as dignified a stride as he could muster. He kept his gaze forward, knowing his entrance would spark whispered conversations. As usual, nervous glances passed between the patrons and a suspicious quiet descended upon the room.

They knew something. Every aching bone in his body suspected a secret was being kept here. But how to discover it? That was the real challenge. He'd been at it for weeks, with no luck.

He couldn't understand why.

"Can I get some service here?" he said loudly, stepping up to the bar. He lifted his leg and swung himself onto an empty stool, banging on the counter. "Taking your afternoon naps, are you?"

"We'll get to you in a moment," the barkeep said. "You're not the only one here today, Mr. Skaggs."

Skaggs gave a look up and down the bar. Apart from himself and pair of sorry sods seated nearby, there wasn't anyone else but those at the tables.

"Don't suppose you could pick it up a bit? How'd you be if you had to walk around all day on a bum leg? You'd be starving for a drink right about now, I swear it."

The barkeep's eyes rolled, but he put down his glasses. "What can I do for you?"

"Gin. And don't you skimp on me," Skaggs warned. "I want a full glass if I'm paying full price." He pulled a few coins from his pocket, setting them on the table.

The barkeep took them and poured Skaggs a glass. He was turning to leave when Skaggs protested.

"Don't you turn your back on me like that," he barked. "Was I done with you?"

"Is there a problem here?" Liesel stood in the doorway. Her expression turned unpleasant as she caught sight of Skaggs.

"Your boy here is begrudging me service. Is this the way you treat all your regulars?"

"I'm not sure you qualify as a regular," Liesel said coolly. "The way you carry on I'm fairly certain you never will."

"Know my name, miss?" Skaggs snapped. "Know my face? I bet you do. Then I'm regular enough. Is my money not as good as yours? Or the next man's?"

"Did you need anything else?" The barkeep was visibly losing patience.

"Just the respect every decent man deserves!"

The barkeep groaned and stepped into the back. Liesel took his place. She exchanged an apologetic glance with the nearby patrons, making no effort to mask her distaste for Skaggs.

Skaggs glowered at her.

"Can't get anything around here without some sod giving you trouble for it," Skaggs muttered, taking a gulp of the gin. His lip curled in disgust at the bitterness, but he quaffed another nonetheless.

"Only trouble you get from us is the trouble you bring through that door with you," Liesel said. "I'm not in the habit of turning away those who find themselves in dire circumstances, but your patronage has been nothing but unpleasant. Consider yourself warned."

"Oh," Skaggs feigned fear. "What you gonna do? You gonna throw me out? You gonna sic the constables on me, are you? Go ahead. While they're here, let's have them give you a shakedown as well. Turn this place over a bit."

"Whatever for?" Liesel looked confused.

"Don't play coy with me," Skaggs growled. "I've been coming here long enough to know something ain't right. I've had my eyes on you for some time. You're hiding something."

Liesel's lips pursed, and she focused on tidying the bar. The other patrons took a sudden interest in Skagg's conversation and leaned toward him.

Skaggs saw it. He read it. He'd struck the right cord.

"Yeah," he sneered. "I knew there was something going on. So, what is it? Not a black-market hub, I reckon. You're too prissy to dabble with the likes of them, aren't you?"

Skaggs gave her a slow once over, then caught her eyes.

"You're the fighting type—says it on your sign. Kind of person who needs a little action every now and then? Getting tired of the same old day in, day out? Bet you this scrap with the colonies excites you, doesn't it? Gets the blood pumping."

"You're talking nonsense," Liesel warned. "You might want to look to that."

"Or maybe it's not just interest," Skaggs kept on. "You think they're in the right. Don't you? You sympathize with them. Feel for their plight? Think it unjust what they been through? And now… you want to do something about it."

With every question, he read the response in her eyes. Saw the truth she tried to withhold from him. Saw her clear through those guarded hazel eyes.

It was his gift.

"Forgive me," he grinned wickedly. "You're *doing* something about it."

Skaggs picked himself up off the street with some difficulty. His forearms were rough where he'd caught himself after they'd thrown him out, and his cheek was sore where she'd struck him.

"You're no longer welcome," Liesel warned from the entrance. "You steer clear of the Pub & Brawl next time you come creeping this way, filth!"

She tossed his cane on the ground and slammed the door behind her.

Skaggs rubbed his arms and touched his cheek gingerly. She'd pay for that, he swore. He swore it to every unholy entity he knew, which was quite the list.

"A pox on the whole lot of you!" he shouted back.

He'd exposed the tender spot, alright. There lay the woman's great secret. She was involved somehow with the conflicts overseas, if his gut could be trusted. And Skaggs, despite his sundry flaws, prided himself in his ability to read people.

He'd have to pick at that spot a bit more before the week was out.

Regardless, he'd have no more luck in this part of the Basin—not for a few days at least. He decided it best to take a break for a while and let hostilities cool before trying again.

He knew one establishment that'd never turned him away. Taking up his cane, he turned in the direction of the bay and sauntered off under the glares of the passersby.

"Ah, Skaggs. It's good to see you again," Bracken said, welcoming him as he hobbled toward the bar. "It's been a few days. I was beginning to worry something had happened to my most distinguished patron."

"Spare me the jabber and get me a bottle of whatever is strongest," Skaggs grumbled, setting down a few coins.

Bracken chuckled at his curtness, but swept away the coins. "You'll understand if I can't get you your usual. Times are a bit lean." Bracken set a bottle down in front of Skaggs. "Might think about pacing yourself to make it last."

Skaggs grumbled as Bracken left to greet another patron. It wasn't ideal, but it was enough to nurse his bruised pride.

"Tough day?" a young man next to him asked.

Skaggs eyed him. He was a scrawny thing, frail under his otherwise bulky coat. His eyes were red, and he sat hunched low over his drink. When he spoke, his words were saturated by the thick slur of alcohol. Clearly, this one had been dragged through the mud a while, but Skaggs wasn't used to people initiating a conversation, and he recoiled at the interest.

"What do you care?" he snapped, taking a greedy gulp from his bottle.

The young man shrugged.

"I suppose I don't. It's just nice to talk to someone new once in a while."

"What about you?" Skaggs asked, though he didn't much care.

The young man nodded. "Whole life."

Skaggs rolled his eyes as the kid reached over the counter, picking a bottle off the wall and pouring himself another glass.

"Well," Skaggs grumbled. "Aren't we the privileged one?"

"Bracken knows I'm good for it," he explained. "I've been coming here a lot lately."

"How fortunate for you," Skaggs said, not trying to mask his sarcasm. "You don't happen to know if they're hiding anything stronger behind there, do you?"

The young man reached into his coat and produced a metal flask, offering it to Skaggs. "Something of my own make I keep on hand for days like this."

Skaggs took and uncapped it. Whiffing the contents, he grinned at the strength of the fumes and dumped a liberal amount into his glass before handing it back.

"Cheers."

Skaggs drank deeply, the new concoction raking his throat like no alcohol had before. For a moment, he was afraid for the damage it might do, but the viscous blend turned warm and comforting in his stomach. He felt an empowering glow spread through his limbs, and he smiled.

"You, my friend, are quite the mixologist," Skaggs said, taking another, smaller, sip.

"It comes with the territory," the young man shrugged. "Almost all alchemists know a thing or two about mixing drinks."

Skaggs choked on his gin, the mixture catching uncomfortably in his esophagus so that his neck seized up and his expression turned skiwampus. He coughed forcefully to clear his throat and struggled for his breath.

"You... what?" he choked out.

The young man looked at him with concern. "Are you alright?"

"Yes," Skaggs strained. "Don't worry about me. You say you were

AETHER SPARK · 343

an alchemist?"

"I am."

Skaggs swallowed hard, fighting to still his reflexes as he regained control of himself. After a moment, he could breathe normally again.

"And, you said you grew up around these parts, your whole life?"

"Most of it."

Skaggs' mind whirled, in part because of the strange new alcohol, and because he'd been pricked by a sudden possibility.

"You wouldn't happen to know..." No, Skaggs thought. He couldn't be too forward. Not yet. "...where a fellow could get a batch of that stuff for himself, would you?"

"It's not too hard to make, if you have the ingredients on hand. I could mix you another sometime."

"How about now?" Skaggs asked. "I've got coin, and it would make the rest of the night more pleasurable."

The young man shrugged. "Why not? My laboratory isn't far from here. Did you just want to—"

"I'll come along!" Skaggs insisted. "Save you from having to make a trip back and all. Least I can do for the favor."

"You sure? It's a bit of a walk, and... your leg," he pointed out.

"Never bothered me enough to pass up an opportunity," Skaggs assured him. "And let me get this for you. Token of appreciation for the conversation."

He placed a few more coins on the counter to cover the drinks.

As the young man picked up his carrier and led the way out of the pub, Skaggs' fingers tapped against his chest lightly.

"So, how's it someone like yourself comes to be an alchemist?" Skaggs asked. "I've met a few who I don't believe could mix up twins, let alone a drink like that."

"Just a typical apprenticeship."

"Perhaps I should give it a go. Not too old am I?" Skaggs chortled. "Who's your master?"

The kid didn't respond immediately, but grew solemn as they walked.

"He's dead."

"Oh..." Skaggs fought to contain his grin. "How unfortunate. I'm sorry to hear that."

"It's okay. It wasn't that long ago. I'm still trying to get used to it."

"Well, if your skills are any testament, then he must have been quite the mentor," Skaggs said. "How did he die, if I might ask?"

"He was murdered," the young man said. "On Septigonee's Day."

Skaggs couldn't contain himself, and he had to turn away as his face bent into a wicked grin. He'd found him. He'd finally found Ashworth's apprentice.

CHAPTER FORTY
An Unfortunate Business

*My work has not been without some unforeseen obstacles. But
they have only proved another testament to its providence—that
the will to carry on endured, no matter what was required of me.*

— Excerpt from *Mechanarcissism*

I t was a chill evening, and Stoddard joined his circle of friends for
a gathering at the governor's manor to celebrate his birthday. It
had begun as most social engagements did, with a general greeting
followed by a speech in which various gentlemen praised the governor
in one long round.

Dinner had been provided, in which toasts were made and more
speeches given, until Stoddard was quite ready to call it an end. But, as
tended to happen, the event dragged on, turning to nothing more than
mindless mingling.

Stoddard idly listened to the drone of voices and tried to feign deep
interest.

"If Dempwolf is sponsoring the production then it must be worth
seeing," Timberman's wife was saying with great enthusiasm. "We must
go, Gerald!"

"Of course," Timberman acquiesced, though he did not appear
thrilled.

"How I'd love to see it," Emmaline smiled. "We haven't been to the theater in so long."

"Too many social engagements?" Merryfield ventured.

"A few," Stoddard said. "And my work continues to demand much of my attention."

"Ah, yes," Timberman said. "And how does it go? It feels like forever since we've had an update."

Stoddard winced.

"It's coming along," he managed to say. "A miracle is a tricky thing to replicate."

"Perhaps things will slow down for you in time," Merryfield said. "It's not good for a man to run faster than he has strength; he must take a moment to breath in the finer culture around him. Otherwise, why do we work so hard?"

"I quite agree," Emmaline said, casting a look Stoddard's way. "We should take your advice."

Stoddard frowned, but followed Timberman's example and conceded. "Of course we should, my dear," he said.

What she didn't seem to comprehend was how precarious their situation truly was. Their company had already grown considerably sparser compared to the entourage they'd attracted when he'd first come into the meritocracy. Stoddard had noted each of the figures as they'd drifted away.

He was slipping. Focus was shifting to more timely topics like the coming war, new hairstyles, and which social engagements were being planned for the winter. Stoddard sensed, with great anxiety, the distance which he had to fall if he slipped much further.

"Perhaps you could share with us some of the difficulties you're having," Timberman suggested. "More minds make lighter work, as they say."

Do they say anything about the quality of those minds? Stoddard thought, but before he could respond he was approached by a manservant.

"Pardon me for intruding, but there is a man here asking for you, Doctor Stoddard."

"If it's not one thing, it's another," Stoddard apologized, seizing the opportunity. "Where is he?"

"At the door, sir. He requests your presence with due haste."

"Friends," Stoddard said. "My apologies, but if you'll excuse me a moment."

He followed the messenger through the room, letting out a sigh of relief. People wanted news, and he was having difficulty providing it for them. He feared unless something drastic changed even Merryfield would end their association.

"You didn't admit him?" Stoddard asked the manservant.

"No, sir. I thought it best we have you confirm that you knew him. He has an unsavory appearance, but he was quite adamant that you'd want to see him."

The hair on Stoddard's neck bristled at the description, and he clenched his jaw when sight confirmed what he'd feared.

It was Skaggs.

"Should I admit him, sir?"

"No," Stoddard said quickly. "I'll see him outside. Kindly show him to an empty balcony. I'll be along in a moment."

The man was too bold.

Stoddard fumed as he returned to his party.

"Back already?" Timberman asked. "We were just speculating as to who this mystery visitor might be who's about to steal you away from us—considering all the people worth knowing were already invited to the party."

"We're not losing you to another promising companion, I hope?" Merryfield asked.

"It's no one of great consequence," Stoddard insisted. "Though I am afraid I will have to leave you for a time. It's a matter of business."

"How unfortunate it was able to find you here," Merryfield laughed. "Just when I thought we might have you to ourselves for an evening."

"It's a frequent inconvenience for all of his acquaintances, I'm afraid," Emmaline said as pleasantly as she could, though Stoddard detected the note of resentment for yet another social disengagement. He'd grown quite skilled at them.

"What a busy man you must be," Lady Merryfield said. "Though I hope not too busy."

"For?" Stoddard asked.

"We have been invited to accompany the Merryfields to the opera this weekend," Emmaline explained. "Marietta Ferraro is singing the aria '*La disgrazia di il cuore.*' It's bound to be the cultural peak of the season. I told her we'd be sore to miss it."

"Yes, that sounds like an enjoyable evening," Stoddard agreed hastily.

"Though shall we have a prayer of holding your attention with the diva there?" Merryfield smiled. "Alas, we may never have our own evening with the doctor."

"I promise," Emmaline said, taking Merryfield's hand. "You two will have our undivided attention." She cast a testing glance at Stoddard as she said it, as if to invite him to challenge her.

Stoddard said nothing.

"Thank you, child," Merryfield said. "Perhaps it will be that breath of fine air you've needed, Doctor."

"I'm sure it will be," Stoddard said. "I look forward to it immensely. But now, if you'll excuse me. I leave Emmaline in your most capable hands."

"Will you be long?" she asked.

"Impossible to say," Stoddard said. "I hope not."

He peeled himself away from the party, evading those who looked like they might engage in conversation as he hurried through the estate to the agreed upon meeting place.

As he stepped out onto the balcony, the crisp air brushed over him and he allowed his countenance to fall. There was Skaggs, resting against one of the marble pillars. Stoddard grimaced, but approached the man nonetheless.

Skaggs saw him coming and straightened up.

"I expressly forbade you from seeking me out in public. Much less, the governor's house!" Stoddard wasted no time with pleasantries. "You have *no* business being here. What could have possessed you to appear now? Speak!"

"Ah," Skaggs frowned. "We're going to start on that foot, are we?

Then let me remind you that it's *your* bloody business that I'm about. Do you think I'd come to one of these high-to-dos for any other reason?"

"You are never to seek me out except in the privacy of my study!" Stoddard snapped. He glanced back into the building, but no one seemed to be paying them any undue notice.

"Not even when I have information?"

"Not even," Stoddard growled. "If you have anything to report you can speak to my assistant. That's the only way we'll correspond from this point on."

He turned to go.

"Not even if I had news about Ashworth's apprentice?"

Stoddard stopped.

"Got your attention now, did I? And what if I told you he's well and dandy, and that I happen to know where the little alchy might be right now? That's what you were hoping for all along, wasn't it? Someone who knew what the old man was working on? Well, I've found him. And I've nestled up to him, I have. Nestled up real close."

He eyed Stoddard as he turned back.

"Where?"

"Right under your nose," Skaggs smirked.

"I'm in no mood to play your games," Stoddard warned.

"And I haven't been too keen playing yours," Skaggs snapped. "But, I've done it, and swallowed a heap of trouble for it too. Scrounging around in the gutters on nothing but hearsay. Now if we're done pissing unpleasantries, why don't we get to our arrangement?"

"Let's," Stoddard said coldly. "Where is he?"

"Oh, it must eat you up that I know, doesn't it? You've been after him for, what? Half a year, was it?"

"About."

"Been a test of patience, hasn't it?"

"The greatest test of my patience has come from working with you. Now, do you know where he is or not?"

"I do," Skaggs hummed. "But it's going to cost you a bit more."

Stoddard stepped toward him, his temper nearly at the breaking point. "We will not renegotiate our contract!"

"Oh, but I think we will," Skaggs grinned. "You see, all that wandering gave me time for pondering. I asked myself, what's the use of a new leg except to end up working in some factory somewhere, slaving away for what Septigonee knows is the measliest of livings? Now why would a man such as myself want something like that? Honest, what good would it do? No, I want a decent standard of living... and you're gonna provide it for me."

"I will do no such thing."

"You're in no place to negotiate!" Skaggs was animated. "There is a whole room of your friends just through those doors. One misspoken word and I could reveal you for the monster you really are. You forget that I've seen what you've done. I know your true character."

Stoddard lunged, seizing Skaggs' shirt and pushing him backwards so fiercely that Skaggs nearly toppled as he collided with the edge of the balcony. Skaggs struggled to regain his footing, grasping for anything to hold onto.

"If you know my true character," Stoddard growled, "then you know not to cross me."

"Wait a minute," Skaggs begged. "Let's not do anything you might regret."

"You're testing my patience." Stoddard pressed him further over the edge. "The alchemist. Where is he?"

Skaggs saw it then, behind Stoddard's eyes. He read the thought before Stoddard himself even had it, saw it form in the mind of a desperate man.

"Cheapside," Skaggs whispered. "At a brothel owned by a woman named Margarete. That's where you'll find him, I swear it is."

Stoddard did not loosen his grip, and Skaggs went on.

"He's a gangly chap. Couldn't be more than twenty. And by the looks of him, he's a bit worse for the wear. Life ain't been too kind to him, what with you hounding him. He's tired. Tired and desperate. I reckon you'll find him willing if the right offer was presented.

"Here," Skaggs said, pulling a folded bundle of pages from his pocket. "Everything I've learned about him. Right here. Meticulous, I was. All of it."

Stoddard took the bundle, looking from Skaggs to the pages. The notes appeared detailed enough to follow to the boy's whereabouts. But, could he trust Skaggs' word? That, he was less sure of.

"That's everything I got," Skaggs pleaded. "I swear. Gods above, it is. He's there, at the dame's place. I promise he is. I could fetch him right now, if you wanted."

"No," Stoddard said, loosening his hold and letting Skaggs rise again. "I'll contact him myself. I have no use for you anymore, Mr. Skaggs. You may consider our business concluded. As of this moment, you're no longer in my employ."

"What about my compensation?" Skaggs insisted. "I went to a lot of trou—"

He was cut short as Stoddard rushed him, shoving him with all the might he could muster. Skaggs stumbled backward on his withered leg, his eyes going wide as he tipped headlong over the balcony ledge. His cry of alarm turned to panic, ending abruptly with the sound of his impact upon the stone patio below.

Stoddard crouched on the balcony, clutching the railing, his heart racing. He tried to regain himself as he heard the startled cries from the guests below and calls for the authorities.

He'd had to do it. There could be no other way. Skaggs had forced his hand. Stoddard couldn't let such a liability exist. Not now, when everything hung in such delicate balance.

Despite the way his heart refused to quit pounding, or the cold sensation which filled his chest, Stoddard breathed a labored sigh of relief. Skaggs would haunt him no more.

CHAPTER FORTY-ONE
Accidents

Was I justified in what I did? Is it like they say? Do the ends truly justify the means?

— Excerpt from *Mechanarcissism*

W hat a dreadful business, all of this," Merryfield murmured. "I don't know how Lady Merryfield will recover. She's much too fragile to handle something like this."

"I think all of us will need time to recover ourselves," Dempwolf said. He, along with many of the other guests, had come to hear from Stoddard what awfulness had transpired on the balcony.

"I think so," Stoddard said, still feeling shaken himself as he eyed the constables. They were conducting the investigation, and were there to hear his story as well.

"Tell me, what was your relation to the man?" one of the constables asked.

"No relation," Stoddard said. "Though we had been in correspondence a time or two. He'd petitioned me to perform an operation for him as I did for Captain Harper, only on his leg. It's terribly withered, as you'll see from the body. When I informed him that I was already predisposed and unable to perform the operation, he sought me out and found me here."

"The sheer presumptuousness," Timberman exclaimed, "to seek you at a gathering like this. You were quite considerate to meet with him at all."

"I thought it better to address him than have him cause a scene, given the occasion."

"I appreciate your consideration," the governor said, also standing nearby to listen. "But, be careful putting yourself at the mercy of a man like that on our account. We're lucky nothing happened to you."

"What did happen, exactly?" the constable asked.

"Well," Stoddard continued. "He asked, or should I say demanded, that I treat him. As though I could treat the man there on the spot. I tried to explain to him my predicament, and he became increasingly belligerent. He threatened that if I didn't help him he would do something drastic.

"Naturally, I took this as a threat and feared for my own safety. The man was outside of his mind. Before I realized what he was about to do, he'd flung himself from the balcony."

"The poor man," Merryfield said.

Emmaline remained silent. She had refused to be taken away with the other women, and Stoddard had not had the time to insist as he fielded questions. She had not taken her eyes off of him since he'd returned. He knew she was looking at him, studying him silently. He couldn't bring himself to look at her directly.

Did she suspect him?

"What sort of life must that man have lived to go to such ends?" the governor asked.

"It was apparent the man was in constant pain," Stoddard said. "He must have lost patience holding out for a miracle."

"Well, whatever becomes of man's spirit when he goes, I wish him a fairer turn." Merryfield raised his glass and the company toasted to Skaggs' memory.

Stoddard tipped his glass as well, but let none of the liquid past his lips.

What did become of man's spirit? The question was suddenly queer to him. He'd been working with what he assumed was the nearest thing to spirit that man had discovered. Yet, in the toast he had a moment's doubt, as though despite all of his studies he'd missed something. Something paramount.

Just then a figure came forward that chased the thought from Stoddard's mind.

"Sir," the constables saluted, and Ringgold returned a salute dutifully.

"That was quite the accident, what happened on the balcony earlier," Ringgold said. His eyes bore into Stoddard. There was no emotion in his voice. No play in his delivery of words. Again, Stoddard felt the man laying him bare with his direct manner.

"Yes," Stoddard agreed. "It was."

"How goes the investigation?"

"Nothing is out of place," the constable assured him. "The man was deranged due to prolonged pain from a withered leg and used the event tonight to gain attention. Stoddard's testimony provides sufficient evidence to shed light on the man's background. It was clearly a suicide."

"Very good," Ringgold said, though he frowned. "I suppose all are better for it? All will meet their end in due time." Ringgold raised his glass in a toast. "To a fitting end," he said, and the company repeated his toast and took a sip.

Stoddard felt sick.

"If you all will please excuse me?" he said.

"Are you alright?" Merryfield asked.

"I need some air." Stoddard pushed his way through the group, almost fleeing to the balcony before he realized his error and changed course. Instead, he made his way to the gardens.

He needed to be away. He needed time to think. He'd just taken a man's life, and he'd hardly realized he was doing it. His hands had betrayed him when they'd lunged for Skaggs.

He told himself over and over that there was no other way, but it did nothing to ease the knot tied in his chest. It was one thing to order Harper killed, but to have killed himself...

Stoddard raced through the doors and away from the lighted manor, falling against one of the hedge walls when he was clear of sight. His mind raced and his heart beat in his ears at an unsteady rhythm.

He retched into the hedge.

"Something unsettling about my toast?" Ringgold came down the steps, approaching the place where Stoddard knelt. "Or have you let this evening's festivities get out of hand? Has it only now finally caught up with you? I warned you, men should never acquire a taste for killing. Yet, you seem to have taken to it sooner than I expected."

"I'm not a murderer," Stoddard pleaded.

"Then what are you?" Ringgold demanded.

"I swear; he was trying to destroy me. It was in self-preservation that I—"

"Every man has his reasons," Ringgold interrupted. "Consider the offer of my services permanently withdrawn. From now on, I serve you only as duty binds me to the meritocracy, and that is the end of it. I will not be drawn into the mess you've woven around yourself."

He turned to go.

"You're not going to arrest me?" Stoddard asked.

"You're a gentleman now," Ringgold said with distaste. "Your friends surround you in both high and low places. And I? I'm only a rising duelist. What good could come from my interference in your affairs?"

Stoddard let out the breath he'd not realized he'd been holding.

"But remember this," Ringgold warned, his cape rustling in the breeze which stirred around them. "There are consequences even an elector cannot shield you from. You will not always have people to protect you from the costs of your actions, Doctor."

Ringgold climbed the steps and disappeared into the manor, leaving Stoddard to tend to his troubled thoughts.

CHAPTER FORTY-TWO
Stoddard's Invitation

And to think, for that brief moment I held their secrets in my open hand. How foolishly I handled such an opportunity. How different might the world look now had I simply closed my fist?

— Excerpt from *Mechanarcissism*

Chance held the open letter in his hand, limp at his side as he sat alone in Liesel's kitchen. Everyone was gone out for the evening, leaving him to look after Serge.

That was fine by Chance. He welcomed being alone. Ever since he'd found out about the Resistance, it had become more difficult to speak with his friends. He felt like he hardly knew them anymore.

And they'd grown nosier. Everywhere he turned someone was asking how he was holding up, where he was going, or offering their help. But none of them could help with the thing he needed most; Keller's notebook was still illegible.

He tried to convince them he was all right, but he was having difficulty keeping up appearances. At least when alone he didn't have to hide how he truly felt—how much time he spent longing for an end to it all.

And now, on top of all that, was a letter.

He turned it over in his hands. He'd read it a half-dozen times already. It wasn't a warning, or a threat. Nor was it blackmail. It was an invitation—to an opera the following night. Chance had never been to an opera before, and he had no intention of starting now.

Yet, he couldn't help but be intrigued.

What kind of person would send an invitation like this? He'd always expected the meritocracy would find him. It was only a matter of time. But, if they had, where was the guard? Why hadn't they kicked in the doors and burned Margarete's like they'd burned Ashworth's? What game were they expecting him to play?

Chance took the flask from his pocket and uncapped a few sips, letting the familiar warmth spread through his stomach and to his outer extremities. His mind slowed too, as the sensations washed over him, until he felt more in control. He'd become such an anxious creature; he all but relied on his new brew to function.

Pocketing the flask, he looked over the letter once more.

"Sincerely, Your Benefactor," he read out loud.

Whomever had sent it, it seemed they wished to lend their support. Or else steal a piece of the glory if he succeeded.

Chance decided to check on Serge. He needed someone to talk to. The silence was doing no favor for his thoughts. Rising from his stool, he climbed the stairs to the second floor, pausing when his stomach turned uncomfortably. The pain was sudden, but subsided after a few seconds.

He knocked on Serge's door. He heard the shuffling of bedsheets and a voice called for him to enter. Serge was lying on his back, propped up carefully with a pillow underneath his hip. A small collection of vials and bandages filled the nightstand. Despite being wrapped in a heavy blanket and a fire burning steadily, Serge was shaking.

"Hey," Chance said.

"Hey," Serge responded.

"I didn't wake you, did I?"

"No," Serge stretched, grasping his side suddenly and relaxing again. "I haven't had the easiest time sleeping lately. Come on in." He gestured to the chair beside the fireplace. "I'm dying for some company."

Chance winced at Serge's word choice. He pulled the chair up closer to the bed. "You feeling better then?"

"Not my normal self yet, but I'm on the mend. It's uphill from here if I can just keep these fevers down," Serge said. "There's no need to look so grim."

Chance tried a smile. Looking at Serge's pale face and the small beads of sweat clinging to his brow Chance knew how delicately he clung to life clung. Infection was still a constant threat.

"You've been drinking the tonics I've left you?" Chance asked.

Serge nodded.

"You do look a little better."

Serge chuckled with visible discomfort. "I'm not sure about that."

"You had us scared."

"I was scared too," Serge admitted. He frowned deeply, and the edges of his lips quivered. "Those bloody cogs nearly did the deed."

Chance nodded.

"They could have ended all of this. Everything, in a moment. One bloody ball and—" Serge choked on his words, and he shook with the effort to speak.

Chance offered him the cup which sat by his bedside, and Serge took it.

"I'm sorry," he said between sips. "I don't know why it gets to me like it does lately. It's just..." He set the cup down. "I never realized how fragile this Resistance is. We're just a few of us, but I had myself convinced we were unstoppable. And now I keep asking myself what would become of it if anything were to happen to us?"

"Nothing is going to happen to you," Chance reassured, checking the tonics to see which of them might need replenishing. "You're in good hands here with Liesel, and no one's searching for you. You have all the time you need."

He wished he could say the same about himself. He was thinking about mentioning the letter when Serge turned and looked at him with eyes like lanterns.

"Chance..." His voice was heavy. "I failed them. I failed the Resistance. I've been waiting—waiting for the right moment to set things in motion. Now, I'm not sure there will ever be one."

"It's not over," Chance said. "You've still got Liesel. Simon. Kwame.

And Rhett," he added.

"But without me, what will become of the cause?" he asked. "If I were to go right now, would they keep this alive?"

"Sure, they would," Chance insisted.

Serge rolled over. "I'm not so sure. If there's one thing that's come from this it's that I see things clearer now. Something has to happen, or nothing will. They need a catalyst. Something to bring them together. Something that will move them. They need a symbol burned into their minds. One they can't ignore. One they won't forget.

"No more waiting on gods that don't exist. No more subsisting on words, or holding out for better times to come. The people are everything they'll ever be. We need only the right catalyst to move them. And now—" He grimaced and repositioned himself on the pillow. "—I won't be there to see it when it comes."

Serge's eyes burned with anger, and he shook with effort. Chance was surprised. These were not the eyes of the friend he'd come to know. These eyes frightened him.

He thought back to what Simon had told him, the morning after Serge had been shot. Serge was the only one Simon feared when it came to the Resistance. And for the first time, Chance understood why.

"What's that?" Serge asked, noticing the letter in Chance's hand.

Chance had forgotten he was holding it. "This? This is..."

He hesitated. Serge was under enough stress without Chance adding to it. If he were going to make a full recovery, he needed as much rest as he was able.

"It's nothing," Chance said, stuffing the letter back into his pocket. "Just something I was thinking over."

CHAPTER FORTY-THREE
The Opera House

*A watched pot never boils. But, then again, neither does a
neglected one.*

— Alchemical Proverb

Stoddard and Emmaline arrived outside the opera house later than
they'd agreed. Stoddard had lost track of time discussing with
Arden the possible applications of intelligence. It was far beyond
what Stoddard had ever considered with his—could he bring himself to
say it—*simple* prosthetics.

Arden had clearly been puzzling over what he'd said at their last
meeting, and he'd come back with theories which had left even Stoddard mystified.

It was during their discussion that Stoddard came upon the realization that, more than anything else, he needed fresh perspective if he
was to crack the secrets of the Aether. The alchemists had obviously
approached his same problem from a unique angle, while he'd spent
years stuck in one mindset. He'd not been able to see beyond what was
right before him.

This was why their discovery had such allure; he needed their perspective.

Even as he closed in on the single individual who, he believed, possessed the key to Aether, he had unintentionally secured another. Arden had proven himself a worthy second, offering a fresh pair of eyes to problems Stoddard had wrestled with for years. There was more to Stoddard's work than even he'd comprehended. More to glean, now that it had advanced so far.

Arden had opened his mind to those possibilities.

When Stoddard did remember his prior engagement, he was nearly a half hour late to fetch Emmaline. She received him coldly, as was growing custom. Stoddard returned her coldness with curt duty, opening her door and taking his seat across from her. They exchanged no pleasantries, and she made no attempt to discern what might have delayed him. The excuse was always the same.

Stoddard found himself surprisingly content with her contempt. He was preoccupied as it was, so the silence in the carriage was sufferable. As they wound the streets, he thought of what Arden had asked him.

If a portion of Harper's intelligence could be transferred into Stoddard's prosthetic, then might it be possible to imbue a mechanism with the whole of it?

The prospect was both surprising and simple. Stoddard wasn't sure how it had not entered his mind before. But then, he'd been so long focused on securing and maintaining his sponsorships that he didn't doubt he'd missed things along the way. While Stoddard had had to balance his survival with his work, Arden's free and inquisitive mind had leapt forward with ease.

Perhaps with Arden's help, he thought, his work would have enough promise to retain Sinclair's sponsorship for a long and prosperous career. And with the alchemist's apprentice finally brought in, he'd have a team capable of solving humanity's great dilemma.

"Will you be working tonight as well?" Emmaline asked, bringing Stoddard back into the moment. She wouldn't look at him. She stared deliberately out the carriage window at the passing buildings.

"I have a meeting of some importance, yes."

Emmaline let out a drawn out sigh. "I wish you would leave work where it belongs and not bring it into everything we do."

"My dear," Stoddard frowned, "everything we do is work. Even these social escapades and little diversions are work. You should be grateful I'm of an industrious disposition, or else I might not be up for it."

"And you should be grateful I'm of a tolerant manner or else I wouldn't abide it." She shot him a severe look.

Stoddard looked out his own window. What he'd seen in Emmaline before, he couldn't recall now. All those days he'd thought of her while he'd labored in his workshop baffled him. Now that he had her, all he could think of was work. That was, if you could call what he had as 'having her.' It was a mutual toleration at best.

For what purpose, Stoddard didn't rightly know.

The carriage pulled up to the opera house, and he was quick to exit. They were in no means alone in arriving late. At least three other carriages were in the process of unloading. No one actually arrived on time to an opera. He'd been informed of that the first time he'd been invited to attend one. It was a sign of importance to arrive late. It gave off the perception of having more important things to attend to.

That, and it wasn't uncommon for the divas to go off script completely and usurp the show for their own amusement. It was likely they'd get a very sparse sampling of '*La disgrazia di il cuore*'.

He held open the door for Emmaline, who took a moment to collect herself. When she emerged, she looked in every regard a young woman thrilled by her evening's engagement and happy to be spending it in his company. It honestly shocked Stoddard how quickly she could turn it on and off.

For the briefest moment, he nearly fooled himself into thinking he was happy to be there with her as well.

They were greeted by Merryfield and his wife, who were waiting just inside. Apparently, they too had felt no need to rush and had taken a few turns about the foyer while they'd waited—"to admire the columns," Merryfield explained.

They found their box with no trouble, settling themselves in whilst diva Ferraro sang an aria from no play Stoddard was familiar with. As they were getting comfortable, he cast a glance at the booth across from theirs where the alchemist's apprentice was to sit.

The booth was empty, but Stoddard didn't worry. He suspected Chance, too, would arrive late to send a similar message of importance. He would want to maintain his dignity. To have arrived on time would have seemed too amenable.

As the evening progressed, Stoddard dutifully enjoyed the performance. He identified a few talking points he could use to entertain conversation later. Diva Ferraro was talented, for sure, though she all but ignored the scheduled performance and the maestro was taxed terribly with the effort to satisfy her whims as she performed pieces she was known for.

As she concluded yet another, Stoddard could not resist glancing at the empty booth. He felt his collar grow hotter. What was keeping the boy? Surely there was nothing more important that could require his attention, if he was to believe Skaggs' report.

Stoddard adjusted himself in his seat. The thought of Skaggs brought back uneasy feelings. Somehow, he'd managed to put the whole grisly affair out of his mind with work and his conversations with Arden. He'd nearly forgotten how he'd come by the apprentice's whereabouts in the first place.

"Are you alright?" Both the Merryfields and Emmaline were looking at him queerly, and he became aware of himself. He was clenching his program so tightly he'd nearly twisted it in half. His brow was wet, and he'd all but dug himself into the corner of his seat.

With great effort, he relaxed and tried to appear collected. "I'm fine," he insisted. "Just..."

He couldn't think of any excuse. He glanced again at the booth.

Empty.

"What has gotten into you?" Emmaline scolded him privately at intermission. Stoddard found it nigh impossible to concentrate. He'd spent more time watching the booth than he did the performance. By the time intermission had arrived, Lady Merryfield had declared him a most distractable fidget.

"It's nothing," Stoddard assured, though he was having a difficult time masking his frustration. The booth had remained empty the entire first half of the performance, and he felt snubbed—by a lowly alchemist of all people.

"I've seen you behave poorly before, and this is significantly worse," Emmaline hissed at him. "What could have your attention so much that you can't enjoy yourself with us? Is it truly too much to ask of you just one evening?"

"Do you see me standing here?" Stoddard snapped. "Am I not here with you?"

Emmaline pursed her lips, but said no more.

They retired to the theater's foyer to join the others who were gathering to discuss how they felt the opera was going. Many of the men were meeting for smokes in the gentleman's lounge. Stoddard did not join them, though Merryfield inquired if he'd like to.

He was on edge. He'd meant to meet with the apprentice during intermission, but now he had no way of knowing what the boy looked like. Nevertheless, he kept his eyes peeled for anyone who might stand out as an alchemist. He wasn't sure exactly what that meant, but he looked for it just the same.

There was the possibility that he had simply not shown, but Stoddard found it hard to believe he would not attend. Stoddard's letter had suggested nothing but promise to improve the boy's circumstances as a result of their meeting.

"Not boring you with our company, are we?" Merryfield inquired when Stoddard didn't respond to a question he'd posed. His generally pleasant demeanor had turned anxious. "You look distressed," he observed.

Stoddard shook his head. "Not at all. I was just taken away a moment by... the columns!" he said quickly. "I didn't believe you earlier, but they are impressive."

"You shouldn't let his manner offend you." Emmaline smiled a deceptively pleasant smile. "It's just his way, getting carried off in his thoughts or with some inane detail."

"I was just admiring the splendor of the theater," Stoddard insisted.

"Oh?" Emmaline said, her facade coming down a little. Her voice was strained. "In that case, who could fault you for admiring the theater?"

What had possessed her? Stoddard wondered.

"Has he told you about his work?" she continued. "It's fascinating. What was it that you were telling me about on the way over, dear?"

Stoddard stumbled for a second. Had they talked in the carriage? But then he saw the glimmer of malice in her eyes, and he sensed what she was up to.

"Yes..." Stoddard began. "I was telling her about an interesting idea Master Arden had come up with recently. It's quite compelling. A theory about—"

"Not more theories," Emmaline protested. "Trust me, once he begins on his theories there's no telling when the end will come. We could miss the second half of the performance! Why not tell us about one of your many accomplishments, dear? Tell us about something *real*."

"Well, my work on Captain Harper's prosthetic continues to be a—"

"Everyone knows about that one already, silly." Emmaline batted at his shoulder with a playful hand, though the touch felt all but playful. "Is that your most recent accomplishment, truly? Have you not done anything noteworthy since then?"

"As I said before," Stoddard hissed. "Master Arden and I have been hard at work developing upon certain theories."

"But they don't really count, do they? I mean, they don't exist. They're just ideas."

"All great things begin with an idea," Stoddard insisted.

"Yet, a man can waste away his days with too many silly ones," Emmaline retorted.

"I, for one, can't imagine what it must be like to have a mind like yours," Merryfield intervened, trying to lighten the mood of the conversation. "My accomplishment came from success in commerce, and I'm afraid I have to attribute a great deal of it to good fortune. Yet, you labor ceaselessly developing all of your ideas and theories; it's quite admirable."

"If only he could cease for a moment or two when others needed his attention," Emmaline said.

"A great mind is not so easy a thing to switch off," Stoddard explained, "no matter what the social agenda of the evening. My work follows me wherever I go. It is a curse."

"Born by all in his company," Emmaline frowned.

"Well, my wife and I have enjoyed the tiny glimpses we've had into your method," Merryfield said. "It's given us something to talk about an evening or two since we first made your acquaintance."

"Be grateful it's only a glimpse," Emmaline said. "You can get lost in it."

They stared at each other coldly, but Stoddard's eye was torn away when he spotted a man in a heavy coat near the door. He followed the figure, but the man turned and Stoddard could clearly see the tuxedo underneath.

It couldn't have been the apprentice.

"And there it is. We've lost him again." Emmaline forced a laugh. "Funny how the mind is prone to wander. But, we must forgive him. He's come to expect it of us."

"There are some things that demand one's attention," Stoddard snapped. His voice was harsh, beyond what was considered polite, but he didn't care. He'd grown tired of the game.

"Does it scorn you," he asked, "that I would have more important things pressing upon my mind than you? Than a wasted evening out or some trivial entertainment? If you enjoy these sorts of things that's fine with me, but you'll have to realize that, if these foibles and social escapades are what you really want, it's only through *my* merit that you'll have them.

"As you've been so keen to point out, I've had no great success since my work for the captain. Do you realize what that means for us? For you? It means that at any moment you could lose this whole facade that you've grown so comfortable behind.

"Tonight, I have a chance to turn our misfortune around. You may think me impertinent. You may find me distracted. But, you will refrain from hindering me as I seek to preserve the ties that keep you in your present luxuries. It is my work that makes us!"

Stoddard breathed heavy and fast, his passion carrying him away quite on its own. Emmaline stared at him, motionless. Her eyes were moist, and she ducked her head to hide them from the patrons nearby who'd overheard Stoddard's rant.

Stoddard felt the sting in what he'd said, but only for a second before he dismissed it. If they were to have a future together she would have to face the reality of their situation, and the sooner the better. If anything, it would impress upon her not to make trouble for him publicly again.

"I'm not sure if anyone else feels the same," Merryfield started, "but I think I could do to stretch my legs before we return to our box. Emmaline, would you care to join me?"

Emmaline nodded, not looking at Stoddard as she let Merryfield take her hand and lead her away, leaving Stoddard to fume alone with Lady Merryfield. He snatched a drink from one of the passing servers.

"Doctor Stoddard," Lady Merryfield said privately, once Emmaline was out of earshot. "Are you sure you're alright?"

"I'm fine." Stoddard smoothed the front of his suit. "A bit stressed from work is all, but an evening of music was just the diversion I needed. I feel quite uplifted, in fact."

"Good," Lady Merryfield said, looking doubtfully at him. "My husband and I were just concerned you might be in some sort of trouble."

"As I said before, I'm fine."

She let it be, and didn't pry further. It had been poor timing to have fought with Emmaline in front of one of his more loyal sponsors, but it couldn't be helped. Regardless, Stoddard made a mental note to act less absent and show more interest in his future engagements.

"Which of the arias did you enjoy most?" Lady Merryfield asked, trying to restore civil conversation.

Stoddard stood dumbfounded. He couldn't recall a single one.

Merryfield returned with Emmaline after a few minutes. She appeared to have collected herself, though she was obviously in poor spirits. Nonetheless, she took Stoddard's arm dutifully and drew close to his side.

"Well, now that we've had our stretch, shall we return to our box?" Merryfield asked.

"I'm afraid I won't be," Stoddard insisted. "An urgent matter has come to my attention, and it can't be delayed. Nonetheless, I trust I leave Emmaline in good hands. Would you see that she gets home safely tonight?"

"We will," Merryfield agreed. "Though it will be a shame not to have you for the second half. Are you sure now is a good time to go?"

"It can't be helped."

"Wait," Emmaline said as he began to withdraw his arm. She leaned in close, speaking so quietly that he paused despite his present temperament. "Please stay. Don't go tonight."

"It's unavoidable," Stoddard insisted. "You must understand. I'll call upon you tomorrow."

He saw it then, a sudden relaxation in her chest, a distance in her gaze. Her eyes gave no more hints to her thoughts or feelings as she let go of his arm and took Merryfield's.

Stoddard watched as she was led away, but he had no time to worry about her. He turned to go, fetching his coat and hat from the coat-check, and pushing his way through the doors.

He would see the apprentice tonight if it was the last thing he did.

CHAPTER FORTY-FOUR
Stoddard's Offer

*How could he not see? How could he not understand? I'd call
his mind weak, if it weren't for the infinity contained within.
Perhaps... he saw what I could not?*

— Excerpt from *Mechanarcissism*

Chance staggered as he walked, the unevenness of the paving compounding his inebriated state. He'd lost track of time again, and it was well into the night as he made his way back from the pub. Each night found him returning later.

Surprisingly, light was coming from Margarete's windows. She'd probably stayed up waiting for him, Chance guessed. He knew what that meant. Another lecture. Another argument.

He decided it would be best if he slipped in from the back... again.

A sharp pain seized Chance's side, doubling him over as it struck. Clutching his stomach, he clenched his teeth and set his jaw in a futile effort to ride out the pain. It was near unbearable the way it paralyzed him, sending tendrils through his spine to his extremities.

After a minute, the pain ebbed and he was able to relax his grip on the wall. His episodes were growing worse, and he was having difficulty hiding them when they struck. Margarete had noticed one earlier, but despite her concern and urgings that he'd see a doctor, he ignored it.

Whenever he could, that was.

It wasn't that he didn't appreciate her concern. Quite the opposite, in fact. What grieved him was how often he burdened her with it; anyone could see she had enough to worry about without him.

As the spasms faded to a tolerable level, Chance straightened again. He knew what the culprit was. He just wasn't willing to part with it. Those few moments of chemical liberation were becoming the things he lived for. It kept him on for one more day in this pit.

He decided to take another turn about the block to let his stomach settle completely before he went in. He followed the uneven walk, passing under the towering buildings and their neglected awnings.

His mind swam, making him feel like he was teetering along the edge of some great crevice. Stumbling, he wished he could hurl himself off it. Yet, every time he felt himself come too close, there was always something that managed to hold him back.

Ashworth's work.

Margarete's concern.

Rhett's helplessness.

He cursed them each silently for the steel ties with which they bound him. But, even those ties were deteriorating. He wondered how long they would last.

He stepped over a man who'd taken up a bed in the middle of his path. For a moment, Chance begrudged the inconvenience, but then the thought occurred to him that he could very well be in the same predicament in the foreseeable future. He'd have already been there had it not been for the kindness of others.

Chance let out a labored sigh and stopped. His stomach was still unsettled and walking was only upsetting it more. He breathed in a few deep breaths, when he heard a voice hail him from the other side of the street.

"You there! Boy!"

Chance looked up at the man crossing toward him, half expecting to see a constable's uniform. He was surprised, however, to see a middle-aged man in a costly tuxedo. He carried an umbrella under his arm and looked altogether out of place in the Basin District.

Something about him pricked at Chance's conscience and curiosity. He came upon Chance quickly, obviously in a great hurry to get somewhere.

"You," the man said. "Do you live around here?"

"Aye," Chance responded.

"I'm looking for someone they call Chance, an alchemist from these parts. Do you know him?"

Chance stared at the man, studying his face and the way he looked with distaste upon the street around him. There was an air of arrogance that permeated his manners, but underneath Chance sensed something else.

An undertone of desperation.

This was him, Chance realized—the man behind the letter.

"Bit far from the Spire for a party," Chance said.

"I've no time for idle chatter," the man said impatiently. "Do you know him?"

"Why?"

"I have business with him."

"And what if he has no business with you?" He saw the realization in the man's eyes. *Good*, Chance thought. *Enough games.*

"Where were you?" the man demanded, his voice laced with frustration. It was obvious he was going to great effort to restrain himself from shouting. His eyes bore down on Chance as he repeated the question more slowly. "Where were you?"

"Was I supposed to be somewhere?"

"I sent you an invitation," the man said. "When someone receives such an invitation it is expected he will respond!"

"Well, you found me regardless," Chance shrugged. "Who are you? What do you want from me?"

"My name is Stoddard—"

Chance's hairs stood up on the back of his neck.

"—and I'm here to make you a deal."

Chance circled slowly, his hand pulling back his coat at his hip. This was his supposed benefactor? The man who'd been hunting him all this time? The thought disturbed Chance. If Stoddard had known where he was then where was the law to break down his door and take him away?

"How long have you known where to find me?" he asked.

"Not long," Stoddard said. "You've done well keeping yourself out of the public eye. I give you credit for that."

"You get pretty good at being ignored when you live in the Basin."

"Which you must be grateful for at the moment. You have no idea the lengths I've had to go to find you. Well done, indeed." Stoddard applauded Chance with a few small claps. "But, you must have expected that I would appear sooner or later."

"I'd hoped later. But, I don't expect much from anything anymore," Chance shrugged. He glanced up and down the street. "So, where are they?"

"Where are whom?"

"Your thugs? Don't you high-brow types usually bring some sort of escort when you have business with folk like me? I don't believe for a second you came alone. They around the corner? Waiting for your order to drag me away and lock me up in the Steep? Or are you just going to have me killed?"

"Please," Stoddard scoffed. "I'm no barbarian. Had you been more agreeable and accepted my invitation we'd be having this chat over drinks in the comforts of the opera house. You've never been to the opera house, I take it?"

The pain in Chance's side seized him again, and he winced in his effort to remain upright. Stoddard didn't appear to take notice.

"That was my gesture of goodwill," he continued, "though it was obviously received in the wrong spirit. I don't want you dead. You and I are both forward-thinking men. It would bring me no pleasure to see a mind like yours waste away in the confines of a prison. What makes you think I'd have gone to such great lengths to contact you privately only to see you locked away?"

"Septigonee's Day comes to mind," Chance said. He knew he should be more careful—this was a crucial moment in a dangerous game—but something within him was lethargic.

He wanted this to be the end of the chase.

"Look around you," Stoddard gestured. "There are no duelists. No thugs. I'm unarmed." He opened his coat to show that he had no pistol or sword. "I wish only to speak to you so that we may fully understand one another. Exchange my story for yours, and then we'll decide where to go from here. You have my word that when I am finished you may continue on your way unmolested by myself or anyone under my employ. You'll never have to hear from me again."

He removed his hat and tucked it under his arm.

"Will you hear me out?" Stoddard asked.

Chance stared hard at him. He didn't want to trust him. He didn't want to listen to him. With every word he was forced to hear he had to restrain himself from lunging at him. But what else was in Stoddard's cards? Curiosity got the better of him.

"By all means," Chance managed to say.

"I've no illusion that you and I have pretense for cordial conversation—"

"That makes two of us." Chance stewed at the way Stoddard addressed him, as though he could ever be coaxed into letting his guard down.

"—but for the moment, I want to speak to you as one intellectual to another. Two scientists simultaneously pursuing one goal. Do you know, you and I are not much different? I see myself in you now that I meet you in person. You were apprenticed to your old mentor how long? Four, perhaps five years?"

"Seven," Chance said.

"I was apprenticed for four years to a mechanist," Stoddard continued. "A clockmaker. It was decent work, but I had aspirations far beyond the vision of my mentor. And then, as if fate had conspired in my favor, the good captain returned from war broken. My master was called upon to fix him. I stood by dutifully, watching his frantic attempts at a task so far beyond him. I was there when he stumbled upon the 'miracle' which saved the captain.

"After witnessing that, how could I have focused on anything else? It became an obsession. While my master was satisfied writing it off as a miracle and enjoying the fruits of his dumb luck, I sought to understand it. To dissect it. To replicate it. I inherited his work, and have seen it through to where it is today.

"But I've reached an impasse," Stoddard explained. "A problem which it seems you and your mentor were able to solve with that spark of yours."

"So that's what you want?" Chance asked. "You want to steal my research?"

"Not at all," Stoddard said. "I want to add my knowledge and experience to it. I want you to help me solve this riddle. You and I, we each have a great work to do—an enterprise to see through to the end. Together, we can advance all of mankind in ways unimaginable!"

"Sorry to disappoint you," Chance said, "but I gave up on the Aether spark a long time ago."

"We both know that's not true," Stoddard said. "I know you're conducting experiments. I know you have friends helping you obtain what you need. And I know you're deciphering a notebook that has the answers we're both seeking."

Chance cursed himself and his loose tongue.

"My sources tell me you're not ready to give up just yet," Stoddard smiled. "I also know that you're tired, and worn out from all of this needless cloak and dagger. If you collaborate with me, I assure you your troubles will disperse. You'll be free to pursue your studies without molestation, and have every resource you could ever dream of at your disposal."

"Why should I believe you?"

"Because you and I depend on one another for the thing we can't do for ourselves. If either of us are going to improve our circumstance, the Aether spark is the key. Together we can turn it, and open the way into a new age."

"I don't have it," Chance said.

Stoddard expression grew cold. "Don't lie to me. I *know* you have it!"

"I don't!" Chance insisted. "You've killed the man who knew how to create it. He was the only one who knew. If you want it so badly, you'll have to bring him back yourself and ask him how he did it."

"I didn't kill Ashworth," Stoddard said.

"Of course, you did!" Chance shouted. It hurt him to hear Stoddard deny it. "Who else would be responsible for his death?"

"Don't for a second think I'm the only one who has taken an interest in you," Stoddard warned. "There are other men as eager to seize the secrets you are holding."

Chance hesitated. Was that true? He'd always thought it was one man after him. Who else might be searching for him at that very moment?

"It doesn't matter," Chance shrugged. "The Aether spark died with him. There's no turning back the clock."

"But you were his apprentice," Stoddard urged. "You're familiar with his work!"

"I had no idea what he was working on," Chance confessed, and his voice faltered despite his efforts to appear strong. That truth still upset him. "Contrary to what you might believe about us, we alchemists have a code. We respect each other's secrets. Ashworth's died with him."

"That's not true," Stoddard grinned, though he didn't appear as confident as he had a moment before. "You have been unable to let your mentor's work rest with him. I'm certain of it. With my help, you could finally unearth the secret of the Aether."

Chance clenched his jaw so tightly he thought his teeth might crack. Stoddard was right. Despite how much trouble it caused him, he hadn't been able to let it go. He'd forgotten all about his own work in light of Ashworth's success. It had become an obsession to recreate it—just as Stoddard had his mentor's work.

"I thought so," Stoddard nodded in triumph. "I understand your predicament, Chance, but I extend my proposition. A partnership, you and I, in a joint effort to fulfill Ashworth's final work."

"I don't work for murderers," Chance said, turning away.

"You still think I was responsible for what happened to Ashworth? What happened to Harper?"

"I don't see anyone else here who would profit from it!" Chance shouted.

"And that's where you're wrong," Stoddard said. "*Everyone* would profit from what you have. They've gone to great lengths to discover your identity. If they'd found you, you very well might have been taken to the Steep already. Take it from one who knows, the Spire is not as pleasant a place as one might think. You're fortunate that I was the first to find you."

Chance stood silent. He thought of the rally. Of the raids on Ashworth's home. On Ponti's. It seemed unlikely, now that he considered it, that one man could be responsible for it all.

"I'll tell you what," Stoddard said. "As a token of my goodwill, I'm going to leave you to think on it. If my proposition disgusts you, you can disappear again. Perhaps you'll find yourself a better hole to crawl into. But, if you change your mind, my offer remains available to you."

He extended a card to Chance, who took it reluctantly. On it was printed an address on the Spire.

"I'll leave you to consider your options," Stoddard said, donning his hat. "I have no doubt you'll see reason in time." He didn't wait to hear Chance's response, but turned and crossed the street the way he'd come, self-assurance in his step.

Chance stood still, both confused and frustrated. He felt vulnerable. Felt thousands of eyes on him from every angle. Backed into a corner with no way out. He turned the card over in his hand, not sure what to think.

His stomach seized up again and he doubled over, retching blood on the ground.

CHAPTER FORTY-FIVE
Cornered

When I think of all the times I could have abandoned this path,
I can't deflect the sense of guilt that I not only chose this fate... I
chose it many times over.

— Excerpt from *Mechanarcissism*

C hance leaned heavily on the table in his makeshift laboratory, clutching it tightly to keep himself stable. He shivered in a cold sweat as pain drove through his stomach in steady waves, twisting him as his muscles spasmed under his skin.

It had been a rough night, to say the least. He hadn't been able to sleep, so he'd tried to distract himself with work. But, he'd hardly been able to go for more than a couple minutes before nausea and dizziness would set in and he'd have to rest.

It was a constant battle. One he was losing.

After a few minutes, the pain subsided to a bearable ache, and he was able to straighten up again. All about the desk lay remnants of the curative tonics he'd mixed, to little avail, as well as a few other concoctions he thought might come in handy given last night's encounter.

Some sat half-mixed. He'd sent Rhett to fetch the components he lacked, which left him little to do but wait and worry. Inevitably, the thought of Stoddard's offer assaulted his already weary mind.

He felt trapped, more so than ever before. He thought of running, of going to ground once more and starting over. He could take Liesel up on her offer to shelter him, if she wasn't so tied up with the Resistance.

The thought of seeking out the Resistance directly crossed his mind. He'd hesitated getting involved with them before, after Simon's warnings, but perhaps he'd be safer with them.

Regardless, even if he found somewhere to hide, Chance had already been found out twice. Obviously, he hadn't gone as unnoticed in the Basin as he'd thought. Eyes were turning his way, and if what Stoddard said was true then there were others Chance wasn't even aware of after the Aether spark.

He wasn't sure if he could evade their pursuit much longer.

Chance uncovered a bottle he'd hidden underneath his mattress and uncorked it. The sweet aroma of his special brew greeted him, and he downed the last of the bottle's contents. His stomach tightened as the liquid hit, but subsided in welcome warmth.

It sickened him, even as he drank, how much he'd come to depend on it to subsist. He cursed himself, and promised again that this was the last time—then cursed himself for the number of times he'd promised that before.

Ringgold may have been right, he thought. *Alchemy may be the death of me.*

Sitting down on his bed, Chance took up Keller's notebook and flipped through it. The symbols swam in front of him as his vision wandered. He scratched out one of his notes and paused. What was he going to write in its place? He couldn't remember.

He closed the book. The wait wasn't doing anything to help his nerves. He needed something to occupy his mind. He needed to work, but with the limitations he faced with money, equipment, or components he had lost momentum. He hated that he didn't have a proper lab. He hated that he couldn't buy basic components. He hated everything about his circumstance.

He took Stoddard's card from the table. He'd not been able to bring himself to discard it. The offer, as much as he loathed the thought, was inviting. If what Stoddard said was true—if he could deliver on his promises—then Chance could escape the hell he'd been sentenced to.

He was rolling the offer around in his mind when he heard footsteps on the stairs. Chance straightened up as Margarete peeked into the loft.

"Are you busy?" she asked.

"Nah," Chance said, tossing the card back on the table. "Just thinking." He cleared a spot on the bed beside him, but Margarete didn't sit down. She wandered the room, examining Chance's mess.

"Working on something?" she asked.

"Just waiting for Rhett to come back with a few things from the Exchange."

"Oh," Margarete said. She looked nervous, which was a state Chance didn't see her in often. It put him further on edge. Something was wrong, and he wasn't sure he could handle any more bad news.

"Did you need something?" he asked, trying to cut through the tension.

"No. Not really," she said. "Do you?"

"I'm okay."

"Yeah?"

Chance looked at her long and hard. What was on her mind? Whatever it was, she was having difficulty letting it go. Her eyes wandered over his laboratory, examining its contents and running her fingers over a few of the vials and flasks. She came to his bottle, and he cursed his neglect for having left it out in the open.

She didn't linger too long, however, before moving on.

"Whatever it is, Margarete, you might as well come out with it," he said. "I can tell something is wrong."

"Can you?" he heard her whisper.

She turned to look at him, and Chance's breath caught in his chest. She was beautiful—even with her eyes so sad.

"I heard you last night," she said, "coming in. It didn't sound like you slept."

"I had something I needed to take care of."

"What was that?"

"Nothing," he insisted.

"Really?"

Chance shrugged his shoulders, and Margarete gave a resigned nod.

"I'm worried about you," she said.

"Don't be."

"I mean it, Chance. I'm worried about how you're handling everything that's happened."

"I'm handling it just fine," Chance assured her, folding his arms into himself.

"No, you're not! Stop trying to put on a brave face. I know you don't like letting others see when you're hurting, but you can't hide it forever. Not from me. You've taken on so much with Ashworth's work, and I'm here to tell you… it needs to stop."

Chance looked at her with surprise.

"I've watched what it's doing to you," she explained, "what it's led you to do, and I can't sit idly by any longer." She cast a glance at the empty bottles around the room. "It needs to stop."

"I can't just stop now," Chance said. "I've only barely begun to make progress on it."

"But at what cost?" Margarete asked. "From where we stand, it doesn't look like progress."

"We?" Chance asked, his eyes narrowing. "Who else is spying on me? Rhett? Liesel?"

"We're all worried for you."

"You shouldn't be snooping on me," Chance said. "What I do with my time is my own business."

"No," Margarete said firmly. "Not while you're under my roof. You're one of mine, Chance, and what you bring here affects all of us."

"I'm not going to stop," Chance snapped. "It's my life! It's my choice!"

"If you won't," Margarete warned. "Then you leave me no choice."

"What does that mean?"

"It means that you'll have to find somewhere else to stay. I can't have you destroying yourself under this roof, not when I have my girls' livelihoods to consider. I love you, Chance. But I won't let you put them at risk."

"You're serious?" Chance asked. She'd surprised him so much he didn't know whether he was angry or confused.

"I wish I wasn't."

"I'm just trying to finish Ashworth's work," Chance insisted.

"That's not all you've been doing. If you were so keen on helping him you wouldn't be so adamant about doing it on your own. Ashworth had help. He accepted help. All you've done is pull away."

"Trust me, no one else wants this," Chance assured her. "And I don't blame them. I'm sorry if you're not happy about it, but I'm not giving up on the spark. Not now. Not ever."

"Then let us help you," Margarete pleaded. "We do want to help, if you'd let us."

"Really?" Chance picked up Keller's notebook and thrust it toward her. "Can *you* read this? Because I've been at it for months and I'm still barely able to make heads or tails of it. None of the other alchemists are about to sign on to help me, after what happened to Ashworth and Keller. They've learned their lesson already."

His voice caught, thick in his throat, and he threw the notebook into the corner. His anger had come upon him so suddenly. He hadn't meant to direct it at Margarete, but it was so close to the surface it was difficult to contain.

"It's the hard truth," he said. "I'm the only one who can finish Ashworth's work."

"Perhaps…" Margarete touched his arm, but Chance didn't feel the comfort of her touch. "Perhaps it's better to let his work end with him."

Chance rose from the bed. "How could you say that? Ashworth cared for you, too. I won't abandon him."

"It's not abandoning him," Margarete insisted.

"That's exactly what it is. Ashworth was murdered," Chance said. "Murdered before my very eyes. And Rhett saw it too."

"Rhett sees what's happening to you, too. He looks to you. He's already lost Ashworth," Margarete said. "What do you think it would do to him if he lost you?"

"If I let it go then they'll have taken everything from us."

"But, if you keep holding on, you may end up losing everything anyway. Don't you see? It's destroying you. It's destroyed everything it's touched. Just... let it go."

Chance clenched his jaw and wrung his hands. If only she knew how tempted he was to do that. The thought begged him every day. And he'd do it if he could.

But...

He glanced again at the card on the desk. It wasn't as simple as she made it seem. He was deep in it. Deeper than he'd ever thought he'd be. They weren't going to let him back out now.

"I see what this is doing to you, Chance," Margarete said. "You're not the young man I once knew—the one who dyed my hair and would dream with me late into the night. He was fine a young man, who lifted others even when it put him out to do it. But now..."

Margarete's eyes were pained, as if it hurt her to say it out loud.

"People change," Chance fumed.

"Not like this."

"Exactly like this," Chance said. "You can't stop it."

"No," Margarete agreed, the last of her hope fading in her voice. "I suppose I can't."

Footsteps were heard as Rhett came scrambling up the stairs and rushed into the room, looking quite put out. Margarete turned away quickly and dabbed at her eyes.

Rhett looked confused. He'd never seen Margarete cry before.

"What's wrong?" Chance asked, realizing Rhett wasn't carrying any bags. "Where are the components?"

"They wouldn't let me in!" Rhett said, exasperated. "I went down to the Exchange and the gate was barred up. There's a huge crowd gathered outside, but they're not letting anyone in."

"What? Why?"

"I don't know. They kept saying it had something to do with the colonies. 'Redistribution of rations,'" Rhett quoted in a voice Chance suspected was an imitation of the quartermaster's.

"What does that mean?"

"I don't know," Rhett shrugged. "But they had dirigibles in the courtyard. It looked like they were emptying the warehouses."

"Did they say when they'll be open again?"

"They wouldn't say anything. Just kept telling us to go home."

Chance stood up from the bed and grabbed his coat and carrier from the hook by the door. The carrier was bulkier, given his recent additions, but he managed to secure it under his coat without too much budge. "Let's go," he said.

"Where are we going?" Rhett asked.

"We're going to find out what is going on!"

"Chance," Margarete said, turning toward him. Her eyes were pleading. *You don't have to*, they told him.

Yes, I do, Chance's answered.

He wanted to say more. Wanted to tell her how much he wanted to listen. How much he wanted her help. But he couldn't bring himself to. Instead, he turned and led Rhett through the doorway.

He'd tell her later.

CHAPTER FORTY-SIX
Barred from the Exchange

*Sometimes, all you need is a little pressure
to get the right reaction.*

— Alchemical Proverb

L ike Rhett had said, the Exchange was in a commotion. A heavy
wind had picked up, blowing in from the bay. The air was thick,
and, despite the billowing clouds which were rolling in, a crowd
filled the street outside the gates. It was growing by the minute as more
disgruntled citizens came running to confirm the rumors.

Chance and Rhett did their best to make their way through the
thickening crowd, which wasn't so difficult for Rhett given his size. He
was good at weaving through legs, but Chance struggled.

As he pushed his way forward, he caught sight of a dirigible struggling to rise up out of the yard laden with crates and boxes. The wind
whipped at its balloon, and men from the ground worked desperately
with their leads to keep it stable.

Chance pushed harder.

"What do you think?" Rhett asked when Chance finally popped out
beside him near the front of the crowd.

"I think, I've had enough of this," Chance said, watching the dirigible cruise away toward the shipyard. He approached the gate where men contended with one another.

"I told you, there's nothing to distribute today," the quartermaster shouted. "Go home! We'll inform you when we open up again. Until then, be on your way!"

"And just how long will that be?" someone shouted. "I've got a business to run!"

"And a family to feed!" another complained.

"What are we supposed to do if you won't sell to us?

"You can't deny us our goods!"

"All goods are first property of the city," the quartermaster said. "They're being redistributed as the city deems necessary. You can thank the colonies and that bloody blockade. When things have settled overseas we'll return to business as usual. Until then, make do with what you have."

"You barely give us enough to make a living on as it is. How do you expect us to feed ourselves on less than nothing?"

"I told you, we'll inform you when we open again. The city will ration goods fairly between the districts."

"And what about the meritocracy?" Chance asked. The quartermaster looked at him, his eyebrow rising.

"What about them?" he asked.

"Are you rationing their goods? Because, by the looks of it, there aren't any dirigibles hauling off goods from the Spire. That seem fair?"

The quartermaster glared at him. "We're redistributing as we see fit."

"As *who* sees fit?" Chance demanded.

"Never you mind."

Chance had had enough. He felt the pressure rising as every injustice, every inconvenience, swelled inside him. It was as though a valve had finally burst. He struck the gate with a clenched fist, shaking it furiously. "You can't do this! You can't just turn us away."

"That's enough!" the quartermaster yelled. "Stand back from the gate!"

"Open the gate!" Chance shouted. He shook the iron gate with all his might. "Open the gate!"

"I'm warning you! Stand back!" The quartermaster signaled to the guard to intervene, but Chance wasn't deterred. He shook the gate again, flailing his weight as he tugged and pushed against the bars. They clattered loudly over the commotion of the crowd behind him.

A searing pain gripped Chance's side as his stomach seized. He doubled over, clutching the bars for support as his strength left him.

Not now, he thought.

"This is your last chance," the quartermaster yelled.

The guards raised their clubs high... but they didn't fall. Something stopped them.

The gates shook again, the sound resonating. Chance looked to his side and saw men and women pressing up against the bars, pushing and pulling together. They were pressed up against him so tightly he feared he might be crushed.

The hinges strained with the added weight, and the sound of bending metal caused the guards to step back in surprise. The quartermaster watched in disbelief as the whole gate began to fold inward. Then, with a sudden lurch, the hinges snapped and the gate came down with a crash.

Chance fell forward as the mob clambered over him to get through. He clutched his side as he tried to move out of the way, but the pain was too great.

For the second time, he was being trampled.

He tucked into a ball, trying his best to protect himself from the stampeding feet, when he felt strong arms on him. Looking up, he saw Kwame and Rhett holding back the crowd while Simon dragged him to a safe spot beyond the gates.

When they were clear of the mob, Kwame knelt beside him and rested a hand on his shoulder.

"You good now?" he asked.

"I think so." Chance appraised himself. Apart from a few bruises and his wrists hurting where he'd struck the gate he was still intact.

"That was a close call," Simon said, and he smiled at Chance. "You may have just been responsible for tipping a mob past their breaking point. You proud of yourself?"

"Actually, I am," Chance said, accepting Simon's hand and rising to his feet.

"What have I told you about picking fights?"

"Sometimes the fight picks you," Chance half-smiled against the pain in his stomach. It still felt tight, but he found he could manage as long as he stayed slightly bent.

"Lucky we see you fall," Kwame said. "Or you be looking from heaven."

"Thanks for that."

"Look at them all," Simon frowned, gesturing to the people pushing through the gate.

The four of them watched from the side as the mob stormed the Exchange and flooded the yard. The guards weren't putting up much of a fight; they were little more than hired thugs. It was one thing to look intimidating from the other side of a locked gate, but in the face of the mob they buckled—unprepared for such an onslaught.

The guards and the quartermaster fled toward a second dirigible still docked in the yard, hoping to get off the ground before they were overrun. They were just climbing up the platform when the mob caught up to them, seizing them with many hands and dragging them down to the ground.

The crew tried frantically to cut the lines, but the mob overwhelmed them too and the dirigible remained grounded.

The whole scene was chaos as more people arrived. The warehouse doors were thrown wide open and pillaged of any remaining wares.

Chance hobbled toward the center of the yard.

"Where are you going?" Simon asked him.

"Taking advantage of the moment," he said.

The three of them followed as he approached the dirigible. People were busy unloading crates, heaving them over the edge and letting them fall. They split open, spilling their contents before an eager crowd. They foraged through it like dogs, bickering with one another as they grabbed whatever they could carry.

Chance felt his spirits fall. He'd thought such a moment would have given him reason to feel satisfaction, watching the meritocracy lose one to the people. But this scene didn't attest a victory—it was just a squabble, and a pathetic one at that.

Just like the factory revolts.

Chance wandered to where the quartermaster was held. The man lay on the ground with his guards, fresh bruises surfacing on their faces. He'd been bound up with a rope and left to wait things out on the sidelines.

"Chance!" Kwame called to him from one of the broken crates. "Look at this!" He held up a set of gentleman's clothes. They were adorned in fine velvet and golden threads. "I never have clothes like this. Me and you all be gentlemen!"

"Get rid of that and go find something useful," Simon instructed.

"Want me to go check for your components?" Rhett asked.

"Sure," Chance said, only half-listening. The boy ran off toward the back warehouse, and Chance watched him go. He couldn't shake the subdued feeling.

Why wasn't he celebrating?

"You're in for it now," the quartermaster sneered. "Oh, you're all in for it."

"You've had it in for us long before now," Chance said dismissively. "About time fortunes turned."

"A lot of good it will do you, I'm sure." The man wiped his bloody lip on his shoulder and stared at Chance. He gave him a queer look as realization crept over his face. "Wait a second..." he said. "I know you! You're that two-bit alchemist, the one who worked for Ashworth!"

"What of it?"

"Never took you for the thieving type," he said. "Can't make your way in the world, so you take it out on us who can? Is that it?"

"You've stolen from us for years," Chance said. "Just returning favors."

"Tell me, what's your plan from here?" the quartermaster asked. He snickered at the look on Chance's face. "I thought so. Nothing more than a band of pillaging slag. Curse you and all your lot." He spat at Chance's feet. "Just you wait until the soldiers get here. You're all in for it then."

"You ever seen what desperate men will do if you push them too far?" Chance snapped. He wanted to lash out at the man, but Simon grabbed him before he could.

"Wait," Simon said, his grip firm. "He's right. We shouldn't stay here long. Pretty soon this place will be overrun with soldiers. It's best if we aren't here when they arrive."

"Time to take and go," Kwame said. "Each man after his own head?"

"No," Chance snapped.

"What?"

Chance glared at the scene before him, the sickness pitting deeper and deeper in his aching stomach. Serge's words came to his mind; the people really were lost—trying to survive from day to day. He'd been right. Chance saw it clearly before him. Their opportunities passed them by, and would continue to, as long as they kept looking after themselves.

Something had to give. Chance had little to give anymore, but he had nothing else to lose. That accounted for something in his book.

"Is that all you want?" he asked, turning to his friends. "A handful of *things*? Back to the same life you've been handed to wait out the next abuse they decide to send our way? Is that honestly enough for you?"

Chance looked from face to face. Each had trouble looking back at him. Apparently, his words struck a chord.

"Well it's not enough for me," Chance continued. "Not anymore. I'm tired. I'm tired of all of this. Of living within the bounds that *they've* set for us. I'd rather take my life into my own hands than leave it to be decided by this cursed city."

He turned on Simon.

"Isn't this what you've been looking for? A moment like this? Isn't this what your little Resistance has been praying for all this time?"

"Perhaps," Simon consented, his voice holding onto worry. "But, I can't see this going any differently than it did with the factory workers. We'll bar ourselves behind these walls and maybe—just maybe—we could mount a resistance for a while. But, they'll mass a force strong enough to punch a hole through us before nightfall.

"We may be together right now, if you can call this mob 'together,' but against a trained military we won't have a prayer. These aren't soldiers." Simon gestured to the people around them. "They're just common folk. These walls will become our tomb."

"Then we don't stay."

"Right," Simon said. "That's what I've been saying."

"I mean we don't fight here," Chance clarified. "We won't wait for them to come deal with us. We'll go to them, right up to the Spire so that they'll have to listen to us."

"A fight isn't going to end well wherever we are."

"Then what is it you are organizing for?" Chance asked. "What is the point of your Resistance if not this, right here? Or are you just a bunch of cowards whose dreams are greater than your resolve?"

"I want to believe it's possible more than anyone," Simon defended. "Believe me. But the people are not unified. This is a mob. They'll loot and they'll pillage, but when trouble shows its head they'll run with whatever they can get their hands on—and that'll be enough for them. They're not soldiers; they're just a band of desperate men."

Chance grinned. "Exactly."

Simon looked confused.

"We don't need soldiers," Chance explained. "Look at these guards. They folded the moment things got tough, and why is that? Because they don't believe in this. They aren't invested in any of this, any more than the few meager scraps they're paid for this job. But these people, we're in the thick of it. All of us.

"We've all woken up to the same lot and felt frustrated by the ridiculousness of the Spire's regulations. There's not a single one of us that hasn't been taxed near the breaking point, and if we could tap into that feeling—tip it past the breaking point—think what could happen. You'd have a city full of men and women better than soldiers!"

The three of them stood quietly. Simon shuffled in place and Chance saw the battle raging visibly in his mind. Kwame looked as though he were holding back tears. He threw the clothes on the ground and stepped forward, taking Chance's hand in his.

"My people be fighting across the sea for long and long. Is time a fight is here to Hatteras," Kwame said. "I fight!"

Simon looked hard upon the two of them, shifting on his good leg as he thought it through. Finally, with a deep breath, he stepped forward. "You're mad," he said. "You realize that?"

"I think I'm figuring that out," Chance smirked. "Yeah."

"There's a good chance none of them will go along with whatever you have in mind."

"But there's always a chance," Chance winked.

Simon couldn't help but smile at that.

"Alright then. I'm with you." He took Chance's hand.

They were only a few, drunk on the moment and up against dizzying odds, but it was a good feeling not being alone.

Chance drank the feeling in deep.

"We'll need to get their attention somehow," Simon said. "How do you reckon we're going to do that? Look at them," he gestured.

The people were still tearing into the warehouses, ransacking anything that wasn't nailed down or locked up—and even then, sometimes. How did one speak to a mob? Chance didn't have the slightest idea.

A symbol. Serge's voice entered into Chance's mind clearly. *They need a symbol burned into their minds. One they can't ignore. One they won't forget.*

Chance saw it then—his opportunity.

"I have an idea," he said.

"Great! You want to tell us what it is?" Simon asked.

Chance didn't, just in case Simon tried to talk him out of it.

Running to the platform where the dirigible was docked, he pulled three of the lanterns off their hooks before racing up the stairs. At the top, he knelt down and lit the burners until they were going strong, then threw one as hard as he could on the airship's deck.

The oil spilled out of the lantern as the casing cracked, sending a coating of liquid flame across the wooden planks. He grabbed the second, and repeated the process.

"What you doing?" Kwame cried, seeing the flames as he came aboard the ship. They'd followed Chance up the platform and all three looked with horror as the second fire started.

"Are you insane?" Simon said. "You'll ignite the balloon!"

Chance paused to acknowledge them. "Exactly," he said, then threw the third and final lantern down.

The ship was burned steadily, the wind whipping the flames and spreading them across the dry wooden planks. A few men who'd been foraging below deck popped up in alarm and raced off the ship at the sight of the fire. Kwame and Simon did as well, stopping on the platform with obvious reservations as they pleaded with Chance.

"Well don't just stand there," Simon urged. "Come on!"

Chance admired his handiwork, watching the flames creep further along the deck. They couldn't wait for him any longer, and they hurried down the stairs. He watched them as they backed away to a safe distance.

"Chance, get on from there!" Kwame called.

"You're acting crazy!"

The people had noticed the flames and a cry of alarm spread throughout the yard. They grabbed the last of what they could from the piles below and backed away, their eyes on the burning ship.

As Chance gazed down on them, he saw Rhett with his arms full of components. His big eyes were turned toward Chance, his expression full of concern.

This was it. This was the moment Serge had been looking for. Chance was going to be their catalyst.

It was now or never. He gripped the rigging tightly and stepped up onto the prow. The dirigible shook in the wind, but Chance held on tight. All eyes were on him, the crazy kid clinging to a burning ship, waiting to see what would happen next.

He had the stage.

"Look at you," he shouted. "Look at what you've become. Gutter snipes. Bilge rats. Bickering amongst yourselves for the scraps left behind by the meritocracy. Is that what you are? Is that really what you are?"

There was a general muttering and glancing about in the mob. For a moment Chance saw each one of them in his mind's eye. Every one of their faces was discernible before him as they gazed up at him.

"I see more than that," he continued. "I've been in your homes. I've seen how you've suffered. I've suffered with you. Thousands of injustices that the meritocracy sees fit to send our way. And why? Because we let them!

"They've taken my home. They murdered my friend. I watched them come into his home in the middle of the night and slit his throat right before my eyes. Where was justice in that moment? Who stood up to them in our defense? I know I'm not the only one who has been left to suffer injustices like these.

"I say we take our grievances to the Spire! Force the meritocracy to heed our voice until they end the abuse of Hatteras' citizens!"

The crowd was visibly resistant, but Chance kept on.

"I see here men and women who've slaved all of their lives to make this city what it is, and at the end of the day does the meritocracy give you anything in return? A home? If you call a gutter a home. Some bread? If their tossings are enough to sustain you. They've given us *nothing* and demanded *everything*. Even our very lives. That's not enough for me. Is that enough for you?"

"At least it's a life," someone called back.

"If this is what we call a life, then I welcome death with every accommodation," Chance said. "At least in death we're not meant to suffer any longer."

His words fell upon the crowd with gravity, and he fought to see through his tears. The silence which settled upon them was profoundly sober.

"When will we have another opportunity like this?" he asked. "Will they give it to us? I promise they won't. It's time to make your own opportunities, not wait for them to decide your fate."

"They're too many," someone said. "We can't fight an entire city."

"We *are* the city," Chance cried. "They've worked so hard to make us feel like nothing more than strangers in our own homes, begging for the scraps when we should be feasting on the fat of our labors.

"It's not about fighting them. It's about having our voices heard upon the Spire. We can't keep complaining about our misfortunes and blaming it on the tides when the ones with the power to turn them are sitting up there right now!

"But, if it came to a fight," Chance continued, his voice solemn, "I'd rather have a hundred desperate men than a thousand of their soldiers. They've given us our greatest freedom, because in taking away the quality of our lives they've stripped away our fear of death. We're driven by something deeper. Desperate men have nothing to lose and everything to give.

"If we won't speak up against the thousands of injustices they commit each and every day, then I say they are right. We are slag, and they're free to do what they will with us. But not me. Not anymore. It's time to show those cogs they can't ignore us anymore!"

The fire behind him had spread until it covered the entire deck. Chance felt the heat on his back, but he kept his gaze on the crowd, waiting for some sign they'd heard him—that they were with him. Yet, all he saw in their faces was fear and hesitation. They didn't know what to do. They were as lost as he was.

But, he'd meant what he'd said, and he'd fixed himself to his course. Even if he had to do it alone, he would march to the Spire and face the meritocracy, come what may.

"Do what you will then," he shouted, "but I've had enough!"

Chance uncoiled one of the ropes on the deck and slung it over the side. He hopped over, gripping it tightly as he slid down to the ground. It burned his hands, but the pain was hardly comparable to what he'd endured thus far.

When he touched down, he tossed the rope away and walked through the crowd, his eyes harsh and unforgiving. He cursed them silently for their cowardice as he passed.

Many of them lowered their eyes, not able to meet his.

The dirigible flared up behind him in a deafening explosion that shook the whole yard as the balloon finally caught fire and ignited the gasses inside. People screamed and shielded their eyes. A plume of brilliant flame erupted into the air and the ship below came crashing down to the earth.

Chance didn't look back. He kept his gaze forward as he trudged toward the gates. Kwame, Simon, and Rhett hurried to join up with him.

"That got them a look," Kwame smiled.

"A lot of good it did though," Simon frowned. "I told you they'd be hard to convince. It's not the right time."

"What are you going to do now?" Rhett asked, struggling to carry all the components as he kept up.

"I'm going to meet them," Chance said. He didn't stop walking. "I'm going to meet the meritocracy. I want to see their faces this time."

He knew it was foolish. He understood he'd be taken and killed for what he'd done and was about to do, but he didn't care. He had nothing to lose. He had nothing he wanted but an end.

And end to it all.

As he walked, he realized that Simon, Kwame, and Rhett were still with him. They'd matched his pace and were looking ahead.

"This isn't going to end well," he told them. "I know that. You don't have to come with me."

"This is my fight," Kwame insisted.

"I told you, I'm with you," Simon said, not deterred. "As foolhardy as it is, I'm with you. I've fought enough battles for Hatteras over the years. Perhaps it's about time I fought one on the right side."

"Rhett," Chance said. "Go home."

"Welch said there'd come a time when I'd need to ignore what you told me to do." He looked up at Chance with eyes aged beyond his years. He threw the components down, letting them break. "I think that's now."

Stubborn kid, Chance thought. But he didn't argue. If the boy wanted to make this his fight, he had as much right as anyone.

Their little group passed through the gate in silence, and turned up the serpentine road. The black pillar of smoke from the burning dirigible rose like a banner over the bay, signaling to the rest of the world what had transpired.

There was no hiding now. They'd know he was coming.

He wondered briefly what was taking the guard so long to respond. They should have descended on the Exchange long ago. Perhaps, fortune was really on their side.

It was then that Chance heard it, the sounds of many footfalls on a paved street. He glanced behind him and couldn't quite believe what he was witnessing. Whether out of curiosity or something more, the people had followed him through the gate and were falling in behind him.

Against all odds, the people were following *him*.

CHAPTER FORTY-SEVEN
The March on the Spire

These ripples I send out into the world... I fear how they may reappear.

— Excerpt from *Mechanarcissism*

They followed the serpentine road, their hodgepodge mob, climbing higher through the city as they marched on toward the Spire. Chance was genuinely surprised by the response they'd received, both from the people and the city.

What had started as a small hundred at the Exchange had blossomed in a short time into a sizable force. Runners raced throughout the Basin, spreading the news of the crazy kid leading the people in a marched on the capitol, and like rats in droves the Basin-dwellers emerged from every nook and corner to join.

He'd expected the guard to arrive and put an end to it, yet no soldiers had appeared, nor did any constables interfere. Their numbers continued to grow until Chance was confident the city would have a challenge if they tried disbanding them.

Chance and his friends remained at the front of the march. At first their steps had set a cadence for the others to follow, but soon the crowd had set a cadence of its own. It swelled and beat behind them, a breathing entity, so that Chance felt he was being pushed by the mob rather than leading it.

It was both exhilarating and intimidating, being at the front of that force. His confidence grew with it, and he didn't hold back as he drank in the feeling of invincibility which spread through their company.

Not even the approaching storm could dissuade them. The wind had whipped up into a small gale, blowing puffs of dust through the streets. The first drops of rain could be felt; they fell like pins in the gusts.

Despite the weather, however, the mood was optimistic.

They would take their grievances to the capitol and bring their plight before the electors themselves. What would happen then, or how their complaints would be received, no one was sure. Nothing like this had ever happened in Hatteras.

They marched with a resolve to find out.

"Chance! Chance, you sorry sod! It's really happening?" Ponti appeared out of one of the side streets and rushed up, jostling him roughly. "I didn't believe what I was hearing, so I had to come see it for myself. I don't know how you did it!"

"A tide is turning," Kwame smiled.

"Looks that way," Simon said.

Unlike the rest, Simon had grown serious and uneasy the further they marched. But, he'd been true to his promise to stick by Chance.

"I'm not sure what we'll find at the end of this road," he said. "It's unnatural not to have been contested by now. Someone should have stepped in and done something to try and disperse us."

"It takes all of a navy to stop me and you!" Kwame leapt into the air at the declaration. His spirits soared, unrestrained.

"That's just what I was thinking," Simon said. His voice sounded significantly less enthusiastic, and Chance wished he'd try a little harder to mask his worry. "All the same, I'm not keen walking blind into whatever is waiting ahead of us. We have no idea how we'll be received at the capitol."

"I agree with Simon," Chance said. "We should get eyes ahead of us."

"I can go," Rhett volunteered.

Chance hesitated. He still wasn't sure how he felt about Rhett being on the front lines like he was. He thought about telling him to go back once more, but Rhett had already rejected that idea. The boy was growing up. Whether it was his time, or if circumstance had forced it upon him, Rhett was becoming his own agent.

"Alright then, run up ahead and see what you can see," Chance instructed. "Let us know what we can expect. And stay out of trouble," he added.

Rhett nodded. "Aye aye, captain!" He gave a sort of salute and ran off up the street at a sprint. A chill ran down Chance's spine as he watched the boy go.

Captain? How in all the city's misfortunes had he become a leader?

Fate had a sick sense of humor.

"Whatever it is you all are thinking, you're in over your heads."

It was Liesel. She'd come up through the mob and fallen in between Chance and Simon.

"That's what I tried to tell him," Simon said with a weak laugh. "But he's not having any of it."

"I just didn't expect to see you going along with it," Liesel said. "I always thought you were the one with more common sense."

"What can I say?" Simon shrugged. "They boy's persuasive when he tries to be. I'm not the only one who felt so."

"Obviously," she said, looking back at the ever-growing mob. "So, does anyone have a plan? Or are we just winging this one?"

"We talk to them," Chance said, his voice determined. "We take this right to the capitol and demand to meet with the electors. With this many people, they won't be able to ignore us."

"I suppose that's a plan." She didn't sound convinced either.

Chance couldn't understand it. He thought Liesel and Simon would have been more enthusiastic. Yet, here they were vocally casting uncertainty. Weren't they the ones who were part of the Resistance? Hadn't they been waiting for a moment like this to act?

"I'm surprised to see you here, Ponti," Liesel said. "I didn't take you as the fighting type."

"Oh, no," Ponti said. "I'm not a part of this. Just seeing you all off before I find myself a spot in the cheap seats."

He gestured to the spectators along the side streets who had gathered to see the march pass by. Many of them were residents of the Spire. They'd obviously heard about the march and come to see what it was all about. Many of them looked upon the procession with a mix of curiosity and distaste.

"How can you sit and look?" Kwame asked. "Me and you have this fight."

"Yeah, well..." Ponti stuffed his hands in his tawdry pockets. "Maybe I'm not quite as desperate as you all just yet. I like my life, as miserable as it may look—and I plan on keeping it as long as I can."

"I thought you looked out of place here," Liesel frowned. She gave Ponti a dismissive look and turned to Simon.

Chance saw her hand off a belt and short-barreled rifle from under her coat. Simon draped the belt over his shoulder and cinched the buckle tight. Now that Chance looked, he saw Liesel wore a belt around her waist—with two wheel-lock pistols. Even Kwame had produced a single shot muff pistol. He screwed on the barrel and pocketed it again.

"You think there will be a fight?" Chance asked.

"Can't be sure," Simon said, checking the chamber of his rifle and tucking it against his side. "One can only hope they're in a mood to listen, like you said. But a mob is a fickle thing. We're sitting on a powderkeg. The smallest thing could set it off."

"Not to mention the meritocracy and what they have in store for us," Liesel said. "They're probably not keen on having their hand forced. They'll resist it before they go with it."

"We play this carefully and perhaps we can keep things from getting out of hand," Simon said. "*Very* carefully."

"Still," Liesel said, tapping her hip. "Best we be prepared."

Chance rested his hand on the carrier under his coat. If the worst should happen, at least he wasn't completely defenseless.

"They're waiting!" Rhett shouted, racing back down the street. His legs flailed wildly, and he looked as if he might take a tumble at any moment as he pushed himself to his limit. "They're waiting for us!"

"Where?" Simon asked. "How many?"

"All of them!" Rhett wheezed. He joined up with them and struggled to regain his breath. He looked like he'd just sprinted the whole city. "There's a whole... line of them... on the steps...of the capitol... just waiting."

"Well, if any of us had the notion this was going to be easy, we can abandon those thoughts now," Liesel said.

"What we do?" Kwame asked.

"We keep walking," Simon said. "It's likely this mob will turn around the moment they see the opposition. I bet that's what the capitol is betting on too."

"I don't think so," Chance said.

He couldn't explain it, but he was almost certain they wouldn't break. He could feel the force behind him. It felt alive, like it had a will of its own. And there was momentum in it now. It had been building since they'd left the Exchange.

"As long as we don't hesitate, they won't," he said.

"How can you be so sure?" Liesel asked.

"I've seen forces break under less dire circumstance," Simon added.

"Because this is it," Chance said. "This is the real thing. It's the moment Serge was speaking about all this time."

"Well, we'll find out soon enough," Simon said gravely. He pointed ahead.

The street was rounding the southwestern bend that led into the mall. Into view came the pillared front of the capitol building. And there, just as Rhett had described, stood a company of constables and soldiers in dense formation, filling the steps surrounding the capitol.

"Gods above," Ponti said.

Chance felt it too. The soldiers stood unmoving in their line, looking down on the approaching mob. Compared to the hodgepodge Chance led, they cast an imposing presence. It wasn't going to be easy getting past them.

But, Chance still felt the momentum behind him. It wavered slightly when they enter the mall, but the force of it rolled forward. As long as that momentum remained, he could keep walking. It carried him.

"Well, this is where I leave you all to it, I think," Ponti said, giving an overly-compensating comical salute.

Chance caught his eye. He couldn't blame Ponti for wanting to run, but if Chance had been in Ponti's shoes he'd have stayed—if for no other reason than to back up his friends. In that moment Chance realized just how hollow Ponti really was. He had no sense of loyalty.

Chance's eyes must have communicated his feelings because Ponti hesitated. "Sorry," was all he managed to say, and he shrugged helplessly. Then he turned and fled.

"Good riddance," Liesel spat, but Chance felt the void Ponti left behind.

They approached the steps in silence. Only the shuffle of feet could be heard as the mob crossed the plaza. A hundred paces? Maybe more? The walk felt longer than they'd come from the Exchange already. In that silence, and under the stares from the guard, the seconds passed like ages.

They neared the bottom of the steps, and it occurred to Chance that he had no idea how he would get the mob to stop, or if they'd just push him right on through the line. He watched as it drew closer.

Thirty yards. Fifteen yards. Ten yards.

Chance's whole being strained backwards even as he advanced until, as though some unknown signal had gone through the whole of it, the mob slowed to a halt. Chance felt his breath catch. He was caught between two forces, and he felt the pressure squeezing him from both sides.

The constables and soldiers were grouped on the steps, stacked deep and tight so that none would be able to pass between them if they tried. At the top stood the officers and duelists of the meritocracy.

Chance subconsciously scanned their faces for Ringgold, but couldn't make him out. They all looked alike in their uniforms.

"Well," Liesel said under her breath. "Let's see what they do."

The forces stared at one another, no one sure what to do. The rain was beginning to fall thicker, but neither showed any sign they'd noticed. Eyes were trained on one another, appraising the moment.

Finally, one of the officers came forward and looked with disdain on the mob before him.

Chance swallowed hard. It was time. He stepped forward—a step so reluctant it felt like he was walking waist deep in water—and drew the man's hateful eyes to himself.

"This mob will turn back immediately and remove itself from the capitol," the officer shouted. "You have no business gathering here in force as you have. Disperse!"

"Remember," Simon whispered. "*Very* carefully."

Chance nodded, and locked eyes with the officer.

"We have grievances that need addressing," Chance called back. "We wish to speak to the electors about their decision to close the Exchange in the Basin."

"You have no right to demand an audience with the electors."

"We have every right! As citizens of Hatteras we have a right to be heard by our government."

"You think to intimidate us in a hope we'll bend for you? You will not be admitted in such a force. Nor under such circumstances."

"We've never been admitted whatever we've done. You've turned a deaf ear on all but your friends on the Spire. What else could we do?"

"Disperse!" the officer bellowed. "Or we'll have the lot of you arrested."

"You can't arrest us all," Chance said, sweeping his arm toward the sizable mob. "We're too many. So why threaten it?"

"Disperse!"

"Not going to happen!" Chance shouted.

"You wish to force our hand?" the officer asked. "You come in open contestation against the meritocracy—"

"We come to speak with our electors!" Chance insisted. "And if you won't permit that then we'll find another way."

Even as he said it, he knew he'd spoken amiss. He felt Simon tense beside him and the officers face twitched.

"Gentlemen," the officer said, no longer addressing Chance, but those of his own company. "What we have here is an act of open treason. Consider them warned—anyone who does not disperse this instant will be dealt with as traitors to the meritocracy!"

The line stepped forward in unison, and Chance felt the mob shudder behind him—but it didn't break. They were scared, but they weren't broken. Not yet.

"Disperse!" the officer repeated.

"No!" Chance shouted. "You won't get rid of us. Not until you've heard our grievances and righted the wrongs which we've born."

"Constables, draw arms!"

The line of constables stepped forward again, this time drawing clubs from their belts and raising them to the ready. Chance felt the pressure increasing. The moment was so tense he felt his ears would burst under it.

"This is your final warning! Disperse!"

Chance felt it before he saw it. Felt the mob swell behind him as the pressure reached its maximum capacity. It wouldn't hold anymore. It couldn't.

A man charged forward from the mob.

"No, don't!" Chance cried out.

But it was too late. The man hurled an object high into the air. Both sides inhaled, and the pressure became a vacuum. All noise and movement vanished but the slow arc of the device. It came down on the line of soldiers and erupted in a plume of liquid flame.

So, Chance thought in the second that followed. *It's a fight after all.*

CHAPTER FORTY-EIGHT
Poor Timing

What a fool I was, thinking I was in control. Experience should have taught me the danger of the unaccounted variable.

— Excerpt from *Mechanarcissism*

I don't want to fight!" Emmaline said.

"Then what is this all about?" Stoddard asked, impatience dripping in his voice.

She'd burst into Stoddard's office, nearing hysteria, right in the middle of a meeting he'd scheduled with a potential sponsor. He'd had to dismiss the man with little explanation when she wouldn't be removed. She'd demanded Stoddard's time, and begrudgingly he'd consented, though he'd kept behind his desk to ward off the conversation as best he could.

He hadn't succeeded.

"You barge in here and chase off one of the few sponsors who've approached me in months. You refuse to wait even for a moment outside. Do you expect me to believe this isn't going to be a fight?"

"Then perhaps it's time we fought," she said. "Don't you think so?"

"And what good would that do us?"

"If nothing else it would get us *talking* again. I feel like I haven't truly spoken to you in ages."

"Perhaps that's because you've kept enough company lately for the two of us," Stoddard said.

"I've been trying to keep up our social obligations," she defended.

"One of us has to, and you've proven you're incapable of that. It's a miracle you keep receiving so many invitations given how disagreeable you can be."

"Count me fortunate," Stoddard said

"I honestly think you have been. Why else would anyone willingly put up with your unpleasantness?"

"My work is valuable. It's as simple as that."

"You don't think it's something else?" she asked.

Stoddard frowned. He knew what she was fishing for, but he wasn't about to humor her childish need for recognition. He turned back to his work.

"What are you working on?" she asked, prying at him. She wasn't going to let him go. Not this time.

"Nothing."

"See?" she pleaded. "Don't you see it? This is what I've been trying to tell you. You're so closed up. You weren't always like this. What's wrong?"

Stoddard kept his gaze on his desk. She wouldn't understand. She couldn't understand. She didn't know what it was like, what being a part of the meritocracy truly meant. The nightmares that woke him in cold sweats in the middle of the night. It was a balancing act along the edge of a knife.

If she only knew how close he'd come to falling off.

"You spend so much time on it," Emmaline said, "your work."

Her hand drifted over the papers before Stoddard, and he felt the hair on his neck rise.

"I remember when you used to tell me all about what it was you were doing. How we'd sit out by the tree on my father's estate. You'd share with me all the dreams of what you planned to create. How the city would change because of your ideas. And now..."

Her voice faded away wistfully.

"I don't have time for the endless chatter I used to," Stoddard said. "I'm not a dreamer, Emmaline. I'm a visionary. It takes hard work to see that vision become reality."

"And yet, you don't see it, do you?" Emmaline asked softly. "Don't see the reality right in front of you."

"I see my work," he said, gesturing again to the piles before him.

"And nothing more?" she asked, hopeful.

"What else is there?"

"Less than I'd imagined, I think."

Stoddard looked up then. Emmaline's eyes were wet, though she maintained her composure. He remembered the subtle relaxation of her chest the night before, when he'd turned her away, and it clicked in his mind. He remembered why he'd loved her.

Emmaline had always been a strong, if not socially minded, woman. Yet, despite what was expected of her, she'd always retained ownership of her heart. It had drawn him to her so long ago when they'd first met, and lasted the years when they'd been forced apart.

But it was fading, and as Stoddard watched it go out of her he recognized what had been there all along. Her heart was breaking... and Stoddard had broken it.

"Emmaline," he said, his voice softened by her tears.

"I don't know what I was thinking," she said, trying to sound unconcerned. "You've always loved your work. I don't honestly remember a time it hasn't occupied your mind. While I was entertaining foolish thoughts of love, your mind turned on nothing but your creations. And now it turns on what? I can never know."

"Emmaline."

"I mean it," she warned. "It feels like I hardly know you anymore, Jonah."

Stoddard felt her plea pierce him with the use of his name. It had been ages since he'd heard it.

"I loved the man who dreamed with me when I was young," she said. "The one who made me feel like I would be a part of those dreams. You once said to me that all of this would take us to a beautiful future. But, all it's brought us is distance. I feel as though I've lost you."

Her voice broke into sobs.

"Emmaline." Stoddard rose from his desk and took her hands. "I've tried for nothing else than to secure our future together. That's all I've been trying to do. Perhaps it's demanded more of my attention than we'd expected, but that doesn't mean it will always be this way. Things are turning in our favor now, even as we speak. Soon that future will be secured for both of us, and we'll have time again for one another as we once did."

She turned away, but he didn't let her hands go.

"Emmaline, I know I haven't shown it recently, but I do care for you. You remain the only thing I do actually love in this world."

"That's not true," she whispered. "You love your work. More than anything else, you love your work."

"Not more than you," Stoddard insisted.

Emmaline frowned pitifully, but the pity wasn't directed toward herself. She looked deep into Stoddard's eyes.

"Yes, you do," she said. "I know it now. Perhaps I always knew it, and only now realized what it meant. I'll always be your second love." She gave a weak laugh. "I suppose that makes it easier to accept. I don't know why I expected more. It was the same way with my father."

"I'm creating something more for us," Stoddard insisted.

Emmaline nodded, though it was strained. "I know. But... I don't know if I want what you've created."

Stoddard was about to speak, but she silenced him gently with a finger to his lips.

"It's okay," she whispered. "Do what you must. I understand now. I think... I think we love different things."

Stoddard felt the twist in his heart. Her fire, which he'd admired about her, was dimmed. He cursed himself silently that he'd been the cause.

"I hope you find happiness in your work," she said, and turned away.

Stoddard grasped her hands tighter, not willing to let her go. She let him hold her there, though she wouldn't look at him.

"I promise you," he said, mustering all the strength he had to compensate for hers. "Fortunes *are* turning, Emmaline. Our future is here, right now. I've seen to that, and nothing can rip it from us. I'm here. Right here, in this moment. I admit I've been neglectful, and that my work has consumed my thoughts these past months, but you must believe me it's not been my intent—it's never been my intent to lose you. Emmaline..."

He lifted her chin with a tender hand, so that he was looking into her eyes. They were soft, and he saw her desire to believe in his words.

"I'm here again," he assured her. "From this moment I will—"

The door burst open and Emmaline and Stoddard jumped as Donovan came into the room.

"Sir!" he cried, then hesitated when he saw Emmaline crying. He shuffled on his feet, unsure whether to continue or not.

"What do you want?" Stoddard barked, making Emmaline jump a second time. "Can't you see I'm busy?"

"I'm sorry, sir, but I thought you should know. There's been a revolt! A mob has formed and is marching on the Spire even as we speak!"

Stoddard frowned. "The guard will take care of them," he said. "It doesn't concern us."

"But sir," Donovan's words were strained. "The alchemist... the apprentice you met with last night. He's there! He's *leading* it!"

Stoddard heart caught in his throat. Through his mind flashed a nightmare far too real. In it he saw his last chance at discovering the alchemists' secrets snuffed out, his work unraveling, his endorsements withdrawn, and all he'd worked to achieve slipping between his fingers.

The guard would certainly deal with the revolt, and they'd be thorough about it. Particularly if men like Vanzeal were involved.

"You're certain?" he asked, hoping against hope to be contradicted.

"I saw him with my own eyes," Donovan swore.

It was too much.

"Attend me," Stoddard demanded, forgetting his coat entirely and stomping through the door.

Donovan cast an apologetic glance at Emmaline and raced after him, leaving Emmaline alone in the quiet of the study with her quieter tears.

CHAPTER FORTY-NINE
The Clash

When all else fails, duck and cover.

— Alchemical Proverb

Chance heard the shout before he realized what was happening. The constables in the front line dropped to a knee simultaneously as the soldiers behind them raised rifles to the ready. The mob recoiled at the movement, but there was no place to go. Chance felt Liesel grab him by the shoulder and pull him backwards as the soldiers fired.

The sound was deafening as the reports of the rifles tore through the open air. Those at the front took the brunt of it, falling to the ground like a wave crashing—many wounded and others lifeless.

It was only a moment as the shock sank in, but Chance blinked in disbelief as he assessed what had just happened.

First, and most importantly, he was still alive. Liesel had grabbed both him and Rhett and pulled them back so they'd been shielded by others less fortunate. Rhett scrambled away from the bodies, holding his ears against the groans of the wounded. Chance looked at them with disgust, and then dread as he realized exactly what he was looking at.

Kwame lay lifeless at his feet.

The cloud of smoke from the rifles masked the line, but he heard the commands of the officers to reload. The mob pulled back, eager to avoid the next deadly wave of lead prepared for them.

"Get back!" Simon shouted at Chance, pushing him to his feet. "Go! Go!"

Liesel seized Rhett and dragged him away as the soldiers leveled their rifles and again the thunderous peal split the air.

More bodies fell, and the mob broke into full flight.

Chance and his friends did the same, ducking low as they made for the first source of cover they saw—the fountain in the center of the plaza. It felt like they ran forever, and with every step Chance's body remained tensed, expecting the third volley to come at any moment with its deadly verdict.

But it didn't come; not from behind them at least.

It came from in front.

Chance looked up as he neared the fountain to see a man in plain clothes rise up on the rim, a rifle cocked tight into his shoulder. The flash of the muzzle coincided with the shot as he fired once over the heads of the fleeing mob.

The bullet soared true, striking one of the soldiers. He fell backwards, his rifle going off as he fell and sending its bullet high and harmless into the air.

More intermittent shots sounded from across the mall, and Chance saw men and women standing high to return fire.

Members of the Resistance, Chance realized. They had to be. He hadn't realized they'd even joined up with the march.

Their fire covered the mob's retreat and the soldiers on the steps stumbled in surprise at the unexpected retaliation. Chance took the opportunity to breathe in a few grateful breaths.

"Glad you made it," Simon said to the man on the fountain as they ducked down behind him for cover.

"You didn't give us much warning," the man said. "We're still missing quite a few."

"Well, I wasn't planning for this either," Simon said.

"Whether we planned for it or not, it's here," Liesel said, drawing her pistols. "You alright, Rhett?" she asked.

Rhett looked shaken, but he nodded as he hugged the lip of the fountain, cringing whenever a gun went off nearby.

"I told you it might go south," Simon said to Chance.

"And it could still swing further," the man on the fountain said. He knelt down and worked quickly to reload his rifle. "You the kid who started this mess?" he asked Chance.

Chance nodded slowly.

"Well, it's an honor to meet you," he said, shaking Chance's hand vigorously. "Name's Flynn. We'll try and give you all some cover till you can clear the plaza. After that, I'm not sure what good we can do."

"Much appreciated," Simon said, patting Flynn's leg. "You heard him. Best make for the side-streets and get scarce."

"What about you?" Chance asked.

"We'll be fine," Simon said, raising his rifle to the ready.

"We'll hang back here and make sure you have time to get out," Liesel said.

"Then I'm staying with you," Chance insisted. A bullet nicked the fountain above them, and they flinched under a light dusting of stone.

"This isn't just a demonstration," Simon said. "This is a real scrap. People are going to get hurt."

"This is my fight," Chance insisted. "I'm staying, whether you like it or not."

"Rhett?" Liesel asked.

"I'm—" He winced as another bullet whizzed by. "—with Chance," he managed to say.

"Stubborn boys," Liesel groaned. "For neither of you having parents, I wonder where you got it from."

"Here they come," Flynn called from the fountain, rising up again. "Look alive!"

They all turned to look across the mall. An officer on the steps shouted a command and the constables stepped forward, clubs drawn and readied. At a word, they split into four separate lines and charged the fleeing mob, spreading out over the plaza as they advanced. Clubs descended brutally upon anyone who'd been unfortunate enough to fall behind—injured or not.

"They're sweeping the plaza!"

"Bloody tyrants," Flynn cursed.

"If they can keep us disorganized they'll have an easier time quelling this fight. Don't let them divide us!" Simon shouted.

"Haven't they already?" Chance asked. The mob fled in any direction they could to find safety. The fight was clearly out of them.

"Not yet they haven't," Flynn said, raising his rifle and leveling it on the advancing force. "Company, ready!"

In synchronization, Chance saw a surprising number of men and women appear from their hiding places—some behind carts and others inside or atop the booths set up for the open market.

"Give 'em hell!"

Another peal of gunfire tore the air as the Resistance fighters fired into the advancing lines. The volley found targets easily; the constables lay bare and exposed in their formations. Their lines soaked up the bullets like bindings on a bloody wound. Men fell, and the advancing force slowed.

Their clubs were useless now.

"Ha!" Simon laughed. "That gave them something to think about."

"Reload!" Flynn called.

"If you two are staying, you'd best take these," Liesel said.

She handed Chance and Rhett each one of her pistols. Rhett took it reflexively, and Chance grasped his firmly. It made him feel strange, but he shook off the feeling and checked it was loaded.

"I can't shoot them," Rhett said.

"Then don't," Simon instructed. "Fire over their heads if you have to. Just make a show of it. We want them to think twice before they try to advance on us again."

Chance aimed, his arms straight before him. They shook terribly, but he did his best to hold steady.

The soldiers advanced now, reinforcing the constables as they retreated. They fired shots into the booths and carts where the Resistance took cover—shooting at anything that moved.

Simon pulled back as a few shots passed dangerously close to his cover, and Flynn leapt down from the fountain. Now that the majority of the people had cleared out he didn't need the elevation.

"Chance," Simon shouted, firing another round at the advancing lines. "Chance, shoot!"

Chance stared ahead, watching as the men charged. He heard the shots around him from the other Resistance fighters, but he couldn't bring himself to pull the trigger. He was too horrified by the sight of what lay before him. The sight of men fallen. Wounded. Crying for help.

These aren't the real enemy, he thought. *They're just like us.*

He let his hands drop and the gun fell to the ground. Rhett was right. He couldn't shoot. He was a lot of things, he had to admit, but he wasn't a killer.

"Let go of me!" Stoddard shouted, trying to push his way through the line at the edge of the plaza. He'd run as fast as he could from his office. The rain had done little to improve his mood; he was soaked through to the bone. The scene playing out before him did nothing to raise his hopes.

This was no revolt. This was a war.

He saw the soldiers centralized on the capitol steps, unmoving from their posts as they fired in volleys across the plaza. Duelists at the top of the steps shouted orders over their heads, directing their focus wherever they could make out their foe.

That was proving quite a challenge, however. Portions of the carts and structures which made up the open market had been ransacked—torn down and piled up as temporary barriers against the constables who'd attempted to sweep the rebels out of the mall.

They'd been forced to fall back once the firefight had escalated.

Stoddard's eyes swept the scene for a single face, but he couldn't see Chance anywhere. He saw bodies strewn on the ground closer to the steps and throughout the open divide between the two sides. His heart caught in his throat.

Gods that be, he prayed, *don't let one of them be him.*

"I said let me go," he shouted again.

"I'm sorry, sir," the constable tried to explain, though Stoddard made it difficult with his persistent attempts to get by. "I can't let you through."

"It's not safe," Donovan offered from behind, trying to hold Stoddard's shoulder as he struggled.

"I don't care what's safe," Stoddard barked back, trying to slip by. "Constable, there is a man in there I must get to. I must find him before something happens to him. It's a matter of life and death. Please!"

"Right now, the most important matter is keeping you from harm yourself," the constable explained. "I'm sorry sir; I can't let you through."

"Ahhh! Damn you!" Stoddard shouted, letting the constable push him back. Donovan caught him, keeping him from stumbling, but Stoddard shrugged him off.

Stoddard paced back and forth, tearing at his hair as he considered what to do. He couldn't just stand aside waiting for fate to decide what would become of the young man. He was too valuable. He represented perhaps another lifetime of research and study—a lifetime Stoddard did not have the luxury of replicating.

He felt the brutality of each passing second as he watched the scene unfold. He saw one of the rebels rise up on the top of a cart and level his rifle, only to be struck by a few balls and fall lifeless to the ground. Stoddard flinched as he watched each strike.

If he dies, the spark dies with him.

The thought came to his mind with such clarity that it swept him of any inhibitions he might yet have possessed. He had to find Chance. There was no alternative.

Like a man possessed, Stoddard turned on the constable and struck him across the chin, catching him off guard and sending him spinning. The others were equally surprised and before they could stop him, Stoddard was through their barricade and sprinting full tilt into the plaza.

"A curse on you!" the constable yelled after him, watching the mad doctor run for the mall, disappearing in the heavy rain. "I hope we find you under the wreckage when we're done here."

Stoddard ignored the man's calls. Nothing else mattered now. Not more than Chance's life.

Ringgold paced nervously on the capitol steps as he watched the movements of the line. They'd given it their best, trying to secure the plaza, but the resistance they'd encountered had done an exceptional job repelling their advance. And now, with the rain picking up, it was becoming increasingly difficult to see where they were taking fire from.

He swore to himself silently. As long as his men were trapped out in the open on these steps, they were at a terrible disadvantage. Their formation was proving the death of them.

"Sir," Ringgold ventured. "I think we should evacuate the capitol and seek better ground to fight from. If we maintain our presence here we'll suffer undue casualties."

"We remain where we are," Vanzeal said. His voice was strained, though he stood rigid and tall. He looked down on the scene unfolding before him with a look of satisfaction. "We hold this line."

"But if this firefight keeps up we won't be able to—"

"We hold the line!" Vanzeal barked.

"With all due respect," Ringgold insisted. "We have a better chance of driving them off if we relocate to a more covered position."

"You speak as though there were a prayer they could take these steps at all," Vanzeal said. "We will *not* let them seize the capitol. This isn't just about saving lives, Sergeant; it's about delivering a message. We will not be ousted by a band of common fodder. But, if you're so eager to relocate, why don't you join the front and lead the next sweep? Would that suit you?"

Ringgold held his tongue, and Vanzeal glared at him. Turning his attention back to the fight, he shouted orders to the soldiers to shore up their line, which was showing signs of weakening. The men were struggling to remain calm while the enemy continued their harassment.

Ringgold watched too, his eyes scanning the scene with concern. He'd recognized Chance when he'd stepped forward to speak, though he'd looked even worse than the last time they'd met.

He was somewhere out there—whether a part of the Resistance or perhaps, Septigonee forbid, one of the bodies strewn across the plaza.

"What is this about?" Vanzeal barked suddenly, his temper clearly not welcoming any more complications. Two soldiers were climbing the stairs, guiding a third man between them.

"Seized this man rushing the steps," one of them reported. "He claims to have an urgent message for Sergeant Ringgold."

"Do you recognize this man?" Vanzeal asked.

Ringgold considered Donovan for a moment, then nodded. "I do," he said. "This is Doctor Stoddard's man."

"He was waving this," the soldier said, handing over Donovan's white handkerchief.

"You must have lost your mind approaching my men just now," Vanzeal said. "Or else you have a death wish."

"Sir," Donovan pleaded. "I wouldn't have come if it wasn't urgent, I promise."

"What is the matter?" Ringgold asked. "What business do you have with me?"

"Sergeant," Donovan began, his voice quivering. "It's Stoddard. Doctor Stoddard... he's lost his mind."

"Hold man," Ringgold said. "Speak clearly. No sense wasting your breath."

"Doctor Stoddard, sir," Donovan said with great effort to calm himself. "We tried to talk him out of it, but he wouldn't listen to reason. He's inside the mall. He's looking for the alchemist!"

Ringgold expression turned grave, and he looked out on the firefight still raging across the plaza.

"You're sure he's there?" he asked.

"Yes, sir," Donovan assured him. "What's become of him, I'm not certain, but he's clearly in danger."

"One can only hope," Vanzeal sneered. "And what is it you want us to do about it?"

Donovan looked surprised. "To retrieve him," he said. "He's a member of the meritocracy. It's your duty!"

"We are charged with defending the capitol," Vanzeal scoffed. "Not parading around trying to find missing persons. If Stoddard is in the mall then it's likely we'll find him after we've—"

"I will help find him," Ringgold volunteered.

"Sergeant," Vanzeal growled. "You're needed here on the line!"

"I have been charged with the protection of the meritocracy," Ringgold said, rising to match Vanzeal's posture. "As you have been. And that charge extends to safeguarding all gentlemen of the meritocracy. I have a duty and obligation to fulfill."

He signaled to one of his men to attend him, and he turned to leave.

"I warn you," Vanzeal barked, his agitation rising. "If you go now I'll see you arrested upon your return for abandoning your post."

"I wouldn't expect any less," Ringgold said, and took Donovan by the shoulder as he led him down the steps. "Now, where was it you last saw the doctor?"

CHAPTER FIFTY
A Misfortunate End

Perhaps, when this is all over, someone will sort through this mess I've made. Perhaps they'll understand why it was that I did what I did. Perhaps they'll forgive me.

— Excerpt from *Mechanarcissism*

"Curse the day," Flynn lamented as he lay against the fountain's rough lip.

Chance shared his sentiments. It was a grisly scene, and he hadn't been prepared for the cost. The bodies of the unfortunate littered the ground between them and the steps of the capitol. Men and women from both sides.

Not once, but twice the soldiers and constables had tried to advance, but, against the odds, the Resistance had held their positions.

"That sharpshooter had it out for you," Liesel said, tightening the binding around Flynn's arm. He'd taken a round during the second push, just above the elbow. His blood tinted the rain as it ran down his arm.

"Well, they took a piece of me for a souvenir," Flynn chuckled gravely. "Credit to them this time."

"That ought to be enough," Simon said, lowering his rifle. The people from the mob had all but cleared the plaza now, apart from those who'd fallen.

"Nonsense," Flynn said. He made an effort to raise his rifle, gritting his teeth against the pain. "I've got a few rounds in me yet."

"We've laid down enough cover. I think it's time we fell back."

"You want us to fall back?" Flynn asked. "Are you mad, man? Look at them. We're winning this fight!"

"We're not losing," Liesel clarified. "Let's not let this scrap go to our heads. We should head back to the safe-houses and lay low until we—"

"No," Flynn groaned. "We can't just slough off now. Look!"

Flynn strained to lift himself up to get a better angle on the capitol. He was obviously in great pain, but he gripped his arm tightly and did his best to ignore it. He pointed toward the steps.

"That line of soldiers is worse for the wear—you can see it in the way they stand. They ain't had reinforcements come the whole time we've been here. And why do you suppose that is?"

Chance honestly didn't know. It didn't look like Simon or Liesel understood it either.

"Because there *aren't* any," Flynn said. "They're on their own! For whatever reason, that line is all that stands between us and the capitol, and it's not far from breaking."

"He may be right," Simon said. "It's odd the way they've let things escalate. I thought it was intentional, but that doesn't make sense. If it was a trap, they'd have sprung it by now. Perhaps they are spread too thin to deal with us."

"We wait for another day and we may never get a chance like this again," Flynn said. "Look, they don't want to be there, but they aren't moving neither. They're sitting ducks in an open pond in that formation. Whether we intended for this or not, we've got an advantage. I say we take it!"

"I don't know if it's a good idea to push our luck," Liesel said. "And who knows when their reinforcements will come barreling in on us."

Chance couldn't help smiling, even in such a moment. "Since when did you believe in luck?" he asked.

Liesel smiled and waved him off.

"Listen, we can run or we can push our way through to the electors and have a real bargaining chip if those reinforcements ever do arrive.

We take the electors, and we take the city. It couldn't be easier if we'd planned it ourselves."

"The electors have long since fled by now," Liesel said.

"Nah," Simon said, his smiled betraying his rising spirits. "They'll be inside, right where they're supposed to be. Stuffy cogs are too proud to leave."

A bullet zipped overhead, and they all flinched.

"Even if we do manage to take the capitol," Liesel said. "What's to say the Navy doesn't return from their campaign overseas and boot us out?"

"We'll deal with that problem when it arrives then, won't we?"

"Call me crazy," Simon said, "but I'm with him. I think we go for it."

"Me too," Chance said. "I'm in."

"They're still a sizable force on those steps. We're not just walking through the front door."

"I can clear it," Chance said. They looked at him skeptically. "No, really." He cracked open his carrier and showed them the contents.

"Smokers? Flask bombs?" Liesel asked. "Is that a—"

"Yep!" Chance grinned.

"Since when have you started carrying all these around?" Simon asked. "That's not a typical alchemist's kit."

"Since last night," Chance said. "I had a feeling they'd come in handy, and it looks like they will."

"Now I wonder if you were planning this all along," Liesel frowned.

"You're a godsend," Flynn laughed. "What have you been doing here this whole time then? We should have been using that from the start."

"I wasn't thinking," Chance said. "But, if I can get close enough to their line, I think I can break them up."

"We can keep up this rate of fire for a while more," Simon said, "but we'll run out of ammunition before the hour is up. If we're going to rush the steps, we best not dawdle."

"You really think you can open us a window?" Simon said.

"I think so," Chance said. "I'll sneak up there on the left, through the mall. The rain will give me some cover. That should get me close enough to reach them with these."

"A few smoke shields and explosions and they'll be so disoriented it shouldn't be too difficult to persuade them off those steps," Flynn smiled.

"We should split up the work," Simon said. "I'll take a few of these and go around the right. We'll drive them off those stairs from two directions at once."

"You sure you want to do this?" Liesel asked.

"If I can," Chance said, "then I'll do it."

"Fortune keep you, kid," Flynn said. "We'll pass the word along for everyone to conserve their ammunition and wait for the signal. At the first sign of smoke, we'll come charging."

"I'll come too," Rhett offered.

"No," Chance said. "Not this time, Rhett. You stay here with Liesel and Flynn. They'll keep you safe."

The kid's expression was torn.

"Don't worry about me," Chance said. "You'll find me after the charge. Just keep the fire up."

"Better hurry up then," Liesel said, firing toward the stairs before ducking down again to reload. "Every second that passes is time for their reinforcements to get here, wherever they are."

"Alright." Chance and Simon split the contents of his kit, Simon slinging a satchel over his shoulder.

Rhett still looked concerned, and Chance rustled his hair, a familiar sense of pride swelling in him toward the boy. He'd surprised him, and suddenly it made sense why Rhett had gravitated to the Resistance. He had the heart of the sea.

Chance crouched into a readied position.

"It's now or never," Simon said.

"We're counting on you, mate," Flynn said, cocking his hat. He gave a hand signal above his head to the surrounding Resistance fighters to keep up their fire, and Chance heard the rifle reports renew with vigor.

Simon was off, the limp in his gait only slowing him a little. Chance ducked low and crept around the back of the fountain in the opposite direction.

"And Chance," Liesel called to him.

Chance popped his head back up.

"You be careful. They'll be watching for you."

Chance hurried through the mall, keeping out of sight as best he could. He'd taken the wider route, closer to the buildings on the border in hopes that he'd be less noticeable the further he was from the center of the plaza. It afforded him plenty of places to hide among the sprawl.

A bolt of lightning split the sky overhead, striking a nearby street. It made Chance jump and nearly drop his carrier.

His nerves were on edge, and his heart pounded in his ears. The firefight was raging, the sound of rifle reports sounding erratically from both sides. He had to hurry if they were going to have enough ammunition for the charge.

Turning a corner, he tucked underneath an awning and hugged the lip of a table full of jewelry. He paused, dumbstruck. Wiping the rain from his eyes, he stared ahead of him, at what he couldn't believe.

There, sprinting across a gap just ahead, was Stoddard. He was ducking between stalls, his hands shielding his head from the rain, as he made his way in Chance's direction.

Chance knelt there, baffled at the cruel tricks of fate. Of all the people he could have encountered in that moment, he'd never expected Stoddard.

Simon hugged his booth, a fresh volley of bullets digging in around him. They'd spotted him as he'd come up through the mall, and he was pinned down. This close, he was the most attractive target. He heard others of the Resistance trying to return fire, but it wasn't deterring the guard. The sound of metal whizzing overhead remained constant.

He couldn't stay there. He knew that much. It was just a matter of timing when he could move. He scanned the booths and carts ahead, selecting one he thought he could reach during a reload.

Another volley struck the broad side of his booth. Now was his chance.

Simon rose and dashed across the gap, clutching the satchel to his side. His leg twanged, his old injury flaring up as he forced pressure on it, but he ignored it. There were more pressing matters to consid—

He felt a bite through his shoulder, and his whole body spun as if struck with the force of a sledge. He lost his footing and fell, rolling a few times on the uneven cobble until he came to rest a few feet from his cover.

He lay there not moving. Not thinking. Waiting for his senses to catch up with him. He'd experienced something like this before as a militiaman, when he'd injured his leg. The similarity in the feeling hurled him back in his memories. He saw the faces of the men who'd surrounded him then, leaning over him, lifting him to safety.

He'd be alright. They'd look after him. All he had to do was rest. Regain his strength. In a while he'd be as good as…

Something wasn't right. He opened his eyes and reality came rushing back to him as he realized where he was. No one was there to help him this time—just him. How much time had passed? Enough for the guard to reload?

He listened, anticipating the sound he knew would come: the many zipping balls intent to seek him out and put an end to his life.

But, none came. The volleys sounded, but he no longer heard the metallic pings of nearby bullets. Perhaps they'd seen him go down and taken him for dead?

He counted his fortune and lifted himself slightly. His collarbone burned where he'd been struck, and he touched it lightly. His hand came up red with blood; the cursed cogs had got him good.

But this wasn't going to be how he went, he told himself. He still had a task to complete.

Grasping his shoulder with one hand and his satchel in the other, Simon crawled behind a nearby cart. It was slow progress, but he was moving. An ache set into his shoulder, sending a burning pain through his chest. His breaths came in short gusts, and he clenched his fists to ride out the pain.

He kept crawling. One way or another, he was going to get to those steps.

"Stoddard!" Chance called, leaping up from his hiding place.

Stoddard froze where he was, stunned before a look of relief came over him, as though a great fear was lifted from his shoulders. "Chance! Gods above, I hoped I would find you." He breathed deep, recovering from his run.

How did he keep finding him? Chance wondered. The man was relentless.

"What are you doing here?" Chance asked. "Shouldn't you be up there?" He gestured to the capitol.

"Why? Because I have ties to the meritocracy?" Stoddard asked. "I'm a man of science, Chance. As are you. Science doesn't take a side."

"If you say so," Chance said. The thick drops of rain streamed over his face and he blinked through them, not willing to take his eyes away from Stoddard. "I suppose you're going to try and convince me to come with you now?"

"I'm here to convince you not to throw away your life," Stoddard insisted. "I'm putting myself in danger to save you."

"Thanks, but I don't need saving." Chance pushed past him and made to continue on his way.

"You and I," Stoddard said. "We are not soldiers."

"I'm whatever I need to be."

"Yes, you are," Stoddard smiled.

Chance wanted to knock that smile off his face.

"You're a remarkably resourceful young man, Chance. A true opportunist. I've admired that from the first moment I met you."

"Don't pander to me," Chance spat.

"Very well," Stoddard said flatly. "But tell me, why are you so intent on throwing your gift away?"

"I have no gift."

"Oh, poor boy. You poor boy. Your gift is greater than you or I can even comprehend. Don't you understand?" Stoddard pleaded. "The knowledge you carry—the secrets of the Aether—they're more valuable than anything you could possibly do here today. This little feud, whatever it's about, is nothing compared to what's in your head."

"I'm fighting for my friends."

"You're putting at risk one of the greatest scientific advancements since the beginning of this city!"

"Everything there was to know about the Aether spark died with Ashworth," Chance insisted.

"That's not true!" Stoddard shouted. "You can't fool me. You know more than you admit, and my offer still stands. Everything I've learned about the Aether I'm offering freely to you. Just come away from this scuffle."

"Still trying to play the friend?" Chance said. "You must think I'm a fool."

"Not at all," Stoddard swore. "You're a genius, Chance. A protégé of the city. You only need the resources and the right guidance. I can provide those if you'll only listen to me."

"I'm nothing." Chance said it under his breath. He'd accomplished nothing. He'd discovered nothing. He'd saved no one. At the very least, he could do something for the resistance—for his friends.

He turned to go.

"That's not true, either," Stoddard called after him. "I see it in you plainly enough. And Ashworth saw it to. He saw your potential, Chance. He saw what you could become! Why else would he have signed off his entire laboratory to you? He wanted *you* to carry on his work."

Chance stopped abruptly, a new thought interrupting his. How did Stoddard know Ashworth had signed over his property? How could Stoddard possibly have known that?

Then it clicked. The documents. The notebooks. All of Ashworth's research had been seized by Vanzeal… and taken to the one who'd issued the order.

"It *was* you," Chance said, turning slowly. "It was you all along."

Stoddard hesitated, a look of apprehension coming over him as he realized his mistake. "Now listen here, Chance. I—"

Chance was done listening. He was done entertaining Stoddard's lies. Every word from the man was like venom in his veins. It heated his blood and caused his whole being to quake.

As he looked at Stoddard now, listened to his silken words try to talk him down, Chance recalled all of his pain since the Aether had come into his hands. The bombing. The fire. Ashworth's murder. Ponti's home. His deterioration. His friend's concern. In a single chain of events, Chance traced everything he'd suffered to the man who stood before him now.

He'd set the gears in motion and triggered this mess.

Chance's grip tightened around his carrier. If there was anyone in the city who deserved to be punished for what had happened it was Stoddard.

Simon pulled himself up against the wheel of an abandoned cart with his good arm. He was close enough he was certain he could reach the steps with a well-aimed throw. Not an easy feat given his condition.

He was losing blood, and the pressure in his shoulder had spread down his side. He could hardly use his right arm. Positioning himself so that the pressure was off his shoulder, he breathed deep to recuperate strength. He'd worn himself out crawling.

Glancing ahead, he saw the soldiers on the steps were looking worse for the wear. They'd suffered considerable casualties, their numbers thinned and many wounded among them. Nonetheless, they'd held their line. Whomever was commanding those men must have been a force to be reckoned with.

It would be the death of them.

"Prideful, cogs," Simon cursed. They may have been the enemy, but he took no satisfaction in their circumstance. He'd been at the mercy of a commander like those too many times himself.

Looking back at the fountain in the center of the plaza, he saw members of the Resistance popping up here and there, keeping up the barrage on the steps, but their rate of fire was audibly diminished.

They're conserving ammunition, Simon realized. They were running out of time.

He scanned the opposite side of the steps for signs of Chance, but none could be seen. He couldn't wait much longer. They needed to put up the smokescreen.

"Come on, Chance," Simon groaned. "Where are you?"

Ringgold trudged at a quick soldier's step, scanning the booths and carts with a trained eye. They'd searched the area where Donovan had said he'd seen Stoddard last run to, but so far they'd turned up no sign of him.

Ringgold kept a wary eye toward the center of the plaza. He didn't want to draw the attention of the revolutionaries. He was a skilled duelist, but even he had to bow to the deadly simplicity of a rifle.

"Are you certain he came this way?" Ringgold asked.

"I'm positive, sir."

"Where could he have gone." Ringgold held a hand up to block the rain. It was difficult to see. At the rate they were going, the firefight would be over by the time they'd found them.

"Perhaps we should split up," he suggested.

"Excuse me?" Donovan asked. "I don't know if that's the wisest choice. I'm an office clerk, not a soldi—"

Ringgold held up a hand to silence him.

There, down a small corridor of booths, he caught sight of two figures. They were squared off with one another, and Ringgold recognized them despite the rain.

He called out, but a peal of thunder sounded, stripping away any other noise. Ringgold cursed, picking up his pace as he ran toward them.

"Don't lie to me!" Chance snapped. The sound of thunder resounded around them, making Stoddard jump. "Stop lying to me! You killed Ashworth!"

"I told you," Stoddard said. "That was not my fault."

"Harper. Keller. Kwame." Chance spat each name at Stoddard as though it were a bullet. "It's because of you that they're dead. You murdered them all!"

"Chance, I—"

"You've hunted me and my friends for months. You've destroyed everything I've ever worked toward, and now you want to pick at our remains? I won't let you prey upon my friends like you've preyed upon me."

"It's not like that," Stoddard tried to explain. "I'm only trying to—"

"Do you even see what you've done?"

Chance was at his limit. Every fiber of his being was honed on Stoddard, seething with hatred.

"All of this," he shouted, gesturing to the grizzly scene of the plaza, "is because of *you!*"

He couldn't contain his hatred any longer. It bubbled up past his breaking point and his hand tightened on the flask in his carrier. With all his might, he drew it out and hurled it at Stoddard's head.

"No, Chance!" Ringgold shouted. He'd stepped out from between two booths, as Chance wound up.

Stoddard flinched, his arms rising as the flask flew straight for him. There was a blur of red as Ringgold dove forward, throwing himself in front of the doctor. The flask collided against Ringgold's shoulder, bursting at the epicenter and spewing flames across the length of his body. Stoddard tumbled as Ringgold knocked him to the ground, shielding him from the worst of the blast.

Stoddard cried out, writhing in pain under Ringgold's body as he grasped his exposed arm. His sleeve was shredded and burned, the skin below charred instantly from the intense heat. A stub remained where his hand had once been.

Chance had only a moment to take in what had happened before the second duelist was upon him. With a single motion and the sound of springs, Chance felt the cold reality of steel sweep across his chest and he fell backwards against the ground.

"No!" Stoddard shouted through his pain. "No! You didn't! You can't!"

The duelist sheathed his blade and knelt over Ringgold, pulling him away from Stoddard and checking for signs of life. Ringgold remained motionless where he lay, his body horribly burned, his chest unmoving.

"Sir!" Donovan cried as he rushed to Stoddard's side. His expression twisted and he shrunk back momentarily as he looked at Stoddard's arm.

"We have to go," the duelist said. "We can't waste time here. They'll have seen the blast." He seized Stoddard, pulling him away from Ringgold's body.

"Come along, sir," Donovan urged, doing his best to help. "Let's get you away from here."

They both leaned forward and lifted Stoddard from the ground. He wasn't a heavy man, but it was difficult to grip him. Donovan let out a cry of alarm as some of Stoddard's skin slid off where he was holding him.

"For the sake of our lives," the duelist barked. "Hold him!"

Donovan grasped firmer and they lifted him again.

"No!" Stoddard cried, fighting against the pain and their strong arms. "You have the wrong man," he insisted, pointing to Chance. "Save him! Save *him*!"

He kicked and struggled, but the pain got the better of him and he felt his strength drain. Defeated, he watched helplessly as he was dragged away. Chance's body faded from view behind them and Stoddard wept openly, surrendering to the cruel trick of fate as his last hope was lost from view.

CHAPTER FIFTY-ONE
The Secret

The master alchemist may not have the power to change lead to gold, but they will have changed—either making heaven of a hell or misery from a gift.

— Alchemical Proverb

Chance lay on his back, sucking in short gasps of air as his mind fought to catch up with him. He was having a hard time grounding his thoughts in the moment; they spun dizzily around him. Everything seemed to be racing by and he closed his eyes to try and block it out.

He tried to draw in a deep breath, but no matter how hard he tried the air never seemed to stay with him. He strained to move, but he felt pinned against the rough stone.

After struggling for a moment, he gave up and sank back into the ground. The pain was too much for him. He lay still, listening to the distant sounds of the battle and watching the flickering glow of flames as they clung stubbornly to one of the nearby booths.

Even in the rain, they refused to be snuffed out.

Chance's mind swam, as if it drifted through murky water. Occasionally a wave of thought crashed down around him and he felt himself dip below its surface, only to return to this same place again as his vision cleared and he sputtered for a breath.

He thought of the Resistance. How would they take the steps now that he couldn't clear the way?

He thought of Liesel. He'd never come through on his promise to pay her back for all the help she'd given him..

He thought of Rhett. Who would look after him if he couldn't?

He thought of Margarete. He'd never apologized for what he'd put her through. Never told her how much deeper his admiration for her went.

He thought of Ashworth and Harper, and wondered where they were now. Had they learned anything more about the Aether since they'd gone.

And he thought of Ringgold. About the argument they'd held onto for so many years. It seemed so pointless now. School. His apprenticeship. Their godforsaken need to compete with one another. All of it.

His head lolled to the side and he saw Ringgold's body only a few feet away. It lay limp and lifeless, half-draped in the blood-red cape. His face was uncovered, however. His eyes were closed, his burnt expression one of unexpected peace.

Why would you do that? Chance asked silently. *Why would you try and stop me, Ringgold?*

Of all the misfortunes he'd endured, this was the cruelest of them all. At the very least it would be his last.

Chance felt his eyes sting as tears clouded the horrible vision before him. A tender mercy. Turning away, he looked into the sky. The sun was shrouded entirely by the blackened clouds which churned overhead. Every so often he'd see flashes of lightning, though the sound of the thunder was fading with the battle.

And then Chance was confused.

Light was coming through the clouds. He blinked through the rain, trying to focus on the light as it grew. It shimmered between the drops like dust falling from a sill, swirling in slow prismatic waves. He tried to follow the particles, but they faded in and out so that he couldn't tell if it were one continuous stream or several moving patches.

For a moment he thought it was drifting toward him... but that wasn't right. He looked harder. The light was moving away from him. It was escaping through the clouds.

Chance followed the trail. His eyes were getting heavy and he struggled to keep them open as he searched until he was looking down at his chest. There, concentrated around the gash, he saw the light bleeding out as he exhaled. It drifted like wisps of smoke, mixing with the rain in a gentle blend of blues and golds.

Chance couldn't help a faint smile. "So, that's what Ashworth meant," he mused, and his eyes closed for the last time.

EPILOGUE

It's clear to me now that the only thing I leave behind is a broken world, and my part in breaking it.

— Excerpt from *Mechanarcissism*

Stoddard trudged down the narrow lane with determined, yet unfamiliar, steps. Though he wore the typical costume of a Basin-dweller, he'd not been this far from the Spire in years. He had to trust his gut and let the general flow of the crowded street guide him in his search.

He walked in silence, even as the streets around him buzzed with ruckus celebration and revelry. Men and women abandoned all pretenses of concern or responsibility as they flung themselves about wildly—drinking, dancing, and debauching.

Stoddard, however, felt none of the celebratory contagion which had spread through them, moving them to sudden outbursts of felicity. Despite the changing times, they were otherworldly to him in their blatant disregard for propriety.

But then, unlike the Septigonee's Day celebrations from before, this wasn't just a momentary lull from the routine misery. This was a celebration of their fortunes turning for good.

Nothing could have contained them if it tried.

Spotting a promising establishment tucked neatly away, he crossed the street, almost being trampled by an impatient carriage carrying a collection of inebriated youth. Patrons exited with heavy and unsure steps, their tongues rolling loose in their mouths.

Exactly the kind of services Stoddard was looking for.

Slipping through the door, he was assaulted by the pub's ripe flavor. The room was stuffy and cluttered. Some attempts had been made to spruce it up, but the general atmosphere remained unsavory. People crowded together, bumping up against one another as their boisterous conversations spilled over and mixed in the slurry of smoke and soot which hung in the air.

Stoddard was careful not to disrupt the pockets of patrons as he swam through the thick air, keeping his gaze low to discourage any spontaneous conversations which might arise.

At the bar, he snatched a vacant seat. Casting a glance from side to side, he swept the room once for signs of familiar faces, but none were to be seen. It was unlikely anyone would recognize him in this part of the city.

He allowed himself to relax.

"Be with you in one moment," the man behind the counter said as he finished up with another customer who was counting out an odd number of coins.

Stoddard didn't mind the moment to settle in. It felt like months since he'd truly been able to breathe. Everywhere he went nowadays he felt severe, probing eyes on him.

He rubbed the top of his gloved hand nervously. He never thought he'd regret so much his once affiliation with the meritocracy.

"Sorry for the wait," the barman said, squaring off with him. "I'm not sure our paths have crossed before. Blake Bracken is the name. But, call me Blake, your eager and willing host. Now, what can I do for you on this fine day?"

"Just a drink," Stoddard said. "Whatever you have on hand. It's not really meant for a celebration."

"I've got something for most men's taste," Bracken said. "However, by the look of you... perhaps you'd enjoy something a bit finer?"

Stoddard head snapped up, his body rising from the chair reflexively.

"Don't worry," Bracken assured him in friendly tones. "I won't make any trouble for you. I'm not above old gentlemen types like yourself coming through my doors. A man is a man as much as a drink is a drink in my books."

"Thank you." Stoddard settled back into his seat, though his nerves remained on edge. If the barman was able to pick him out from among the crowd so easily, he worried who else might. Perhaps his guise wasn't as common as he'd supposed.

He cast a few wary glances at the patrons nearby, but none of them seemed to pay him any mind. They were buried too deep in their drinks.

"How about a brandy?" Bracken asked.

Stoddard nodded and Bracken poured him a clean glass. Stoddard laid out a few coins on the table, a faint winding and grinding of gears heard as he did so. Bracken's eyebrow raised, but Stoddard withdrew his hand quickly and took the glass with his other.

"So, what brings you to this part of the Basin?" Bracken asked. "On a day like today, no less."

"Does a man need another reason than a drink to visit a pub?" Stoddard asked.

"I suppose not," Bracken said. "Take no offense to my asking. To be honest, it's refreshing to find a soul who still has some decency in their demeanor. Ever since that bloody uprising, men have gotten heads the size of blimps—even if their pockets ain't holding but thick air. But, I understand that you're guarded. Can't say I envy your type these days."

Who was this man to speak so boldly? Stoddard wondered. It reminded him a moment of—

He shook his head and polished off his brandy in a single motion. He didn't want to think about the old world. Those memories haunted his thoughts in his every waking moment. Not today, he told himself. He was determined to be free of them for one day.

He passed the glass back, and Bracken refilled it. Again, the sound of gears could be heard faintly as Stoddard took it back.

"Don't get me wrong," Bracken continued, glancing at Stoddard's hand curiously. "I'm no worse off, now that the common man has got a share in what the meritocracy was holding onto. Lot of wealth to distribute, and I can't complain about my cut. Keeps my baby's walls standing tall," he said, gesturing to his establishment.

"It doesn't look like it's done much..." Stoddard trailed off. It wasn't wise to criticize his host, but he was growing comfortable with Bracken's openness. It was refreshing.

"No offense taken," Bracken waved dismissively, discerning his thoughts. "I know she ain't pretty. Things may have improved some, but that isn't a reason to get a high brow. That type of thing has gotten to men's heads. How long will it last, I wonder? It's difficult to say. Fortunes are always turning, and can only be divided so many ways. That's the tricky thing with fortunes: sooner or later, everything runs out."

"I suppose."

"Between you and I," Bracken said. "I'd have been just fine if things had stayed the way they were, and the meritocracy was still in power. World was simpler then. You knew who a man was when he came through your door. And, more importantly, so did he. Everyone's so blasted eager these days.

"But here I am rambling about my own affairs. What of you? How's fortune favored you this past year?"

Stoddard looked deep into his brandy. "I honestly can't say."

"Well, I assume if you're still around then you're through the worst of it," Bracken said. "Can't say I agree with all the changes which have come about, or the treatment of the gentlemen of the old world. But, someone's got to pay, I suppose.

"To think they got by on a fluke," Bracken chuckled to himself, though he didn't seem amused. "I'm not much of a gambling man myself, but, if I was, I would have liked to have put my money on that day. Navy repelled by Selaria. A hurricane blowing in from the sea. And all the while, the revolutionaries seizing the moment like it was a gift from Septigonee herself. Never would have expected it. If there was ever a coincidence, that wins them all. Or are you the kind who believes in fate?"

Stoddard breathed a heavy sigh. "I don't know if I believe anything anymore."

Just then, a man fell backward and bumped into Stoddard's chair. Stoddard turned to avoid being shoved, his drink sloshing up over the lip of the glass and splashing on his gloved hand.

"Watch it now!" Bracken scolded the man.

Stoddard was already up. He'd shoved the man back and, in a swift motion, removed his glove before the liquid could soak in. There, in plain sight of all present, Stoddard's hand lay exposed. It glinted in the artificial lights. Across each digit ran thin metal frames. Each bent as naturally as a hand of flesh might as he examined it to ensure that each were still dry. As his hand moved, the clear sound of winding gears and the clicking of tiny levers could be heard in the silence which had fallen on the pub.

Stoddard sighed in relief. None of the liquid had gotten through the glove.

Only then did he remember his audience. He glanced about him, his gaze meeting the shocked looks of the patrons as they stared at him with a blend of awe and horror.

Shoving his hand deep into his coat pocket, Stoddard dropped a few more coins on the counter and pushed roughly through the crowd. Without a word, he hurried through the door and down the street, eager to leave the place behind.

"Did you ever see a thing like that?" someone whispered after a few seconds.

"Never in all my days," Bracken said.

ENJOY THE BOOK?

Thank you for taking the time to read my debut novel, *Aether Spark*! It's been quite the journey writing it, and a thrill sharing it with you.

I know, you likely have many questions left unanswered. Trust me, it drove me crazy that I couldn't fit it all into just one book. Like what becomes of Rhett without Chance? How did the world change after the meritocracy fell? And does Stoddard ever get his comeuppance? There's much more to discover, and plenty more misfortunes to brave as the story continues in the next installment:

Aether Construct: Book Two of the Clockwork Calamity

I'd love to hear your feedback. Please consider leaving a review wherever you bought this book, on Amazon, or on Goodreads. com. Indie authors like me work hard to create stories for you to enjoy, but our success is in large part due to our readers. When you review your favorite authors, you help ensure the release of future books.

And, if you'd like to send feedback directly to the author please visit **www.nicholaspetrarch.com/contact**.

THANK YOU TO MY PATRONS!

This book was made possible in large part because of my patrons over on Patreon. They generously helped offset some of the production costs and improve the overall quality of the publication.

Special thanks to:

Amanda Rasmussen
Jared Peiffer
Scot Seitz
Brian Dilts
Stacey Cole
Thomas Speck
Wendy Speck

Without all of you this book
would never have turned out so well

If you are interested in learning how you can support future books from the author, as well as gain access to exclusive perks and rewards as a distinguished patron, visit:

www.patreon.com/nickpetrarch.

ABOUT THE AUTHOR

Nicholas is an indie author raised in the sylvan mountains of Pennsylvania, currently residing in the rocky hills of Utah. Married to his muse, Nicholas writes science fiction, fantasy, and other stories with a fantastical element.

A late bloomer to the writing scene, Nicholas dabbled in high school and college writing poetry, short fiction, and starting the occasional novel. The thought of making writing a lifetime pursuit, however, remained aloof until a singular conversation with Orson Scott Card at graduation when his professional ambitions turned toward storytelling.

The road to authorship took some time, sifting through the slew of good and bad advice that exists on the internet and struggling to support himself while he studied. Another chance encounter in the throes of this struggle, this time with Brandon Sanderson, set him on the journey of completing his debut novel, *Aether Spark*.

When it came time to choose a publishing option, Nicholas opted to take the indie route for the opportunity it provided to learn the many aspects of writing and publication—taking it as a personal challenge to pave a way in which future writers like himself can find success in their own writing endeavors.

Connect with Nick on Instagram, YouTube, Facebook, and Twitter **@nickpetrarch**, and at **www.nicholaspetrarch.com**